PRAISE FOR GWEN RIVERS

"Gave me all the feels: AMAZING"

— BOOKGRYL, AMAZON REVIEWER

"I freaking LOVED this book!!! FINALLY, a book that's WORTHY of the five stars."

— SWATHI, GOODREADS REVIEWER

"So book 1 was utterly brilliant, book 2 surpassed even that..."

— ELISA, AMAZON AU REVIEWER

THE IMMORTAL QUEEN

THE IMMORTAL QUEEN

GWEN RIVERS

ELEMENTS UNLEASHED MEDIA

THE IMMORTAL QUEEN

THE UNSEELIE COURT BOOK 2

An Uncrowned Queen....

Nic Rutherford never wanted power. Yet now she's responsible for hundreds, alive and departed. Keeping the supernatural army separate from the humans for the sake of both races is no easy task. With the help of Aiden—the disgraced god and part time werewolf who must obey her every command— Nic plans to reign in the Wild Hunt and recover the lost souls she bartered away. But will her new life magic be enough to save what she lost?

A Fistful of Doubt....

Nicneven's last reign ended in heartbreak and disaster for the fae world. Aiden is a patient hunter and he will do whatever it takes to restore Nic's faith in herself. But the closer she grows to him, the more Nic fears she is courting her own doom.

A Dangerous Test....

The fae call it the gauntlet- the harrowing challenge to turn a mortal into one of the forever young. Many who enter are never seen again. The lucky few who do survive are forbidden from telling its secret. Can Nic overcome every obstacle and win the coveted prize of immortality? Or will she die in the attempt?

PROLOGUE

Definition: To run the gauntlet:
1. A punishment endured by convicted military personnel and inflicted by his/ her fellow soldiers, usually in the forms of beating, clubbing, whipping, etc.

2. To suffer an onslaught of criticism from various sources at once.
3. The test to become forever young, to prove oneself worthy of immortality to Underhill. Many who attempt it are never seen again.

4. All of the above

CHAPTER 1

THE SPECIAL HELL

The worst three words in the English language are without a doubt, the ones spoken by the handsome prowler in my bedroom. "Time for school."

"How did you get past my aunts?" I mumble and burrow deeper under the covers, doing my level best to ignore the half-wolf, half-god that equaled one giant pain-in-the-ass alarm clock.

"You left the window open." Aiden gestures to the slit in the windowsill where sure enough, there is a one-inch crack. "I took it as an invitation."

Aiden's abilities include turning himself into nothing more than a collection of sparks. If he ever decides on a life of crime, he'll be the world's best cat burglar. "I'd tell you to go to hell but then you'd literally have to do it."

"Someone's in a mood. Training go that well last night?" Aiden, fresh from the shower and smelling of cedar, sage and his own unique wild scent, plops himself down on my bed. His weight makes the entire mattress quake and my sore muscles scream in protest. He tosses back the covers, exposing me to the late summer morning breeze that hints at cooler weather. The boxer shorts and tank top I sleep in provide no real barrier from the chilly air.

Or from Aiden.

I hiss and swat at him. Regret accompanies the groan that bubbles up as the aches and pains in my muscles intensify. "Freda's a sadist."

A chuckle from the werewolf. "Probably why the two of you get along so well. Turn over."

I glare up into his leaf green eyes. "Why?"

He's all normal innocence, eyes wide, dark hair neatly combed. The picture-perfect all-American teenage boy, and about as trustworthy. "I'm going to give you a massage."

Yeah, right. "You've gotten way too handsy with me since you figured out I'm not

going to kill you." It isn't an idle remark. I have killed people, several of them in fact, most recently a jealous fey queen who wanted my head on a plate.

In my defense, she started it.

"Who says I have to use my hands?" He makes a grab but I dodge him and sprint for the bathroom. The lock clicks. A rumble of masculine laughter emanates from the other side of the door. "Next time then, my little queen."

"In your dreams," I call through the oak.

"Every night," he murmurs, totally unashamed to admit such a weakness.

I rest my forehead against the door and press my palm to the scarred wood. That was close, too close. I *want* Aiden's hands all over me almost as much as he wants to put them there. But a physical connection will complicate an already overly thorny relationship.

No time to dwell on that now. Instead, I turn to the shower and set the water to tepid. Even though I crave lingering beneath a scalding spray, something needs to cool my blood, so I can face the world calm and collected. As the Ice Bitch.

A pang goes through me. It was a nickname that my best friend, Sarah Larkin had given me what felt like a lifetime ago. Sarah died last spring, in a head-on collision with a downed tree. It wasn't until Sarah was gone that I realized how much she meant to me and how much I regretted not sharing my darkest secret with her.

Namely, that I am a sixteen-year-old serial killer. A punisher of evil incarnate. A hunter of men.

And that's not even the half of it.

Clean and shivering, I step from the shower and wrap one towel around my hair, another around my body before tip-toeing to the bedroom door and opening it a crack. Not that I suspect Aiden is lying in wait for me. Better safe than sorry.

No sign of him. The window is still open, the sheer curtains dancing in the morning breeze. I shut it and turn back to make the bed. It's then I see it, the lone pink rose on my pillow. My heart kicks up as I retrieve the flower. It's perfect, the petals still tightly closed but soft as a newborn's cheek. There's a note, too, four words written in spidery scrawl on a page torn out of one of my notebooks.

It's not all bad.

I blow out a sigh and plunk the rose in the glass of water on my nightstand. Aiden's right, it's not all bad. He's the most understanding potential boyfriend an asexual sixteen-year-old girl could ever hope to have. He doesn't try to pressure me or convert me. He's willing to wait until I am ready, even if that means we never have sex. He just wants to be with me, whatever that entails.

I'm not sure what that says about his sense of self-preservation, since I can kill a full-grown man with a kiss. And since my adoptive parents are two of the Fates who give him the hairy eyeball at every opportunity.

Fully dressed in cut off denim shorts and a black tank top, I stare at my reflection in the mirror. "This is stupid," I tell the petite blonde with narrowed blue eyes. "I have better things to do than repeat the tenth grade."

A knock sounds on the bedroom door. "Nic? Are you ready?"

I open the door to Jasmine, the elfin twelve-year-old strawberry blonde cherub whose mother gets off on subjecting me to some of the most gruesome physical challenges known to the forever young. Jasmine grins up at me, practically vibrating with excitement. Today is her first day of school. Ever. And she couldn't be more thrilled with the prospect. Picking out school supplies with her took a ridiculous amount of time. She lingered over every notebook, tested every pen.

I wonder how long her enthusiasm will last. In my experience, public education has a way of dulling the edges of the sharpest minds.

"There you are." This from Chloe, the gorgeous red-haired Fate who today smells like cupcakes. "Breakfast just hit the table and coffee will be ready in five."

"I'm the queen of the Unseelie Court," I point out. "It's undignified that I have to repeat a grade."

Chloe, usually the more understanding of my aunts, shrugs me off. "You should have thought of that before you dropped out of school halfway through last semester."

"And you're not the queen yet." This comes from Addy, the fatalist of our little trio. She peers at me over the top of her glasses, her brown braid bristling like a cat's tail. "It's a title you have to earn back."

"All the more reason I should stay here and train with Freda," I say but no one is listening, instead, gathering around the table for pancakes topped with late-season strawberries and fresh whipped cream.

Frustration makes me grind my molars. How am I supposed to rule the Unseelie Court when I can't even get my family to hear me out?

Someone raps on the front door.

"Don't open it," Addy grumbles from behind her laptop screen.

Chloe sets down her fork. "We have half an army camped in the field, we can't

ignore the door all day." She pushes back from the table and rises.

The hinges groan as the farmhouse door swings inward. Chloe casts the newcomer a black look and her cupcake smell shifts to one of burnt toast. "Oh, it's you."

"Told you so." Addy doesn't bother to look up.

Aiden stands there, wearing the same blue jeans and black t-shirt, military-style combat boots he'd been wearing the first day I'd seen him at school. As a part-time wolf, Aiden's need for clothing is limited and so is his wardrobe. While I appreciate his minimalistic style, I've been ordering a few more pieces suitable for high country fall and winter. I am, in many ways responsible for his basic needs, the same way I'm responsible for Jasmine's education and the aforementioned army's support.

Aiden bows formally to my aunts. "Ladies. I've come to escort the queen and Lady Jazz to school."

His speech is unnecessary, we agreed on the details weeks ago, but Jasmine grins in delight, loving the nickname. Aiden's courtly manners enchant her, unlike her mother who still harbors ill will against him for things that happened in my past life.

"We know that," Chloe snaps.

"Come in," I call. "Have some breakfast."

There's a spark in Aiden's leaf green eyes as he crosses the threshold. The way I phrased the invitation had been worded as a command. And when I issue him a command, he is unable to refuse.

He chooses a seat beside me, takes the plate Jasmine passes to him and loads it with seven pancakes. Under his breath he mutters so only I can hear, "I know what you're doing and it won't work."

"I assume you brought your own syrup." I grin at him, safe in the knowledge that he won't try any of his shadier tricks with my aunts and Jasmine present.

Aiden might not be willing to break bread with two of the women who had ruined his life on more than one occasion, but his oath to me leaves him with no choice but to obey. It's a power I hate having over him. Our relationship is made up of a series of whacked-out power struggles. I've been needling him lately to encourage him to drink the magic syrup that will break the connection between us once and for all.

"I'd rather have the strawberries. One last taste of summer." There's a wicked gleam in his eye as he says the words.

I jolt in my chair as a memory surfaces, not one from my current lifetime.

I am lying on my back in a meadow, long dark hair falling over my shoulders to cover my naked breasts. Aiden, also naked, is kissing his way down my body. The last rays of sunlight bathes our bare skin in an amber hue.

"I wish we didn't have to leave," I murmur, my hands fisted in his rumpled hair. It's clear from the state of dishevelment that it isn't the first time I've done so.

"It's not over yet," he kisses the inside of my thigh, his eyes molten with lust. "One last taste of summer."

"Nic?" Jasmine's voice breaks me from the reverie.

I turn to her and realize I've completely zoned out, the effects of my cold shower long gone. "Sorry, what was that?"

"Mom said you should stop by the base of operations before we go. Nahini wants to talk to you first thing."

I turn to Aiden. "Did she say anything to you?"

He shakes his head. "I would have told you if she did."

Excitement builds in my belly. "Maybe she's found them."

Nahini is third in command of the Wild Hunt. A tribal wise woman with the inborn grace of a dancer and the heart of a warrior. Until recently, she controlled the souls of wicked men who were sentenced to the Hunt as punishment. Unfortunately, those souls have been MIA for several weeks, including Nahini's brother.

"Don't get your hopes up." Chloe cautions me. "The souls might have moved on, or been consumed by the Veil."

I spear a few strawberries viscously. "I know. But their disappearance is my fault." In one of my impulsive decisions, I'd traded their afterlives for the soul of my former best friend.

"Nahini doesn't blame you, Nic." Aiden puts a hand over mine. The gesture doesn't go unnoticed by the rest of the table.

Uncomfortable with the gentle affection and their scrutiny, I pull away from his comforting touch. "I should probably go if I'm going to speak with her before we leave."

"Should we come with you?" Jasmine jumps up, nervous energy effervescing from her like bubbles in a champagne glass.

I glance to her half-filled plate. "No, you two should stay and finish eating. Meet me down at HQ when you're finished and we'll drive into town together."

Aiden's lips twitch as he picks up on the ring of command in my voice. His lids lower, a dark promise of retribution for abandoning him with the Fates and his twelve-year-old fangirl.

My backpack waits on the bench seat by the door. I pick it up on my way out. The thing is worn but sturdy. It holds some sentimental attachment for me as well as books. I carried it into Underhill, the mystical fairy realm on the other side of the Veil, on my quest to save Sarah. Slinging it over my shoulder feels like the beginning of a new journey, its weight a subtle reminder that I have all the tools I need at hand.

It might be a lie, but at least it's a comforting one.

HQ IS the rundown staff quarters about a half-mile from the farmhouse. Members of the Wild Hunt have used a combination of magic and the limited supplies on the farm to fill in the gaps in the collapsed roof and make the space somewhat livable. There are several rows of bunk beds, shower stalls with running water and enough electricity to keep the refrigerator and microwave operational. To me, the space is spartan and barely habitable but it's about all the Hunt can handle. The fey and modern technology don't mix.

In the beginning I'd offered to buy them whatever supplies they needed, even hiring humans to build a new bunkhouse. Freda had said, with some pride, that the Hunt would do what they always did and make do. It was enough for them to have a place to stay, to pitch tents and shelter the hounds, horses and birds of prey. I'd been relieved by this answer. Magic is easier than having a slew of contractors wandering around the property, asking questions about all the odd folk with armor and penchant to kill first and ask questions later.

Nahini is in the small room she claimed as her own space.

It sits adjacent to the main sleeping quarters. Close enough for her to oversee the troops, but still set apart. Freda and Jasmine have taken over the potting shed on the far side of the training pitch, but someone had to keep an eye on the troops and Nahini had volunteered.

Inside, there is a camp cot, as well as a mat on the floor. The latest book she'd borrowed from my personal library is sitting on the cot, the pages carefully marked with a leather strip. *Treasure Island* again. I make a note to get her an e-reader, as she's been through all of my print books at least twice already. Unlike the fey, Nahini is a turned human and has no inborn magic, only forever youth granted by Underhill. With practice, she could use modern technology.

Her weapons are laid out on the dented metal desk. Two long knives, a coiled whip that looks more like a long vine with thorns than anything manmade, and a series of daggers. Nothing on the walls, no decoration or personal effects. The Wild Hunt travels light.

Nahini is seated on the mat, posture regal. She wears only a sleek black bodysuit, her armor polished and lined up along the far wall. Her feet are bare, the soles pressed together. Sunlight streams through the evergreen boughs, dappling the light against her smooth dark skin in exotic patterns. Her riot of braids falls halfway down her back. I glance up to see that some sprite had encouraged several trees to grow directly over the hole in the roof, the leafy canopy is so thick it provides decent cover, while still being part of the natural world.

I rap lightly on the open door and her lids flutter up.

"My queen," she moves to stand. "How fare thee?"

"I'm good." I pat the air, indicating she should remain where she is. "Jasmine said you wanted to see me. Is it about your brother?" I can't keep the eagerness from my voice.

She settles easily back into position. "Not yet. There have been more thefts."

Damn. Not the news I'd been hoping to hear. "Who is it this time?"

"Melrock and Gil."

Names I'm unfamiliar with. "What did they take?"

"Food mostly, a brown sack of it right out of the trunk of one family's transportation. Also, some fabric left hanging outside."

The residents of Underhill didn't have an industrial revolution. They subsist on a barter system, trading goods for services, usually magical services, and mostly they obtain things like food, clothing, and weapons by stealing from humans. A hard habit to break, apparently.

"Food and clothing. Don't they understand I will provide whatever they need?" The Fates aren't flashy with their wealth, but after existing over several mortal lifetimes, money has a way of piling up. We could certainly feed and clothe the army if they would just learn to ask instead of take.

"I don't think it's about needs, at least not their immediate needs," Nahini says carefully.

I prop the sole of one sneaker against the wall. "What do you mean?"

"They steal for sport, to get one over on the humans. And because this is the way they have always survived. What they possess today might vanish tomorrow."

I read between the lines. "You mean if I don't pass the gauntlet and reclaim the throne."

Nahini's dark eyes are solemn. "The immortal challenge is much more dangerous than Freda has led you to believe. Many have died or disappeared in the attempt."

Frustration bubbles up. "Maybe if you told me what exactly to expect in there, I might survive."

The mysterious gauntlet is a challenge I must face in Underhill to become forever young and reclaim the Shadow Throne of the Unseelie Court. All I've been told is that a representative from Underhill will come for me when I am adorned with the markings of a gauntleted hopeful. No one has mentioned what sort of challenges I will face and every time I ask I get the same answer.

The one Nahini gives me with a regretful expression. "We are forbidden from speaking about it."

I can't think about the gauntlet now, not with school looming. "Any suggestions on how to deal with the thieves?"

"Make an example of them," Freda says from the door.

I turn to face my first-in-command. A tall Viking with golden hair which she wears in an elaborate braid. Her falcon helmet is nowhere in sight and like Nahini, she too is in her form-fitting bodysuit. Where Nahini resembles a graceful ballerina, Freda is built like a centerfold. If said centerfold was combat trained with every weapon known to man.

Her eyes are the same icy blue as the waters that surround the small Nordic fishing village where she was born centuries before and hold just as much warmth when she speaks of the traitors. "You've told them you would provide for them year-round and have been good to your word. Their actions undermine everything we are trying to achieve. If there is no punishment, others will follow their example."

During my absence—if you can consider death and subsequent rebirth an absence—Freda had been the de facto commander of the Wild Hunt. She knows how to run the day to day command, how to portion out limited resources, how to keep her warriors in check.

I raise a brow. "What sort of punishment?"

"Flogging," she responds right away. "They need their

hands for battle otherwise I'd advocate cutting one off, as was done to thieves in olden times."

Olden times sound like a bitch and a half. "No."

"My queen," Freda begins.

I hold up a hand. "I'm not beating them for habits ingrained over a lifetime. I've been to Underhill, I've seen how little most of the fey have. Stealing is how they've procured what they need to survive. I can't change that mindset overnight. Think of something else."

"You mean like mortal incarceration?" Freda scoffs. "A few days of leisure lying abed while everyone around them works? More will follow their example if only for the respite. We'll lose what little control we have."

I glance at my phone, checking the time. "Look, I will take care of this in six and a half hours. Jasmine is waiting for me."

Freda's face softens and she falls into step beside me. "Thank you for including her. She has talked of little else over the past few weeks."

"She's a great kid if a little misguided about school." I don't mention that Jasmine hoped to learn how to read so she could teach her mother. Freda is a proud woman that will show no weakness, not even to someone she considers a friend.

"I will see to it that Melrock and Gil are put to hard labor for the day." There's a sneer when she says it, but at least she's listening.

We exit HQ just as a vehicle slows to a stop, kicking up dust in its wake. Aiden is behind the wheel of my battered pick-up truck, with Jasmine on the seat beside him. He hops out when he sees me and bows, his dark hair almost touching the ground. "Your carriage, my queen."

"You better stop that," I say. "You can't do that in school without drawing attention."

He winks, unfazed by my criticism. "I know how to blend in."

He does, too. I've seen it before, the first day he arrived at school. Every mortal we ran across seemed to know him, though they couldn't place when or where. It was as though he had always been a character in the background, or maybe part of the scenery.

When I'd approached him about doing the same for Jasmine so she would have an easier time fitting in with the normals, he'd laughed. "We don't want her to fit in. We want her to stand out. There's no faster way to instant popularity in a small school than to be the new kid."

"But what about her skill level? She can't read."

"Trust me, Nic. No one will notice."

I hope he's right.

Aiden hands me the keys and then offers a nod to Freda. "First."

"Manwhore," she curls her lip at him in disgust.

"Freda," I say, a warning in my tone. "We talked about this."

"Sorry. *Wolf*whore."

Aiden bares his teeth, his expression not something that could ever be confused with a smile.

"Freda," I bark again, physically putting myself between them. "Knock it off. Your daughter is watching."

Freda turns to the truck, where Jasmine looks up from braiding her hair on either side of her head to hide her pointed ears. The commander's lips press together and she nods once.

I grab Aiden's arm and tow him to the other side of the truck. "Time to go."

His gaze is still locked on Freda and I can tell he's thinking about tearing her throat out. "She insults my honor."

"Aiden," I touch his cheek. "Please, let it go."

His gaze falls to mine. "And yours as well by implying you would accept a faithless traitor."

"My honor is just peachy, thanks. And we both know the truth, right?"

The truth that Aiden had never sworn an oath to Brigit, had never been her consort the way Freda and every other member of the Wild Hunt believes. He'd spent years locked in a cage beside the Fire Throne, the butt of jokes, an object of scorn. And he'd sacrificed his freedom to keep me safe.

His expression relaxes somewhat, and he brushes his knuckles along my cheek. "We do."

"If you tell them the why of it," I begin.

Aiden shakes his head. "It won't make a difference. Freda and I have never gotten along. She blames me for your death."

Judging by the haunted look in his eyes, Freda wasn't the only one who blamed Aiden for my demise.

"Suit yourself," I sigh. "We need to go."

Aiden presses his lips to my forehead and hands me the keys. "It will be all right, Nic."

Easy for him to say. No one would know Aiden was repeating a semester of school. I, on the other hand, went from being the girl no one noticed to the basket case too emotionally distraught to finish tenth grade after her best friend died in a car accident.

If my intention is to solidify my cover as a drama queen, I'm well on my way.

The drive to school takes about fifteen minutes. Jasmine peppers us with questions the entire time. So far, her experience with school comes from television and movies, which she takes as gospel. There's some trouble explaining to her the difference between real life and pretend for entertainment.

Today she's focusing on practical musings. Where the cafeteria is located, how long does she have to get from one class to another and should she raise her hand if she knows the answer to a teacher's question.

"No," Aiden and I say in unison.

"But I might know some answers." Jasmine glares between us. "I'm not an idiot."

"Of course, you're not." Jasmine is clever and one of the best fighters I've ever seen. I've taught her basic cooking and I've read to her every night. Already she recognizes a few frequently-used words. Her handwriting is awful, but she's a quick study.

"It's not about if you know the answers," Aiden cautions her, "What we know to be true might not be the same answers the mortals are used to."

"Just watch and listen in the beginning," I advise her. "We'll keep practicing your reading at home. You'll figure it out quickly."

"Do I look all right?" She fidgets with her purple and white striped tunic top again, rechecks her braids.

You better take this one. I think at Aiden. *Male approval will go farther.*

"You are radiant as the sun," Aiden tells her.

"Really?" Jasmine is blushing but looks pleased by the compliment.

"On my honor." Aiden bobs his head and then thinks to me, *You could outshine the stars, my queen.*

Flattery will get you nowhere. But even as I think the words at him, I feel my own face flush.

All too soon, I park the truck at the edge of the gravel lot. Jasmine watches as students spew from the big yellow buses and funnel into the concrete and brick buildings. Her small hand slips into mine, as though afraid I will disappear in the crowd.

"You'll do great." The words sound hollow in my own ears. She had built this moment up in her head so much, how could reality not disappoint?

She nods and unwilling to prolong the moment, I pop the door and slide to the ground. Aiden whispers something in her ear and a laugh bursts from her. He opens his own door and offers her a hand and she takes it without hesitation.

Freda may not trust Aiden, but her daughter has no such reservations.

Together, the three of us head up the cracked concrete steps and through the open glass doors. The building is already buzzing with noise and activity. Jasmine's eyes are wide as she tries to take it all in. "There must be a million people here."

"Only about four hundred including the teachers," I correct. In terms of modern-day schools, ours is on the small side, with the seventh and eighth grades shoehorned into the same building as the high school.

"The good news is, this is the first day in the building for all the kids in your grade." Aiden puts a hand on her shoulder. "You won't be the only one overwhelmed."

Jasmine nods, eyes round.

"Do you want us to walk you to class?" I ask.

She shakes her head. "No. Better if I do it on my own."

Brave girl.

The warning bell rings. I put a tentative hand on her shoulder and squeeze. Aiden, who is much more affectionate by nature, wraps one arm around her shoulder. "Remember what I said."

Jasmine giggles and then squares her shoulders and trots off.

"You're not helping her crush one bit, acting that way." I glare at him.

"Jazz knows my heart is devoted only to you." Aiden

smiles fondly after the girl. "It's innocent and she needs people to be kind to her. We all do."

I study him out of the corner of my eye and wonder if he's talking about me or himself. "Do I want to know what you told her?"

He drapes an arm over my shoulders, the gesture somehow more intimate than what he'd done with Jasmine. "That if anyone gives her any shit, we know plenty of creatures that would be happy to eat them."

A snort escapes. "That's probably not the best way to deal with conflict."

He shrugs and keeps a hold of me as we walk toward homeroom. "Still effective. And it reminds her that someone has her back. She'll need that today."

I notice several people glance our way as we pass by, but the looks of pity I'd been dreading are nowhere in sight. A few smiles, one wave from a girl who'd been in my American History class. It dawns on me that by sticking so close, Aiden's shielding me from the gossip about Sarah, giving people another bit of fat to chew. At the same time, he's pretty much staked a claim on me in front of the rest of the school. He might as well have peed a circle around me. "Tricksy wolf."

Aiden blinks down at me, the picture of innocence. "What?"

"Everyone will think we're going out."

He frowns. "Going out where?"

"No, I mean that you're my boyfriend."

He raises a brow. "And you don't wish them to have this impression?"

I shift away, uncomfortable. "Not really."

"Then you want to keep me a secret." His face closes up. "You're ashamed to be seen with me."

"It's not that." I hunt for words to explain why I don't

want to make such a public declaration when I feel someone's eyes on me. It's not a glance of curiosity like the others. No, this one is malevolent. I peek over my shoulder, trying to spot whoever is making all the fine hairs on the back of my neck stand on end.

Students passing in the hallways. The glint off Vice-Principal Steinburg's greasy black hair as he speaks with Coach Dunn, who must be pushing seventy but sees no reason to retire. Laughing, talking, yelling. No one paying any special attention to us.

Still, I feel like I'm being stalked.

"What's wrong?" Aiden's wolf instincts are on high alert, his pique forgotten.

"I'm not sure. I just feel like we're being watched. By something… other." It's the best explanation I can give.

He scans the hall with a brief glance that I know misses nothing. "I don't see anyone out of place. Doesn't mean no one is here though."

I take one more look in the bustling corridor, searching for signs of something unnatural. Magical. Anything that doesn't belong. Whatever it is, it's well hidden. "That's what I'm afraid of."

CHAPTER 2

SOMEBODY CALL WEBSTER'S

The morning drags like a dead body through the woods. If I thought my classes inane the first time through, having to repeat them all this semester is a study in mind-numbing boredom.

"Why won't they just let me get my GED," I complain to Aiden as I root my lunch out of the brown paper bag. Same fare as always, almond butter and honey on wheat, an apple and a bottle of water. It looks so normal, set out on the battered cafeteria table. Almost as though the events of last spring didn't happen.

Except Aiden is on the other side of the table, not Sarah.

Aiden, brave soul that he is, opts for a hot lunch. There's something brown, something gray, and lots of oozing. Not exactly a meal fit for a god. He pokes at the gray stuff with his fork. "Is it really so bad, being here?"

"Yes," I wrinkle my nose as he takes a bite. "Ugh. How can you eat that stuff?"

He shrugs. "It's better than starving."

"Debatable."

He holds my gaze, his green eyes hard as emeralds. "Trust me, Nic. Any food is better than starvation."

An image surfaces of the first time I'd met Aiden when I could count his ribs through his bruised and bloodied skin. Shame burns my cheeks. I'd forgotten he'd been half-starved, reduced to trading his body for scraps. "Sorry, I wasn't thinking."

He nods his head, accepting my apology. "That's part of the reason it's wise to finish school. You need time to build up your knowledge, not just of Midgard, but all the worlds."

I glance down, crumpling the brown bag in one hand. "You're probably right."

He takes the ball of paper from my hand and then laces his fingers through mine. "You were a powerful queen, but an unskilled one who was out of touch with her people and their struggles. You were never cruel, like Brigit, but you hid away from the problems of the Unseelie Court. You did the bare minimum to get by. Learn from those mistakes."

I heave a sigh. "Okay. I'll quit the bitching. It's probably better that Freda doesn't have access to me all day every day anyway. There'd be nothing left but a puddle of goo. Sort of like that." I point at the gray glop on his plate.

Aiden grins and, holding my gaze, forks up some of the stuff and eats it. "Delicious."

I shudder and turn away in time to see of a brown-haired boy a few tables over watching us. His eyes are the color of rich soil, framed by the kind of thick dark lashes most women would kill to possess. He's small and compact, obviously in good physical condition, though his clothing is rumpled, as though he slept in it. His hair is messy, too. He's disheveled and shy. And completely unfamiliar.

"Aiden," I say as the boy hastily turns away. "I don't know him."

He sets his fork down, the tray nearly empty. "What? Who?"

"That boy over there with the dark hair and eyes. He's new." In a school the size of ours, one might not have a name to go with every face, but the faces are always familiar. "He was staring at us."

Aiden follows my gaze. "He's sitting with people from eleventh grade. The seventh and eighth graders have a different lunch period, right?"

I nod. "Besides, look at him. He doesn't look prepubescent to me."

Aiden turns back, his expression intense. "Maybe he's the source of the scrutiny you detected earlier."

But I shake my head. "No. Earlier I knew we were being watched, felt the malevolence of it. I have no idea how long he was looking at us before I noticed him."

Aiden stands, and for a moment I think he's just going to dispose of his tray, but then he looks toward the table. "Stay here. I'm going to go get some answers."

I open my mouth to respond but he's already out of earshot.

"Nic?"

I look up to see Gretchen Hamill, the girl who waved to me in the hall earlier, standing before me holding her lunch tray. "Hi, Gretchen. Do you want to sit down?"

She nods eagerly and sets her tray down. Gretchen is what is referred to as a big-bodied woman, an unfortunate distinction in high school. She's smart, most likely going to be valedictorian of our class, as well as kind, but so socially awkward it's painful for even me to watch.

Having her here is a good cover. And provides a solid distraction so I don't go nuts wondering what Aiden is doing. "How's your first day going?"

Unlike Aiden, she didn't get the hot lunch. She has a ham

and cheese on worthless white bread and pears in syrup so thick it's more sugar than actual fruit. "Okay. It's good to see you back in school. I stopped by your family's clinic once in the spring, but it looked all closed up. I thought maybe you guys had moved."

A chill goes through me and I want to ask when exactly she'd been at the farm. Had she seen or heard any sign of the Hunt? I can't ask outright without arousing suspicion. "No. I just needed some time. You know. After what happened to Sarah." It isn't a lie, but I let Gretchen draw her own conclusions.

"I'm so sorry about Sarah. I know you guys were close." It's genuinely meant, not the hollow platitudes people offer because it's the right thing to do.

Unfortunately, I never know what to say to the condolence givers. No reaction seems appropriate, but it seems rude to say nothing so I settle for murmuring, "Thanks."

She nods and ducks her head. "So, I guess you're a little behind with classes and everything?"

Massive understatement. "I flunked second semester."

She takes a bite of her sandwich, swallows and says, "You know, you could probably set your schedule to double up. That way you can graduate with our class. I'd be happy to tutor you."

I tilt my head to the side, studying her. First, she drops by the clinic and now the offer of help with school work. Why this sudden interest in me? Is she what she seems, a lonely girl who needs a friend and believes I'm in the same boat? Or is there something more going on?

Something of the paranormal variety.

I decide to play along, see if she possesses some sort of secret agenda. "That'd be great. Aiden's not big on homework so I doubt he'll be any help."

"Are you two like, together now? An actual couple?" She asks, her eyes bright. From gossip or something else?

"We're taking things slow. No labels. We have…similar interests though." Like stalking and killing, vengeance and magic. You know, the usual. To get the topic shifted away from my nonexistent love life I ask, "What about you? Are you dating anybody?"

"Me?" she laughs as though I've made some sort of joke. "Who would want to date me?"

"Lots of people. You're smart, kind, easy to talk to." I don't know her well enough to elaborate further.

She glances down at the table, cheeks turning red. Her lack of confidence bothers me. In many ways, Gretchen is like Sarah. Years of other people's abuse has undermined her self-worth. Sarah's behavior had been overtly destructive. Drinking, drugs, promiscuity. I wonder if the girl in front of me is set on the same destination, just by way of a different heading.

"Ladies," Aiden plops down on the seat beside me. "Miss me?"

"You know I never miss," I tell him even as I think, *what did you find out?*

His eyes meet mine for an instant and a single word echoes in my head. *Later.*

"Gretchen doesn't believe me when I tell her that there are plenty of people, even in this backwater town, who would be happy to date her."

"More than happy. Thanking their lucky stars to find such a goddess." Aiden flashes his killer smile to close the deal.

Gretchen's face turns redder than a tomato. "I'm sort of focusing on school right now."

Aiden nods. "Wise as well as beautiful." There is nothing patronizing in his tone, he means every word. Gretchen looks up at him, her lips part as though she's witnessing the most beautiful sunrise.

A flash of irritation goes through me but before I can say anything, the bell rings. "Let's go, Casanova. We better move or we'll be late for P.E. See you later, Gretchen."

"Call me, if you want. About the tutoring," Her face shines with a happy flush.

"Tutoring?" Aiden asks.

"She offered to help me catch up." The words come out as a snarl.

"Nic, what's wrong?" Aiden snags my arm and steers me out the flow of traffic and into an alcove.

"Nothing. Other than we're going to be late." I try to push past him but he places a hand on either side of my head, effectively trapping me.

He ducks down until his eyes meet mine. "No one will notice. Now, what's going on?"

The words escape and fly free, jettisoned out of me on a gust of emotion. "Do you have to flirt so freaking shamelessly with every female you encounter?"

He blinks. "You asked me to tell Gretchen the truth. That's what I did."

"You're just so…." I wave my hands in vague circles while hunting for the right words. "Over the top."

A slow grin spreads across his face, as though I've given him some sort of present. "You're jealous."

"I am not," I try to push him away but he's as immovable as a brick wall. "Don't make me order you to move."

He cups my face in his hands. "Know this now, my queen. My heart belongs to you, whatever you decide to do with it. If my manner causes you distress I will try to be less, over the top, in the future."

"It doesn't cause me distress, smug bastard." I grit out.

He taps the side of his nose. "I can smell the lie. You best practice honesty, if you are to be immortal again."

The forever young can't lie, though they can and do twist the truth until it's barely recognizable. What a fey says and what she means might be on opposite ends of the spectrum. I like lying, it's a skill I've honed well over the years and the thought of giving it up disturbs me almost as much as Aiden's shameless flirtation.

He steps aside, tucking his hands into his pockets, looking way too self-satisfied for my liking.

"You're incorrigible," I inform him.

"*En*couragable," he shrugs, that smile still on his lips.

"That's not even a word."

"Sure, it is. I just used it. It means, I'll take encouragement in any form wherever and whenever it appears." He shrugs, but his nonchalant manner is spoiled by his goofy grin. "When it comes to you, Nic, I'll take whatever I can get."

THANKFULLY, the second half of the day picks up the pace and soon the dismissal bell rings. I stash my books in my locker and go to meet Jasmine on the front steps.

"How'd your day go?" I ask when I spy her exiting the building.

"Great." She beams at me and then Aiden. "So much fun. And I made friends."

A few girls pass us on the way down the steps, waving to Jasmine and calling out that they would see her tomorrow.

"Damn, Jazz. You could show Nic a thing or two on social interaction." Aiden casts her a wink.

I glower. "Are we leaving soon? Or are we just going to stand here all day? I have things to do."

Jasmine's face falls and I feel like a total bully, something that wouldn't have concerned me a few months ago.

Feeling awkward, I put a hand on her shoulder. "Jazz, I'm sorry."

"It's okay," she says in a small voice.

"No, it's not. I don't deserve to be let off the hook when I act like an ass. In fact, I'll make sure your mom knows so she can take it out on me during training. Come on, I'm sure she's waiting to hear all about your first day."

Jasmine nods, her smile returning and I am halfway down the steps when I realize Aiden isn't with us.

"Do I owe you an apology, too?" I call out.

"No. But I have something I want to check out. I'll meet you back at the farm." He strides off toward the buses as though he has every intention of boarding one.

There's a sharp stabbing pain behind my right eye. I still don't know what, if anything, he discovered about the unfamiliar boy who'd been observing us. Nor had I gotten a chance to talk to him about the punishment for the two members of the Hunt who'd been stealing. Or ask his advice about Gretchen. And I have math homework as well as training. Will the torture never end?

"Fine, be that way," I mutter and turn back to Jasmine. "So, was I right about your reading?"

She tosses her backpack into the front of the truck before hoisting herself in as if she'd done it every day of her life. "No one noticed that I'm behind. My friend Kayleigh invited me to her birthday this weekend. It's a sleepover."

One day. Jasmine had been in our school for exactly one day and already she's been invited to a sleepover. I've lived in the same town my whole life and never once had such an offer been extended.

And why does that bother me all of a sudden? It never had before. I'd intentionally kept my distance, to disguise myself. Maybe Aiden's observation about my lack of social graces burrowed beneath my skin. More likely it's the insecurity that I don't possess the skill set I need to rule the Unseelie Court. Queens need to be diplomatic, to talk to people, not just kill them.

I don't want to be another Brigit.

"That's great, kid," I say and shift the truck into gear. "What's Kayleigh's last name? I might know the family."

"Hamill."

My brows furrow, but I force my face to relax, not wanting to spoil her joy any more than I already had. What are the chances that Gretchen decides to traverse the thorny wall I've built around myself at the same time her little sister befriends Jasmine?

And where the hell is Aiden when I need him?

Jasmine chatters the entire way home, about her teachers, her classes, the other students. The picture-perfect middle school girl. Except she's half-fey and can kill any of her classmates with less effort than I expend on trig. For my part, I ask a few questions to keep her talking though my mind is on other matters.

Aiden was right at lunch. I'm not ready to rule. I can't even decide what to do about two thieves in the Wild Hunt. Freda wants to punish them but to me, what they did isn't all that bad. They filched a bag of groceries, who cares? Someone with a properly calibrated moral compass would say that stealing is wrong, regardless of the reason.

Good thing I don't have one.

The bigger problem is exposure. The farm is magically concealed from Underhill and her inhabitants by the Fates. But any human can access it. Many do regularly, because of Addy's vet clinic on the far end from the house and the Hunt's camp. Which means mortal authorities can drop by and ask questions about thefts in the area. A rash of kleptomania might draw attention we can't afford."

A sigh escapes. "Your mom is right."

"She usually is." Jasmine doesn't seem bothered by my abrupt change in topic. "What about this time?"

I fill her in on the theft and sum up, "I need to make examples of them. If mortal law enforcement starts asking questions, we'll have to make some tough choices."

Jasmine considers it another way. "Maybe you don't have to hurt them to punish them."

I frown. "What do you mean?"

"My social studies teacher was talking about something called community service. We can gain extra credit by volunteering in soup kitchens or nursing homes or animal shelters. She says sometimes criminals are ordered to do community service to make up for their misdeeds. What if you order Melrock and Gil to spend time helping humans, to make up for the things they stole?"

My lips part. "And that way they can see that some humans do without too, same as they do. Jazz, you're freaking brilliant. If it wouldn't kill you, I would kiss you."

She beams, then reaches for the radio. "I need to catch up with my mortal music lessons. Kayleigh and the others were discussing some singers at lunch like I should know who they were talking about."

Some autotuned garbage blares out of the tinny speakers and I cringe. Normals music isn't something I've ever developed an appreciation for either. Sarah used to turn on the radio whenever we drove together. She knew the words to every song, and belted them out off-key. I prefer reading and quiet for contemplation to the background noise pollution.

By the time we reach the farm, Jasmine is humming along to the refrain, her natural melody much better than Sarah's. I wonder if that comes from her nymph heritage, and make a mental note to ask Nahini during our next fey study session.

I park the truck in front of the farmhouse. Freda is sitting on the steps, using some sort of crystal to sharpen the edge of *Seelenverkäufer*, the blade that collects souls for the Veil.

"How did you fare?" She asks as Jasmine climbs from the truck and runs to meet her.

"Very well, *Jord*."

"And did any comment on your illiteracy?" Freda's chin goes up, her posture that of a mother ready to slay any demons who tried to harm her precious offspring.

It must be incredibly difficult for her, knowing Jasmine wants to read and being unable to teach her. I've seen her hands clench in frustration whenever reading was necessary. She was born into a world where survival was paramount and living past thirty was considered old age. Taking time to learn anything beyond the basics to survive was considered a frivolous waste.

"No one noticed, just as Aiden and the queen promised."

Freda's shoulders relax infinitesimally. "I am glad."

I put a hand on Jasmine's shoulder. "Go on in, I'm sure Chloe will have chocolate chip cookie dough ready for baking. It's our first day of school tradition." Mostly, it's an excuse for Chloe to get her chocolate fix and to hear some normals gossip. She's an absolute drama junkie as well as an unrepentant chocoholic.

Jasmine dashes up the steps, the screen door bangs shut behind her.

"Training in one hour!" Freda calls after her. Her smile fades when she turns to me. "Have you come to a decision about the thieves?"

"I have," I tell her about Jasmine's idea regarding community service.

Freda's blonde brows form a tight v as she considers it.

"Asking them to help mortals who they consider to be favored by the gods? They will hate that more than the flogging. You will be known as a ruthless queen." Her lips turn up in a predatory smile.

"Just the look I was going for. Let me drop my stuff and then we'll tell them together."

Freda stands and sheathes the sword. "I can inform them of your decision."

But I shake my head. "No. I won't be the sort of ruler who passes a sentence without looking her subjects in the eye. I want them to know me. To know I will punish them if I must but also that I am involved in all that takes place."

Freda nods, the light of approval shining in her eyes. "As you say, my queen."

I move up the steps and into the farmhouse. As expected, Chloe and Jasmine are busy spooning cookie dough onto a baking sheet.

"The trick is to work in a little extra flour," Chloe says, a smudge of white on her rosy cheek. I can't tell if the vanilla scent belongs to her or the batter. "It makes them super soft. Nic, grab a spoon."

"I can't. Some royal duties need my attention." I set my bag down and snag a water bottle from the fridge.

"But it's tradition," the goddess of spinning destinies whines like a constipated mule.

"And you're observing it and passing it on." I gesture to Jasmine.

Chloe pouts. "Fine. But if we eat all the cookies before you get back you have no one to blame but yourself."

Jasmine giggles, eyes shining with mirth.

I head into my room and change into Pilates pants and a sport's tank, knowing it's unlikely I will return to the house before training. Sore muscles protest and I wince. Every time I feel as though my physical condition is improving, Freda finds a whole new muscle group to torture.

When I exit the house, I see Nahini speaking to Freda. In the late afternoon sun, her iridescent armor shimmers like dragon scales. She dips her head respectfully when she sees me. "My queen. Freda has informed me of your plan."

"Technically, it's Jasmine's plan since she's the one who suggested it. Do you think it's a good one?"

Nahini nods. "I do. The Hunt needs to respect mortals and their property. To see them as similar instead of different. To view them as people instead of prey."

I nod, feeling only slightly hypocritical. Most mortals are categorized in my mind in terms of threats, useful cover or prey. "Ironic that I'm the one to teach this lesson."

Being a serial killer and all.

The three of us fall into an easy stride, Freda on my right, Nahini on the left.

"You've always served justice," Freda says.

"If I was such a terrific ruler, how did Brigit manage to convince the Unseelie lords to attack my summer residence?"

"There's a difference between just and popular. And you were never that, at least not with the lords."

The pressure behind my eye intensifies. At this rate, I'll have a full-blown migraine before sunset. "And is this move going to make me enemies within the Hunt?"

"You already have an enemy," Freda growls. "We still have a traitor in our camp. Someone was sneaking *Seelenverkäufer* to Brigit."

"Any luck in the search?"

"I've ruled out a few of the newer members who don't have connections. But that still leaves dozens of us." Her gauntlet covered hands clench in frustration.

Seelenverkäufer, the blade of souls, was entrusted to Freda after my death. Someone had been stealing it from her tent and transporting it to the other Unseelie queen for her unnatural experiments in reanimating the dead. My first in command has made it her personal mission to ferret out the traitor in our midst and bring him or her to justice.

"They're immortal fey. They can't lie. Why not just ask each one directly if they took the sword?" It might be a stupid question, but it seems like the most straight forward approach.

"If word spreads that we're looking for a traitor, he or she might run before we have a chance to interrogate them. We don't just need to find out who was helping Brigit, but also how they did it and if there are any others." Nahini's words are soft and sure.

"We are hunting one of our own," Freda says as we approach HQ. "An immortal hunter. And our greatest weapon is that the spy or spies aren't aware that we are after them."

"So, who do we trust completely? I want a list."

"Myself and Nahini of course. Tad, Leaf and Gwendolyn."

"That's it? What about Alric?" I name the handsome Spriggan fauna master who helps Addy out with the veterinary clinic.

Freda's cheeks flame. "I haven't ruled him out."

"But he's your number one fanboy. Err...fan fey? Surely he wouldn't betray you or the Hunt."

Nahini chuckles. "I tried telling her that. If we can ascertain his innocence, we can have him use the birds and beasts of the Hunt to help us keep watch."

I study Freda a moment. "Why not enlist his help?"

Freda stops and stares at the ground. She doesn't say anything, but I see a muscle

jump in her jaw. "You're worried it's him."

"One of his half-siblings is of Brigit's line. His father was

one of her consorts. They are fighting for the Fire Throne."
She swallows hard. "If it is him, I'll have to put him to death."

My mouth goes dry. "Freda…"

"I know it's unwise to delay," she studies the ground beneath her boots. "I should do it and get it over with, one way or the other. But I can't bring myself to contemplate killing him. Even if we have no future."

I exchange a glance with Nahini, whose lovely features are soft with sympathy. Alric's father expects him to become a consort to the queen of the Shadow Throne after his tenure with the Wild Hunt. If his half-sibling won the Fire Throne and Alric did move into a position of power, his family would essentially rule the entire Unseelie Court. Of course, this won't happen. I've told my first that I'm not interested in Alric, and have no intention of choosing a consort or upholding Unseelie traditions. But I don't sit on the Shadow Throne yet, won't until I pass the gauntlet, so my reassurances don't go far.

"Freda, if it is him, I'll do it myself. I'm the leader of the Hunt, not you. The burden falls on me."

She swallows, then nods. "Forgive my cowardice."

"You are many things, Freda. But you are not a coward. Let's handle Melrock and Gil and then the three of us will clear Alric. Together."

"Together," Nahini says and extends a hand for me to take.

Freda exhales and puts her own hand over the top of Nahini's. "Together. As we always should have been."

CHAPTER 3

SPIES AMONG US

"Your wolf has returned." Freda doesn't lower her sword from the attack position as she addresses me. "He's devouring you with his eyes."

I don't turn toward the crowd gathered to watch our sparring session. Instead, I step to the side, sword raised to block her inevitable strike. "That just makes us even then, since Alric has been eye-humping you for the last two hours."

It's true. After the confrontation with Melrock and Gil—who'd been both reluctant and insulted at their punishment to work in a soup kitchen over the weekend— we'd gone to see Alric.

I don't mince words. "Did you take *Seelenverkäufer* from Freda's tent?"

"No," he responds, eyes guileless and mystified.

"And have you ever arranged for someone else to take the sword of souls?" Freda pushes.

"Of course, not." Alric's gaze shifts from Freda to the sword handle poking up over her shoulder. "It's right there."

Freda's shoulders sag. Not a full-on slump, but a minuscule easing of tension visible only to those who know her well. I wonder how many sleepless nights she's spent worrying that Alric was the traitor, imagining that she would be forced to kill him.

"My queen?" The gold flecks in his brown eyes seem to shift as his gaze roves from me to Nahini before resting on Freda. "First? Is aught amiss?"

Addy was in the storage room doing supply inventory but otherwise, the clinic is deserted.

I look to Nahini, then to Freda. "There's no wiggle room in his answers, right?"

Freda shakes her head, her blonde hair coming out of her braid in curling wisps. "No. He has no courtly slyness."

"More to appreciate." Nahini stops just short of saying I told you so. "We can trust him with the whole story."

So, we do.

Alric agrees to use his connection to the birds and beasts to watch Freda's quarters. A falcon or hound could observe comings and goings much more casually than posted guards and animals, and as he pointed out, won't accept a bribe.

Then we'd gone on to training.

Freda's grin flashes a moment before her sword. It isn't, *Seelenverkäufer,* which she hasn't practiced within weeks, at least not since our training "got real". Translation: when she needed to fight back to win.

I see the move before it happens, the way she taught me, and fall into a blocking stance. She lands three blows against my sword in rapid succession then ducks beneath my return swing. I anticipate the move, and swipe out with a roundhouse kick, knocking her to the ground. She's down for only an instant, then arches her back in a graceful maneuver and springs up to land back on her feet, sword poised for the next attack.

We clash again and again, neither of us gaining much ground. I'm gratified to see sweat forming on her brow. She must work for what had been an easy victory a few weeks ago. She feigns a swing from the left when I know she has every intention of kicking out to the right to trip me up. I'm on to her tricks though, and back up enough, take two steps and leap over her blade, flipping in midair to land behind her. She whirls, only to have the point of my sword at her throat.

A spattering of applause from the onlookers. I don't look their way. Don't back down, don't budge an inch, waiting. Her sword drops to the dust. A laugh escapes Freda as she puts her hands up, followed by a murmured, "I yield."

I duck as the second attack comes from behind me. Nahini rolls over the top of my back in a graceful summersault. Her two long knives are out and crossed before her by the time her feet touch the ground. Freda retrieves her sword and I am faced with level two, trying to disarm and beat them both.

So far, an impossible task.

Nahini is fast, where Freda is strong and the two have worked in tandem for the better part of two centuries. They separate, Freda moving left, to my weaker side while Nahini circles right. There's no way to keep an eye on two opponents at once, so I follow Nahini with my body and gaze. Freda is stronger, but also larger and slower than both Nahini and myself. It makes her somewhat easier to track. Nahini, I'm convinced, can turn to smoke if she so chooses.

There are no war cries as they lunge. The attack is silent and if they'd wanted it to be, deadly. I defend against Nahini's quick jabs and throw my body weight to the side to avoid the powerful blow from my First. I have only one weapon, no way to put the second opponent down. At least not yet.

Nahini slashes out with a knife. I jump back, doing a mule kick into Freda who lunges forward. The blow makes contact, though it isn't the direct hit I'd intended. She staggers back but still holds her sword. I duck low to avoid Nahini's slicing cuts, the daggers glinting in the late afternoon sun.

We continue for several moments, me landing blow after blow on Freda while dodging Nahini's attacks. She moves like the tide coming in on the beach, one hit surging against me like waves against the shore. Eroding my flagging energy, wearing me down.

Nahini's speed is unearthly. Like Freda and myself, she was born a mortal. But unlike my fatal kiss, her gift is that of swiftness. She moves like a dancer, no motion wasted, every one graceful and deadly. I can't beat her.

So, I let Freda do it for me.

I allow Freda inside the protective circle I'd created with my sword and kicks, pretending to drop my guard. She takes the bait and charges at the same time Nahini slashes out. I dive out of the way, hitting the ground hard on my left side. The movement is completely inelegant and totally effective.

The two warriors crash into each other, Freda barreling down like a freight train, Nahini too off-balance to move out of the way in time. Her daggers are poised wrong, and I see the panic in her eyes, the worry that she's about to unintentionally stab Freda.

She drops them.

They go sprawling to the ground. Freda's sword is still in her hand, but Nahini is defenseless and trapped beneath her.

My side aches like a bitch, but I scramble up in record time and step on Freda's wrist, so she can't raise her sword against me. Then tap each of them with two fingers. If this had been a real fight to the death, those taps would have been my Goodnight Kiss.

Elation fills me. I won. I beat the two best fighters in the Wild Hunt *at the same time.*

"I think that's enough for today." Freda grunts. "Mind getting off my wrist?"

"Sorry," I step back and then drop my own sword, and offer them each a hand up.

This time the hoots and hollers from the crowd are much more enthusiastic. I turn to face them, unable to keep the grin of elation off my face and meet Aiden's leaf green eyes.

Well done, my queen. He beams at me with pride even as his mental voice caresses me from the inside out.

Time seems to slow and stretch between us, our connection pulling taut, crackling with energy. I sway a little, all my soreness replaced by something else. A growing hunger. Primal urges. I want to run into his arms, can see it in my mind's eye. Throwing myself at him, letting him pick me up and spin me around to celebrate the moment of victory.

Together. Forever.

The cawing of two crows from the stand of birch trees shatters the spell like a dropped glass ornament on a concrete floor. Freda claps me on the shoulder. "You won. Once. Tomorrow we'll try it again and next time I won't be so easy to fool."

I shake my head, trying to dispel the last shards of that bizarre vision. "Then I'll have to come up with something else."

"Always so confident." Freda removes her hair from her braid, the golden fall catching the late afternoon's rays. Behind her I see Alric clench his fists as he watches her.

"Now that you know he's on our side," I begin but she raises a hand.

"I know where you're going with this and…I can't." She shakes her head. "I'm just relieved he's with us."

"Who's with you?" Aiden approaches from behind and is standing so close I can feel his body heat.

"Alric," I murmur as his cedarwood and sage scent fills my senses.

Aiden tilts his head to the side. "Why would you think otherwise? He's always been loyal to the Hunt."

"A few weeks ago, I never considered that we had any who weren't loyal to the Hunt." Freda's features are taut with strain. "We need to deal with the reality that is, not what we wish it to be."

Aiden watches her walk away and then turns to me, his gaze going to where my left arm is crooked and pressed tightly into my sore side. "You're injured."

"I'll be fine." Having cracked my ribs before, I know it isn't serious. Probably just some bruising. "Nothing a hot shower can't fix. Where have you been?"

I start walking toward the house, knowing he'll follow. After a brief pause, he does, catching up to my slow pace easily. "I was checking out our new friend. The one who was so fascinated with you earlier."

"And?"

"He got off the bus on the opposite side of town, about ten miles from here. He was the only one at the stop, though there was another boy waiting for him. I got off at the next stop but by the time I tracked back to where he'd exited, I lost them."

"What do you mean, lost them?" We're nearing the old barn and I head toward it, my stride purposeful as though I have business there.

"No scent. No tracks, nothing to follow." Aiden scans the area. Seeing no one nearby, he scoops me into his arms and carries me inside the barn.

"Hey." The protest is automatic, almost by rote.

"No one's looking. Hold on to me." His green eyes glint with mischief.

I grip him around the neck, pressing my sweaty body

against his. It isn't a carnal move, merely one of self-preservation because I know what he's going to do. Sure enough, my body comes apart, drifting upwards in a shower of sparks.

I've traveled with Aiden this way before, molecule by molecule. We become weightless, able to drift on the wind. The breeze that's coming from the west, the direction of the sinking sun carries us off. We are caught up in an air current. It pushes us to the east, over the Blue Ridge Mountains.

In this form, my senses are dulled. I can't smell the scents being carried on the air or feel the wind on my skin. I have no skin, no nose, no anything, yet I am somehow still Nic Rutherford. And Aiden is there too, his floating embers mingling with mine until there's no way to tell the two of us apart.

After an interminable amount of time, we drift back down to earth, forming where we touch first. It was like that before and I don't know if that's because it's easier to tell us apart that way, or it's his sneaky way of getting me to cling to him a few moments longer.

With Aiden, it's hard to tell.

"How do you do that?" I breathe as our upper bodies continue to reform.

His hands are on my waist and he makes no move to release me. "I'm really not sure. It's transmutation of some kind, changing solid living matter inanimate and then back. Mostly it's about removing water from the body, making it light enough to float."

When I frown up at him, he goes on. "People are made up of a great deal of water. Water's heavy, deadweight that's tied to the earth. Take out the water and transport is much easier. I just pull moisture from the air to replace the water when we reach our destination."

I'm watching his mouth, only half-listening to his explanation. Being so close to him, breathing in his scent, the sage, cedarwood and wild heat of him, it's almost impossible to ignore the current that sizzles between us.

"Nic," I see it in his eyes, the animal hunger. "I want you."

It's true. So close, I can feel the firm length of him pressing into my hip.

And gods help me, I want him too.

Without conscious thought, my hand snakes up the back of his neck, fingers furrowing through his thick dark hair. I stand on my toes, tugging him down while reaching up to meet him.

He breathes my name again and then his lips are on mine, molding and shaping them in an intimate crush. He tastes of cinnamon gum, and an addictive kind of heat and each small sip only makes me crave more.

My hands become restless, eager to explore the terrain of his broad shoulders, the tight muscles of his arms, the lean-ness of his torso. His own hands caress along the length of my spine, only adding fuel to the blaze within me. I bunch the cotton of his t-shirt in my hands, pulling it almost franti-cally from the waistband of his jeans.

He tears his mouth away from mine, sucking in oxygen. "This isn't why I brought you here."

"I don't care. You've been teasing me for weeks." I rest my forehead against his chest.

A laugh rumbles out of him. "Have I then?"

"You know you have." My tone is irritable, frustrated.

He tilts my chin up so he's staring into my eyes. "I didn't mean to, love. Truly."

I fix him with a level stare. "Then what is it you want, if not to drive me crazy?"

"To protect you. To keep you safe."

"Is that all?" I whisper.

The perfect arches of his dark eyebrows draw together.

"You sound disappointed. Maybe you need to tell me what it is that you want, Nic."

I suck in a breath and confess the truth that's been eating at me for weeks. "I want to know that you're here because of me, not because of her."

We both know who I'm talking about.

His grip on my waist tightens. "Nicneven is dead."

"I know that. I also know that you believed I was destined to be exactly like her. Isn't that why you swore your oath to me again? I don't want you hanging around because of a promise you made to someone else or out of misplaced sense of guilt."

He blinks as though I've shocked him. Maybe I have. The more I get to know Aiden, the more my attraction grows. Where once there was only scorched earth in my heart now there is fertile soil. But the feelings taking root within are not a pretty garden full of flowers and butterflies. No, true to form, what's been growing in my heart is a snarl of poisoned vines, like those in Underhill's Dead Forest, waiting to attack. Jealousy, possessiveness. Ownership.

I want him to belong to me and me alone. And that scares me more than anything else. It's one thing to snuff out the flame of life, another entirely to dictate when and where that flame can be lit and who it can warm.

Suddenly, Aiden's head whips to the side. "Did you hear that?"

I seize the distraction with both hands. "Hear what?"

He mutters an oath in a language I don't comprehend, then lowers my feet until they touch the ground once more. Retrieving his discarded shirt, he pulls it on, then pulls me down behind a scrubby rhododendron.

"What…?" I ask, my blood still racing around in my veins, my head still foggy from lust.

Aiden points and lowers his mouth until his breath tickles

the fine hairs around my ear as he speaks. "That is why I brought you here."

From our hidden spot, I can see only more fields, nothing more remarkable than browning grass and dead leaves fluttering off a river birch. I'm about to tell him so when the light shifts, a craggy mountain face growing from the earth.

"Is it an In-Between?" I ask, referring to the places where one can cross the Veil into Underhill, the realm of the fey.

He nods and covers my kiss swollen lips with one hand while thinking at me, *Don't speak out loud.*

The green hill grows until it's about thirty feet high. The ground shakes beneath us. I fall to my hands and knees and only Aiden's vice-like grip keeps me from sprawling on the ground.

It's a fairy hill, from one of the courts, Aiden thinks. *Only the royals hold enough power to cross this way.*

My gaze slides back to the hill. The shaking stops, but the movement goes on, moss clinging to the rock slithers, vines outline something that looks like a doorway. An entrance to our world from Underhill. *Who's coming through? Which court is it?*

I don't know. We're close enough to the change in power that it could be either summer or winter, Seelie or Unseelie. This explains why that brown-eyed boy vanished so suddenly earlier.

And why he'd been looking at me so intently.

The moss and vines finish their readjustment. A loud scraping sound fills the deserted clearing and then I see the arch of a doorway, glowing with a hypnotic light.

We have two choices. Aiden turns and holds my gaze. *Confront whoever emerges directly or follow them and see what they're up to. The decision is yours.*

My heart is racing as I stare back at the door. I'm sneaky by nature and my impulse to spy wars with my need for answers. With Aiden by my side, it wouldn't matter if one of the Seelie kings strode through that newly made door with murder on his mind, the wolf would protect me with its life.

Yet even though fey can't lie, they have a way of twisting the truth until up is down and black is white.

We follow them. I think to Aiden. *Find out exactly what they are up to and then we can bring the might of the Hunt down on them if need be.*

He nods, green eyes glinting and simultaneously, we both turn back to face the doorway. We're both facing it head-on as a cloud of sparkling golden dust erupts from within, like someone stepped on a puffball mushroom. There's no time to react, to run, it overtakes us with the speed of thought. Aiden's hand close around my wrist to shield me with his body.

But the wave of glittery sunbeams surrounds us, permeating our clothes, our skin down to every pore. I brace myself, expecting it to hurt.

It doesn't. Instead, a wave of euphoria passes through me. Someone giggles.

"Nic," It's Aiden's voice, but he sounds…different. "Are you all right?"

"Never better," a sloppy grin steals over my face and I sway in his hold. His arm tightens around me. "You don't always need to be so worried about me. I'm a big tough girl, can tie my own shoes and everything."

He doesn't respond to the last statement. "I need to get you out of here. Try not to breathe."

"That'd probably kill me." Probably comes out sounding like proly. Am I slurring my words? Another giggle and I'm shocked to realize it's coming from me. "What is this stuff?"

"Intoxidust. Come on, I think I see an opening."

This statement has me snorting with mirth. Aiden foists me up over one shoulder in a fireman's carry and hauls my giggling carcass from the center of the cloud.

We jounce along for an interminable time, me no more than dead weight. Finally, he stops near a creek and lowers me to the ground before scooping some water up in his palms to splash his face. Then he cups more water and splashes me with it.

"Hey," I take a swat at him, several seconds after the water makes contact. "What're you doing?"

"Trying to clean the dust off your skin. You'll only feel its effects as long as it's in contact but the longer it lasts, the worse the recovery." He splashes me again.

I stumble into him, gripping his hands to keep him from any more water sports. He's so close and I can't help but bury my face against his t-shirt and take a deep breath, eyelids growing heavy. "Mm. Amazing."

Aiden tilts my chin up, green eyes scrutinizing my face. "Your pupils are the size of quarters. You're completely intoxicated. Come on, we need to bathe you in the stream."

I sigh and lean into him, glad someone else is calling the shots. "I don't wanna be the boss of you."

"You've made that abundantly clear." His tone is dry as he bends down to tug off my boots.

"Shouldn't you at least buy me dinner first?" I'm no help. My arms and legs feel like foreign weights that I don't have the strength to operate. I end up curled over the top of him while he removes my footwear and socks. "And how come you're not affected?"

He stands and reaches for the hem of my t-shirt. "I am. I just have a higher tolerance than you do because I've been pixed before. Still probably couldn't pass a sobriety test."

"Pixed?" I repeat. "As in pixies?"

"The dust doesn't actually come from pixies. They collect it in the Unseelie catacombs." His eyes are trained on my breasts as though he can see through my sports bra. "We used to dose ourselves after festivals and…"

"Are you rambling?" I ask, charmed by the idea.

He blinks, then makes an efficient tug to yank my yoga pants down to my ankles. "Go get in that stream."

But I'm much more interested in moving closer to his body, enjoying the intoxicating effects of the dust and picking up where we'd left off. "I'm too cold. Warm me up first."

"I'll go with you, how's that?" With a grunt Aiden picks me up again and carries us into the stream.

"No, I want—," I claim his mouth in a hungry kiss. My fingers revel against the smooth flesh of his stomach. With a groan, he acquiesces, tongue lapping against mine, hands cupping my face to hold me still.

Soon the shirt is in my way, the fabric frustrating me as it obstructs my progress. I don't know if Aiden senses my growing agitation or is only experiencing his own, but he withdraws from me long enough to whip the shirt over his head.

His skin is so hot beneath my fingertips, so smooth pulled taut over the hard ridges of muscle. His abs and pecs, biceps and triceps are perfectly formed, drum-tight and ready for whatever demands he makes of his body. The perfect weapon, honed via the hellish flames he's endured. With only inches between us, the wild scent of his skin is overwhelming, like a drug spicing the air. I sway on my feet while I explore the entrancing terrain at my leisure.

"Nic," he breathes my name and I can't tell if it's encouragement or protest.

I move closer into him, my hands curling around to the equally exquisite dips and hollows of his back. My stomach brushes against the hard length between his legs and he gasps into my mouth. The sound delights me, and I repeat the contact, intentionally this time, wondering what would break the iron fetters of his self-control. His hold on me tightens, his hands slide down my back to grip my ass in both hands, holding me against him. What would it take to make Aiden wild with lust, with desire? What will drive him to the point of no return?

Aiden's hands slide lower still until he's got one hand around the back of each of my thighs. He lifts me up, encouraging me to wrap my legs around his waist, my arms around his neck.

The pressure is addictive, him pressed against me just there, the friction and heat making me crave him even more. Dream memories have given me glimpses of what it's like to make love with Aiden. He's fire and magic and all things sex should be. There will be no awkward teenage fumbling, no clumsy exploration with teeth clacking together, hair inadvertently pulled. My wolf will know exactly what to do, how best to proceed, even if I don't.

It dawns on me suddenly that I want more, I want all that his delicious kisses promise. And not just sex. The intimacy. Me, who has never let anyone close, who trusts no one, including the aunts who raised me. And yet here I am imagining that sort of closeness with Aiden. When did that happen?

Without warning, he sets me down in the icy mountain stream. I gasp in indignation as the cold seeps into my calves.

Aiden ducks underwater. The yellow gold dust drifts downstream like a thick layer of pine pollen, glittering in the sunlight.

"Your turn," he emerges wearing only his wet jeans but looking more like himself.

I reach up to touch his face when he reaches for me. His stubble prickles against my fingertips. "I'll tell you a secret. It's not because I don't like you."

He pauses in trying to dunk me. "What isn't?"

"Why I'm such a bitch to you. It's not because I don't like you. It's because I do like you. And that's scary."

"Nic," he breathes the word like a prayer.

"You want to kiss me," I lean in closer, ready, eager for another taste of him. Kissing Aiden seems like the best idea I've ever had. Why didn't I think of it sooner?

"That's the dust talking." He makes a grab for me but I dart away, laughing.

"It is not."

He closes in. "Nic, this isn't a good time for a heartfelt confession. Trust me. You think you know what you're talking about, but—"

I splash him. Not with my hands or feet, but with my fey queen powers, I dump a big bucket of water over the top of his head.

He stands there, staring at me, water dripping off his perfect nose. "I can't believe you just did that."

Neither can I. I stare down at my hands, in awe. I hadn't even thought about it, it had been sheer reflex. Of course, now I have a sopping wet wolf to contend with.

With a growl, he lunges for me. I dodge and then leap to the rocky shore. Alighting on rocks, moving fast enough to stay ahead of him.

But not for long.

He leaps, his body plowing into mine and turning in midair to take the impact of our crash landing on his back. The water is about four feet deep, and he wastes no time rolling with me until my entire body is submerged.

Quickly he helps me up. Wet hair streams in my eyes as I sputter and choke.

"Are you all right?" Aiden pushes the sodden masses of hair out of my face.

"Fine." I sway on my feet. Then the ground rises up to meet me and I know no more.

CHAPTER 4

MISTAKES

Brigit sits atop a throne made of golden fire, her perfect porcelain face marbled with the black streaks that appeared when her Kiss of Life met my Goodnight Kiss. "Oh, sister mine, what have you done?"

Her smile turns predatory. "And how shall I retaliate?"

"You're dead." I can't move. My arms are bound by my sides. "This isn't real."

"First," she muses, not bothering to answer my statement. "I think I'll roast all the skin from your bones until it splits. Cooking the flesh beneath. Then I'll let your wolf eat you up."

A door opens behind her throne and a green-eyed wolf is brought in, foaming at the mouth.

I lift my chin, even as fear makes me want to shrink into myself. "Aiden won't ever hurt me."

"Ah, but after the Master of the Waves is finished with him, Aiden will be gone for good. There is only your wolf."

Aiden, I think. But there is no reply, only a hollow space where Aiden had been.

"This wolf's a killer. He committed fratricide. A fitting mate for you, Betrayer of Underhill. And I doubt he can resist the scent *of cooked meat." The Fire Queen raises her hand and I see the flames surge toward me, melting my clothes, singeing my hair, burning....*

The flare of agony jolts me awake. Consciousness does nothing to still my thundering heart. The wolf that had been sleeping at the foot of my bed, raises his face to meet my gaze with leaf green eyes.

I stare back, heart pounding from that too vivid dream. But it's just Aiden, looking back at me, concern radiating from his alert form.

Nic? How are you feeling?

"Like death warmed over. What happened?"

We were gassed.

Slowly it comes back to me, the fairy hill, the cloud of golden dust emerging from the enchanted doorway.

Acting like a complete idiot. A desperate, horny idiot.

"Did you see whoever did it?" I can't hold his gaze. Heat suffuses my face as I recall how I'd acted like a cat in heat.

No, my attention was focused...elsewhere. Strong stuff. Whoever crossed came through. By the time the dust cleared the hill was gone again.

"Why are you the wolf?" I swallow, my throat too damn dry.

Only way they'd let me stay. Aiden tilts his head at the cracked bedroom door. *Unless you want them in here with us, I suggest you speak to me mind to mind.*

No, I certainly didn't want Addy and Chloe and whoever else was out in the main room coming to check on me. Coddling wasn't my thing and while Addy was matter-of-fact, Chloe would make a fuss.

I'm surprised they agreed to let you stay at all. My mouth is mossy, my teeth badly in need of brushing. There's a glass of water on my nightstand. I flail, but can't seem to force myself upwards enough to reach it.

Gritting my teeth, I stretch toward the water glass and again fall short.

This is ridiculous. Aiden leaps off the bed and between one step and another, transforms himself from wolf to man. *I'm not going to sit here like a lump and watch you struggle.*

I close my eyes, more from exhaustion than to preserve his modesty. Aiden thinks nothing of strutting around naked. Most of the fair folk don't. There was no industrial revolution beyond the Veil. Clothing is a luxury in Underhill, one very few can afford. *You said you were supposed to be a wolf.*

He picks up the glass with ease and hands it to me. His green eyes spark with mischief as he crouches down to meet my gaze. *I won't tell if you don't.*

I down several gulps of water and then take the pain reliever. *Thanks.*

There is silence for a beat. I have no idea what he's thinking, all my concentration on forgetting that disturbing dream. And not reliving the confessions I'd spewed at him earlier. Had I really admitted to fearing my feelings for him? I would cringe but it would probably make me hurt worse.

You like the way I smell. Even his mental voice sounds distinctly pleased.

A groan escapes and I put a hand over my face. *I'm pleading intoxication.*

Worry not. I won't hold you to any of it. Aiden lifts my hand away, threading his fingers through mine.

I stare up at him, unsure.

The things you said while you were drugged. I'm not going to hold them over your head.

Thanks. I think at him again, this time with utter relief.

If... A wicked grin steals across his features.

My mouth falls open. No way. He's going to curb boost me? My eyes narrow to menacing slits. *Are you really going to use my drugged-out babble as* leverage? *Don't be that, guy, Aiden.*

He shrugs, the gesture nonchalant and without mercy. *I spent millennia with the fey. I know the value of a gift. And a bargain well struck. Would you do any less if there was something you wanted very badly?*

He has a point. *And what exactly is it that you want?* I brace myself for the worst.

A date.

I blink. *One date? That's it?*

He nods. *That's it.*

Are you fucking serious? I glare at him. *You could ask me to stop pushing for*

you to break the bond, or blackmail me for whatever else you want. Half of the Unseelie Court. I could kill anyone you wanted dead. And your demand is a night on the town? You don't need leverage for that.

Green eyes sparkle. *I do if I want you to say yes.*

Sensing the trap, I study him closely. *Why is this so important to you?*

Aiden answers my question with one of his own. *Do you agree to my terms?*

How can I not? I don't know which angle he's playing, but an evening out sounds better than reliving the single most humiliating experience of my life.

Slowly, I reach out my hand, offering it to him, palm up. *It's a bargain.*

He takes my hand in his, his touch more a caress than an actual shake. *No kiss?*

Don't push your luck, pal.

The skin around his eyes crinkle up in amusement and I prepare for the next barb in our verbal sparring game when footsteps approach the door. In the space between heartbeats, Aiden shifts back into a wolf so when Chloe pushes my bedroom door farther open, I'm sitting there with his big paw in my hand.

My aunt smells of toasted marshmallows and anxiety as her gaze takes in the scene. "Nic? You okay?"

"Yeah." I release Aiden's paw and turn onto my back.

"Aiden told us what happened." She offers a weak smile. "Intoxispells have taken down the best of us."

I slide a glance at Aiden. "Would you mind giving us a minute?"

Silently he pads to the door and out into the other room.

"What's up, Buttercup?"

"I need to ask you something about Aiden."

Her jaw is set and I see hellfire blaze in her pretty blue eyes. "Did that wolf try something? Because I swear I will make him suffer—"

"No, Chloe. He was the one who kept his head. But it's more a question about…" I trail off, not sure how to voice what I'm feeling.

She plops onto the side of the bed. "Is it time we had the sex talk? Is wittle Nic feeling a funny tingling *down there?*"

"Can you be serious for two seconds, please?"

"One, two. Time's up."

I groan and throw an arm over my eyes. "This was a bad idea. Especially when I'm hungover."

Chloe laughs. "Okay, no more shenanigans, I swear. Do you, like, have questions?"

I pick at a stray thread on my comforter. "How do I know if it's me he really wants?"

Her face sobers and her scent changes to something that smells lemony. "Look, kid. I'm not living with my sister because I'm aces in the love department but there's one piece of advice I can give you. Don't get screwed with a hard-on meant for someone else."

I roll my eyes, then wince in pain. Freaking hangover. "Classy with a capital K."

"I mean it. If you think he's using you as some sort of

substitute, kick his furry ass to the curb. You deserve someone who will love you for the little sociopath you are."

"Thanks, Chloe."

She shrugs. "Obviously, Addy and I know you can do better, but we respect your choices."

I give her a level look. "He's the son of a god. There really *isn't* much better."

She sniffs. "I'll keep my opinion to myself."

"That'd be a first." I sigh and snuggle back into the pillows.

She pushes some hair behind my ear. "You've been training too hard."

"I want to beat the gauntlet. To become forever young."

Chloe arches one perfect red-gold eyebrow. "Do you really?"

I hadn't at first. When the possibility of me taking up the Unseelie Shadow Throne had been broached I'd wanted nothing to do with it. But now….

"I have things that I need to fix, from my last life."

"No one is keeping score, Nic. Most of the Unseelie, most of the fey for that matter, don't know you've been reborn. You could have a clean slate."

"I've never had a clean slate, though. You know that. I started killing when I was six years old."

Chloe glances away, but not before I see the troubled shadow in her eyes. "I should let you rest."

I reach out and grip her arm. "What is it?"

She licks her lips. "You killed before that."

"What?" I stare up at her. "How would you know that?"

"It's why she abandoned you."

She. Meaning the third sister fate. The one who supposed to be my guardian. All thoughts of discomfort fade away. "Tell me what happened."

"Nic, it's late. You have school tomorrow."

"Like I give a shit?"

She huffs out an exasperated breath, her scent changing to something more sour than sweet. "Look, it was a long time ago."

"So was everything else. But it's still impacting my here and now. How am I supposed to face this series of unknown tests if I don't know who I am or where I came from?"

"Addy should be here for this." Chloe makes one last-ditch attempt. "Let me run and wake her up—"

My voice goes up several decibels. "And have her side with you?"

Outside the door, Aiden growls low in his throat. He doesn't like the idea of anyone, even the aunts who've raised me, ganging up on me.

"If you're going to eavesdrop," I tell him, "You might as well come back in."

He nudges the door open and stares at the two of us. Chloe casts him a withering look but he simply stands there, unafraid and unmoving.

I put my hand over hers, no longer scared of physical contact the way I'd once been. "Please. How can I make an informed choice if I don't know how it all went down?"

She exhales wearily. "Fine. But this isn't exactly a bedtime story."

I nod and settle in, doing my best not to leap out of my skin. Over by my bookshelf, Aiden curls up on the braided rug, his green eyes watchful.

Chloe nods in his direction. "Your wolf brought you to the three of us as a babe."

"How did he find you?" I interrupt.

"We were...more accessible before, for those who knew how and where to look. He told us that you were the Unseelie Queen of the Shadow Throne and had been reborn as a mortal. He said he had been your consort and the father of your unborn heir and it was his job to keep you safe until you came of age and could reclaim your birthright. He asked us to raise you, to keep you safe. In all the history of the world, no being, god, immortal or man ever entrusted us with an innocent life or asked for our help so directly. We could have refused. It is not our place to interfere with the course of things. But we have threads just like any other. And ours has in the past, become entangled with those of mortals and the fey."

I look to where Aiden has laid his head back down between his midnight paws and is feigning sleep. "Why did you send him away?"

One green eye cracks open.

"We agreed only on the condition that your fate is hidden from us. We knew that if your wolf, your Aiden, was part of your life, then your past would never fully abandon you. It's difficult enough to overcome struggles from your own life-time, but to cope with what a previous incarnation did?" She shakes her head. "It's too much, even for a mind as powerful as yours."

"And he agreed." I look back at Aiden.

You deserved a fresh start, he thinks.

And you didn't? Aiden had suffered for almost the entirety of my mortal life at the hands of Brigit and her Unseelie Court.

He doesn't respond, his eyes sliding shut once more.

"So, he left you in our charge," Chloe continues, unaware of our silent communication. "And then we divvied up the task of raising you. At first, we all tried living together. It was a nightmare. We were used to moving around, going where we were needed when we were useful. A nomadic existence isn't easy, especially not with an infant in tow. We fought constantly and you were always crying, always needing something. So, we decided to split up, each of us taking you for a year. I was supposed to be the most nurturing of us, the most patient. I had you first. We went to that cottage in the Black Forest, the one where you were found. It was your first home. When I was needed out in the world, one of the others would come to relieve me, but for most of your first year, it was just the two of us. Then Addy got you year two, and so on."

"And your other sister?"

Chloe stares out the window. "Her name was Lachesis. Sissy. She had you year three, starting on your second birthday. And believe it or not, she loved you as much as we did. I could hardly wait for your third birthday, for my next turn to be with you. You'd changed so much in such a brief time."

I open my mouth to tell her a year is plenty of time for a mortal child to change but then shut it again. When a being is as old as the world itself, a year probably doesn't feel like a long time.

"So, I had you for your fourth year and reluctantly turned you over to Addy for your fifth. Sissy showed up for your sixth birthday and everything seemed fine. We had no idea that she would wipe your memories of us and abandon you."

"And why did she leave me?" My pulse pounds. "What did I do wrong?"

"She'd taken you out to see other people. It's something we all did during festivals because you were very isolated and we wanted you to see civilization, even if you couldn't be a part of it on a regular basis. Your magic had yet to manifest and we couldn't risk having you expose yourself until you could control your gifts.

From what Sissy told us later, she had taken you to an ice cream shop. You were sitting outside, eating and she ducked in to get a napkin. When she came back you were gone. Every parent's nightmare, even for one of us."

"Someone had abducted me?" I ask as Aiden growls from the floor.

Chloe shook her head. "No. Apparently, you had seen a boy running through the crowd, all bloody and bruised. You took off after him. And his father cornered the two of you in an alley. The man was drunk, Sissy said. She could smell it on him, even after...what happened.

"I killed him." It's not a question.

She confirms it. "According to the boy you'd been protecting, yes. Sissy panicked, wiped the boy's memories and yours as well and brought you back to the cottage. She didn't know anything, didn't see that it was your kiss that killed him and because she'd erased your recollection of the event, you couldn't tell her how you'd done it."

"And did she tell you, or Addy?" I ask. "What I'd done?"

"Yes," Chloe says. "We knew she was freaked out and we'd made plans to go get you, to move you to a more secure location. One on one obviously wasn't working anymore, not if your powers started to manifest. But we were delayed. And Sissy..."

She pauses and takes a deep breath. "I won't make excuses for her, Nic. She stole your memories. She abandoned you in the woods with no food, no water, only the clothes on your back and then left the cottage in ruins so even if you did find your way back, it would provide no real shelter. She meant for you to die in the forest so your killing power wouldn't be unleashed on the world, at least that's what she told us when we caught up to her."

"And you killed her for it. Your own sister." Sensations war within me, rage at the third adoptive mother I can't remember, sorrow for Chloe and Addy, and above all, overwhelming gratitude that they hadn't sided with Lachesis and decided to give up on me, too.

Chloe nods, her scent like bitter coffee. "You have to

understand. Our oldest and most sacred law is to not interfere with the natural progress of mankind. You were reincarnated for a reason, brought to us for a reason and we agreed to take you in for a reason. Even if she didn't actively try and kill you, she engineered a set of circumstances designed to take your life. She left us with no choice. We cannot interfere, or the fabric of the world could unravel."

I swallow. "Is there any way for me to regain those early memories? The way Nahini taught me to follow the threads to my previous life?" It wasn't something I'd thought much about, until now.

But Chloe shakes her head sadly. "I don't know. When a Norn does a memory purge she doesn't erase just the mind she's scrubbing, but all the events that led up to it. It's not a power we use often because it affects so many lives, for even the smallest event. That boy, the one you saved? He has no memory of you, the alley or how his father died. The time is a complete blank. For him, it never happened and his mind will most likely try to fill the void with mundane events. Laundry, dishes, a trip to the grocery. You could pass by him on the street and he wouldn't experience so much as a flicker of recognition. Your mind is different though. Not fully mortal, not fully fey. It could be that even with the purge you might remember things in time even if they aren't complete memories."

I lean back against the pillows. "Thank you for telling me."

"Nic," Chloe begins.

"I'm tired," I say to forestall her. "Can we talk about this tomorrow?"

"Okay." She nods and heads for the door, but pauses to look back. "She did care for you. The same way Addy and I do."

Just not enough to overcome her fear. "Night."

Chloe shut the door and a moment later I see the light flick off in the kitchen. There is the click of sharp claws on wood as Aiden paces around the room. The mattress dips as, still in wolf form, he slowly pulls himself up beside me, taking care not to jostle me.

He meets my gaze, his eyes seeming to be lit from behind so they glow in the dark. He doesn't think at me, doesn't ask whether I'm okay. I reach out to stroke his fur and after a long moment he lays down beside me, offering the only comfort I'll accept.

I close my eyes but sleep doesn't find me until dawn.

"You sure you're up for this?" Aiden asks as he parks the truck in the school lot and glances over at me. "You can always change your mind."

I shake my head, wincing at the pain. "What am I supposed to do at home, sit around and brood? There are things that need investigating here." Like the brown-eyed stranger and the fairy hill.

It had been decided at breakfast that morning. A shower had made me feel more like myself, washing away the pixing and the conversation with Chloe. Not to mention the make-out session with Aiden. Wearing a baggy purple t-shirt with a pair of glitter red lips on the breast pocket over black leggings, I'd secured my hair in a braid and felt almost normal.

"You look like *Jord* with your hair done that way." Jasmine, her own hair a riot of red curls, studies my outfit with interest.

"In my wildest dreams," I circled the table to my usual place.

Aiden, freshly showered and shaved, pulled out the chair for me. "No way to improve on perfection."

Nahini and Freda were there as well as my aunts and Alric's falcons and hounds prowl around outside to guard against eavesdroppers.

I let Aiden and Addy fill them in on the details, concentrating all my efforts on buttering my toast with the barest amount of movement possible.

"Why didn't you say anything yesterday?" Freda's blonde brows are drawn together, her jaw set at a menacing angle. "We could have set a watch."

"Whoever is using the fairy hill knew we were there, sent the dust out as a diversion." Aiden sets a bowl of oatmeal down in front of me. "They have the location under surveillance. Your troops would end up fornicating on the hillside."

Freda's countenance darkens and Chloe barely stifles a laugh.

"It's wise," Nahini's tone is calm. "To keep the existence of the fairy hill quiet, at least until we can flush out the spy. For all we know, the fairy hill is where they cross into Underhill."

"My thoughts exactly," I said and reached for my bowl of oatmeal. "We need to go about school and training, all business as usual."

Underhill could take me as soon as I wore her mark.

"Worry not, my queen. There are things we can do to help you prepare." Nahini had said with a soft smile. "I will work with you on borrowing powers from the fey of the Unseelie Court as well as mental shielding and preparation. And we need to go over Unseelie politics as well."

"Something to look forward to," I grumble now and pop open the door to the truck.

Aiden is out and around, there to ease my descent to the ground. "What did you say?"

"Nothing." I reach back in for my backpack but he plucks it from my hands and slings it over his own shoulder before taking my hand in his. "Hey, isn't it enough for you that I let you drive my truck?"

He captures my hand in his. "It's never enough for me."

"Just let me know if you feel the need to mark me in any other way." I stare down at our intertwined hands but don't pull away. "I'd prefer not to be surrounded by a circle of piss."

"This is for your benefit," Aiden explains.

"Sure, it is." Still, I hang on to his hand.

"You two are so cute." Jasmine beams at us in pleasure, then rushes ahead when she spies Kayleigh.

I stare after her wide-eyed. "Did she just call us cute? I am *not* cute."

"Of course not." Aiden's wide grin contradicts his words.

We head to my locker. If Aiden has one, I have yet to see him use it. He carries a green five subject notebook and a pencil, and somehow manages to have whatever he needs for individual classes on hand. Of course, he isn't here for educational purposes.

"Any sign of our friend from yesterday?" I move slowly, to give Aiden time to survey the hallway and the throngs of students passing by.

His glance is casual even as he puts a hand on my shoulder. "Not yet."

He appears troubled. "What's wrong?"

"The boy from yesterday. He blended well. *Too* well."

Understanding dawns. "The way you did."

Aiden nods once. "You were the only one to notice he was out of place. That takes a strong sort of glamour. More than what a typical fey would possess."

"And combined with the fairy hills that lead directly to the courts…." A chill goes up my spine. "You're thinking we're dealing with one of the Seelie royals? Wardon or Soladin?"

"Or perhaps one of the fey lords from the Unseelie Court." Aiden shakes his head. "We just don't know enough yet."

"I guess that means I'm bait." I don't know how to feel about random fey wandering around my hometown, my school. "I don't know if I'm ready for this."

Aiden stares down at me. "I'll protect you."

"That's not…" I slam my locker, frustrated. How can I make him understand that it's not me I'm worried about?

"Everything will work out," Aiden puts an arm around my neck, drawing me into him. "Let nature take its course."

A wave of dizziness washes over me and I hear a woman's voice as though she'd whispered in my ear. *It's not in your nature.* Each word hits me in the gut like a physical blow, knocking the wind out of me. I stumble and would have gone down on my ass if Aiden hadn't been there to catch me.

"Nic? What's wrong?"

"Give me a minute." I blink, the fluorescent lights searing my retinas. Everything is too much, almost overwhelming. What brought that on? After-effects from the pixie dust most likely.

"Ms. Rutherford? Is everything all right?"

I blink up to see Vice Principal Steinburg staring down at me. The man looks like some sort of half-starved bird of prey, thin to the point of gauntness. He has a long beaklike nose and a pointed chin. His hair is black as a raven's wing, except at the temples where the pepper is mixed with a decent amount of salt. Either his hygiene regimen doesn't extend to washing his hair or he uses some oil-based product on it because it always looks wet. And he doesn't smell that great either.

"Sure," I plaster a stiff smile and lean more heavily into

Aiden's hold. The last thing I need is for the veep to think I'm high and do a locker search.

"Mr.…?" Steinburg's blue-gray eyes narrow on Aiden.

"Jager," he supplies helpfully, though his attention is fixed on me.

"Would you run and fetch the nurse? She should be in her office." The veep puts one hand on my back shifting my weight from Aiden to himself.

"I'm fine," I protest around gulps of air. My knuckles turn white where I clutch Aiden's arm, silently begging him not to leave. I don't want to be given over to tender school custody.

Aiden licks his lips, his expression worried. "I'll be right back, Nic." He breaks into a flat-out sprint, knocking into several students who have the misfortune of getting in his way.

The bell rings and the halls empty out. The veep guides me to an empty classroom "Come, sit down."

"The nurse," I glance back in the direction Aiden has gone.

"I'll flag her down, if necessary. You should get off your feet in case you faint."

There's a buzzing sound in my ears and I still feel as though I'm laboring for breath. Part of me doesn't want to take deeper breaths. He positively reeks, like an old outhouse sitting abandoned in the sun for a full decade. Sitting seems wise. I allow him to usher me into the empty room, only realizing I've made a mistake when I hear the door close and the click of the lock.

"Nicneven, at last." The creature who I'd believed to be a mortal begins to melt away.

CHAPTER 5

YOU DON'T SEE THAT EVERY DAY

For a moment, I understand Dorothy's horror when the Wicked Witch of the West melts before her very eyes. Except I haven't tossed a bucket of water, did nothing to instigate the horrific display happening ten feet away.

Imperfect human skin and dark greasy hair ooze like sap from an injured tree to reveal feathers the color of midnight. The nose I'd once thought of as hawk-like reveals an actual hawk's sharp beak, the long arms transform into wings, the legs no longer end in sensible shoes but wicked looking talons. The being is still humanoid in shape, though its eyes are as cold and merciless as a bird of prey.

"Who are you?" I'm still not seeing straight and watching the bird creature emerge from beneath the human flesh doesn't help.

"Nicneven," the voice transforms along with the appearance. It's higher in pitch, with the inflection sharper, more menacing. "Somehow, I was expecting more from the Ice Bitch."

"You knew me?" My heart pounds in the face of this new threat. "In my last life?"

"Only by reputation." Wings spread wide, blocking the door, the only exit. "Rumors in the courts say you were reborn mortal. That you do not recover from injuries like the fair folk. I didn't believe them. After all, how could you kill Brigit if you are of mortal flesh?"

I back away from him—her—it—until my back hits the cinderblock wall. "What do you want?"

The creature makes a sound I can only assume is a laugh. "Why? Are you willing to bargain for your miserable life? You, who decimated an entire nest of my kind?"

I opened my mouth, then shut it again. What can I say? That I have no memory of decimating anybody for any reason? It's not like I can claim innocence, being a serial killer and all. Judging by the predatory gaze in those midnight eyes, no excuse will get me out of this unscathed.

It lunges for me, but I duck beneath the nearest desk, my training kicking in. The desk is ripped away, flung across the room like a ball of paper. I scramble under the next, but don't pause, hunting for a weapon or at least better cover. Neither is to be found.

I stay a hair ahead of it, moving just before it is about to strike. I'd won against Freda and Nahini, but that hadn't been life or death. Somewhere in the back of my mind, I knew it wasn't real. This creature means business. What good will besting them do me if I don't even make it to the gauntlet?

Crawl. Toss. Crawl. Toss. This goes on until my back presses against the far wall. I pause a moment, frantically trying to come up with a plan. As far as I can tell, the creature has no exposed skin. Nowhere for me to place my deadly kiss.

The desk above me is violently ripped away.

Great wings flap, stirring the air in the small room and

lifting the creature off the ground until those sinister talons are at eye level. Will it rip me apart as I huddle here? Or perhaps sever my head from my body and take it as a trophy.

"Any last words, Queen of the Shadow Throne?"

I raise my arms. It's an instinctive gesture, to protect my face from oncoming harm, but as I do, the wall behind me explodes inwards.

I am tossed through the air and slam against the opposite wall even as the funnel of a tornado swoops inside. The bird creature shrieks but the winds of the funnel are too powerful. With no purchase, it is sucked into the swirling vortex in a flurry of feathers.

I struggle to hold on to anything nailed down so as not to suffer the same fate. The wind whips papers through the air, pulls desks and chairs out through the hole. I grasp the doorknob even as the gale pulls me horizontal from the floor. Over the roar of furniture being relocated I can hear someone pounding on the door.

"Nic!" Aiden bellows.

"I can't hold on!" The words are ripped out of me, sucked into the ravenous funnel.

"You can control it," he shouts. "Focus on the air. Get the feel of it and it will become yours."

"How?" I shout. My hands slip on the door handle.

"Describe it to me. What does it smell like?"

"Death," I bitch, but then pick up other scents. "Ozone. Churned earth."

"What does it feel like?"

"Energy, power." As I say the words I experience them in my veins. One hand slips but I don't panic, sensing the same power inside me as the tornado swirls above.

The wind dies down, my feet touch the floor. And then all is quiet.

"Nic?" Aiden asks.

"Yeah," I pant, unable to believe the destruction in the room. Or that where moments ago I was sure I was about to die, now I am alive and relatively unharmed. I sink to the floor, panting.

"Can you unlock the door or should I bash it in?"

Reaching up, I turn the handle until the lock pops, and then roll away so Aiden can push through.

He takes one look at the room, at me on the floor, then crosses the hall and pulls the emergency fire alarm.

"You can't do that," I gasp even as the sound rings out.

"I just did." He's back at my side in an instant even as the hallway fills with students. "Can you stand?"

I nod and he helps me to my feet. Between one heart-beat and the next, we fall in with the crush of exiting students.

"Where's the nurse?" I ask, realizing that he's alone.

Aiden half carries, half drags me down the concrete steps and we maneuver our way toward our homeroom teacher, Mrs. Bates, who's frowning at her clipboard.

"There you two are." She gives us a cursory once over and then frowns. "Where were you?"

"Looking for the nurse. Nic wasn't feeling well, but I couldn't find her." Aiden answers both my question and the teacher's at once.

"She doesn't come in for another half an hour." Mrs. Bates is shaking her head. "And why did no one tell me a drill had been planned for today?"

Aiden slides me a sideways look. I am just as incredulous. Did no one else notice a tornado ripping a hole in the side of the school?

"May I take Nic over to the bleachers so she can sit down?"

Mrs. Bates squints at me through thick bifocals. "Just stay in sight."

"Of course." Aiden flashes her an easy smile even as he helps me hobble away.

"Well done." He's much better at managing people than me.

But Aiden doesn't appear to have heard the compliment, already too busy with the self-flagellation. "I shouldn't have left you. Steinburg attacked you?"

"Whatever it was, it attacked me." I do my best to describe the birdlike creature and its massive grudge.

"A Valkyrie," Aiden growls loud enough that several other students look our way as we pass through the knot of people. The fingers on his free hand flex.

"Say what now?" I pull him further away for more privacy. Fire trucks come roaring into the lot, distracting the onlookers. "Valkyries are real?"

He gives me a well, duh kind of look.

"Aren't Valkyries supposed to be all beautiful shield-maidens who serve Odin by selecting which warriors to spirit off to Valhalla? The thing I saw was heinous and smelled like an open sewer."

"They don't serve Odin. They serve Freya, who is a jealous sort. Can't keep any sort of competition around. She likes her handmaidens to be plain or homely to enhance her own beauty. Though she will bestow them with glamour to help recruit the souls of the slain. The part about Valhalla is true, but what many people forget is that the Valkyries don't just select who will serve from the slain, they select who will survive the battle."

I suck in a sharp breath. "Like my aunts?"

"Similar, though their powers are limited to the battle-field. They've grown restless in recent decades. Too few wars, too many idle claws looking to serve up trouble."

"So why was it after me? Do you think Freya set them on me?" Slowly, I ease down onto the bleachers. Facing Brigit had been terrifying enough, I didn't want to tangle with a goddess.

But Aiden shakes his head. "Freya's asleep, all the Aesir and Vanir are, except for Heimdal, the watchman. No, whatever the Valkyries are up to, it isn't on behalf of the gods."

That is only somewhat reassuring.

"My main concern is that Valkyries usually hunt in pairs." Aiden glances around at the throng of milling students. "And if they're able to don a glamour, they can hide in plain sight."

"Do you see Jasmine?" Worry spikes through me as I scan the crowd for the nymph girl who is my responsibility.

He nods. "She's with her class. Was Steinburg new to the school?"

I shake my head. "No. He's been here for years. At least since I've been here. Why?"

"A glamour that comes from another being's magic won't last more than a few days. Chances are the Valkyrie took his place recently."

"Would it have killed the real Vice-Principal Steinburg?"

"I have no idea. Outside of a battlefield, it's rare to find Valkyrie on this side of the Veil. Without magic to cloak them, they are extremely conspicuous. The other one will be nearby, hoping to catch you alone, though after this demonstration of your power, it'll be more careful."

"My power?" I blink up at him. "Why do you think it was me?"

Aiden blinks down at me. "You mean, you didn't summon the tornado?"

"I don't know. I mean, I didn't do anything intentionally."

"What were you thinking about, when it attacked you?"

"The Wizard of Oz," I say. "It was a stray thought, the way the glamour came off, it melted, the same way the wicked witch did in the story."

"I'm familiar with it." Aiden frowns. "Didn't the girl in that story get swept up in a tornado?"

My lips part. "You mean I summoned it, just by thinking of that story?"

He nods once. "Your powers are getting stronger the closer we come to Samhain. Another reason the second Valkyrie will act quickly."

I'd summoned a tornado out of the clear blue sky to battle a Valkyrie with a grudge. By accident. "I could have killed someone."

He looks at me, brows raised. "You did kill that Valkyrie."

"Unintentionally, I mean. Setting a tornado loose on a school? I had no idea I could do that."

Aiden's expression turns grim. "We'll speak with Nahini about accelerating your mystical training, though the power over air is unique to you."

"Did I ever tell you how I learned to control it before?"

He shakes his head. "No. You never spoke much about your early life. Your focus was on the future, not the past."

From our vantage point, I can see the wake of destruction left by the tornado. What if the second Valkyrie comes after me in the gym? Or the cafeteria? I might kill hundreds of innocent students, trying to protect myself from the next attack.

Thinking of students in the cafeteria made me recall the boy with the brown eyes who'd been staring at me yesterday. "The other boy, the stranger you followed to the fairy hill. Do you think he could be the other Valkyrie?"

He considers for a moment. "It's possible."

I scan the crowd. "Have you seen him today?"

"No."

I huff out a breath. "What now?"

Aiden puts an arm around my shoulder. "We keep vigilant and wait."

❄

"THE KIDS ARE STOKED," Jasmine says when we finally get the all-clear to leave school grounds. She hops up into the cab of the truck and then leans down to give me a hand up. "Second day and we're out before lunch. And none of them seem to care why."

I take her hand and grunt as Aiden boosts me up. It's not exactly a dignified position and I'm fairly certain my wolfish companion is enjoying it just a little too much.

Once I'm situated, Aiden shuts the door and then circles to the driver's side. "The modern teenager is a remarkably resilient creature. School bombs, threats, riots in the streets. They accept it with nothing more than a shrug. Adults are the ones who are rigid and inflexible, who are shocked by everything. Children accept as the way the world works."

"What really happened?" Jasmine asks.

"A tornado." I lean against the window and watch the flashing lights. "Apparently I summoned it."

"Why?" Jasmine flicks on the radio and thankfully, switches away from the top one hundred looking for news.

"A Valkyrie came after her," Aiden says tersely.

I'd called Freda and Addy to let them know what had happened. Freda had told me to give Jasmine enough information to satisfy her without bogging her down with the details.

"A Valkyrie? Really?" Jasmine looks at me with wide eyes. "I've never seen one."

"You're not missing much," I say just as the newscaster's passionless voice switches to a practiced somber tone.

A freak weather event has shut down the local junior-senior high school this morning and stumped local meteorologists. A tornado touched down, decimating a classroom shortly after seven AM, while school was in session. Luckily the room was empty at the time and no injuries have been reported. Tornados are not frequent in the high country and no tornado watch or tornado warning was in effect at the time of the occurrence. The last reported tornado watch was Wednesday, May 24th, 2017. Before that—"

Aiden clicks off the radio. "Good old mortals. They're going with the old freak weather event."

"How long do you think school will be closed?" Jasmine's tone is anxious.

"Possibly through the end of the week," I tell her.

"So long?" Her face falls.

"Don't worry, you can use the extra time to practice your reading. We'll try some new audiobooks." I'd been purchasing books as well as the accompanying audiobooks to assist her with reading and pronunciation.

She nods but remains quiet for the rest of the trip to the farm.

Aiden parks in my usual spot and insists on helping me down, in case I feel dizzy again. I haven't told him about the voice or the odd feeling that had accompanied her words. *It's not in your nature.* Did that have something to do with the Valkyrie? I scoot to the edge of the seat but pause before I can take his hand.

"What is it?" He studies me from head to toe. "Nic?"

"I keep thinking about Steinburg." I meet his green gaze. "How did it know to take the place of a teacher? You said the glamour only lasts a few days."

He moves closer until he's standing between my spread knees. "Do you suspect Brigit's spy has something to do with it?"

"School started yesterday and the Valkyrie makes its move today. The Hunt is here at the farm, and the place is mystically hidden besides. At school, I don't have those same protections. Someone is noting my movements." To anyone looking on, it would appear we were sharing a tender moment, not discussing espionage and assassination attempts. "We should go to the veep's house, look for clues."

Aiden doesn't appear thrilled by the prospect of looking for the wayward vice principal. "Do you know where he lives?"

"No, but he has a Siamese cat. Addy will have his address on file in the clinic."

"The other Valkyrie might be lying in wait for us there," he cautions. "I should go alone."

"It's after me," I remind him. "It might not reveal itself to you. At least this way I don't have to worry about it coming after me at school. Plus, if it is there, we could trap it and maybe unearth the spy's identity. Two bird creatures, one stone—so to speak."

Aiden reaches up a thumb to trace my lower lip. "And the dizzy spell?"

"Probably just the after-effects from the pixie dust."

"Will you let Addy check you over, just to make sure?"

"She's a vet, not a doctor," I groan.

"She's the closest thing we have to a physician." He appears worried.

"If it will make you feel better, fine."

Though it's a short walk from the house to the clinic, Aiden insists on taking the truck. I don't argue since I'm hoping to get the all-clear from Addy and head out right afterward.

Addy's busy in the office, but Chloe is seated behind the reception desk, a stack of files by her elbow, a game of spider solitaire up on her computer screen. She smells like cherries today, a scent that typically means she's exhausted. She looks me over with a quick glance. "A Valkyrie, really?"

"It's not like I woke up and said, gee, today seems like a stellar day to get attacked by a giant bird woman."

"Smartass," she gripes. "Everyone is okay though?"

"I felt a little dizzy earlier, but that was before the attack. Probably just overtired."

"I thought you said it was a result of the pixie dust." Aiden narrows his gaze on me.

"Or that." Changing the subject I turn back to Chloe. "Do you know anything about Valkyries?"

She drums her bright pink fingernails on the desk. "Yes. They're foul, grasping creatures. Sort of a combination of kleptomaniacs and hoarders with personal hygiene issues."

Which explains the smell. "The one that attacked me said I destroyed a nest of them in my last life. Why would I do that?"

"They probably took something you valued and you retaliated."

"*Seelenverkäufer.*" I look to Aiden who nods in confirmation.

"It was before my time at your court, but I heard stories. You rode the Hunt on midwinter's day into the high hills where the nest was and scourged the lot of them from the oldest crone to the newest hatchling."

Sounds like me, rather the old Nicneven. "Great, just what I need, more shitty judgment calls from my last life cropping up to bite me on the ass."

Chloe stands and circles the desk. "So, what's the plan?"

"We're going to check out the vice principal's place." I don't elaborate further. "I need Steinburg's address of record."

"After Addy gives you the all-clear," Aiden insists. "At least let her take your vitals."

"I'll get her." Chloe rises, then pushes the tin of chocolate chip cookies across the desk to us. "You didn't get any of these, yesterday."

"It's eleven in the morning," I tell her.

She blinks. "What's your point?"

"You need help." I hand the tin to Aiden, who can always benefit from a few extra calories.

Chloe disappears into the back, and a moment later returns with Addy in tow.

"A Valkyrie? We better make sure your shots are up to date," Addy grumbles.

"I'm starting to get the impression that no one likes these creatures." I follow her into one of the examination rooms. Thankfully Aiden doesn't follow.

"Not much there to like," Addy says. "They're excellent soldiers but without a true leader, they make trouble."

"Some people have said the same thing about me."

Addy washes her hands at the sink and then dons a pair of exam gloves. "Who?"

"Aiden's grandmother." I try not to flinch when she presses the cold flat disk of her stethoscope beneath my shirt until it rests on my bare flesh.

Addy listens for a minute before removing the stethoscope and reaching for my wrist. Eyes on the wall clock she adds, "Well, you're an acquired taste."

"That's putting it mildly. So, am I gonna make it?"

She shines a small penlight into my eyes. Hissing, I cringe away.

"You didn't hit your head yesterday?"

"No, nothing like that."

"And you ate fine this morning." She steps back, frowning. "Describe the dizziness. Did it come on suddenly?"

"Yes. Aiden and I were talking and then I thought I heard a woman say, it's not in your nature. After that everything went sort of sideways." I stop short of telling her about my reaction to the words.

"It's not in your nature." She takes off her glasses, her gaze going unfocused. "It might be some sort of spell, though the phrasing isn't that of a classic curse. And there was no one near you?"

"You mean other than the giant bird creature in disguise?" My tone is dry.

"Valkyries can't cast spells. I think you're probably fine for now, just take it easy and let me know if anything else unusual happens."

"Easier said than done." Unusual is my new normal.

"Nic, I mean it." Addy pushes her half-moon glasses up further on her sharp blade of a nose. "You're still mortal. You can die."

I tilt my head to look at her. "Do you know when I'll die?"

Addy, or Atropos as the Greeks called her, was the Fate responsible for severing the threads of life for mortals and gods alike. I must assume that she also deals with former fairy queens turned teenage serial killers.

She shakes her head. "Even if I had that knowledge—which I don't—I wouldn't tell you. It would be considered tampering with the divine plan."

"Which you will not do. Funny though, that the three of you agreed to raise me. Or doesn't that fall under the subheading of tampering."

She turns away. "The moment your wolf asked us, we could no longer stay neutral. Our destinies were entwined with yours whether we took you in or not. Perhaps it was selfish but…"

"But?" I prompt when she doesn't finish.

"We wanted a closer look. It's a terrible thing, to be alive and unchanging. Unattached to any yet responsible for all. To watch all those around you grow from a tiny helpless creature to a force of nature. To see them grow old and die and to witness their loved ones mourn, never truly understanding the depths of their loss. Even the fair folk die eventually, though they don't age. Until you came into our lives, until our sister died…we were alive but without life." She stares at the wall, though I'm certain she sees something else entirely.

"Do you regret it?" I ask. "Having me instead of your sister?"

It's a stupid question, one I really don't want an answer to. Yet it's out there now, jettisoned from the dark corner where I'd stashed it.

She swallows, shakes her head. "I regret what we had to do to her. But you're our family, Nic. One of us."

We aren't huggers. Laughter is acceptable, as well as healthy doses of sarcasm and snark. But physical affection has never been part of my world, at least not until Aiden came into my life. He's always looking for a reason to touch me, not sexually, but in support. To lace his fingers through mine, or to put a hand on the small of my back. To brush a stray lock of hair out of my eyes. And I soak it up like a sponge.

I wonder if Addy longs for that sort of supportive touch, for the pure affection the same way I do. Slowly, I reach out and put a hand on her shoulder. She turns, eyebrows lifting in surprise. Her hand comes down over the top of mine. We stay that way for a long moment.

"It will be all right," Addy tells me. "Everything happens for a reason. You'll see."

I'm not sure if that's a prediction or just her confidence in me, but Aiden knocks on the door, interrupting the moment and I don't have the nerve to ask.

CHAPTER 6

SOUL WALKING

The address Mr. Steinburg had on file with the vet's office is an apartment complex on one of the main thoroughfares on the outskirts of town. While I'm eager to investigate, Aiden talks me into delaying.

"Wait until nightfall. If things go sideways, we'll want the cover of darkness."

"You mean, in case I start manipulating weather patterns by accident," I grumble.

It's a sore spot. I have a world of power within my grasp and no idea how to control it. Even my own innate abilities, like manipulating air and spirit, don't come naturally. If I can get a handle on my magic, maybe I wouldn't be so apprehensive about the upcoming gauntlet.

"We don't want to be seen," Aiden neatly dodges the question and instead, takes a different tack. "Involving the mortal authorities never ends well. Particularly for those of us with blood on our hands."

"The authorities will all be busy at the school. You saw the lights." It's a token protest. I know he's right to wait for nightfall. I want to get it over with though, before I lose my nerve completely.

"Let's check in with Alric," Aiden suggests. "See if his beasts have learned anything that can help."

But Alric isn't in the bunkhouse and no one we ask seems to know when he left or how long he's been gone.

"Let's check with Freda and Nahini," I suggest. "They might have dispatched him on some errand or another."

Freda and Jasmine are in the training yard, working with longbows. Jasmine is barely tall enough to keep her bow end from touching the ground, but her accuracy makes up for her small stature.

"Excellent," Freda says, casting her daughter a proud glance. I never get an excellent out of her. The highest praise she's ever given me begrudging, "You're improving. A little."

Considering I almost took out a patrolling fey and his mount when I first used the bow, I can hardly get any worse. Luckily, I am a better swordswoman than I am an archer.

"Have either of you seen Alric?" I ask as we approach them.

Jasmine lowers her bow and shakes her head. "Not since last night, right after supper."

"Freda?"

My first moves to the target and extracts the arrows from the canvas with sharp uneven yanks. "Not today."

Aiden and I exchange a look.

"They had a fight," Jasmine volunteers.

Freda freezes for an instant, her hand around the shaft of an arrow. She rounds on her offspring, blonde braid cutting the air like a whip. "Jasmine! You were eavesdropping?"

"Yes." The petite redhead appears completely unapologetic. "I saw you sneak down to the lake in the middle of the night, so I followed you."

Freda appears torn between aggravation that Jasmine

took it upon herself to spy on her mother, and rattled that the girl managed to get the drop on her. Finally, she lets out an indignant huff of air and grumbles, "Well, don't do it again."

Jasmine shrugs and unstrings her bow. "Then don't sneak out."

Freda watches the small figure skip off down the hill, her expression a mixture of irritation and grudging admiration. "That child will be the death of me."

"About Alric," I say. "If your disagreement is personal, just say so. I don't want to invade your privacy. But do you have any idea where he might have gone?"

Freda turns to me, her expression troubled. "It's possible that he crossed the Veil."

Aiden takes a step closer to her, his tone a low growl. "Why would he do that?"

"To see his sister." Freda doesn't back down from Aiden's fierce demeanor, though she swallows when she looks back at me. "And possibly to spy on his father and the workings of the court."

I gape at her a moment. "Spy?"

"I told him it was a foolish idea." Freda spits the words out like they taste bitter on her tongue. "Told him his father will know what he's up to, but he wants to make it up to you. To prove himself loyal."

"To me?" I raise a brow. "Why would he think I doubt his loyalty?"

Aiden places a hand on my arm. "Because of his connection to one of the heirs to the Fire Throne. And because you three questioned him yesterday."

"We had to," I protest. "To make sure."

But my wolf shakes his head. "Nic, you don't understand. You took a shot at his honor. A fey male won't take that lightly. Especially a soldier in the Wild Hunt."

"I told the idiot he had nothing to prove," Freda mutters. "Told him you trusted him as far as you trust anybody."

I pick up the censure in her words. "What's that supposed to mean?"

Never one to back away from a challenge, Freda puts her hands on her hips. "Do you trust me?"

The question takes me by surprise and I stutter. "I…I…."

"How about Nahini?" She presses. "Or the wolf here? Personally, I wouldn't trust him with dinner, never mind my back, but you've always shown a preference for him. I would think a certain amount of trust is only natural."

Beside me, Aiden tenses. Out of the corner of my eye, I can see that he's completely still, possibly even holding his breath.

I open my mouth but words fail me.

"You see, we are all loyal to you, Nicneven. And not just because you are our queen. We know you will put the good of the Hunt and the Unseelie Court above your own needs or wants. Unlike Brigit and the kings of the Seelie courts, you don't see us as tools to be used. You know what we are, people who can fight and die. Who are willing to fight and die for you. The problem is, you don't believe that basic truth. And we feel your mistrust, all of us. It chips away at our honor, bit by bit. And a warrior without honor soon doesn't see the point of fighting."

"It's not like that." I try to catch Aiden's eye but he's staring at the ground. "You don't understand what you're asking me."

"I'm not asking for anything," Freda says. "I am only high-lighting the reasons why Alric feels he should risk his life to bring you information without your asking. Why he would defy my order to stay put. Believe me, he will be punished for his insubordination, regardless of the reason."

I watch as she deposits the practice arrows in a nearby

quiver and then strides back down the hill toward the bunkhouse.

"Do you feel the same way?" I study Aiden carefully.

"I know why you are the way you are," the artful dodger responds with his posture still rigid.

I don't let him get away with it. "That isn't what I asked."

"I know." He looks over at me, unclenching his fists to tuck a stray piece of hair behind my ear. "Does it bother me to know that you don't trust me, even after all we've been through together? Yes. But it is the way it is and I need to believe that in time, you will let down your guard."

I stare into his leaf green eyes. I want to tell him that I'm trying, that I really do want to have the same sort of faith in him that he has in me. But wanting to feel a certain way isn't the same as possessing the capacity.

It's not in your nature. Is this what the woman in my mind had been talking about? My inability to trust?

"You're so closed off," he murmurs. "Trapped in a prison of your own making. I would endure the sentence with you if you would just let me in."

"I can't." The word is a whisper. I don't offer excuses or phony promises. "I'm sorry."

He smiles sadly. "Not now. But someday soon, you will decimate the walls that keep you contained. And when you do, my queen. There will be no stopping you."

NAHINI IS WAITING at the bottom of the hill. "You want to practice your magical skill set?"

I share a glance with Aiden then nod to her. "It's past time."

"Then follow me. Wolf, you may come, but only if you don't interfere." Nahini isn't nearly as hostile toward Aiden as Freda. The two aren't exactly friendly but they have a grudging respect for each other.

Aiden surprises me though when he shakes his head. "No. I'll find you when it's time for us to go out, Nic."

I frown as he walks away. "I think I hurt his feelings."

"Put it out of your head for now," Nahini advises and strides off in the direction of the barn.

I admire her composure and ability to compartmentalize. Even though her brother's soul is missing. Nahini is too much of a professional to let it interfere with her job.

We enter the barn, the familiar summertime smells fill the space. Nahini skillfully clambers up into the hayloft and after a moment, I follow. I'm not sure what magic we can do up here, but keep my reservations to myself. Nahini knows what she's doing. I crest the ladder and take a seat facing her, mimicking her crossed-legged pose.

"Clear your mind," Nahini instructs. "You need a blank canvas to create a masterpiece."

Though I try to do as she says, my mind buzzes with questions. "I don't understand how magic works."

"Magic doesn't work. It exists."

I exhale audibly. "I'm used to science and the explanation it provides, not backwater mystical beliefs with no reason to exist."

"They do have a reason though, just one beyond mortal understanding," Nahini replies patiently. "All living things have primal drives, urges to help it survive and to perpetuate the species. Some are basic, like instincts. The hair rising on your arms, the flesh creeping on the back of your neck when you are being followed. It's a warning. Magic is simply the abilities buried beneath those instincts, the actions."

"How can I tap into abilities I've never seen used though?"

"You grew wings and flew with them. You called a

tornado down upon an enemy. How is what I'm talking about any different?"

I let out a sigh. "You make it sound like I did those things on purpose. I didn't. I didn't even know they *were* possible until I'd already done them."

"So, seeing is believing?" She arches an eyebrow.

It's on the tip of my tongue to respond with a yes. I don't. Arguing with Nahini isn't productive. Instead, I retrench. "I'm still not sure how—"

"Don't focus on how. The laws of nature aren't inflexible to those who respect them. Magic is just science that is beyond current human comprehension. There is a great deal mortals don't grasp. The fey have learned that understanding isn't as important as acceptance. An immortal accepts the way things are and works with what she has been given."

"You're saying, I shouldn't look a gift horse in the mouth."

Nahini scowls as she does when I roll out an aphorism. "What mount have you been given?"

"Never mind." I take a deep breath, shove all my misgivings aside and then look around the room. "What do you want me to do first?"

"Air is your inborn power. Try to send a breeze through this space. A cold breeze, from the north."

My teeth sink into my lower lip and my gaze shifts to the glassless window. In the distance, the beings of the Wild Hunt are moving about their days. "What if I accidentally summon another tornado?"

"Don't consider it," Nahini warns. "Acknowledging the possibility opens the door to doubt and when you doubt yourself, mistakes are made."

Great. I close my eyes the same way I have the other times I've used magic. The taste of the air is warm and thick with the scents of hay and old wood. I breathe it in and then search farther. Out to the trees, the lake, the house. The tang of late summer is ripe on the farm as the sun bakes the ground. The smell of fey and hawks, horses and hounds comingle alongside that wild, pulsing whiff of ozone I associate with magic use.

I push my senses farther, hunting for the cool breeze Nahini requests. It's out there somewhere, waiting for summer to give in to its final death throws and herald the oncoming cold season.

My season.

I don't know how long I sit that way, sorting through scents and air currents in my mind. I lose track of my body, the hardness of the floor beneath me. I am scattered across the globe, traveling on the four winds.

A gust so strong it practically knocks me over, blows in through the window. Hay is caught up in a whirlwind and is carried up to the rafters. I gasp as the north wind tugs wisps of hair free from my braid almost playfully, like a puppy eager for attention.

I grin in triumph. "I did it."

Nahini nods. "Well done."

All my doubt evaporates, all my questions are forgotten. "Show me more."

We work together all afternoon. Nahini is a patient teacher, much more dedicated than any I've had in school. By the time night begins to fall, I have frozen a hay bale, then melted it with the heat from the sun, which radiated from my palm. I've also managed to soul walk. That is, to detect the spirits of all living things on the farm.

"Each soul has its own unique signature," Nahini instructs.

With my eyes closed I can feel the pulsing blue energy clustered around Addy's clinic, the bunkhouse, the farm-house, but also in the field and trees. Some of them move, others are completely still. "I can't tell them apart. They all look like blue blobs."

"Perhaps fingerprint is a better comparison. Souls are made of air, though not the air we breathe and the way they come together is as unique as physical appearance or mental acuity. Your element is air, which is why you and those of your lineage have been entrusted with the Wild Hunt. Focus on a soul and you will recognize its uniqueness."

I scan the area I know to be the farmhouse, looking for anyone I might distinguish. With the trees and grass out of the way, I have an easier time detecting individual shapes. The blue outlines are too fuzzy to separate male or female, though there is a bit of height difference. I inhale, narrowing my focus on one blob apart from the others, the striations in the energy ripple in a familiar way. Almost as though two souls are woven into one.

"Aiden." I open my eyes and see Nahini before me. "Aiden's on the front porch of the farmhouse."

She tilts her head to the side. "How do you know?"

"It's like there are two souls within one form. The energy patterns are conjoined but move in different directions."

Nahini nods. "You're right. Study him and you'll be able to pick up some of the nuances between animal spirit and human."

I close my eyes again and focus on Aiden. I'm hardly an expert, but his energy outline appears to be brooding. Or at least part of him is—the part that has man-shaped shoulders. The wolf is lounging within him, though ready to leap up at a moment's notice.

Someone else comes out onto the porch. The color is lighter, more innocent than Aiden or the wolf, as though untainted by the world. Jasmine, I'd bet my left boob on it. She sits down next to Aiden, as though trying to engage him in conversation.

"There's something else," I say to Nahini after a moment of studying the two patterns. "It isn't just the wolf. He's different from Jasmine somehow. His energy is...heavier."

"You're right." She doesn't explain why. "Now, look for Chloe or Addy."

I linger on Aiden a moment longer before skimming over the landscape in my mind to the clinic. Now that I know what I'm looking for, it's easy to distinguish between animal and humanoid. There are three people in the clinic, and two of them....

"Their energy is white, not blue."

"The Norns aren't tied to the Veil. Much as the water on the earth's surface gives the planet a distinctly blue look, the Veil gives all souls a blue reflection. Except for those souls who aren't a part of the system. It's why even the gods fear them. The rules do not apply to them."

"Where did they come from?" I ask, curious.

"No one knows. Fey scholars have researched and studied, looking for the answer to that question for eons. I doubt even the Fates themselves know. None have been bold enough to ask."

"Everyone really fears them that much?" Sure. Addy could be gruff, but my aunts were both marshmallows deep down. Way, way, *way* deep down.

Nahini tilts her head to the side. "Haven't you seen demonstrations of their power?"

I had. An image of their swirling eyes and deadly pronouncement pops into my mind. If that had been all I'd ever seen of Chloe and Addy, I would be scared of them, too.

Wanting to change the subject I ask, "What about creatures like the Valkyries? Can I soul walk to detect them?"

She nods. "Look for something similar in appearance to Aiden, although not two souls, but a mortal-animal hybrid.

They'll appear misshapen, even while hiding in a mortal guise."

Well, that would make it easier to find the other one, even if it is still using a glamour. "Is this how you've been searching for the dead souls missing from the Hunt?"

The beads in Nahini's braids clack as she nods. "Yes. They are more difficult to distinguish than souls tethered to bodies. They dissipate quickly when not held up by an iron will. The Wild Hunt keeps them intact, though not always visible."

After soul walking myself, I can see that her task is essentially searching for several needles in a multitude of haystacks. Every blade of grass, every tree and animal possess the same color aura as the missing members of the Hunt. And Nahini must scour the entire world tree, Yggdrasil, to find them.

"Maybe I can help."

She shakes her head. "It will take time, my queen. And you have much to do, many obligations."

She isn't wrong, but still. "Those souls are my responsibility. Tell me what to look for and I will set aside time every day to search."

Nahini's eyes widen slightly, but a small smile curves her lips. "As you insist."

She explains her grid method search for the souls of the Wild Hunt as we walk back to the farmhouse. "You're looking for a cluster of untethered souls. They won't have any discernible shape, not like a tree or a horse or a mortal. It would be simpler if the souls of the damned were black, like in all the stories. But they aren't. Only the Fates have different colored souls."

"Where do I begin looking?" My muscles, stiff from sitting still so long, start to relax as we move.

"I've been casting out to the far-flung spots where untethered souls congregate. Like calls to like. Large cities, especially near cemeteries or hospitals, where their mortal bodies passed."

"Don't innocent souls move on?"

Her lips twitch. "Are you asking about an afterlife?"

I guess so. When I nod she explains, "Souls are as individual as the beings they inhabit. Trees, plants, even animals don't tend to linger, but are absorbed into the Veil. It's the next natural step. They don't have the same feelings as sentient beings, that there are things left undone. They know they have given their all and it is time to go. People leave loved ones they want to say goodbye to, or regret over a mistake. Remorse and a feeling of unfinished business will keep a soul in this world for a time, but eventually, they understand that they can affect nothing on this plane and be forced to accept their new reality. That's when they move on."

I drink in all she's said. "What makes the souls bound to the Wild Hunt different?"

"For one thing, the Wild Hunt is the damned soul's new place. Those who have been selected to serve forfeit the right to linger the way a free soul could. They were handpicked by you, in either this life or your last, and will serve until you dismiss them to the Veil."

"Is it possible that's where they've gone?"

"Possible yes, but unlikely. The Veil isn't mending itself. If it absorbed all the souls from our missing dead, the hole would have sealed up by now."

"The hole." With everything else going on, I'd forgotten about the tear in the Veil that separates the mortal world, what Aiden referred to as Midgard, from Underhill, the land of the fair folk. "Where exactly is it?"

Nahini stops and turns to the west then points to the sky. "Several hundred feet above the surface."

"Could a plane fly through it?" That would be one hell of a ride, a connection between Atlanta and Louisville that ends up in the hall of giants, or the dead forest.

She begins walking again. "It's possible, but it's lower than most of the human aircraft fly. Freda sent scouts to monitor it. So far the only reported crossings are birds."

I stop dead.

"My queen?"

I look her in the eye. "Valkyries can fly, but can't wield magic."

She blinks. "Yes, of course."

"No one reported them crossing." I look around quickly and move closer to her so I can whisper. "Our traitor stood guard duty over the tear when they came through. How many have been assigned to watch the tear?"

Nahini's dragon scale armor shimmers in the late afternoon sun as she turns to face me. "Maybe half a dozen. If you're right, that narrows our pool of suspects considerably."

Out of the corner of my eye, I see Aiden heading in our direction. "I need to go take care of the other Valkyrie. Have Freda call a meeting for midnight with the scouts. One way or another, we'll catch the traitor tonight."

CHAPTER 7

VALKYRIE VILLAGE

"Are you sure about this?" Aiden asks as he stops the truck in the lot of the apartment complex where Vice Principal Steinburg moved after his divorce six months ago. It's a U-shaped building with a central office in front, with two squat buildings sitting on either side of the parking area.

"It's not too late to change your mind." He puts a hand over mine and squeezes gently.

"The Valkyries came here for me." I stare out the window to the second-floor apartment. "And we need to find out who helped them."

Aiden studies me closely. "You look a bit...amped up."

"I want to hunt." My fingers curl into fists. "It's been weeks since I've hunted or killed."

"And you miss it?" he asks.

"Miss isn't the right word." The need for it claws at me like a wild thing held in by nothing but my ribcage. If I don't let it out periodically, it will consume my heart. "I don't know how to describe it without sounding like a monster."

He offers a small smile. "Takes one to know one."

I look over and hold his gaze. "I'm trying to be everything I'm supposed to be and I'm failing. No one expects me to do the one thing I'm best at doing. I don't know how to lead, how to negotiate with the Seelie kings, how to do anything but kill."

"Nic, no one expects anything from you," Aiden says softly. "You can forge your own life."

His words are tempting, the offer to turn my back on the crazy mess that is Underhill. Yet, how can I? When I know all the things I did wrong before, that I've done wrong in this life. The tear in the Veil, the loss of the souls I damned to the Wild Hunt, the instability of the Unseelie Court. There are freaking Valkyries disguised as people I know. How can I ignore everyone and everything without trying to set it right?

All this goes through my mind but I don't say a word of it to Aiden. Instead, I pop the door to the truck. "Let's do this."

He's out of the truck and around before my feet touch pavement. "Stay behind me."

"I'm armed," I hiss.

"And unprepared," he retorts. "You identify the creature and I can cripple it so you can interrogate it. You already battled one Valkyrie today and barely escaped with your life. Let me help."

His green eyes seem to glow in the dim light, lit from within. "Just don't barbecue it before I give the order. Or in front of witnesses. We don't need law enforcement poking around in here."

"As my queen commands," he murmurs and then heads up the rickety wooden stairs to the second floor.

These aren't the best rentals in town. Most of the inhabitants are college students who can't afford better or recently divorced. Steinburg's door is at the corner unit. No lights at all and no sound. It's possible with the Valkyrie is gone thanks to my tornado and the place is as vacant as it appears.

Aiden scrunches his nose in disgust. "Do you smell that?"

I inhale deeply. "Nothing out of the ordinary. Why? What are you picking up?"

In the dim light cast from a streetlamp, I see his muscles clench. "Shit and rotting

meat."

"There goes my appetite."

He hesitates. "From the amount of both, I think there's more than one inside."

"How many?" I ask just as an eerie cry echoes from somewhere below.

Aiden grabs my arm and tries to pull me away. "An entire nest."

At my blank look, he clarifies, "A dozen or more."

"All in this one little apartment?"

He shakes his head even as he grabs my hand and pulls me toward the stairs. "You don't understand, Nic. They've taken over the apartment complex."

"What?" I glance back over my shoulder. "What about the people who were living here?"

"Where do you think the rotting meat smell is coming from?"

Horror fills me and I glance back at the apartment complex. "There are at least twenty apartments here." Even if only half of them are occupied by one person each, that's double-digit homicide.

Also known as mass murder.

"We need back up," I say. There's no way Aiden and I can handle a dozen—or more—Valkyries on our own.

The cry comes again, part bird of prey, part woman scorned and completely blood-chilling.

"They've scented us," Aiden shouts, whirling around. A

blade appears in his hand, a sword conjured of pure fire. I draw my own shorter blades. We stand back to back as the first aerial attacker swoops toward us.

Aiden strikes with the fiery sword and the Valkyrie screams in pain. One wing is ablaze as it flaps up. The smell of barbecued feathers drifts toward us on the wind.

Its cries have alerted the others though and doors open all over the apartment complex. Some are human-shaped, others in the befouled bird-like forms. When I shift my vision to the soul walk however, the creatures all have the same avian hybrid glow.

"There isn't a mortal among them." My words are snatched from my throat by a sharp gust of carrion scented air. "Not left alive anyway."

"Nic, focus!" Aiden shoves me to the side an instant before two Valkyries try and sink their talons into my arms. They cry out in frustration, but Aiden's fire sword is there, cooking the flesh from their putrid forms on contact. They fall to the pavement at his feet.

"Nic?" Aiden's eyes are on the circling predators, even as he reaches down to help me up.

"I'm fine." I bite out the word.

"Don't try any of your tricks right now," he cautions, once again putting his back to me, the fire sword up and at the ready. "They're fast and determined but not organized. We need to dispatch them quickly before more mortals get caught in the crossfire."

He's right about their lack of systemization. If the Valkyrie's attack had been coordinated, we wouldn't have stood a chance. But these creatures don't possess the discipline for a planned assault. Their numbers dwindle further with each attack.

Aiden's skill with a sword rivals Brigit and perhaps even Nahini. His every movement is fluid, purposeful, as though he fights like this on a regular basis. Wherever he swings, a Valkyrie loses a wing, a foot, some even their lives.

I am less graceful, but make up for it with sheer savagery. These…things crossed into *my* world, showed up in *my* town and killed an entire apartment building full of people. The rage helps focus my mind as the bloodbath continues. They grow frantic, crying out as they swoop over our heads, talons clutching, wings flapping, determined to take us out or fall in the attempt. They don't stop, don't retreat, but keep coming.

Within five minutes all the Valkyries lay dead or dismembered. The ones on the ground cradle stumps that held wings or feet, their gazes malevolent.

Aiden scans the skies one last time before turning to assess me. "Did they scratch you?"

"A bit." Blood oozes from the scrape on my forearm where one made contact while I was finishing off its compatriot. "It's not bad though."

"Valkyries are filthy beasts. We need to get those cuts cleaned up so they don't get infected."

"There's a first-aid kit in the truck." I survey the fallen survivors. "You can go get it while I get some answers."

He hesitates, taking one last look around the blood-soaked parking area before jogging off to the truck.

"Who let you cross?" I ask the nearest Valkyrie, this one missing half a wing.

"Go to hell, she-demon," it spits at me.

I smile at it, my predator's smile, before spearing it through the eye with my sword.

"Anybody else want to be uncooperative?" I call out while its body twitches on the end of my blade. I yank the weapon free and turn in a slow arc so they can all see me. My skin crawls, and I can feel their scrutiny. Along with…something more. "I'll let you cross the Veil if you answer my questions.

If not…," I make a show of watching the blood drip from the point of the sword onto the ground.

Silence. Even the moaning stops.

"Tell me who let you across," I lower the sword to my side and do a slow pivot on my heel. "And where the one posing as Steinburg got the glamour."

"And you'll let us go?" This comes from one of the Valkyries in the back. Her foot is missing and she cradles a smaller creature in her lap, its eyes staring sightlessly up at the night sky. From the blood trail behind her, it's easy to see that she crawled over to where the other fell. "Why should we believe you?"

I level my gaze on her. "Because I'm not giving you a choice. Either tell me what I want to know and live or die protecting a traitor's secrets."

She glances down at the dead one, a wing passing over the eyes, before looking back up at me. "I don't know the name of the one who let us cross. Female, brown hair with a streak of silver woven into a braid."

"And the magic?" I prompt as Aiden returns carrying the medical kit. "Who provided the glamour?"

"The giantess, Angrboda."

The first-aid kit clatters to the ground. All color drains from Aiden's face and his glowing green eyes burn hotter. "What did you say?"

"She came to our nest and told us of the tear, offered to help us cross the Veil undetected." The Valkyrie coughs and blood speckles her mouth.

"Out of the goodness of her heart?" I snap, dividing my attention between Aiden, who looks ready to wolf out at any moment, and the Valkyrie.

"No, she asked only that we take care of the threat to the Unseelie Court on this side of the Veil." The Valkyrie pants, her breath growing shallower. She shifts the body of the miniature Valkyrie in her arms to reveal a deep gash.

She's dying, I realize. Belly wounds are excruciatingly painful. It speaks highly of the creature's strength of will that she can negotiate with me while she dies.

"You will keep your promise, Ice Bitch? I will have your fey word on it."

I look to Aiden but his attention is turned inwards.

"What's your name?" I crouch down so that we are eye to eye.

"I am called Nightweaver."

"Are you the leader of these people, Nightweaver?"

When she nods, I hold out a hand. "I vow to you, I will see your people safely taken back through the Veil, given property to colonize in the way they see fit. If you will join the Wild Hunt."

Her black eyes flare wide. "What?"

"I want your word that you will serve me in the Wild Hunt."

"Nic," Aiden snaps out of whatever trance he's fallen into at my words. "What are you saying? There's never been a Valkyrie in the Hunt. They belong to Freya. And you can't just let them go. Think of all the mortals they've killed."

I glare at him. "I need to accept all the help I can get. Didn't you say that?"

"This wasn't what I had in mind," Aiden growls. "The fey of the Hunt won't like it."

"The fey of the Hunt can fuck off." I snap, my focus on the dying creature. "Do we have a bargain, Nightweaver? Your eternal help for the eternal safety of your people?"

I hold out my hand and after the smallest hesitation, she places her claw in my grip.

She coughs, more blood flecking her lips. "Agreed, Ice Bitch, though I doubt my service will be for long."

"Think again," I say and press my lips to her bloody ones. "You have been found guilty."

Around us there are gasps as Nightweaver's body sags, her hand going limp in my hold. My deadly kiss sparks hot on my own lips and I feel her spirit slip from her body.

"You killed her?" Aiden breathes.

"She agreed to serve. And as you pointed out, I couldn't let her go unpunished after decimating this place." Though I am speaking to him, my own gaze focuses beyond. I watch as Nightweaver's soul tears free from its fleshy prison.

What is happening to me? The voice isn't mental, not like when Aiden communicates with me mind to mind. It's more like a sighing breeze passing through dry leaves, something that I didn't know existed until it slips by.

"You tied her soul to the Hunt." Aiden's tone is full of awe.

I nod. "The souls I bargained away to Brigit. And because Brigit was fey, I'm sure her clause is open-ended. Any new soul will belong to her, too."

Aiden is gaping at me, his expression pure shock. "She'll lead us right to the rest of the dead."

"Grab your keys." I'm already on my feet, heading for the truck, barely daring to hope. The soul drifts higher from the ground, not flapping the way the great wings did when Nightweaver lived, but almost as though it's a balloon filled with a gas lighter than the surrounding air. I can make out the general direction though.

"What about the Valkyries?" Aiden spares them a glance as he turns the truck's engine over.

"They have until first light to cross back into Underhill." My words are loud enough so all can hear. "Then my people will burn this place to the ground."

Lower, so only Aiden's sensitive ears pick up on it I murmur, "Freda can supervise their departure and covering this up so we don't alert the mortal law. We need Nahini with us though, in case we do find the souls we're looking for."

The hairs on my arm stand on end and I scan the area, feeling hunted.

"What is it?" Aiden's head jerks up.

I scan the dark tree line behind the apartment complex, looking for anything out of place. The Valkyries chose their hideout well, the buildings are set back from the road with their backs to the trees a large force couldn't sneak up on them. But someone is out there. I'm sure of it. All the small hairs are up on my neck.

"Nic?" Aiden follows my gaze.

"Nothing." We don't have time to investigate, not if we want to follow Nightweaver's soul to its final destination. I'd leave it to Freda to track whoever lurks in the woods.

"Which way am I going?" Aiden slides behind the wheel and the truck roars to life.

Once inside the cab, I check the sky again, watching as the Valkyrie's soul drifts even higher. "West."

"That's toward the tear in the Veil." Aiden throws his arm over the back of the seat, whips the truck around in a broken K turn, before shifting to drive and pushing the pedal to the floor.

I already have my phone out and am dialing. "I know. Nahini will have to meet us there."

THE STEEDS that belong to the Wild Hunt are fast and aren't confined to roads the way my truck is so neither of us is surprised to see Nahini waiting below the tear in the Veil.

"Has she gone through yet?" I slide to the ground as soon as Aiden shifts into park. "We lost sight of her at the edge of town."

Nahini scans the skies, then shakes her head. "No, nor do I see any sign of her or feel the presence of the other souls."

"What happens if we cross through the tear?" I stare up at the sky, looking for the telltale flicker that moves like a curtain in the wind. The Veil between worlds is thin and time spent In-Between feels endless. But there is no unnatural movement. The night is dark with only a sliver of the moon visible through the scudding clouds.

"It's not like the In-Between." Aiden's gaze is steady though I can feel his anxiety through our connection. "There is no transitional space. Just chaos."

Nahini's eyes are on the sky, not the frantic sweep I am doing but a thorough scan. "If we cross now," she warns, "We may not have time to return before your rule begins anew on all hallows eve."

Time moves differently in Underhill. What feels like a day to us might be a year in the mortal realm, or perhaps only an hour. And it's foolish to cross with no provisions. No change of clothes or food, only the weapons we have on us. If given a choice I would like time to prepare, to strategize with the aunts and Freda, make plans and pack.

But this is the first real chance we've been given. A wicked soul damned to the Wild Hunt doesn't come along every day and my to-do list is already full without digging up another.

"I have to fix this." With my focus on the souls around us, I can see the tear. It isn't just a void or a rip but something with an enormous amount of suction, like curtains caught in a vacuum cleaner. "Not just reclaiming the dead of the Hunt but the tear as well. The Valkyries killed dozens of innocent people because of this thing. I don't care how much time passes here, we need to make this right."

Aiden takes my hand. "We will."

I turn to Nahini. "Then mark me for Underhill."

Her big dark eyes grow bigger. "You're sure you are ready for the gauntlet?"

"Not even. But I won't risk missing my chance because we don't have a reliable clock. You said once I was marked, Underhill will take me when she sees fit, is that right?"

Nahini nods and extracts something from her saddlebags. A knife. "It is."

"Then mark me."

"Nic," Aiden breathes my name like a prayer.

"You can't talk me out of this." I set my jaw, pretending to be ready for what is to come. Fake it till you make it.

"I'm not trying to." With one hand he grips the steel, holding it until a curl of smoke emerges. Sterilizing the blade. I see the metal glow red gold as though it had been heated over a fire but it returns to normal as it cools. His brilliant green eyes glow bright in the darkness. "I'll do whatever I can to stay by your side."

I search his face. His expression is set. He's just as determined as I am.

"Are you ready?" Nahini says.

In answer, I roll up the sleeve on my right forearm, exposing the skin there. My sword arm, marked for service to Underhill.

Aiden takes my free hand in his and lowers his forehead against mine. "Don't look."

I squeeze my eyes shut. The sight of my own blood makes me dizzy, a wimpy trait for anyone, especially a serial killer, and ridiculous compared to the mess we'd just left at the apartment complex.

Even without seeing the action, I can feel the slicing of the blade, quick sharp marks to form an edgy sort of U shape. The rune for Underhill.

My eyes stay closed and I breathe in Aiden, the scent of

cotton from his shirt, his own unique blend of earthy heat and wildness.

There's a rustling sound as Nahini retrieves something from her saddle bags. I inhale when my second sprinkles some sort of powder over the fresh wound, murmuring in an unfamiliar tongue. Then she covers the wound with a gauze pad and binds it with purple vet wrap she must have filched from the clinic.

"There," Nahini points to the east. "And just in time."

Sure enough, the bizarre hybrid soul of the Valkyrie moves towards the tear, caught up in the current of its powerful pull.

"Will you ride with me?" Nahini is in the saddle before I can bat an eyelash and offers her hand.

I shake my head. "Aiden can't see the spirit world, I need to stay with him." His sparks and embers form can become weightless and lift us up off the ground and through the Veil.

He squeezes my hand as though trying to convey a message, but I can't look away from Nightweaver long enough to ask him what it means.

"Now, before we lose, her." Nahini makes a clicking noise to her mount and the steed kicks off from the ground.

The odd dissolving sensation that accompanies Aiden's magic engulfs me from right to left, where our hands are still clasped. My body is pulled apart and my senses disappear. Even so, I sense Nightweaver and the tear above, its pull as great as the vortex of my tornado.

Up, up, up we swirl like leaves eddying in a twisting stream, our momentum getting faster the higher we climb. I can't feel its tug, can't feel anything by normal human standards, but it is all around me.

Madness swallows us whole.

Though I have no physical body, it feels as though a thousand shards of jagged glass are scraping across my skin, leaving bloody rivulets in their wake. If I had a mouth, a voice, I would cry out, but I don't have access to those things in this form. Even if I could scream I might not remember how, the pain pushing me past the point of sanity, or comprehension, beyond words.

And then the chaos whispers a single word to me, its tone greedy and ravenous.

Thousands of souls cry out for what they once were, what they seek to be again, what they desperately wish to consume.

Life.

That's what it wants, the toll it's trying to forcibly extract. My life, mine and

Aiden's and Nahini's. The Veil itself demands life, not just more untethered souls that makes up its fabric but to forcibly rip a soul free from a living being, to gobble up the very essence of life.

Let go.

It's Aiden speaking to me mind to mind, not the Veil. He's struggling, I can feel him yanking on me, trying to shove me free. If given the choice, he will stay if it means Nahini and I can cross unharmed. The stupid hero wants to sacrifice himself for me.

So, I don't give him the choice.

Wrapping what there is of me around what there is of him, I hang on for dear life and force myself to endure the pain, the madness, what feels like the end of all things until darkness swamps me and pulls me under.

CHAPTER 8

UNDERHILL

"Don't leave me." *Tears stream down my face as I watch her pick up her bag. We are in the darkest part of the woods, a place I have never been before. I cling to her skirts. "I'm scared."*

"I don't have a choice." Her curly blonde hair is a lion's mane around her pointed face. Usually such a calm and tranquil face, but now she's upset, her eyes bright with fervor, motions sharp and jerky as she wrenches free of my grasping hands.

"Sissy please," I hunt frantically for something else to say, something else that will change her mind. "I'll be good."

She turns to me then, blue eyes colder than the sharpest winter gust. "You don't have it in you. It's not in your nature."

"Please, I don't want to be alone." I cling to her skirts, imploring her again, desperate.

She puts her hand on my forehead and issues a one-word command. "Sleep."

"Please," I murmur, fighting the darkness, too afraid that when I wake up I'll be alone. "Don't leave me here. I'll be good, I swear."

"Nic? It's all right. I'm right here." Aiden.

The sound of his voice drags me back to consciousness. The very last place I want to be as the aches and pains pile up like cordwood. Everything throbs, my head all the way to the roots of my hair and my feet to the tips of my pinky toenails, plus everything in between.

I try to open my eyes but the light streaming in beyond the closed lids is bright enough that I know sheer agony awaits.

"She's coming back." Another voice, low and melodic. "My queen? Are you damaged?"

"Hurts," I wheeze out the word and then roll to my side, tucking my knees up in the fetal position.

"What does?" Aiden's hand alights on my shoulder. "Nic, what hurts?"

I shrug away from his touch, wanting nothing more than to be alone. The panic I'd relived moments before. Sissy. I'd remembered her, remembered the day she'd abandoned me. *It's not in your nature.* "Everything."

"Leave her, wolf." Nahini's tone is light, but even that is more than I can bear. "She will come back to herself in time."

I can feel Aiden vibrating with tension, uneasy at my pain, wanting to help. To fix whatever's wrong with me. My anguish impacts him in a way that goes beyond empathy, almost as though he experiences it right alongside me. Another wave of agony washes over me, and my thoughts scatter like leaves before a hurricane. I can't worry about him right now.

Time passes and the pain, both physical and emotional, fades. I don't know if I drift off again, but the next time my eyes open the light isn't nearly so oppressive. Textures are starting to register again. The grit of sand beneath my cheek, coarse and warm. The air carries the tang of the sea and in the distance, the sound of waves crashing as they meet the shore.

And deeper than that there is a pulse, throbbing in time to my own. Only this one surrounds me. I can feel the pull and push, like a tide made from the air. It caresses my face, throbs in the wound on my arm.

Underhill. She knows I'm here, that I've come to face the gauntlet.

Slowly, not moving a single muscle more than necessary, I crack open one eye. I am still curled up on my side, my face pressed into a dune. The light is low with the sun making its descent toward the ground. A few feet away, Aiden sits facing not the surf but me, though his eyes are closed.

"Hey," I croak.

His lids lift though he doesn't otherwise move. "Are you any better?"

"Think so." The words whisper from between cracked lips.

He assesses me a moment then reaches behind him for something. A canteen, I realize.

"Where did you get that?"

"Nahini had it in her saddle bags." He crawls closer and then tips the canteen so I can drink.

The water is warm, though the taste is marvelous, from our own well back at the farm. I swallow greedily, but he takes it away before I am ready and screws the cap back on.

"Easy. This needs to last you awhile. I already used enough of it when we cleaned you up." He touches the bandages on my forearm where the Valkyrie scratches are now covered by gauze.

"Where's Nahini? And Nightweaver? Did we find the missing souls?" I struggle up, needing to see more of the world around me than my limited view of the beach.

"Go slowly." Aiden reaches under my arms and guides me into a sitting position. He shifts so my back can rest against his chest. My own living wolf recliner. "Be careful. I have your medical kit but would prefer not to have to use it again so soon."

Fully propped up, I take in our surroundings. Waves and sand, surf and the sinking sun. No signs of houses or other people, mortal or forever young. Out of the corner of my eye I see more dunes rolling like their own sort of waves behind us. They are tufted with sea grass but otherwise there is nothing. No rocks or trees, just endless open rolling hills of sand. The terrain is completely unfamiliar and even with my soul vision, I spot nothing to help us.

"Where are we, exactly?" I whisper. "And where's Nahini?"

"She's following Nightweaver. She'll come back here as soon as she locates the other souls, though she left us her saddle bags. There isn't much, but if you're hungry there are a few apples." He shifts until his legs are on either side of me, providing maximum support.

"I'm good." Food is the last thing on my mind, my head aches and my stomach is too unsettled for digestion.

He eyes me. "Are you really?"

He means my flashback. The hollowness in my chest expands, my promise rings in my ears. *I'll be good.* I would have done anything to get her to stay, to give me another chance.

And Sissy's response is a fresh wave of torment. *It's not in your nature.*

My voice is flat as I say, "I don't want to talk about it."

"Was it your mother?" His voice is soft, gentle.

"Which one?" Technically I have two, though I can't remember either. The one who gave birth to Nicneven, Queen of the Shadow Throne and the one who brought me into this world as Nic.

"Your mortal mother died," he puts a hand on my arm.

When I look at him sharply, he withdraws "I checked, in

case you were curious."

"I'm not." It's only half a lie. I am curious but there's no time to indulge myself.

He's silent a moment before changing the subject. "As to our current location, I can't be sure but I think we are in Wardon's territory."

"Wardon, the Seelie king?" One of the two.

"Master of the Waves and your male counterpart, Samhain to Beltane. He has a castle beyond the great desert at the point where the sea touches the sky where he lives on his off time." Aiden's tone is grim, as though this isn't good news.

"Master of the Waves," I grumble. "Nicer ring to it than The Ice Bitch."

He lets out a soft chuckle. "Maybe we should steal his PR person."

I sigh and lean into him, lulled by the steady beat of his heart.

He smooths my hair away from my face. "Are you feeling better?"

"I think so." Though I'm still not sure what happened.

"In that case," his voice drops to a low growl that makes all the hairs on the back of my neck stand on end. "What the hell were you thinking back there, holding on to me that way?"

"That I wasn't about to let you be all noble and sacrifice yourself to that thing." I snap. Pain makes me irritable under the best of circumstances, which these certainly are not.

"You could have died," he snarls.

"And what about you?" It's odd, having a seething wall of muscle at my back and not considering killing him. I want to look him in the eye, but turning isn't an option with my head still swimming.

"You are the priority, Nic. The Veil craves a fresh soul and it doesn't care whose—a mortal's or a god's."

"But it didn't get any, not even Nahini's horse. We beat it so I don't understand why you are so upset."

His hands clench and unclench on his knees. The skin over his knuckles turns the palest white. "It was sheer luck that it gave up. Another minute and it would have ripped you apart."

"But it didn't." I huff. "You need to stop thinking of yourself as the redshirt."

"The what?" My reference confuses him.

"Redshirt. It's from *Star Trek*, a science fiction show. Sarah used to make me watch endless hours of it. When we get back, I'll show you a few episodes to prove my point. The unfamiliar character in the red uniform is always sacrificed on the mission." Though it pains me, I shift until I can see his face. "You aren't disposable, Aiden. Not to me."

His eyes meet mine, green chips of emerald melting to a somewhat softer expression. Slowly, his hands relax.

"Thank you, Nic."

"For saving you from your own noble streak?"

He shakes his head. "The Veil wouldn't have killed me. I was born a god, remember?"

"Then there was no real danger." No wonder he was angry that I'd stopped him.

"I didn't say that. It wouldn't have torn my soul from my body, but it would have fed off my soul while I writhed in agony in an effort to repair itself. Like being eaten alive and never dying. Wishing for an end that wouldn't come."

My lungs aren't working right. I try to inhale, fail and make a second attempt. Better. "And you really wanted me to let you go to that?"

"At the time? Yes." One hand strokes down my hair. "Right now, I'm glad you didn't."

He doesn't say anything, just continues to caress my hair.

I feel a little foolish, letting him pet me this way, but it feels too delicious to abandon just yet. "So, what exactly were you thanking me for earlier, if not for saving your life?"

"For including me."

I turn to face him. When I raise one eyebrow he elaborates. "You didn't ask or order me not to cross the Veil with you, even though I couldn't see the souls. You stayed with me even though you had good reason not to bring me with you."

"I never even thought of it," I admit. "Including you was instinctive."

"That's what pleases me so much. You are beginning to rely on me." Pride radiates from him.

"Just because I've accepted the inevitable reality that you aren't going to go away doesn't mean I trust you or anything," I snap.

"Tell yourself that, my queen." There is smugness lacing his every word, the fiend. "As often as you want."

FULL DARK FALLS yet there is still no sign of Nahini or anyone else.

"What if something happened to her?" I can barely see Aiden in the dark. The moon isn't up yet and a heavy cloak of clouds obscure the starlight. "She might not be able to get back to us. We can't wait here forever."

"We won't have to," Aiden points to what I think is the east. "Someone's coming."

He's on his feet in the span of a heartbeat, with me positioned behind him. Blinding orange light flares as his fire sword once again materializes from his hands.

"It might be Nahini returning." The fire creates a small bubble around us but beyond it there is only blackness.

Aiden doesn't respond, his shoulders tense, his blade

dancing in the breeze.

I scramble to my feet, though I am weaponless, save for the magical gifts that I can't control. Besides, using magic in Underhill is...tricky. The consequences are always murky, some good, some bad and a mortal magic wielder never knows what the price will be until after the deed is done. I might conjure another tornado, only to have Aiden sucked up into it, leaving me alone to face whatever is heading our way.

I hear them as they draw closer, more than one set of feet pounding across the sand. The light from the flaming sword makes me feel as though Aiden and I are in a fishbowl. Whoever is coming our way is doing so in the darkness with no concern about stumbling on uneven ground. Only fey, like those of the Hunt, would be so sure footed.

What appears no more than ten feet away isn't beautiful and ethereal, like the fey that I have seen. They are hideous, lumpy creatures, with large knobby hands and feet, bulbous noses and flat dull eyes. Their skin tone is the color of wet granite and looks just about as impenetrable.

"Trolls," Aiden grumbles.

Trolls? I want to ask what a cluster of trolls are doing on the beach. At least a dozen of them form a perfect an inescapable circle around us with deadly precision.

One steps forward, a man with a long dark braid falling over one shoulder and a neatly trimmed goatee. He appears less dull witted than the others, but that's not saying much. He studies Aiden's stance, before dismissing him and looking down at me. "You are Nicneven, the Risen Queen of the Unseelie?"

Risen Queen? A step up from Ice Bitch I guess.

I hesitate, unsure if I should confirm my identity. If I say yes, will they try to kill us? But if I say no they might kill us anyway. And I have no doubt that they can, if they so desire.

The shortest stands a head taller than Aiden and I get the impression that while they seem slow, it's just a front to lure us into complacency. Not only am I in no shape to help Aiden fend them off, they exude a confidence that is much deadlier than the Valkyrie's blind rage.

I put my hand on Aiden's back, feeling the tension in his muscles. "I am. Who are you?"

"Galfin Dunn, commander of his majesty's ground troops." The troll has a nasal quality to his voice, like his sinuses are clogged. "He sensed your presence in his realm and dispatched us to find you as soon as the sun went down. He wishes to offer his hospitality."

"Hospitality," I repeat the word, my voice giving it a suspicious edge.

The trolls wait, holding all the cards. They appear unarmed, but again, my instincts scream that it's only a deception.

It's most likely a trap. I hear Aiden's voice in my head.

It's an effort to speak to him, to divert any attention away from the threat posed by the trolls. *Wardon doesn't have to lure us in though. He could have had these guys stuff us in sacks and drag us before him or kill us outright. So why bother to make the offer?*

He wants something. Aiden's grip on his sword tightens.

Look at us, we're in no shape to take on these creatures. I don't doubt for one second that they will kill us if we refuse their king's "hospitality".

Aiden doesn't respond, leaving the decision up to me.

"We accept his majesty's generous offer," I say.

Aiden's sword sputters and then vanishes altogether, leaving us in the dark.

It takes several moments for my eyes to adjust but when they do I see Galfin Dunn and one of the other trolls kneeling in the sand. "Climb aboard."

Aiden turns to look at me, his green eyes glowing in the dark. "Think I'll run alongside."

Galfin Dunn scoffs. "No fey can keep up with a troll."

"Good thing I'm no fey," Aiden says and shifts right out of his clothes.

The trolls grumble and fall back as the black wolf with the glowing green eyes emerge. They shift their massive bodies as though unwilling to touch him. The second troll rises slowly and shies away from the massive black wolf, her eyes round with wariness.

Aiden sweeps them all with an even gaze and then turns to face me, his expression completely wolfish. He knows he's the greatest predator here and his smug satisfaction says *now, they do, too.*

"Are we ready then?" I pick up Nahini's saddle bags and Aiden's clothes before approaching the still kneeling but much more nervous seeming Galfin Dunn. "Don't worry, he's mostly housebroken."

Galfin Dunn rises up, perching me on his shoulder and then turns around. "Move out!" He shouts to the trolls around us.

They take off into the dark night. They are fast, faster than most horses. Though gracelessly shaped, their long legs hold power that launches them with each step. To my right, I catch the gleam of green eyes as Aiden runs alongside them, his paws softer on the beach than the heavy thuds of their feet.

I'll make you pay for that. His voice rumbles in my mind.

Wind tugs at my unbound hair and sea spray coats my skin. There is something so exhilarating about the momentum combined with the darkness that a thrill shoots down my spine. A laugh bubbles up as I meet Aiden's gaze again. *Something to look forward to.*

CHAPTER 9

The sun is just peaking over the horizon when the trolls slow their mad dash. All my aches and pains have returned in full force after hours of being jostled against Galfin Dunn's unyielding body. Aiden was smart when he said he would rather run. It seems to me the troll leader does his best to jounce me about as much as possible.

Who knew trolls could be so passive-aggressive?

"There." With his ape like arm sprinkled lightly with crisp brown hairs, Galfin Dunn points to a distant cliffside.

"Where?" I ask, squinting. There is nothing up there that I can see other than a sheer drop-off.

"Just wait for it."

I'm in no mood for waiting or guessing games but it's not as though I have much of a choice in the matter. I stare at the spot he indicates as the sun continues to rise.

Are they going to turn to stone, do you think? I ask the wolf. That was the legend about trolls, that if they were caught in the pure light of the sun, they would turn to stone.

Aiden assesses the trolls. *They don't appear concerned. If they work for Wardon, they probably have some sort of mystical protection, at least in Underhill. I can't see the Master of the Waves employing an army that can't move during the day.*

A glint draws my attention. It's not just the crashing waves, but a reflection as though the sunlight has been captured and reflected from glass.

Perfectly transparent glass.

Aiden comes up beside us. *It's completely camouflaged from view. Anyone who didn't know it was here would go right past it.*

He's right. The glint is coming from the uppermost level, a breezeway between two towers all made entirely of glass, beneath it, hewn from the cliff face, is the home of Wardon, Master of the Waves, who sits upon the Gray throne of the Seelie.

A lone figure stands on that breezeway, his dark cloak flapping like a banner. He's too far away to make out but all the hair on my arms rise as he lifts both his hands above his head and water fountains from the sea in hundred-foot-high spouts, like a geyser set in the middle of the ocean.

No sooner does one jet crash down then another erupts, further out. It's like a series of fireworks without the fire or the explosives, just water churning up high in a massive demonstration of power.

He turns as two huge spouts erupt, almost like dolphins jumping into the air. Though I can't see his face, I feel him smirking at me.

He's doing it on purpose. I am sure of it all the way down to my marrow. He's out there to show off his considerable mad skills for my benefit. To impress me? To intimidate me?

Either way, it sets my teeth on edge. I know better, especially in this place where I am a mortal—translation easily broken. A queen yes, but still a mortal amidst the forever young, all of whom have more practice with magic than I. But my temper takes over.

The breeze off the sea is gentle. I delve into it, going deeper, yanking at the air that surrounds us and stirring it to life. There is a storm several miles offshore, one with no path to the land. I yank it toward me, toward him, the Master of the Waves who makes a tragic mistake and turns his back on the ocean. Of showing off and expecting me not to do the same.

The trolls shout and point as they see it coming, the water rushing for their liege lord. He turns and in my mind's eye, I can almost see the smug smile flash freezing on his arrogant face.

The spouts combine in a wall of water, a tsunami that crashes over the top of his haughty head.

The castle is well made, the glass solid enough to withstand the force of that water. And to his credit, the king holds his feet, doesn't get sucked back into the sea with the tide. But he's soaked to the skin and maybe it's my imagination but I do believe I see steam coming out of his ears.

The trolls are speechless, gawking at where their now saturated king drips atop his palace.

I hope no one had a window open. Aiden comes up alongside me, bumping his body against my leg.

My grin fades alongside my moment of satisfaction. The reality of what I'd just done sets in. *I could have hurt someone. I wasn't thinking.* Just like with the tornado at the school.

If he can't protect his own gods' damned castle from the sea, he shouldn't have built it so close. Aiden's tone is matter-of-fact. *It's good that he knows you aren't helpless going in, Nic. He's an arrogant as and he was trying to intimidate you. You got the best of him, so this round goes to you.*

Our escort exchange looks and then Galfin Dunn sets me carefully on the ground. "We should bring you in through the front. His majesty will wish to see you."

"After he dries off," one in the back mutters.

There are sniggers amongst the rest of the lot, but Galfin Dunn shoots them a sharp look and they quiet.

My knees almost buckle as I slide off and to the ground, but Aiden is there, transformed back into his human form to support my weight. A wave of *something* is crashing through me, the same as the wave of water crashed over the palace.

My hands ball into fists, nails sinking into my skin. There's a pounding in my temples, my blood races thick and hot. Anger, though that's much too mild a word for it.

Rage.

"Nic? What is it?" Aiden rubs my back in a slow, gentle manner.

I take a deep breath in an effort to calm the surging wrath. All I can smell is his sage and cedarwood scent. He's naked. I study him and the feelings morph, though are no less demanding.

I want him, desperately.

The price. I hiss mentally as shudders of need wrack my body.

Hold on to me.

I shake my head and push away. Who knows what I'll do if I don't put some distance between the two of us? *Put some clothes on. Now.*

He gives me a hurt look, whether from the rebuff or the order I can't tell, but he moves toward the saddlebags where I'd stashed his jeans and t-shirt.

I close my eyes and swallow, trying to ignore my rampaging libido. *Underhill, you sick bitch, why are you doing this to me?*

The walk isn't far, but it stretches on for what feels like an eternity. I'm twitchy, vacillating between wanting to hit something and wanting to have my wicked way with Aiden in front of the trolls, Wardon and anyone else who might be looking.

The sun rises higher. My body grows tenser, the emotions spilling through my bloodstream like an overfilled cup. Tension bunches the muscles in my shoulders and I vow not to use magic again unless it's a life or death situation.

I'm strung too tight, spoiling for a fight, a fuck, maybe both. Aiden casts me a couple of uneasy glances but keeps his distance. I grit my teeth, wanting to run, to scream. This is *not* the ideal way to meet one of the other royals.

After what feels an age, we cross under the glass portcullis into the sandstone courtyard. The gate stands open but is only wide enough to allow one troll through at a time. I pass through behind Galfin Dunn and try to distract myself by taking in the new surroundings.

The castle itself is comprised of a series of seven buildings with the smoothness of sand sculptures. The twin towers connected by the glass walkway are the tallest, just high enough to peek above the sandstone cliffs. With the castle built on a peninsula one faces to the east, the other to the west. Beneath them are four squat buildings, maybe three stories high that branch out around the central courtyard. The seventh structure is a single-story, longer than all the others combined and seems to be the congregating place for the trolls. There is no sign of masonry of any kind, almost as if the place is carved from one solid mountain of sand. With effort, I reach out and brush my finger along one wall. The texture is that of hard-packed sand. Like Wardon sculpted his home to be a life-sized sandcastle.

That's it, I realize with a start. That's exactly what he'd done. Wardon must have used his water gifts to deposit enough sand for the buildings and borrowed enough fire from one of his courtiers to superheat the silica into glass. The entire structure is a testament to his abilities.

And I thought a little storm would intimidate him?

Tents are pitched around the open courtyard, the colorful

fabrics flapping in the morning breeze. As Aiden said, the courtyard is dry and the fey and trolls within moving about their business don't look as though the tsunami from moments before affected them at all. Wardon must have urged the water back out to sea before it could reach the lower levels.

There are dozens of creatures in the courtyard. A few have set up what looks like a sort of market place. Baskets of vegetables and fish, wheels of cheese and jugs in an assortment of sizes and shapes are on full display as well as jewelry made from shells and sea glass, bundles of driftwood and other odds and ends.

Something about the picture strikes me as odd, but it takes me several moments to realize what it is. The sellers are fey, and the trolls are their customers, though I don't see any sort of currency changing hands.

A big man with iridescent scales not so different than some of his basket's contents sidles up alongside the trolls in our group. "May I interest you in fresh oysters?" His voice is thick with the sounds of Dicken's London streets.

"Not now." The troll, this one just as congested as Galfin Dunn, doesn't even make eye contact.

"I've got clams too, dug fresh at low tide." The scaled fey tries again, his large bulging eyes hopeful. "Make an excellent chowder. I'll give you a sample."

"I said bugger off." The troll shoves the shellfish hawker hard. The man loses his balance, and ends up on his ass in a tide pool. His tray of wares lands upside down in the sandy muck.

"Hey," I bark, stepping between the troll and the fey, rounding on the former. "What's your damage, assbite?"

The creature glares at me. "What's it to you, mortal?"

He says mortal like it's a dirty word. And that pisses me off. So, I shove him, once, with all my might. He doesn't budge, of course, he outweighs me by at least 500 pounds and his center of gravity is spread over two well-planted feet. He laughs and several of the others join in.

I see red. That tears it, one dead troll coming right up.

"Nic!" Aiden grips me around the waist lifting my feet off the ground. "Don't."

"Let go of me," I snarl. "I want to kill him."

"If you do, they'll kill us," he whispers the warning low for my ears only.

I suck in great lungsful of sea air. What the hell is wrong with me?

"You okay?" Not waiting for an answer, Aiden releases me before crouching to collect the spilled shellfish.

The scaled fey blinks at him, taken aback, either by his handling of a fey royal or his assistance. Perhaps both.

"How much?" Aiden asks, righting the tray and depositing his handfuls onto the driftwood container.

"For what amount, milord?" The scaled creature scrambles up and takes the tray from his proffered grip.

"All of your inventory." Aiden digs into Nahini's saddlebags and extracts a small bundle of coins. "Will this cover it?"

"Yes, milord." The fey nods eagerly. "That is more than enough. Thank ye, kindly."

He tries to return some of the money but Aiden waves it away. "Keep it. Courtesy of Queen Nicneven of the Unseelie."

The fey hands over the tray and then dips a reverent bow in my direction. "Thank you, milord. My queen, it is an honor to be in your presence."

Behind me, a troll snorts but I ignore him and move toward Aiden.

"Just what," I hiss at him out of the corner of my mouth, "Are you planning to do with this stuff?"

"I hadn't gotten that far." Aiden's grip on the tray tightens. "I just didn't like the way the trolls treated him. That was at least a day's worth of merchandise for that man and they would have left it to rot in the sun."

We turn back to where we left the trolls, only to see them on their knees, their heads ducked in reverence.

The creature standing before them has blue-gray skin and a shock of hair the color of seafoam. His face is ageless though his colorless irises are an ancient silver. His body is lean and spare, that of a swimmer, all smooth sleek muscle. His clothes are simple and elegant, loose white linen trousers and a blue-gray tunic. Power thrums around him billowing like his cloak in the sea breeze.

He's bone dry and there is no sign of the toll the magic took on him, but I recognize him at once as the figure from the balcony.

"Queen Nicneven," His lips are a lighter blue than the rest of his skin and they part to reveal two rows of shark-like teeth. His voice is straight out of merry old England too, but cultured, like that of the aristocracy. "I'd heard you came back...altered but I had no idea that meant mortal."

Be careful. Aiden's warning is unnecessary. I recognize a predator when I come face to face with one.

"King Wardon," I hold his gaze, unwilling to back down, especially with my blood still thrumming with a tribal beat of death and lust. Still, I force myself to be polite. "Thank you for your hospitality. My traveling companion and I appreciate your assistance."

Activity in the marketplace grinds to a stop, all the beings freezing in place to watch our exchange.

"The pleasure is mine." He moves closer, not walking so much as gliding like an eel through the water. "May I ask what brings you into my territory? And so close to our transition to power?"

He extends an elbow, those silver eyes glittering. I read once that a sea snake's venom is much deadlier than its land-dwelling counterpart. Wardon's fathomless gaze informs me that while I may have my Goodnight Kiss, he's been playing this game much longer.

"It's a long story," I offer a cool smile though I place a hand on the proffered arm. "And it's been a long journey to get here."

Touching him is like dumping icy water over my raging hormones. I barely stifle a sigh of relief as they scurry into some dark corner for a time out.

"Indulge me over dinner then." Wardon leads me up the sandstone steps that lead to the east-facing tower, the one overlooking the sea. "I'll leave you and your...companion to rest and recover for the day." He claps his hands and two tiny winged fey appear. Wingtip to wingtip, they are no bigger than one of my hands. They look like stick insects with long noses and fingers, their bodies almost skeletal.

"My pixies will see you to your room." Wardon raises my hand to his lips.

A kiss is never just a kiss, at least not when it comes to the kings and queens of Underhill. Lip to skin contact can be a fatal mistake. According to Nahini's teachings, the Master of the Waves commands the Kiss of Madness. Unlike my victims who are tied to the Wild Hunt, those who suffer Wardon's kiss lose the ability to distinguish reality from imagination. They hear words that aren't said, see things that aren't there and are often driven to taking their own lives.

I snatch the appendage away before his blue-gray lips make contact. His eerie eyes sparkle with victory at my retreat. His gaze tells me he wouldn't have used his gift against me, but my flinch reveals my fear. A weakness.

I let him have it. Let him celebrate this minor victory. I am at his relative mercy and though we've just met, I get the feeling that the Seelie king wouldn't react well to another defeat.

He's immortal, I am not and we're in his territory uninvited, surrounded by his people. There are times to advance and time to retreat and this is one of the latter.

The pixies tug at my hair and I turn my back on him and follow the creatures up the spiral staircase. The sky overhead is revealed through the glass domes, the sun as bright as it is outside. The view from up there must be incredible, but between fatigue and my innate sense of modesty, I hope we aren't going to be housed in one of those transparent spaces.

Luckily our guides head into a room about halfway up. The walls are the same color as the sandstone exterior, the texture visibly rough. Curtains of woven seaweed billow back from the open window. Just before it, there is a large bed, its frame hewn from driftwood, with a thick mattress atop it. Strings of seashells hang from the ceiling in one corner with a large white tub partially obscured by the makeshift partition and a blue-green driftwood fire blazes in a sandstone pit beside it. The only other stick of furniture in the room is a large wardrobe on the opposite wall.

"Here we are," one of the pixies squeaks, its voice thin and reedy as the other flits about the room. "The wardrobe will provide you with whatever you require. Let us know if you need anything. Someone will retrieve you for dinner."

"Whatever we require?" I ask.

She flits up, a bit of sparkling dust falling on the floor beneath her. "Clothing, towels, extra blankets for the two of you."

"The two of us?" I say as it suddenly dawns on me that Wardon had said room. As in singular. "Wait!"

But they have already departed.

"Did you pick up on Wardon's pause around the word companion?" Aiden offers me an apologetic smile and sets down both the saddlebags and the tray he purchased from the scaled fey before turning to shut the door. "It's just a small step away from consort. He knows who I am."

"Do you think it's safe to talk here?" I mean aloud and from the understanding light in his eyes, he knows it, too.

"I think so. Wardon likes his games but spying on you within his own walls doesn't pose much of a challenge. If I were to hazard a guess, I'd say he already knows exactly how we came to be here, who we're looking for and probably what we ate for dinner last night."

I crouch beside the tub, awed to find it made from half a clamshell. A giant clamshell, roughly the size of a Volkswagen bug. I run my hand over the smooth contours. "This is incredible."

The sink on the wall behind it is also made of a clamshell albeit a much smaller one. There is a sandstone partition with a toilet that looks relatively standard, thank the gods.

"This is a strange blend of items from the modern mortal world and fey magic." My hand finds the faucet and I turn it on, smiling to see water pouring into the clamshell tub. "How did he do this?"

"Chances are Wardon's crossed the Veil, carried some things back and other's he's recreated from memory."

I stand and glance about the space. "Does he really expect that we'll sleep here today?"

"Sleeping isn't why he provided us one room." His gaze locks with mine. "Would you care for the first bath?"

HEARTBEAT. Heartbeat. Heartbeat. More than the thought of hot water brings my blood back up to temperature. It zips through my veins like quicksilver as I realize that not only are Aiden and I sharing a room, but that there is no door to separate us. No solid wood to come between us, to keep us from touching, kissing and doing everything else I've imagined doing with him.

Things I *remember* doing with him.

My lips part but no sound comes out. I've grown accustomed to his presence, comfortable with being close to him. His cedar and sage scent, the feel of his skin as he takes my hand. It's as though out of the two of us, I'm the wild animal and he's the one doing the taming, getting me used to him. I see the acknowledgment in his green eyes, along with the hunger. Usually, he keeps it on a tight leash but I can tell that he's thinking the same thing I am.

This room is made for intimacy. For sex. It's too easy to picture our naked bodies writhing together in the oversized tub, or on the massive bed. In the home of one of the most dangerous fey alive no less. I'm not thinking about Nahini, the lost souls of the Wild Hunt, the upcoming gauntlet or whatever Wardon wants from me. No, I am thinking about Aiden, about touching his naked body and having him do the same to mine.

The situation has forced us to make a giant leap ahead. One room, one bed, one bath. Nowhere to run or hide. His desire plain, his expression questioning. I watch as he licks his lips, his gaze seeming to drink me in.

My own body is sending me mixed signals. Fight or flight, wanting and fearing. Remembered passions from the stream and my past self, mix with a lifetime of denial. It's a shock to realize how mistaken I've been. I'm not asexual, the way I once thought, at least not entirely. Aiden's accepted me, made me trust, made me remember. Made me crave him in a way I never thought possible.

The feeling is exclusive to him, to Aiden. Wardon is exceptionally well made, if unusually colored. Alric too is a perfect physical specimen. But I hadn't felt a flicker of attraction for either of them any more than I ever had any of the boys at school.

"Gods, what is *wrong* with me?" I put a hand to my spinning head.

Aiden's there in an instant. "Tell me what's going on."

"It's like I have zero control over my hormones." I look at him, lean muscles on display and lick my lips.

He puts a hand to my forehead, checking for fever. "You're burning up. Is that why you picked a fight with a troll in the middle of a clutch of them?" Without asking, he scoops me into his arms and carries me to the bed.

"A clutch?"

"A group of trolls." He places me flat on my back and eases down beside me.

The heat radiating from his body has me frothing at the mouth. "Do you think the price of the magic I used here made me sick?"

"I've never heard that before." His fingers move to my wrist. "Your pulse is racing."

"Mmmm," I breathe, my eyelids growing heavy as his scent envelopes me.

He tilts his head. "You said hormones. Are you...turned on, too?"

I stroke his forearm, loving the smooth glide of his tanned skin under my fingertips. "Like a damn lamp. It's weird, I keep switching between extreme rage and extreme lust."

His lips compress as though he's fighting a losing battle with a smile. "I...uh...think I know what's wrong with you."

I struggle upright, needing to get closer to him. "Really? What?"

"Testosterone poisoning."

I freeze seconds before swinging a leg over him. "Are you joking?" Sure, Aiden possesses a mischievous sense of humor that can sometimes border on diabolical, but now is hardly the time.

The expression on his face doesn't appear playful though. "I'm serious, Nic, though I could be wrong. But your... urges... seem in line with testosterone overload, at least the way I've experienced it." He nods down to where my hands are balled up in the elegant bedspread.

I force my hands to relax and shake my head, burrowing deep into denial. "No, it can't be."

But Aiden's focus turns inward. "That's why Wardon was showing off. He wanted you to use magic, and have you off-balance, dealing with the after-effects of wielding your powers. He had no way of knowing what the consequences would be, but it was worth the risk if it gave him an advantage."

Sitting still proves impossible. I leap to my feet and start to pace the room. Moments earlier it seemed spacious enough, but now it feels like the walls are closing in. "We need to get out of here. *I* need to get out of here."

Aiden catches me and pulls me into an embrace. It's not affection so much as for restraint. "It's okay. I've got you. We'll figure something out."

I lean into him, but he smells too damn good. My hands start roving over his back and my body flashes hot then cold. I'm too turned on, too overloaded. Growling in frustration, I shove away from him. "Gods, how do you deal with this? I can't hold a thought. I want to...?" I want him to tear his clothes off, but I just barely stop myself from blurting it out.

"What do I do?"

He catches me again. "Without some sort of human hormone treatment? There are only two possibilities. You need a release. Either a fight or...." His gaze slides to the bed.

I back away from him, even as every molecule in my body

stretches and prepares to sing the hallelujah chorus. "Oh, no. No. I'm not going there. Especially not here."

He nods, his expression somber. "Then hit me."

That draws me up short. "What?"

"You need an outlet to burn it off. Take it out on me."

He's serious. "I'm not going to beat you. That's sick."

Says the serial killer to the werewolf.

"It won't have been the first time a woman has done so," his tone is quiet.

I stare at him at a loss. "And are you going to hit me back?"

He glares at me. "Of course not. I'll dodge if that helps, restrain you if necessary, though I won't be able to really hurt you without the wolf—" He chokes off, looking away as though ashamed.

Aiden had been forced to hurt me before, physically in order to save my life. The act had traumatized him and his wolf took control, threatening all those around us. And here he is, willing to risk it again, to let me hurt him in order to help me.

In that moment, with the golden seaside light streaming in on him, he'd never been more irresistible. Maybe the hormones are to blame, but I throw myself at him, knocking him onto the massive bed. I cover him like a blanket, my lips ravenous for his, needing him closer, needing to feel him.

He doesn't respond immediately, that iron will still in place. I'm busy kissing my way down the side of his tanned throat when he murmurs my name and asks, "Are you sure this is what you want?"

I whip my shirt over my head in answer and drop it on the floor. "Just kiss me, Aiden. We'll figure out the rest later."

With a growl he rolls me under him, pinning me to the mattress beneath his delicious weight. Good man.

I lose myself in the taste of him, hot and hungry. He

nibbles my bottom lip. I fist my hands in his hair. His tongue sweeps into my mouth as I claw down his back, loving every sensation. We crash into each other, one kiss after another like waves upon the beach outside. It's too much, it's not enough. I want to drown myself in the mysterious and alluring fathoms of Aiden.

His skin is hot to my touch, his body moving in a rhythm both foreign and familiar. My own responds to him, arching, aching, needing. His hand skims along my ribcage, settling over the lacy cup of my demi bra.

"I like this," he toys with the lace. "Did you wear this just for me?"

"Yes." While normally it would have stung my pride to admit that I'd dressed with him in mind, I'm beyond caring.

A soft growl rumbles in his chest. The sound is pure masculine satisfaction. "I'm trying to go slowly—"

"Don't," I gasp as I yank his shirt up, craving the contact. "I don't need slow…I need…I need…."

His gaze is searching my features, for what, I have no idea. "You need slow. You crave release but this is new."

I shake my head. "It's not, I remember. From before. Those damn memories have been plaguing me for *weeks*."

"It is new, for your body." His clever fingers pluck at a nipple through the lace.

An involuntary cry escapes my lips as pleasure spirals down inside me. "More."

He chuckles then rolls to one side. "As my lady commands. But slowly. I want to savor you and I need you to like this."

My lips part but before I can argue, his hand glides beneath the fabric of my bra. Without the barrier, the sensations are a thousand, a million times stronger. I make some sort of strangled sound and arch fully into his palm.

He withdraws his hand. I sit up, ready to lodge a protest

but his fingers move to the back clasp of my bra. "I want to look at you while I touch you. Is that okay?"

I nod jerkily, a riot of emotions going on inside me.

He unfastens the hooks and reflexively, I hold up my hands before the undergarment can fall away. He reaches for me again, cups my face in his big palms, his gaze locked on mine.

"Trust me, Nic," he breathes between soft, slow kisses.

"I do." I lower my shaking hands.

Aiden doesn't rush, he's much too accomplished a seducer to pounce. His thumbs graze along my jaw bone, down my neck. His kisses are deep, thorough and make me forget my nervousness, stoking the fire within. He slides the strap of my bra over my shoulders, peels it from my arms.

His lids grow heavy as he withdraws to look at me. "Gods, and I thought you were beautiful before."

"I was," I say, hating the image of my dark-haired former self and all her perfect curves. Compared to her I'm kinda pretty—in the right light. The perverts that I'd offed never complained.

But the way Aiden's drinking me in… it makes me think he hasn't gotten the memo about my appearance being less-than stunning. He doesn't look disappointed. *His* hands are shaking as he reaches to touch me. The spark of contact as he caresses my bared flesh makes all my worries evaporate like the water left in a tea kettle.

The heat is building, too. Every pull and tug on my sensitive nipples creates an echo in the pit of my stomach. And lower. Much *much*, lower.

He dips his head, taking one tormented tip into his mouth.

My blissed-out mind churns out a word I'd never thought much about before this moment. Desire. I've wanted before. Yearned. For superficial things. I've had cravings, felt the need to stretch, to sleep, to kill. But nothing can match the sexual hunger that's tearing me apart from the inside.

My head thrashes on the pillow. It has to end. I never wanted it to end.

His tongue teases and then relinquishes, and, moving to my other breast, sets in on that side, while his fingers continue to torment the wet peak. He's diligent, patient, fanning the flames of feeling until they threaten to overtake me. Ravenous, I've been starving for this contact. It can't get better than Aiden's hands and mouth on my bared breasts.

And then a hand traces down, following the seam of my jeans to the center of feeling. He presses in with the heel of his palm in a deliberate maneuver.

I shatter. There's no other way to put it. All that coiled tension breaks like a mirror under the onslaught of a sledge-hammer. The pleasure so sharp it hurts, ripping a cry from my mouth. Leaving me in pieces. Sharp jagged little bits of Nic are scattered everywhere.

And that scares me.

The fear grounds me back in my body, still hot and sensitive, vulnerable and exposed. I don't want to open my eyes, to look at him after what he'd…what we'd just done.

Will he expect more now…will he want…everything?

"Nic?" He lifts his head to look at me. "Did you just…?"

"Yeah." My eyelids squeeze shut.

"Was that the first time you…?"

"Yeah." And yes, under the right circumstances, even a serial killer can blush. Reality is crashing back down and it's a bitch and a half. I wriggle out from under him, doing my best to ignore my bobbing breasts, the same ones he'd been licking and sucking only a few altering heartbeats ago.

My hands are shaking again, not from nerves but from agitation. No way do I want to struggle to put my bra back on but damned if I can find my shirt.

I spot it, over near the door and move to retrieve it.

Aiden catches my arm. "Is it over? Have the urges passed?"

What urges? Oh, right, the testosterone poisoning. I'd forgotten all about it. "Yeah." My voice sounds thin in my own ears.

"Are you all right?"

"I'm fine," I snap, jerking my arm free and diving for the discarded shirt which I hold up like a shield between us. Sand still clings to it, abrading my already sensitive nipples.

He lets go. "Why won't you look at me?"

"I'm not ready," I blurt. It's the only thing I can say. The truth, if not the entire truth. "To do anything else."

He stares at me a moment, his thick eyebrows pulling down. His lips part as though he's going to say something but then he clamps them shut. When he does speak it's a lackluster, "Okay."

I want to ask what he was going to say. Was he angry? Did he think me a tease? But I can't seem to move, can't do anything but clutch at my sandy shirt and stare at him.

He chucks a thumb at the exit. "I'll wait outside."

I sag when the door clicks shut behind him, though in relief or disappointment is anyone's guess. I need something to do, to distract myself. My gaze falls on the tub. A bath, I could use one of those. I stand, drop the shirt and turn on the tap before stripping out of my sand encrusted jeans. Carefully, I remove the vet wrap from the Valkyrie scratch and my rune. The wound around the scratch is still red, the skin beyond that a hideous blue-black, but I don't think it's infected.

The rune is completely scabbed over, almost healed.

The water is only about a third of the way up the clamshell but I climb in any way, busying myself by investigating the collection of bottles lining a small indent beside the tub. One smells of coconut another eucalyptus, a third sandalwood. Shampoo or soap of some sort. None smell as delectable as Aiden, but I haven't bathed since before the encounter with the Valkyries and work a decent amount of lather up for my skin and hair.

Though I'm tempted to linger, I worry over Aiden standing out in the hall. He deserves an explanation. Problem is, I don't have one. I'd been so caught up in the physical bliss, my first climax. When it ended, all the other things had crept back into my mind. Self-consciousness at my body's release, and the indignity of desire. I had barely recognized myself as I begged, *begged*, him to keep going, to keep touching me.

Once clean, I drip to the wardrobe and fling open the door, thinking towels. Just like the pixie claimed, the shelves are lined with fluffy white terrycloth. I pick one up and study it. Standard issue towel, though much fluffier than ours, since Chloe inevitably adds too many dryer sheets. I shut the doors to the wardrobe and think, clothes. Lo and behold, the towels are gone and in their place, several dresses hang. I frown. Dresses aren't my first choice, a little too inconvenient if I need to run or fight. And the shoes. Broken ankle central.

I return my focus to the wardrobe. How does the magic work? Is it sentient? Reading my mind somehow? Or is it just a storage facility? From the outside, it looks like a regular piece of furniture but the inside completely rearranged itself.

After drying off, I wrap the towel around my sopping hair and another around my body before padding to the door and opening it a crack.

Aiden stands there, his back to me. And he isn't alone. A purple-skinned fey woman with waist-length hair black as a raven's wing is eyeing him like he's an item on a buffet table and she hasn't eaten in weeks.

"You know where my room is," I hear her purr. Her

accent is much different than any of the fey or even the trolls I've heard here. It's sultry and rich, flavored with Latin spice which adds weight to her invitation. "In case you change your mind."

I blink. Freaking really? Where did she even come from?

"I won't," his tone is definite.

"Oh, but I hope you do." She reaches out and though I can't see, I get the feeling that she's dragging her silver nails down his bare chest. "You look like you could use a little fun."

I open the door wider, until she notices me standing there. She raises one eyebrow as though to say, *can you blame me for trying?*

I don't but I don't have to like it either. "He's good. We're good, though we could use a bottle of wine. Be a doll and get us some?" I loop my arm through Aiden's and pull him back through the door, slamming it with excessive force.

"Do you know who that was?" Aiden asks, his eyes wide.

"No, and I can't say I give a flying rat's ass." I snarl.

"She's Wardon's seer."

"Seer? Like his own personal fortune teller?"

"Much more than that. She's his most trusted adviser, a noble in her own right." He shakes his head. "And you treated her like the help."

I put my hands on my towel-covered hips. "Well, she seemed so damn eager to be of service, I figured I'd throw her a bone before you did."

"Are you jesting?" He stares at me, a muscle ticking in his jaw. A sure sign of frustration. "After what just happened, you still don't trust me to be true to you? You have no faith in me."

"Don't be ridiculous," I whirl toward the wardrobe, uncaring of what's in there, just not wanting to continue the conversation while wearing only a towel. "I have faith in you. You wouldn't be here if I didn't."

Even though they are impractical, I can't help but admire the series of shimmering gowns in varying ocean colors, from the palest gray-green to blue so dark it is almost black. Though there are no tags, I have the feeling all will fit as though tailored just for me. A pair of black satin elbow-length gloves rest in a box to one side. And the shoes....

I pick one delicate pump up, marveling at the colors, the play of light off the transparent surface. A few pairs are greenish tinged, others blue, still others completely colorless. "Is this...?"

"Sea glass," Aiden confirms, coming up beside me.

His nearness rattles me, almost as much as Wardon's easy use of magic. "Why would he do this, build this place and furnish it with his magic? Wouldn't he have had to pay the price each time?"

Aiden shakes his head. "All of Wardon's magic comes from his mind and is fueled by the sea. He can create anything he wants out of his element without paying Under-hill's price."

Carefully, I set the shoe back down and meet his gaze. "So, why can't I do the same?"

He offers a small smile. "You probably will, once you pass the gauntlet. Underhill doesn't know what to make of you, a mortal able to wield magic. You're a queen but not yet a ruler and until you run the gauntlet, you will continue to struggle here."

"But I could do it before? Use magic for everything?"

He curls a finger around a tendril of hair that escaped my towel turban. "Not everything, but you could craft items from snow and ice, from shadows and air and even souls. The Veil had no need to repair itself, because you sealed up any rips or tears with half a thought."

And now there is a giant hole in the thing and no one to mend it. At least not until I get my abilities back. If I ever do.

"Your display earlier probably fooled Wardon into believing that your magic still comes so easily," he continues. "Your loss of temper might prove beneficial."

Dread fills my stomach and I can't look him in the eye. "Until the trolls tell him how volatile I was afterward."

"They might not. Trolls can't wield magic any more than Valkyries. They don't understand how it works and most don't know about the cost. It's likely that if Wardon doesn't think to ask them, they won't volunteer any information about your condition."

"We need to find Nahini and the rest of the Hunt and get the hell out of here before he does." I hesitate, again peering into the depths of the wardrobe, trying to decide which gown to put on.

Aiden chooses for me. "This one," he says, selecting a gown so pale blue it's almost white. Ice blue. "It matches your eyes."

His own eyes are hot, though I'm still too much of a novice at emotion to tell if it's from temper or lust.

"With my pale hair and skin, I think it's more likely I'll look like a corpse," I mutter.

"Please," the word is quiet, not a plea so much as a simple request. "I want to see you in it."

"Okay." I need to wear something to dinner and it's really the least I can do for him, after the emotional roller coaster ride from earlier. The closest I'll come to apologizing. And yet, it's not enough.

"I didn't mean…," I stop, suck in some air then blow it out in exasperation. Damn it, why can't I just articulate my thoughts? "About earlier…."

He kisses me lightly on the cheek, his green eyes alight with hope. "Believe me, Nic. You have nothing to worry about."

My lips part and I'm about to ask what he's referring to,

when he turns and, with typical ease, strips out of his jeans. I suck in a breath. No matter how many times I see his bared flesh, I can't get used to it. My gaze is locked on his perfect form as he strides to the alcove and passes through the curtain to the clamshell tub.

It takes effort to drag my eyes away, to focus on something other than the churning mess of feelings clamoring inside me. I take the dress, gloves, and shoes to the far side of the room then lay them on the bed before turning my back and dropping my towel.

A low growl fills the room. He's watching me, taking in the sight of my naked body. That curtain is no real barrier to his keen eyesight. I can feel his gaze sliding down my back, over the flare of my hips, down my legs and then back up, taking his measure of every dip and curve.

My nipples stiffen again, the reaction having nothing to do with the temperature of the room. I want to look at him, want to peek over my shoulder and catch him ogling my body the way I scrutinize his.

But we have other things to think about, more important things. If only I could recall what they are.

We're supposed to be resting. Sense dictates that I take a nap, rebuild my reserves before my next run-in with Wardon. But the idea of climbing naked into this bed, of Aiden also naked and wet in the tub….

The temptation is too great. As is the fear.

I pull the gown over my head, adjusting the spaghetti straps so they fall in straight lines crisscrossing my shoulders. The gown is slit high on the right thigh but otherwise, it clings to me like a shimmering second skin. Once it's in place, I remove the towel from my head and step into the shoes then pick up the gloves.

"I'm heading downstairs. Meet me when you're ready."

"No, Nic, wait!" There's some splashing as he lunges from

the tub, but I'm already out the door and halfway down the stairs.

Aiden fears for my safety, I know this and I probably should wait for him. True, Wardon poses an unknown threat but being locked in that bedroom with Aiden wet and naked and wanting me is far more dangerous.

CHAPTER 10

AN OFFER

The fact that my hair is still wet and slicked back from my head seems to fit in with the seaside palace. I've never been much of a beach person but the view of the rolling waves is hypnotic and treacherous. Much like Wardon himself.

I meet a pixie on the stairs. She starts, probably to find me outside of our assigned chambers. A shower of bright yellow dust falls to the floor beneath her. Glittering like sand.

"My companion is still getting dressed. I thought I would look around while I wait."

"Of…of course, your majesty," she stammers. Her voice is higher, less sure than the one who'd shown us to the bedchamber earlier. "Would you care to wait here for him?"

"We can go down." I decide to use her unease to my advantage and poke around. Wardon has home turf advantage after all. Something needs to even the odds. "How long have you worked here?"

"I was hatched here." The pixie flits ahead, her dust turning an embarrassed pink, the color of a maiden's blush.

"Hatched? Like from an egg?"

She nods. "A moon egg along with my seventy brothers and sisters."

"Seventy? Is that typical?" At her nod I add, "Family reunions must be confusing as hell."

"Most pixies don't live into adulthood," she says. "Only five of my siblings made it past the first year. It's why so many of us are born because so few of us survive."

We pass by a window. The sun is high in the sky now. Down below the sounds of the marketplace have increased. "Tell me, how come it seems like the fey marketplace is set up to serve the trolls? And why can they move about in the daytime? I thought they didn't possess any magic."

"They don't. But the trolls serve the king as the royal guard. To curry favor with them can mean acknowledgment from his highness."

I wonder at the arrangement. Wardon can draw on fey powers, it's what makes him a Seelie king. He's lavish with using his own, this castle is a testament to his vanity. All the Seelie fey, from Samhain to Beltane are sworn to serve him. Why go to so much trouble to enlist trolls to his royal guard, to grant them the ability to move around under the sun and set them up in a position of power over his subjects?

"Nicneven."

As though stepping from my thoughts, Wardon appears at the bottom of the stairs. I dip my head in acknowledgment. He offers me a hand down the last few steps.

"Aren't you becoming in my finery." There's a slight lilt in his voice, a brogue though it's difficult to pick up. I'd missed it earlier.

The king smiles and there is no warmth in it. "I thought for sure you would be…resting. Have you worn your consort out already?"

"I have more important things on my mind than…rest." I put the same emphasis on the word.

He raises one brow. "I admire an ambitious woman. Come to my study and we can discuss your needs over a drink."

Though touching him makes my skin crawl, I allow him to escort me down the long corridor, my glass pumps clicking steadily on the sandstone floor. Wardon's feet are bare and silent beside mine.

He opens the door and ushers me inside. The décor is much the same as my upstairs room. Driftwood shelves and furniture, seagrass curtains, glass candle holders. The main difference is the double doors leading out to a balcony that overlooks the churning sea. It is here Wardon leads me, settling me in an intricate driftwood chaise before retrieving two sea glass tumblers from a glass sideboard. "Rum or mulled wine?"

"Water," I counter, unwilling to shed one ounce of my inhibitions in this place. Well, one ounce more than I'd already done. I need every advantage I can get.

The sun is high in the sky. Large palms flank the patio, providing adequate shade. He hands me the glass and then turns to take in the view. "Magnificent, isn't it? Much warmer than you're used to, I'll wager, even this time of year."

I study him out of the corner of my eye. It's unclear if he's referring to the old Nicneven who lived in an ice palace or to Nic the mountain girl. Questions abound. How much does he know about me? Was he the one who pixed us from the fairy hill?

I am not a game player. Unless you count hunting and stalking as a game. But word games and political machinations aren't my forte. I decide to put my cards on the table. "What is it you want from me, Wardon?"

He flashes that shark's grin. "And what makes you think I want anything?"

"You didn't send your trolls out to collect me just for the pleasure of my company," I take a sip of water.

"Perhaps I just wanted the chance to see if the rumors are true."

I quirk a brow. "Rumors seldom are."

"I'm not so sure." He pulls up a chair beside my chaise, and leans back, steepling his fingers while he scans me. "You look different from before, as rumor reported. Smaller, younger and obviously mortal. But the gauntlet will take care of most of that."

I raise an eyebrow. "It's going to make me bigger?"

He laughs. "Not in body, but in spirit. I have yet to see a mortal reach immortality that didn't overflow with a sense of purpose. Only the strongest survive, you are aware."

He doesn't wait for my response but continues. "No, it's going to make you harder. The gauntlet breaks a soul down to its core and builds it back up again. Life is hard and unending life is harder still. It takes something unbreakable to go up against the vastness of forever."

It takes all my self-control not to react to his description. A sense of purpose? I have been set on this path by others, those who want me to reclaim the Shadow Throne. Wardon apparently believes I have what it takes to come out victorious. Is he mistaking hardness for coldness, determination for pride?

To distract myself I ask, "What other rumors have you heard?"

"That you continue to serve in the same capacity, collecting diseased souls to serve the Wild Hunt. That you have no mortal compassion, no feelings for anyone and are completely self-serving." He raises a glass, his filled with an amber liquid. "My kind of woman."

I drink to his toast sans argument then set my glass aside. "And where would a Seelie king hear such gossip?"

Quicksilver eyes glitter. "From my spies, of course. You don't think Brigit was the only one keeping tabs on you?"

I offer a tight smile, even as the image of the brown-eyed stranger who had been eyeballing me in the cafeteria surfaces. "And why go to the trouble of spying? What is it you hope to gain?"

Instead of answering, Wardon sets his empty glass aside and stands. "With Brigit gone, I am the oldest monarch in any of the courts. That role comes with certain responsibilities. To uphold tradition and continue to rule as I always have or, if the situation warrants it, to create new and more suitable roles. The lives of the fey have not markedly changed for eons with magic being the dividing line between the haves and have nots.

The fey courts were split before mankind even crawled from the ooze yet most of our people live in squalor. You have spent time in Underhill, surely you know of this plight."

I nod once, refusing to ask another question until he answered the previous one.

"One monarch is dead, with no obvious heir to claim the Fire Throne and the Unseelie nobles squabble like children over a teacake. The Shadow Throne sits empty, awaiting your return. The two thrones together make up the Unseelie Court. I want you to claim them both and then unite with me to take the Green Throne from Pan's heir. Four thrones, two rulers."

I blink at him. "You want to unite the fey?"

His thin lips curved upwards. "Imagine, ruling both the Seelie and the Unseelie together."

My stomach feels hollow, and not just from lack of food. "By together you mean…?"

"I want you to marry me."

I stare at him, my lips parting. Out of all the things he could possibly say… "Why marriage? Why not simply a truce?"

He gestures back through the open glass doors to the driftwood shelves that hold rows and rows of books. "I've been studying mortal history. Many great empires united through marriage to form lasting alliances. If it works for the mortals it can work for us as well. Imagine it, Nicneven. All the fey united under one banner."

My heart is thundering in my chest but outwardly I am calm. Cold. The Ice Bitch. "I'm surprised you didn't propose this to Brigit."

"I did." He says without an ounce of remorse. "Why do you think she murdered you in the first place?"

"You did what?" Aiden's hands are fist at his side, the knuckles white.

Apparently, he'd appeared on the balcony in time to hear the confession. Fantastic.

"Ah, here's your wolf. Now. If the two of you will excuse me, I have some royal matters concerning the transition of power to attend to." Without waiting for a response, he makes to sweep past Aiden. For his part, Aiden is perfectly still, a predator ready to strike. He's a hairsbreadth from tearing out Wardon's throat.

I do the one thing I swore not to do. I use our bond to command him. *Aiden, stand down.*

He swings his murderous gaze to me.

Not here. I shake my head slightly in warning. In the glass door, I see Wardon's lips curve up in a self-satisfied smile. Obviously, the fey King wants the two of us to fight. Why can't Aiden sense the trap? He's supposed to be better at this than I am, my guide in navigating the quagmire of fey politics. Yet he's playing right into Wardon's hands.

Play along. I mentally project to Aiden. "I find I am feeling fatigued. Will you escort me back upstairs so I can rest before dinner?" The tone is a little bit entitled debutant, certainly not me, but if Wardon wants a show, I'll give him one.

Aiden's jaw clenches, but he offers an arm. "As her highness desires."

Don't be an ass. I think at him, though I keep my eyes staring straight ahead. *I'm not considering his offer. He's a power-hungry psychopath who teamed up with Brigit to have me killed. Don't look relieved, I'm sure someone is watching.*

Aiden immediately schools his features back to the same tenseness and leads me out into the hall.

He's an idiot if he thinks you won't take that bit about him convincing Brigit to murder you personally, Aiden says.

I dip my head in acknowledgment of a finely dressed group of courtiers as we pass in the hallway. *Right? I hold onto grudges like they'll be back in vogue. Not the best way to pad a marriage proposal. I can't figure out what his actual game is though. What is it he really wants?*

We ascend the steps and I sag once the door to our bedchamber closes. "I'm sorry I ordered you."

He huffs out a breath. "I'm sorry you had to."

"You need to be smarter than that, Aiden."

He looks away and his Adam's apple bobs. "I know. You ran out of here so fast and the thought of you out there alone and unguarded in the viper's den made my wolf rise. I had to fight the change before I could come after you. And then to hear that bastard admit that he practically took out a hit on you—" he breaks off, shaking his head.

"Hey," I say. "It's all right. I see him for what he is and he doesn't scare me."

"But I do." Aiden keeps his distance, his heart in his eyes. "I scare you into running."

I swallow and look away. "Now's not the time for this conversation. We have more important things to focus on, like finding Nahini and the spirits of the Hunt."

He flinches and it isn't until that moment that I realize how my words might have sounded. "Aiden, I didn't mean—"

"That I'm not important? No, I already got that update, thanks." He stalks to the door. "Stay here, I'll be back before dinner."

"Aiden, I didn't mean—" I say but the door is already closing behind him.

"That could have gone better." I slip my feet free of the sea glass shoes and shuck the dress off before crawling into bed. Though my body hurts and I am physically exhausted, sleep doesn't come right away. The sheets are scratchy against my bare skin. I get up and pad over to the wardrobe. A layer of pajama fabric will help. But instead of the t-shirt and yoga pants I was hoping for, I am faced with rows of lacy undergarments. Baby doll nighties, merry widows, and sexy lingerie in every color of the rainbow that have little to do with sleeping.

With a resigned sigh, I reach for a sheer black camisole and matching thong, probably the least revealing of the garments. After dressing, I head back to the bed and do my level best not to think myself crazy.

I hate the doubt and uncertainty. Even when not in the throes of a full-blown panic attack the feelings are there, lurking just below the surface, a geyser ready to erupt at any time. And Aiden is usually the one catching the brunt of my bad temper.

He's right, I had been jealous earlier, to find that fey vixen sniffing around him. I didn't even like when he flirts with mortals like Gretchen, never mind a forever young seer. If there's a green-eyed monster in this relationship, it certainly isn't Aiden.

He'd described his own jealousy to me, how he felt in my last life when, during my fertile time, I had to sleep with fey nobles. How had he endured it, knowing that another male was touching my body, using it, trying to intentionally plant immortal life in my womb? I can't even stand to see him *talking* to another woman.

If I'm honest, my envy has very little to do with Aiden's behavior. I heard him turn the seer down. It isn't his fault that he's flawless, that his body is made for long sweaty sessions between the sheets. Yes, he's respectful to every woman he meets, even Freda, who treats him with contempt. And that kindness made him even more appealing than his sexual magnetism. Both traits I lack.

Even though he makes my skin crawl, Wardon really is a more fitting match for me than Aiden. I understand his cold ruthlessness, the fact that his soul is nothing more than bare branches scraping against glass. Aiden is warmth and light and life, the opposite of the Seelie king. And of me.

The lace on the camisole abrades my nipples, still sensitive from our earlier romp. I groan and then turn over. And then there are these damn foreign urges, the sensations that course through me whenever I look at Aiden, or get a hit of his wild scent. Twice now, I've been lost in the madness of sexual need. Hell, just having him *look* at me a certain way is enough to ignite my desire.

Something has to give. I know it and Aiden knows it. Eventually, I'll have to either give in to the urges or shut him down entirely. We can't continue indefinitely in this half state, both together and not together. It's making me crazy, wreaking hell with his control.

I am playing with fire, in every sense of the word.

I can't be what it is Aiden wants me to be, open with my

body, honest with my thoughts, trusting with my heart. The knowledge is there, deep in my guts. I can't be free with my body, to trust him with it, to let my guard down so much. He says he can accept a non-sexual relationship. Maybe he even believes that's what he wants. Yet every time we are alone together it's as though we're dangling a match over a keg of gunpowder. Eventually, there will be an explosion and we'll be lucky if the blast doesn't destroy us both.

I roll onto my side. What happens when Aiden comes back, lies down next to me? Will he reach for me? And if he does, will I go into his arms?

I surge upright and sprint to the wardrobe thinking *pillows.* I fling open the door and grab a giant armful of pillows and dash back to the bed, dump my load and head back for another.

Cocooned once more in bed, I start stacking a wall of pillows around my scantily clad body. It feels silly but a physical barrier might buy me time to think before I attack him. Task done, I flop back onto the bed and try not to think about having sex with Aiden.

It isn't fair to string him along this way. To use him whenever a fey spell turns me on, then shut him down when the danger passes. What's the other option, though? To set him free, let him move on to someone else, give his devotion to another. Maybe a goddess. My fists clench at the thought of him in some golden beauty's arms, kissing her the way he kisses me, caressing her as he touched me, being everything to her that he once was for me.

In a way, my aunts had been right to insist that Aiden keep his distance from me. You can't miss what you don't remember. For if I had never encountered him perhaps the memories of my past life would have stayed buried and I would have gone on with my mortal life, never knowing what I was missing.

And then there's the very real possibility that I won't survive the gauntlet, won't make it to immortality. Everyone around me, even Wardon, seems sure I will make it, that I will come out the other side ready to pick up where I left off.

I'm not so sure.

No matter how many times I try to picture it, I can't see myself sitting on the Shadow Throne. Can't imagine ruling the Unseelie fey, dispensing justice. It's like trying to fit a square peg into a round hole—no amount of force is going to make it fit.

I don't want to die but neither do I want to live forever as an immortal queen. Why are those my only options? My mind is like a bumblebee in a jar, ricocheting off an invisible prison, unable to find a way out.

Eventually, exhaustion has its way with me because the next thing I know the door to the bedchamber groans and Aiden pads inside. The cream-colored tunic and pants he's wearing are wrinkled and crusted with sand around the ankles and his hair appears windblown.

Green eyes meet mine. "I'm sorry, I didn't mean to wake you."

"It's okay." I sit up and half a dozen pillows topple from the stack.

Awkward silence.

He shuts the door, comes into the room. I struggle upright, wishing I had come to some sort of decision about how to approach him, to tell him the truth he needs to accept.

"I think I know where Nahini has gone," Aiden says.

That pulls my mind from the downward spiral into self-pity. "Where?"

"The valley of lost souls."

"Sounds promising." When he frowns I add, "For the missing members of the Hunt. How far is it from here?"

"About two days overland on foot. Faster if you can convince Wardon to lend me a horse."

Tossing the covers back, I set my feet on the floor, ready to go. "You mean us a couple of horses, right? For both of us?"

He shakes his head. "You should stay here."

"And why is that, exactly?"

I expect him to say something about how it's too dangerous for my mortal self. Truth be told, all of Underhill is too dangerous. But he surprises me.

"You should consider his offer."

My mouth falls open. "The offer of *marriage*? The one you were fuming about not even an hour ago?"

He looks away, the green of his irises focus elsewhere. "Wardon would be a powerful ally, something you'll need to combat whichever of Brigit's progeny lays claim to the Fire Throne."

"You're joking, right? Tell me you are kidding."

He doesn't respond, doesn't as much as twitch.

I stalk towards him. "You actually want me to marry the bastard who suggested to Brigit that she should kill me in the first place?"

His lids lower somewhat, his voice sounds detached when he speaks. "Brigit is dead. Things are different. You're different and pretending you aren't won't help us."

"I'm not attracted to Wardon." I raise my chin.

A muscle jumps in his jaw. "It doesn't matter."

"Like hell it doesn't," I snap.

"What he's proposing is a political alliance. You've seen the fey of Underhill, see how they struggle. Forever young beings that die of starvation and exposure. You could put a stop to that."

"By becoming Wardon's broodmare?" I snap.

"You said you wanted to make things right," Aiden snaps

backs. "To make up for your past sins. This will let you do so without fey bloodshed."

"So, instead of sleeping with hundreds of fey I don't desire, I only have to sleep with one? You know what the difference is between a queen that marries for position and a back-alley whore? Some high-end fabrics and a warmer place to do the deed."

"An alliance in the Seelie Court could make a difference come Ragnorok," he says quietly. "You'd be able to do something to stop the end of the world."

"And that matters more to you? You'd trade me for the rest of the world?"

His face closes like a shop at the end of the workday. Take your business elsewhere, his expression says. We're no longer interested. "In a heartbeat."

My breath hitches, as though he's hit me in the diaphragm. Here I thought I would have to find a way to let him down, to set him free. Had he been looking for his own escape all along or is this a recent development?

I turn away from him, not wanting him to see my loss of composure. Or the pain that's ripping through my system like jagged glass.

"Fine," the word comes out thin, but audible enough that I know he hears. "I'll get you a horse. Do you need anything else?"

"I'll make do." His tone is detached.

I nod, then straighten my shoulders. Through the window I can see the light purpling, the shadows growing longer. Almost dinner time.

"I better get downstairs," I say. "You should go."

He doesn't respond, doesn't protest at all. The door shuts quietly behind him. There won't be any chasing after me this time, no mad dash to keep me under guard. I'm a commodity now, valuable only in what he can buy with me.

Peace and a happily ever after for everyone else. Funny, though I always knew Aiden was the altruistic sort, I never imagined he would sacrifice me. And here I'd been worried about using him.

I pause in a shadowed alcove and press my back against the wall, covering my hand with my mouth so my distress doesn't draw any attention.

I've never been so alone. Or so afraid.

CHAPTER 11

DINNER WITH KILLERS

Wardon readily agrees to give Aiden not only a horse, but an armed guard of trolls to accompany him. "The Valley of Lost Souls is on the edge between my lands and Brigit's. There are new skirmishes popping up every hour." He explains as he pours me a glass of sparkling white wine on the patio outside his study. "We wouldn't want anything to happen to your…companion."

My smile is tight but my hand remains steady as I take the glass. "Are there any serious contenders?"

"Rodrick's daughter has the best claim." He says this as though I should recognize the name. "And he has both the magic and the forces to help her hold it. There's an immense amount of pressure from the court to have the new monarch settled before Samhain."

"Rodrick was Brigit's consort?"

"Yes, and my spies have told me he's been meeting with Soladin." Wardon taps a long finger against his glass. "You have no idea the level of threat the Lord of the Land poses to us."

"Is he really so dangerous?"

Wardon nods. "More so than any who have held the green throne before him. He is beloved by many of the Seelie fey."

"People liking him is a problem?"

"It is when what he says contradicts the way things are done. He's already shirked the tradition of bedding noble females. His *male* lover is his sole consort and he refuses to take another." Wardon's tone implies he thinks fidelity is one step above defecating at the breakfast table.

I make a noncommittal noise, then ask "But your offer indicates that you want to change some of the long-standing traditions, too."

"Out of necessity for our subjects." He clinks his glass against mine.

I sniff at the glass.

"It's not poisoned, I assure you."

"I never thought it was." My face might crack from all the phony smiles.

The wine is light and crisp on my tongue, the bubbles bursting with little pops of fruity flavor. "It's very good. Thank you."

A fey with iridescent silver scales and gill slits at the side of her throat pauses in the doorway. "Dinner is ready, my king."

"Very good. Send word to her majesty's companion that a riding party will meet him in the stables to accompany him on his journey."

"Yes, sire."

Wardon offers me his arm and, setting down my glass, I curve my hand around his elbow and allow him to lead me to the dining room, footsteps light, heart heavy.

I still can't get my head around Aiden's abrupt change in

behavior. Had Wardon threatened him, or me? With a bit of distance, it occurs to me that he hadn't tried to communicate through our bond. The power thrumming off the immortal being at my side thickens the air around us, as though we are walking through viscous liquid. Even if I hadn't been worried about the potential side effects of magic use, I don't have anywhere near the kind of control he does.

The servant, who has arms but no legs or feet that I can see is obviously well trained. She makes no noise as she moves through the hall. Occasionally I see the gill slits at her neck flutter. Does she breathe through them, the way a fish does, even while on dry land?

I wish I had the freedom to ask without belying my ignorance.

The corridor ends, the scaled servant bobs a perfect curtsey and departs. Two liveried fey, one with horns, one with a long birdlike beak step forward, pivot at a ninety-degree angle and bow to us. Wardon inclines his head and they fall back into place, each grasping a handle on the opaque glass door. They pull them open and stand aside as Wardon leads me into the grand dining hall.

There are no hints of the sea beyond the door. A silver candelabra sits in the middle of a massive mahogany table. The matching chairs are padded with rich brocade cushions. Gilt edge mirrors and paintings hang from smooth walls. Some of the paintings are seascapes, others of dignified looking royals. Wardon's ancestors, judging from the strong resemblance he bears to them.

Silver plates gleam in the candlelight, crystal water goblets sparkled. Gold utensils sit on navy napkins. The forks have three prongs apiece, like miniature tridents. Above us, the silver and gold dome is cracked open to the jewel-toned evening sky. Thirteen crows circle ominously as though something is dead below. The birds unnerve me for some reason and before I can think about it, I send a gust of wind to disperse them.

"Impressive, is it not?" If Wardon noted my magic use, he didn't comment on it.

My head is pounding, my latest side effect of magical use. I really need to stop calling on my abilities unless it's an emergency. What were we talking about again? Oh, the room.

"I've never seen anything like it." It isn't a lie. Everywhere I look, unchecked opulence abounds. Precious metals, rich wood, and fabric. A monument to vanity, a giant pat on the back for his royal highness.

An image of the oyster seller in the courtyard below flashed in my mind. One of these forks would feed him for a year. It's amazing the place hasn't been overrun by the starving Seelie.

Maybe that's why Wardon keeps the trolls around? For protection?

The king pulls out a chair at one end of the table for me. I sit. It's been almost thirty-six hours since I ate, though I have no appetite. What else can I do? I want to give Aiden plenty of time to clear out before I go back to our room for the night.

My room, I mentally correct.

Servants appear, carrying platters of fish, baskets of bread, steaming bowls of vegetables in a lemon butter sauce. They line up before the king first, dishing up the choicest fish, the greenest greens before trekking down the length of the ridiculously long table to me. Wardon cocks a brow when I wave away the fish, but doesn't comment. Instead of setting the remaining portion of food on the table, the servants move off to the wall, place each dish under a matching silver cloche, then stand ready in case we ask for seconds.

"Ah, there you are, my dear."

Wardon stands, pushing his chair back and turning to the door to the opposite side of the hall. I follow the direction of his gaze in time to see the purple-skinned fey, the one who'd been flirting with Aiden earlier, sweep into the room.

Her emerald green gown shimmers as she walks, round hips swinging with every step. The color goes well with the unusual hue of her skin as well as her dark hair. I don't miss Wardon's appreciative slow scan of her lush curves, the way the thin fabric seems to mold itself to her every asset.

Ah, so that's how it is. I recognize the look, it's the one Aiden gave me when I first put on the fancy dress.

I bite my lip to keep from frowning as a thought surfaces. Odd how he didn't even seem to notice my skimpy night-wear during our last encounter.

"Harmony, may I introduce Nicneven, Queen of the Shadow Throne and future ruler of the Unseelie Court. My dear, allow me to introduce Harmony Goldfeather, seer to the Gray Throne."

"We've met," I say shortly.

Wardon blinks, whether at the revelation or my tight tone, I have no idea. Harmony, for her part, offers a syrupy smile. "That's right. You were the one with that delightful werewolf earlier. I envy you, traveling with him. You must have seen so many amazing things." Her tone is low and husky, full of innuendo.

"Not as many as you, I'd wager." I spear a broccoli floret on the end of my golden fork and pop it into my mouth.

Wardon appears pleased, as though he's scored front row seats at a mud-wrestling contest. "Harmony's the first seer in over a millennium. It is a rare gift, one of the ancient texts tell us only manifests in times of profound change. I was fortunate to hear about her before any of the other rulers and spirit her away to my castle by the sea."

"You are most clever, my king." Harmony beckons the server with the fish forward and the man practically trips over his oversized furry feet to reach her side.

"It's the only gift a royal cannot claim from his subjects." Wardon states. He's not easy to read but I'm fairly certain this is wistfulness in his tone.

"And one I wouldn't wish on you, sire." Harmony takes a delicate bite of fish. "The visions are most disturbing to one's sleep. Sometimes I have trouble rising in the mornings due to insufficient rest."

"You see everything that is going to happen?" I ask, curious despite my dislike of her feline manner.

She shakes her head, one dark curl falling over a bare purple shoulder. "The future isn't written. It's not like reading a page of a novel. Choices and decisions of key figures will lead to a more likely outcome."

"For example," Wardon cuts in. "I asked Harmony what would happen if you consent to marry me. If we could successfully merge the courts into one solid ruling body."

"And?" I quirk an eyebrow, knowing her answer wouldn't matter in my ultimate decision.

"And I told his majesty that a marriage is the only way to unite the fair folk."

Harmony takes another of her delicate bites. I doubt she can taste anything, the portions on the end of her fork are all but invisible.

"Was it also your guidance that led him to urge Brigit to kill me?" I fight to keep my tone even.

Harmony raises a brow, but it is Wardon who answers. "Before her time. Harmony is around the same natural age as you are yourself, at least in this life. Harboring a grudge still, are we?"

Ass muppet. "Hard not to take it personally when

someone shows zero remorse in planning your death," I say sweetly.

Wardon throws back his head and laughs. It isn't a pleasant sound. "Oh Nicneven, you do delight me so. Did you experience regret for those you bound to the Wild Hunt?"

He has a point, but I refuse to give it to him. "So, it's all forgive and forget, is it? Sorry, I'm not made that way."

Wardon sets his fork down. "Nor am I. You did terrible things in your last life, atrocious acts of war against the Seelie. A year before your untimely demise, there were raids on our fishing villages here along the coast. Seelie citizens lost their livelihoods, their homes. Some were raped, and murdered. You and I both held our respective courts at the time. I beseeched you to banish the fey responsible to the far side of the Veil, to exile them from Underhill. You refused to discipline the Unseelie, saying in a terse missive that 'might makes right.'"

His expression morphs as he speaks, a flash of rage appears on his face, the first genuine emotion I've seen from him.

I stare at my plate to hide my ignorance even as I try to scour my fractured labyrinth of past life memories for proof that he's telling me the truth, the way Nahini had taught me. Nothing surfaces. The lack leaves me to think that if I had heard about greedy Unseelie preying on Seelie fishing villages, it hadn't been something I'd devoted time to contemplating. My throat tightens. I knew I'd been selfish in my last life but this...

"Obviously you had sanctioned the raids," Wardon continues, his face smoothing, his tone glib once more. "If not beforehand, then after. What choice was I left with other than to seek out the other Unseelie queen, the ruler of the Fire Throne? She wanted to help, was eager for an alliance, but could do nothing while you ruled at the same time as I. It was not my hand that killed you, Nicneven. I merely suggested you should be replaced by a queen with more compassion."

"And you thought Brigit would fit the bill?" I don't bother to hide a snort. "That she had more compassion for the Unseelie than I did? How many did she slaughter in my household, how many stood in her path as she cut her way to me?"

"Lost lives of the Unseelie are not my concern." His tone is frigid. "Protecting my people is."

"And did the raids stop after my death?" I ask. Had it been worth it for him, to get in bed with Brigit?

He picks up his water goblet, takes a sip, his gaze not meeting mine. "They've stopped now."

The trolls. That has to be why he employs them, to end raids. From what I saw in the courtyard, Wardon has only traded one problem for another.

We finish dinner in relative silence. Harmony chatters a bit about unfamiliar names and places I've never been, but she's nothing more than background noise. Distantly it occurs to me that out of the three of us, she's the only one sitting here who hasn't admitted to cold blooded murder.

I barely eat, my stomach in knots over both of Wardon's revelations. I need to talk to someone about all this, to find out if the ruler of the Gray Throne speaks the truth. Rape, murder, villages burned to the ground. Might makes right. In what universe? How could I have been so ambivalent? Even if they hadn't been my people, they had been people. And yet I hadn't spared them a second thought.

At last, the king pushes back his chair and stalks down the table, offering me his arm. Silently, I take it. Harmony falls into line behind us.

Wardon escorts me to the foot of the stairs. "I will take my leave of you, Nicneven."

I study him a moment. I don't trust him, not at all. If anything, his tale made me even more wary of him. This is a being who won't hesitate to decimate any obstacle in his path. If I refuse his marriage merger outright, he might again see me as only an enemy. And with my allies too far away to help, I can't afford to have him turn on me.

"Thank you for your hospitality," I say instead.

"Rest well." He nods, his semi genial mask back in place. "Come, seer."

Harmony meets my gaze for just an instant, and then replaces me as the king's arm candy.

Slowly, I trudge up the stairs to my room. As awful as dinner had been, at least spending time with Wardon distracted me from my worry over Nahini, my heartache over Aiden.

I reach the room and look around. A blue-green fire blazes in the hearth. Had a servant laid it in anticipation of my return? Or perhaps the room sensed the chill that sinks into my bones. I move toward it, hiking up the dress so I can sit down on the floor. Wood shifts and pops as it burns and I lose myself for an endless time in the dance of the flames.

I MUST HAVE FALLEN ASLEEP STILL STARING at the fire because the touch rouses me. It's light, like a butterfly's wing, but insistent. My eyes pop open and in the smoldering light from the dying fire I see a figure looming over me in the dark room.

I lunge upwards and clonk heads with the shape, having misjudged the distance between the two of us.

"Ouch," I say at the same time the other person cries out. The sound is feminine, though there's no way to tell if the cry is one of pain or just astonishment.

"What are you doing in here?" I hiss, rubbing lightly on the bump that is already forming on my forehead.

"Trying to save both our necks."

The voice is familiar, though it's more disgruntled than I've heard it so far. Harmony.

I drop my hand, squinting at her in the darkness. "What do you mean?"

"I mean," she says, reaching out a hand and pulling me to my feet in a surprising show of strength. "That Wardon has your wolf imprisoned. Without his protection, you are completely vulnerable."

"Aiden?" I blink, trying to clear the fuzziness from my mind. "That can't be right. He sent Aiden off after our other companion."

"No, he had the shifter he sent to convince you to wed him off." Harmony says this as though I am a bit slow. "I warned him that your attachment to your wolf would keep you from accepting his suit."

My lips part. Of course, no wonder Aiden had been acting so oddly, encouraging me to accept the Seelie king. Because it hadn't been him, just some shifter in disguise. When will I learn not to believe everything my eyes tell me in Underhill? "So Wardon decided to clear the playing field of all competitors. Is Aiden all right? Is he hurt."

"I'm not sure." The seer lets go of me and turns to the wardrobe. She flings back the doors and chucks a pair of leather pants in my direction. "Here, put these on."

"I don't do dead animal pelts." I toss them back to her.

Though I can't be sure, I'm vaguely aware that she rolls her eyes at me before stuffing the pants back into the wardrobe and shutting the door. "Then come over here and pick your own clothes. Something suitable for rough terrain."

My foot catches on the edge of a piece of furniture. "Ow. I can't see my hand in front of my face in here."

Harmony snaps her fingers and the fire blazes to life. "Hurry up. The guards will be changing shifts soon. This is our only opportunity."

With the illumination I see that she's wearing leather pants identical to the ones she flung my way, as well as a leather utility vest. The buttons start just below her cleavage and then stop above her naval so the vest flares to either side, exposing taut purple flesh. She wears hiking boots and her black hair has been slicked back into a thick rope.

"Why are you helping me?" I ask.

"I'm helping myself," she counters. "The king has kept me within this castle for my entire life. I wish to be free."

Fey can't lie. No immortal who passes through the gauntlet can either. But they can twist the truth, omit key facts until the listener believes they have heard something much different than what's been said.

I don't trust Harmony not to lead me into a trap. For all I know she could be setting me up for Wardon to catch me sneaking away, and then demand her freedom as a reward. But if Aiden really has been imprisoned, I need to take the chance.

After another moment of studying her wardrobe I think about what I want to wear, envisioning it in my mind's eye before opening the wardrobe. The jeans are faded on the thigh and broken in, the tank top stretchy. The parka is long and baggy, with multiple deep pockets, but also waterproof. Good against the sea spray.

"*That's* what you're wearing?" Harmony's eyes round as I don my androgynous ensemble.

I sit down to pull on thick woolen socks. "Who am I trying to impress? Certainly not you, technicolor Barbie." I lace up the hiking boots.

She snorts. "Not that I'd have anything to do with a scrawny murderess like you regardless of what you wear."

Oddly, her genuine bitchiness toward me reassures me. With both Aiden and Wardon, she'd been a simpering flirt. If she were leading me into a trap, I doubted she'd bicker with me beforehand.

Sporting clothes much more my speed, I close the wardrobe, picture what I want and then open the doors once more to reveal a replica of my beat-up backpack. The weight is decent and I don't have to look to know that the magic closet has provided all the supplies I requested. First aid kit, matches, toothbrush and toothpaste, hairbrush and deodorant, change of clothes, refillable metal water bottles, and a week's worth of protein bars for me, or a meal for Aiden. A very handy gadget, this wardrobe.

"If you're done, your majesty," Harmony says with a sneer in her voice.

I turn to look at her. "Where are your supplies?"

She quirks a perfectly sculpted black eyebrow. "Immortal, remember? Besides, I actually ate at dinner. Figured it would be the last hot meal I got for some time."

I ignore her barb and brush past her into the hall, backpack over one shoulder. "Which way?"

"Left," she holds her hand aloft. At first, it appears as if she's holding a torch of some kind, but then I realize the red gold flame dances in her naked palm.

She catches me staring. "My father was once a contender for the Fire Throne."

I raise an eyebrow. "I thought you were a seer?"

"I am. The ability to see the future is earned, not bestowed."

"Earned how?"

"Crossing into the underworld and returning," She casts me a level look. "You have to die to earn it."

"Mind if I ask how?"

"I drowned as a child." Her tone is flat, indicating the subject is closed. "The fire wielding abilities are more…active though not so powerful as some. I can manipulate fire, but I cannot conjure it."

We descend a spiral staircase, much less grand, dark and pokey compared to the main set that leads to the entry hall. Servant stairs, I guess.

"Aren't you worried we'll run into someone?" I ask.

"Not at this time of night. The only beings still awake are the trolls and we'll hear them coming a mile away."

We reach the bottom of the stairs and abruptly Harmony's torch winks out and she throws an arm across my chest, shoving me into the stone wall.

"What is it?" I hiss.

"Someone's coming."

Then I hear the footsteps, steady and coming closer. See the flicker of another torch on the wall ahead. So much for no one being awake.

"It's him." Harmony's voice is full of fear. "The king."

I don't bother to ask how she knows. Whether it's because she recognizes the sound of his footfalls or has one of her future visions doesn't matter. I believe her.

A quick glance around. No convenient alcoves or tapestries to duck behind. "Let's go back up the way we came." Doubtful the king will see fit to use the servant's stairs.

I start inching in that direction when a second set of footsteps, light and barely audible come down the sandstone steps.

We're trapped.

CHAPTER 12

THROUGH THE MAN'S EYES

Six Hours Earlier...

Aiden runs along the beach in his human form. His mind churning and restless as the sea. He wants to kill Wardon, craves tearing the bastard's innards out with his teeth. The Seelie king's blood would slide down the back of his throat, sweeter than any wine. And then he would lay the severed head at his queen's feet and she would smile in that way she did that never fails to send sparks through his veins, ramping his body up to bed her.

He runs faster, away from the castle, needing to burn his need down before he sees her again. It seemed so easy, back when she told him she had no desire for sex. No desire for him. Though he missed the physical intimacy, he would rather have her, hale and healthy. Content with herself and with him.

But she isn't content. Her need spices the air, pheromones charging him up until he feels like he will explode. And when he'd touched her earlier her pleasure had been so intense, her taut body so responsive, he thought he might go over with her.

Then afterword she'd been on the verge of panic. Damn Underhill and her wiles. He had no way of telling what had been honest desire and what was an overload of hormones. Nic treats her desires as if they are unnatural. And maybe for her, they are. She'd never experienced sexual pleasure before, he knows that much. And the two times she had let her guard down, there had been magical interference.

Maybe he should have stayed away from her, not awakened her body, not let her know with every breath that he wants her, craves her. Better he be denied that for Nic to believe herself to be flawed. That she is broken to crave release. He wants to help her, to ease her body as well as her mind. The way she does for him.

Usually.

What wouldn't I give to truly know her? The more time he spends in her company, the less he understands. She's so different than her previous incarnation. Nicneven of the Unseelie Court of Alba was cold, as though her heart had been coated with permafrost. And while Nic can be icy too, he senses a lurking fire beneath the layers of frost. A fire she shares with no one. An inferno he wants to throw himself into until it consumes him.

Earlier though she'd infuriated him. First with believing he would spurn her for another and then by considering the Seelie king's outrageous offer. Doesn't she see what the bastard was trying to do? Lay claim to the entirety of Underhill without lifting a finger. He knows from past experience that Wardon is dangerous and not to be trusted. Only a fool trusts a fey, court be damned. All his instincts scream for him to pluck her from the castle and run. A Seelie king who used trolls as hired thugs to keep his subjects in line is not an ally worth having, regardless of the magic he possesses.

Aiden slows to a stop, turning on his heel and scenting the air for any hint of Nahini, the souls of the Hunt, anything that will help them accomplish their mission so they could return to the mortal realm. Nic doesn't have much time to prepare for the gauntlet and every day that passes here is one day less that she can train.

Nothing on the wind. Not the rich jasmine and lavender that belongs to Nahini, not spirits of the Hunt who to him smelled of dried blood and musty air, not even her horse. Where could she have gone?

He's all but abandoned the hope of talking Nic out of the gauntlet. The stubborn female feels it her duty to become forever young and reclaim the Shadow Throne, to throw away the gift of a mortal life and responsibility only to herself. What worries him most is that obligation isn't enough to compel one through the gauntlet, not if the forever young humans are to be believed. Many who attempt the immortal challenge die, others vanish into the mists. He's been asking around the camp, trying to find out as much about the process as he can. Freda's lust for power and Nahini's need to stay with her brother had gotten them through. What could Nic desire enough to save her?

Aiden tips his head back, letting the sun beat down on his face. If only he could do it for her. It doesn't matter what the challenge would be, he would overcome anything to return to her. If only she felt the same for him, he wouldn't be so unsettled.

He closes his eyes for a brief moment and inhales. The briny sea air expands his lungs but even at a distance, he picks up traces of her own unique feminine heat. His mate. He could follow her winter apple scent across Underhill, beyond the Veil, through the very marrow of the world itself if he must. Perhaps he could go through the gauntlet with her....

The sound of thundering feet breaks into his musings. That's odd, no sign of trolls. He should have smelled them in any case. Maybe he is imagining it. He whirls in time to see a portal open not six feet away. Only beings of great power could travel by portal. He makes to shift—he's faster on his feet as the wolf—but a series of small projectiles erupt from the swirl of broken time.

Elf darts. One strikes him in the shoulder, another in his side. He grips the serrated shafts and pull. Muscles tear, skin shreds but creatures that used elf darts typically poison the arrow heads. Better to have a few extra gashes. With the small arrows free, he throws himself to the side to avoid a second volley. His intention is to hit the ground and roll, but his limbs are sluggish and don't respond. He collapses face first onto a dune.

Get up. His wolf snarls at him. The beast senses danger, its instincts not something he can reason control. *Get up or I'll take over.*

Aiden doesn't bother responding, conserving all his strength in the attempt to rise. He can't though he manages to roll onto one side. The poison is spreading, every beat of his heart pushing it through his bloodstream, circulating it throughout his body. It doesn't matter what sort of poison coats the arrows, his rapid metabolism will burn through it, given enough time.

Time, however isn't on his side. Two trolls bound through the portal, each swinging a barbed chain above its head. The chains ended in three wicked looking claws. His heart thunders at the sight and he commands his body to get up, to shift.

Let me, the beast within him growls. *Let me out and I'll devour them whole.*

It's no idol threat.

Neither are those whirling chains. But no matter what they have in mind for him, Aiden still fears the beast he carries within himself more. He struggles to a sitting position, though his left arm, the one below where the elf dart had struck him, feels dead.

Let me protect her, the creature beseeches him. *She is my mate.*

Yes, but who will protect her from you?

The chains fly through the air. The claws sink into his back as the heavy iron manacles wrap around him, pinning his arms to his side. He doesn't cry out, the pain is tolerable, all his focus on keeping the wolf at bay. It claws him from within, desperate to rend his flesh and anything else that stands between it and Nicneven.

"Got ya," The troll draws up beside him, the other one a pace behind. "I expected more of a fight out of you."

He recognizes the creature as the one who'd shoved the shellfish seller, the cruelty in his flat black eyes is unmistakable.

Aiden doesn't answer or ask why they are doing this to him. He doesn't need to. The trolls may have been given carte blanche when it came to the Seelie fey, but he's a visiting emissary from the Unseelie. That they are coming after him with such drastic force means Wardon had condoned it.

Nic, he thinks although she's too far away to hear his mental projections. *Be careful.*

THE TROLLS BRING him to a cave on a spit of land some distance from the castle. He recognizes the area, it is one they'd passed by in the darkness. He'd marked it as they'd passed as a potential hiding place in case he and Nic needed a place nearby to hide.

The cave is damp, the waterline from the most recent high tide wetting the sand several steps within. The place smells foul, dank like mildew and rotting sea life as well as hints of despair. From his vantage, dangling between the trolls he can see more iron chains hanging from the ceiling. A large meat hook sways ominously over an open pit. The cave has a single clear purpose.

Torture.

The trolls drop him like a sack of meat onto the stone floor. He grunts, his teeth clattering on impact.

"You're pretty tough for a shifter." The troll leans down, narrowing its coal black eyes on him.

Aiden doesn't respond or correct them on their assumption that his wolf is merely another form.

The troll rights itself until it's looming above him like a pile of boulders. "Don't worry, we'll break you. Even if it means we gotta drag your little blonde companion in here and hang her from that hook."

"No," the protest slips out before Aiden can stifle it. *Must not rise to his bait.*

"Too easy, Dav." the other troll grunts. The thickness in his voice makes him sound even more stupid than the other one. But just because they are dumb, doesn't mean they aren't dangerous. "I thought he'd be a challenge."

"Don't worry, shifter, that's only a last resort. Plenty of steps between here and there. Strip him."

The chains are removed from Aiden's legs first. He tries to kick but his muscles barely respond. It's as though the limbs have gone numb. Soon though, soon he will have enough strength back to kill these fuckers.

If they didn't poison him again first, of course.

The leader, Dav the other one called him, takes a curved

knife to the inner seam of his trousers. The blade goes slowly as though in anticipation, the tip brushing over his skin. It moves up his leg in a sick sort of caress, leaving a thin red line in its wake, a bloody reminder.

Aiden swallows hard as he recognizes the light in the troll's eyes, the dark desire there. He isn't just following orders, he truly wants to hurt Aiden. And the more pain, the more he, Dav will enjoy it.

He sucks in a breath when the blade reaches his crotch, coming close enough to shave the hair off his balls. The troll smiles, satisfaction radiating from him like a sun. "Oh yes, I'll break you. I can almost hear the snap."

Aiden affects a bored tone, casting his gaze to the troll's own reproductive equipment. "Jealous, are you?"

The second one laughs, but Dav's eyes darken. "You're no better hung than a mortal. I'll show you a real—"

"Get on with it." The other grunts impatiently. "He'll be here any minute."

Dav's lip pulls up but he continues down the other leg, his movements more efficient. Aiden's mouth is dry, he's afraid to breathe and truly considers letting his wolf loose. Sexual violation or castration isn't something his wolf will endure. The change will burn the rest of the poison from his system, of that he is sure. Would it be better to give over to the beast now?

Cold sweat breaks out on his forehead. How many lives will he obliterate before he regains control?

They remove his pants—the mocking of his body and man-sized equipment constant—before rechaining his knees. They don't bother removing the shirt, just cut it off above and below the wrapped chains. Aiden calls on his fire magic, intending for it to radiate out from his skin and burn the sadistic bastards to ash. Nothing, not even a spark. Whoever made that poison concoction knew their business, knew just how to take him down, make him helpless.

Angrboda. The Valkyries said it was her who gave them the glamour. The treacherous giantess was one of very few who knew enough about Aiden's curse to subdue him. Even though they had been uneasy allies for millennia, he harbors no doubt that she will turn on him, for the right price.

Footsteps sound, not the stomping that would indicate a troll but the steady thud of boots on stone. Whoever the he is, it appeared his arrival was imminent.

He had expected the king or at least a familiar face, but instead a large fey he doesn't recognize strides around the corner. A yellow orange skin fey, almost seven feet tall. No clothing, though judging by the healthy amount of flesh on his bones that is his preferred state rather than due to lack of magic. His hairless dome gleams in the torchlight. He had no eyebrows or even eyelids, his golden stare unblinking.

"You're late," Dav snapped.

The fey looked at the troll in obvious distaste and when he speaks it's in a clipped, accent-less manner. "I haven't agreed to do this, yet."

Theirs is obviously an uneasy alliance. Perhaps he can use that to his advantage.

"Oh, you'll do it." The second troll responds. "Your king wills it."

"The king has access to similar powers. Tell him to do it himself."

"The king has more important obligations." Dav tosses a small bag. It lands with the obvious clink of coin at the fey's feet. "He's paying good money for your services."

The fey bends down, scoops up the bag and opens it. "I want double this."

Dav hisses but the second fey holds out an arm. "That is more than you would earn in a year as a court entertainer."

Aiden blinks. A court entertainer is a member of no particular court, obligated to no throne. Like the Wild Hunt, they are autonomous wanderers who travel the lands in search of stories and songs in both Underhill and the human realm. They have photographic recall and were sometimes used in criminal cases as well. Their shape changing abilities allow them to blend in with the mortal population and do what amounted to a one-man theater troop able to reenact any event perfectly. What in all the worlds could a being like this have to do with Aiden's abduction?

The fey tosses the bag nonchalantly back to the troll. "This job is beneath me and I am under no obligation to accept, king or no. Unlike yourselves, I am not some thug for hire. Double the price or find yourself another thespian."

Dav exchanges looks with the other troll. "Don't do it, Rok."

"Do you want to tell the king we failed?" Rok snaps. He lobs the bag back to the fey. "Half now, half when the Ice Bitch agrees to wed King Wardon."

The wolf surges within him and for once, Aiden is in total agreement with the beast. His magic surges, then extinguishes, like a match lit in gale force winds. He tries again, and again.

"Dose him again," Rok commands.

They don't bother with the elf darts. Dav simply grabs a fistful of his hair, forcing his head back at an unnatural angle until his lips part. The troll pours a bitter liquid down his throat. It isn't hot but it burns the delicate tissues of his esophagus on the way down. Aiden chokes, trying to force the brew back up, but gravity is against him.

Dav releases him. He sags in his chains. The entertainer steps forward, reaches out a hand to touch Aiden's face.

"Don't do this." Aiden's speech is slurred. "Please."

The fey doesn't respond, doesn't indicate he even heard

Aiden's cry. The lidless golden eyes are cold and flat as they scan him.

Then comes the pain.

It's as though his blood boils within his veins, as though a million shards of glass rip through his innards. Agony so sharp it is almost sweet. Aiden loses track of the others, of everything but the sensations burning through him. The wolf struggles to take over, to revisit the pain on the one inflicting it tenfold. It craves the crunch of bone between its jaws, the knowledge of life extinguished.

It is that part of him that recognized its mate in Nic. The serial killer and the remorseless hunter. The animal knows it's kill or be killed. It greatly admires the predator within her. She's his match in destruction and death, the one that would rule upon a throne of bones beside him at the end of all things. The beast tears at him, shredding Aiden's control. She's in danger. He must fight them, must kill them all.

But the white-hot agony tears through them both, no enemy to grapple with, just wave upon wave of unending pain.

When he finally comes to, the wolf in him is sluggish and slow to respond, whether from the drug or the struggle, he doesn't know. His body is slick with sweat, his mouth dry. He can't hear anything above the gallop of his heart. The wolf curls in on itself, no longer fighting to be free. Conserving its strength, knowing its moment will come. His vision blurs but he makes out the outline of the fey entertainer.

The air around him ripples and then it is as though Aiden is looking into a mirror. The dark hair, the green eyes. It's him, a perfect copy of him, albeit one looking less ragged around the edges.

"Incredible." Dav breathes.

Roc stomps over to a stone outcropping, picks up a

bundle and heaves it at his doppelgänger. "An exact replica of what he was wearing. You have all you need?"

The fey wearing his skin pulls the clothing on. "His flesh memories are…odd. There's something more to this being than my abilities can read."

"Are you trying to back out?" Dav asked in a low voice. "I warn you if you double cross us—,"

The shifter shakes his head. "No. Simply that there are too many experiences within the man to copy. I had to pick and choose, so I focused on the ones pertaining to what he knows of her. Her weaknesses, her insecurities, her desires. I will be able to manipulate her with what I've gleaned."

"She won't," Aiden wheezes, lungs still constricted from pain. He can't get the rest of the sentence out.

Green eyes turned on him. "Believe me? I assure you, she will. According to your own flesh memories, you've been struggling to gain her trust for weeks. Trust is a fragile thing, slippery to hold and easy to shatter."

"Please," he implores the creature, unashamed of begging. "Don't do this."

Rok interrupts. "You know the script. You're heading for the Valley of Lost Souls, she must stay behind and accept Wardon."

"Are the ones she seeks actually in the Valley of Lost Souls?"

"No idea." Dav shrugs. "Does it matter?"

"Only if whoever they are return and spoil the ruse. Loose ends have a way of tripping one up." The entertainer nods in his direction. "What of him?"

"Once you convince her that he is abandoning her, return here. We will kill the wolf and return his body to her. Abandoned with no way to cross back through the Veil or finding her companions, she will have no choice but to accept the king's generous offer. Wardon will bind her to him and once the king has claimed her magic and title, she will meet with an untimely accident. No loose ends to trip over."

With one final glance at Aiden, the shifter departs with a promise, "I'll return when it is done."

Aiden closes his eyes, praying to whichever god might still favor him that Nic would see through the imposter. No matter that his wolf was in a near frenzy at the thought of Nic in danger, he had to keep it in check, to stay put, no matter what the trolls do to him.

For now.

A hand grips him roughly by the hair and he looked up to see Dav's menacing face looming over him. "Now for the fun part."

CHAPTER 13

ENCOUNTERS IN THE DARK

I flatten against the wall, one arm going out to hold Harmony back. The gesture is a futile one, seeing as how either Wardon or the person coming down the stairs will have to pass no less than a foot from us in order to continue on their way.

The scrape of stone on stone fills my ears and a fresh gust of sea air wafts into the close space of the corridor. It's coming from in front of us, from the direction of the Seelie king. There must be some sort of alternate exit. Either that or the king created one specifically for his use. His footsteps continue, now tracking away from our hiding place. On impulse, I grip Harmony by the wrist and dart after him.

The door, which is really more of a gap in the sandstone is collapsing in on itself, sealing the passageway shut. Beyond it lies more darkness, save for a bobbing blue-green light, more magic wielded by the king no doubt. I have all of two seconds to decide and, then dropping Harmony's wrist, dive through the hole into the waiting blackness.

I hear her gasp and a moment before the hole closes entirely, she follows my lead, landing directly on top of me.

All the air is forced from my lungs but our collision is near silent. The scuff of the stone would have covered any noise of our pursuit.

"What now?" The seer hisses in my ear.

I shove her off me and automatically check for damage, relieved when I find nothing beyond a few scrapes. Clambering up, I dust myself off, jaw set in determination. "Now, we follow him."

To her credit, Harmony doesn't argue. Not that I thought she would. Having alerted me to Wardon's deception, the seer had placed all her eggs in the Queen Nicneven basket and has no choice other than to hope I wouldn't drop the aforementioned basket.

The light from Wardon's magic glowing orb is barely visible, though it seems to be descending. Feeling my way with the toe of one boot, I tap the ground ahead of me, searching for the distinctive edge of a step. There is none though the ground does slope downhill. A ramp then. Perhaps to cart heavy goods into the sandcastle?

Whatever its original function the tickle of dust against my sinuses and the eerie brush of cobwebs on one searching finger tells me the passage is seldom used. Chances are good that we won't run into anyone else. Unless Wardon decides to do an about-face of course.

Careful not to make any noise, I start down the ramp, keeping one hand on the rough sandstone wall and my gaze affixed to the bobbing blue-green light ahead. I hear the creak of leather as Harmony falls in behind me. No hunter, the seer's breathing on my neck is loud enough to wake the dead. But with my ears open, I can detect the roar of the ocean, which should conceal our pursuit.

There's no way to tell how long we walk, all I have to count are my erratic heartbeats. Whatever Wardon is up to, the king obviously doesn't want witnesses. Otherwise, why take such a secretive route out of his own home?

And I would further assume that whatever his aim, I suspect it has something to do with me or Aiden or Nahini. Or all three.

Our decent into the abyss continues, with only the bobbing aqua light to mark the distance between us and the king. The roar of the ocean grows louder, thunderous and it seems to be coming from…overhead? I glance up at the same time as Harmony breathes, "We're beneath the sea."

I swallow and eye the rough-hewn ceiling, hoping that it's structurally sound. Not that we have to worry overmuch about drowning. Too far from either end, the smallest crack in the infrastructure will lead to us being crushed beneath tons of seawater.

Okay, well nothing to be done other than to continue on as we had been.

After another immeasurable span of time, the floor beneath our feet begins to even out, the crashing of waves subsides. We must be beyond the sandbar then or too deep down to hear the waves hitting the shore. Neither thought is comforting. Gradually the slope starts to rise. The incline is slight at first, so much so that I wonder if I am imagining it. Where the hell is Wardon heading? I wish I had a map of Underhill, though deep down I knew it would do no good. The fey realm changes and shifts at will. Where a mountain range might exist today, a swamp could be tomorrow, the land beneath our feet as prone to relocation as the beings that tread upon it.

I look up and freeze. The flickering light winks out. We are in total darkness.

Harmony grips my hand. Hers is clammy. She squeezes once and then let's go. I read her nonverbal message loud and clear. Maybe Wardon knows we're following him. Perhaps he's lurking up there in the dark, ready to spring out at us like some sort of ghoul.

Even if he is, there's no going back the way we came. Taking a deep breath, I surge ahead, willing this purgatory to end.

Aiden, I call out mentally. *Hang on.*

There is no reply. But a few more steps and I breathe easier. Wardon doused his light because the tunnel finally ends, depositing us on a beach. After the total blackout, the light from the waxing moon peeping through palm fronds is almost blinding. I pause, giving my pupils time to adjust to the flood of illumination and to spot my prey.

Wardon is nowhere in sight, but I can hear his voice even though the words are indistinguishable. It sounds like he's heading to the left, up the bank behind me.

"...Pay what you owe." Another booming voice demands.

A familiar one at that. Unless I'm mistaken, it belongs to the giantess, Angrboda.

Eager to learn more I scramble up the bank toward the sound.

They are standing on a strip of pristine beach. Unlike the last time I saw her, the Hag of the Ironwood is contained to a more standard mortal size, although she still stands half a head above Wardon. Her blood-red hair is woven into a loose braid. She's clothed in what appears to be some sort of fur bikini, though it isn't molded to her. A strip of fur is wrapped around her breasts, another encircles her waist. Her stomach, arms and legs are exposed, her feet bare where they sink into the sand.

"You'll get him when I have another infusion of magic, not before," Wardon says. "The Risen Queen is stronger than any led me to believe. I need more power to subdue her."

"That," Angrboda says, a sneer in her voice, "Is not my

problem. We had a bargain and you will uphold your end of it. I want Loki's son."

Aiden? Why would Angrboda bother with him? And had I just heard Wardon admit that I possess greater magical abilities than he did? He who created a castle out of the beach around him?

Or maybe he hadn't. If he was somehow siphoning magic from a giantess, perhaps Wardon isn't so powerful as he led me to believe. Maybe his all-powerful persona is just like my Ice Bitch mask. Theater meant to help further his ends.

"I'll give him to you. But the Unseelie queen must see greater demonstrations of my power. She cannot learn that the magic of the Seelie court is failing."

Failing? Is that why Wardon is using trolls as hired thugs to protect his kingdom? To keep order by brute force instead of with magic? Perhaps it is simpler to make the trolls immune to daylight than to use magic for every tiff and squabble. Even if those same brutes abuse his subjects?

"You bore me, Master of the Waves," Angrboda pivots on her heel as though to walk away. "You will get nothing more from me until you've met my price."

"I have more to offer. I'll give you the spirit caster," Wardon calls out at her retreating back.

She slows. "The one of the Hunt? Nicneven's third? What would I do with her?"

My breath catches in my chest. Nahini. Wardon's had her all along.

"Ransom her. Steal her abilities. Carve her up for stew. The choice is yours, my lady. Consider her a gift. To tide you over until I have secured the Unseelie queen."

Harmony touches my leg, causing me to nearly jump out of my skin. I slither back down the bank and move away from Wardon and the giantess. "What?"

"I know where we are," she says.

"Good for you." I glance over my shoulder back toward where we'd come from, more interested in the rest of the conversation between Wardon and Angrboda.

Harmony grabs a strand of my hair and yanks. *"Listen.* We are on the outpost island. There is a lighthouse over there, you can see the light when it turns our way. And see there? That's where the sea dragons nest."

"As fascinating as all this is," I begin but she barrels on ahead.

"And over *there*," she points to a high cliff about a mile away, as the crow flies. "Is where the king keep prisoners."

My breath catches. "You're sure?"

She nods. "The trolls like to brag about how they torture enemies of the crown. Some, like Galfin Dunn, are honorable. Many are not. They delight in pulling their victims apart a piece at a time."

Aiden. I take two steps toward the peak before my brain kicks in. I freeze and throw a glance over my shoulder, back toward the beach where Angrboda and Wardon may or may not have concluded their bartering. With my third as their bargaining chip.

Angrboda, like all the other giants, possess great deals of magic and knowledge. Enough to travel the distance of Underhill in a heartbeat. Herself and whoever was with her. If Wardon hands Nahini over to the Hag of the Ironwood, we might never get her back.

But can I really leave Aiden to whatever suffering he might be enduring at the hands of the trolls? The imposter came to me hours ago. Who knows what sort of shape he's in, what they've done to him over the intervening time.

It feels as though my body morphs to metal and two equally strong magnets are pulling me in two opposite directions. My friends, both in peril, both of whom I'd let down.

Can I really choose to help one, knowing it could mean death
—or worse—for the other?

If only I know what state they are each in. Nahini has
been missing the longest. She might be in worse shape.
Wardon must have incapacitated her somehow in order to
keep her under lock and key. Aiden has his wolf as a trump
card, he might have escaped already.

But what if he didn't? What if he can't? What if it is
already too late?

This dithering is getting me nowhere. I need something
that will break the tie, a glimpse into the end result, a way to
see the future…

My gaze shifted to my companion. "Are both of my
companions being held in the same place?"

"No." The seer shakes her head. "Wardon won't trust the
trolls to guard her. They are…brutal to female prisoners."

"Then where?" I begin but she cuts me off.

"I don't know where she's being held, only that she's in a
stasis of some sort."

"If I go after Aiden, will I lose Nahini?"

She stills, her eyes going unfocused, the pupils shrinking
to pinpricks. "Yes. As well as the rest of the Wild Hunt."

"And if I wait here for Nahini?"

"Your wolf will die," she confirms.

Shit. Shit. Shit. My lids squeeze shut. "How do I choose?"

HARMONY TOUCHES MY ARM. "There is a way to get them both
back. Though neither
will be as you remember them."

Her words sound both ominous and hopeful. "How?"

"Give the king what he wants. Agree to marry Wardon."

My jaw drops. "What?"

187

"He will not wed you until after your gauntlet trial and you claim the Unseelie thrones, but he will agree to return your people as a bride price."

The thought makes my stomach twist. Not only because I find the Seelie king icky, but he's also a bit of an idiot. Borrowing magic from Angrboda to pay for troll protection and using my people as payment. How can that possibly turn out well?

"What of his deal with the giantess?" I ask. "He promised to give Aiden to her."

"Eventually." The words are sly, a treacherous sparkle reflects in her eerie eyes. "He stalls because he knows you will pay more for the wolf than she ever will. And he can simply hand the wolf over, fulfilling his bargain, then have the trolls shoot her with fey bane or another poison to drain her magic."

"But she's been helping him." Though I still don't know why.

"Giant magic is temporary, Wardon wants magic that will last."

"I don't understand. What exactly is his end goal?"

Harmony swallows. "Magic follows the life cycle of the fey. When we are born we have the potential for magic, just as we have the potential for walking, talking, dancing. As we grow, the muscles become stronger, allowing us more control over the magic. But as we age, they sometimes break down. Even for the forever young, overuse of magic means no longer being able to wield the power we could in our prime. This loss is devastating, especially to one like Wardon, who leaned so heavily on his magic use for centuries."

"He told Angrboda that the magic of the Seelie was failing," I say.

"No, it is his own abilities that deteriorate and he fears his loss of power. He's done…unspeakable things to keep it. It is that which he hopes to reverse."

I raise a brow. "So, he's having some sort of midlife crisis? I'm supposed to be his trophy wife?" Ick.

She ignores my snarky comments. "Long ago, it was fore-told that if the Seelie and Unseelie courts ever joined together, the combined magic could overthrow even the gods. Wardon is counting on that, which is why he will give you your people back. It's the only way to save them both."

"Let me get this straight. You're saying that either I sacri-fice one of my friends…or my freedom? To the fey who convinced Brigit to murder me?"

Harmony nods. "It's the only way."

My molars clench. Aiden would tell me not to do it, to give him up so I could be free. Nahini would fall on her sword as well. I'm not nearly so altruistic. But I've already murdered one fey ruler, why not another? After he gives me what I want, of course.

"Okay," Meeting Harmony's gaze, I blank my expression to keep my long-term plan to myself. I still don't trust her, and the fact that she's suggesting I kowtow to Wardon's wishes makes me twice as wary.

She nods, appearing relieved. "Just in time. He returns."

Sure enough, the Seelie king appears on the ridge from the beach. I can't see his face, the moon is at his back, silhou-etting him in its luminance. He starts when he sees us. Good, that means I tracked him without his knowledge, even with an amateur like the seer in tow. Whether it is attributed to my skill or his distraction, it doesn't matter. I snuck up on him once, I can do it again.

Beside me, I feel Harmony dropping into a respectful curtsey. "Sire," she breathes. "Queen Nicneven has an answer for you."

"Does she," Wardon stalks down the slope, as though

trying to make up for the ground he lost. He doesn't know I'm aware of his weakness and as long as he keeps making impulsive decisions in an effort to impress me, I will always hold the advantage.

"I want Aiden set free. As well as my third in command." A thought strikes me. "And any of the dead who belong to the Wild Hunt."

He shifts, then stills, repressing the urge to turn back to the beach. "And what makes you believe any of those things are in my power to give? Or that I will hand them over to you even if I did?"

"Nahini was following a soul I tethered to the dead of the Hunt. Souls I traded to Brigit last spring. And since you and Brigit were so chummy, what with your murder plots and all, I think she gave them to you. And you will return them to me if you want me to agree to your proposal."

I see a flare of avarice in his gaze. Oh yes, he wants me to agree very badly. "You consent?"

"If you agree to my terms. The dead reunited with the Hunt and back under my control. Nahini and Aiden given into my custody. I need them both to help see me through the gauntlet. Or do you still want to pretend you don't know where they are?"

I see him inhale, searching for the trap, the loophole. "You are still mortal. You can lie. What assurance do I have that you won't just take what you want and leave?"

"None. But I can promise you, that if you harm those under my protection or continue to keep them from me, once I reclaim my crown, I *will* come after you with everything I've got. Marriage or war, the choice is yours."

Wardon studies me, then holds out a hand to me. "I agree to your terms, Nicneven."

It's all I can do to keep the starch in my spine, to not sag in relief even as my flesh crawls at his touch. "Where are they?"

"They will be brought to you before moonrise tomorrow after you are blood sworn to me. Come, there are arrangements to make." He snaps his fingers and his bobbing ball of blue-green light swirls into a vortex. A portal. The arrogant bastard is still trying to pretend his magic has no limits.

He offers me an elbow and I am about to take it when Harmony steps forward. "Wait, my king."

He frowns at her as though having forgotten she is there. "What is it?"

She stares at me and I can almost hear her thoughts. She wanted to be free of this bastard. And as much as I don't like or trust her, I can't leave her to rot.

"I want her, too. A seer could be valuable to the Wild Hunt as well as my war plans."

"Agreed." Wardon is almost eager to tug me through the portal, to return to his castle made of sand and finish with his extortion. "My betrothed."

A moment before the portal seals shut behind me, I hear the broken cry of a wolf.

CHAPTER 14

DOUBLE CROSS

Wardon leaves me at the door to my bedchamber, the journey that had taken half the night on foot undone in seconds. Traveling that way must weaken him though, otherwise, he would have done so instead of walking miles beneath the surface of the sea. His weakness is my advantage.

The Seelie King doesn't appear weak, or even strained though. "I will send someone in to fetch you as soon as everything is ready."

Though tempted to give him one of my special kisses and make a break for it, I have to play his game. At least until Aiden and Nahini are safe and the dead of the Hunt back under my control. From the glint in his eye, the Seelie king plans to use my people as leverage up until the last instant.

"Leave the seer with me. As an engagement present." I lift my chin as I issue the demand, daring him to renege on his promise.

A flash of emotion crosses his features. Rage, there and gone so quickly I would have missed it if I hadn't been looking for it. A serpentine smile replaces the look and he waves a hand to allow Harmony to enter the room. "May she serve you as faithfully as she did me."

I hear the warning for what it is, but choose to ignore it and shut the door in my intended's face. "That could have gone better."

"We're both still alive," Harmony says quietly. "That's what's important. Thank you."

I don't answer her directly, instead shucking my backpack down by the door and then sit on the bed to pull off my shoes. "Would he have killed you if I hadn't claimed you?"

"Yes." There is surety in her voice, shadows in her gray gaze.

If she hadn't answered me directly, I might have killed her myself then and there. "And will you be loyal to me and the Unseelie court?"

A nod. "You won't keep me in a cage."

She's right, I detest the idea of being held against my will. It's why I'm always so careful when I hunt not to leave a trace behind. And I will never trap someone else that way, no matter how they might wrong me.

I may be a serial killer, but at least I have standards.

I meet her gaze head-on. "I promise you, your life will be your own. You can serve in my court or go on your merry way. And if you betray me, I will kill you. Fair enough?"

She doesn't hesitate. "Agreed."

I turn my attention to our current situation, wondering what to expect. "He mentioned a blood oath. What is that?"

Harmony goes to the wardrobe and opens the doors, extracting a padded stool. She sets it down across from my position on the bed before answering. "A covenant, an unbreakable one. He's going to call on his potion masters to mix your blood with his and add it to a vat of poison. After it has set, you will each drink half the poison and then swear your oath to one another. If either of you breaks your vows, the poison will be released and you will die in agony."

I blow out a breath. "And let me guess. If one of us kills the other...?"

Harmony nods once. "The same fate."

"Not big on trust, is he?" A ball of ice forms in my stomach at the realization I

may be forced to marry the gods' damned prick.

"Wardon takes no chances. Even if you were already immortal, he would insist upon the oath."

Restless, I rub my hands down the length of my denim-clad thighs then stand up, and pace to the window. The night is dark, the ocean crashing mere feet away. Aiden is out there somewhere, I can feel his presence. Is he hurt? And what of Nahini? Has Wardon held her captive since the first night we arrived here? I hate to think that the evil bastard is getting one over on me, on my friends. "There must be another way."

A knock sounds at the door. At my nod, Harmony stands, crosses the room and then lifts the latch. The door swings inward. One of the pixie servants bearing a tray three times her size drifts into the room. Judging from her careful balancing act, pixies must have strength like ants, able to lift things much heavier than their own body weights. "His royal highness thought you might be hungry."

I sniff, wrinkling my nose in distaste. The aroma indicates something undeniably fishy, not exactly my go-to midnight snack. Undoubtedly the Master of the Waves was testing my vegetarian resolve. Asshat. There is a steaming pot though and unless it's some sort of meat-based broth, I'll enjoy the liquid's warmth.

I take the tray from her and set it down on the bed. "Thank you."

Instead of leaving, the pixie waves her wand so the door

slams behind her. The instant it's closed, her shape…disintegrates.

There's no other way to describe it, one minute the pixie is smiling at me and the next she's nothing more than a pile of dust.

My lips part. "What?"

Harmony gasps and scuttles to my side. Apparently, the seer didn't see this coming.

The dust doesn't settle though, instead, it swirls into a shape, a much larger shape. I catch a whiff of ozone and there is an electric tingle in my hands, my feet. The body expands, stretching and horrific angles until resolving into the distinctly male form of a naked fey.

He's one of the oddest looking fey I've seen, which is saying something. His skin hue is that of a sunrise, yellow-orange and he has no hair anywhere on his massive body. He bows, the movement elegant in spite of his nudity. "My queen. Forgive the deception, I had no other way to reach you. We must talk."

I blink, once and then again. A shapeshifter. *The* shapeshifter that caused me so much heartache.

"You're the one who pretended to be Aiden. You tricked me." I stride forward, wrapping my fingers around his throat before he can respond. "How dare you show your retched face here?"

To his credit, he doesn't struggle or beg for his life. "My most sincere apologies. They gave me little choice. Please, I can help you."

"And where have I heard that before? There seems to be a rash of defectors in the Seelie court." I want to kill something, desperately.

Harmony rests a hand on my arm. "He's not a member of any court. He's an entertainer."

"What?" I look between the two of them, frowning.

"It's true." The shape changer swallows. I can feel a soft fluttering beneath my hands. Membranes or gill slits. I'm not just choking him, I'm suffocating him and can't be bothered to care.

"I want to come with you," he makes a gurgling noise. "To witness the journey of the Risen Queen."

"What am I, the circus? Everyone wants to run away with me?"

"It's for our histories." His lidless eyes are sincere. "Songs and ballads that will echo through time."

"You helped Wardon manipulate me," I spit.

"I apologize for that. I heard rumors that you were different from before, more concerned with the well-being of the common fey. I had to judge for myself."

"And if I hadn't been? You were all set to marry me off to Wardon."

"No. I only agreed to deceive you to gain access to you. I have a plan," he wheezes. "One to get you everything you want."

I let go of his throat. He stumbles forward, membranes fluttering like leaves in a gale.

"Tell me your plan and then I'll decide whether or not you get to leave this room alive."

Through the Man's Eyes
Two hours ago...

AIDEN.

He hears her voice in his head, feels her concern. She must be close.

Panic wells up and it takes the last of his feeble reserves to fight the wolf, to keep it from bursting through him as it recognized its other half who travels in a separate skin.

The wolf had sensed her presence earlier and fought his way loose, desperate to get to her. Aiden had been too weak, didn't possess the will to restrain the creature and it had erupted from him like lava from a volcano, wreaking havoc. There was no room for shame, no thought in his head other that he must find her.

He doesn't know how many he's maimed or killed, his memories are foggy and bathed in the thick red haze of bloodlust.

The trolls had fought back, fought for their lives. Reinforcements had thundered in. They'd beaten him, struck him with more of those damn darts. It hadn't been enough though, he'd slain all within reach before the poison had dragged him down again.

He awoke as a man hours later, lying in a sticky puddle, his body battered and bruised, still shackled. The remains of Dav and Rok and the others have been hauled away, though their blood congeals on the cave floor. The wolf in him curls up in satisfaction. They'd hurt him, had threatened to hurt his mate.

Pain thrums through his body like a low voltage charge. Both his legs are broken as well as chained. He focuses on his breaths as they shudder in and out of his lungs. Tries to sense her, but she is gone again. There is only darkness. The sticky floor beneath his cheek. He closes his eyes and tries to sleep.

Time passes and he hears her voice in his mind. Aiden takes one breath and then another. He must keep his emotions reigned in, all the shame, the regret, the fear feed the wolf, makes him stronger, harder to control.

Aiden, I don't know if you can hear this. I can't hear you at all.

He tries. Every time he's dragged back to consciousness he attempts to contact her, to tell her that he's still near, that he hasn't abandoned her, didn't rejected her. Would never reject his proud mate.

Apparently, his efforts failed. Even her mental voice projects her worry. Worry she would never show directly to him or anyone else. The damn drugs interfere with their bond in a way time or distance cannot.

We have a plan to get you out. You and Nahini both as well as those we've been seeking.

The dead of the Hunt. Through the haze of pain, hope glimmers. She'd promised to find them and against all odds, she did. Without his help. He's been more of a liability, getting himself captured. One more lost soul for her to rescue.

But his pride in her shines brighter than the loathing he has in himself. She kept her promise. Hope blooms in the arid soil of his heart.

Hold on. She thinks to him. *We're coming for you.*

No. He tries to send back. The word echos around the inside of his skull but goes no farther. It's though she stands on a distant hilltop and shouts into a megaphone. He can hear her but has no way of responding.

The wolf rises up, eager to be with her again. Nose in the air, sniffing, trying to pick up her winter apple scent with his limited human senses. He has more success keeping the beast at bay. It asked a question before settling down again.

Who is helping her?

She'd said we. Said it more than once so he knows it wasn't an error. Maybe Freda and the rest of the Hunt crossed into Underhill in search of her? Or perhaps the Fates?

A shudder of revulsion goes through him at the thought of Nic's aunts helping to rescue him. Of owing the witches any sort of favor. But if they help Nic...

More time passes. He has no way to track it, can't focus

enough to count the seconds or the breaths. He just keeps taking them, enduring the pain of his shattered orbital bone, the missing eye, the broken fingers, and toes. For once his instincts aligning with that of the wolf. He has one job now. Survive.

Eventually, he hears their approach. Two creatures, not trolls, as the ground doesn't shake beneath his feet, just the steady thud of boots on stone. He doesn't lift his head or open his remaining eye. His nose tells him who approaches, with the scent of brine and sea air and magic as distinctive as fanfare.

Wardon, and one of his magicians.

Heat and light come with them. He senses the fire and is surprised to find that it responds to his call. The dampening drugs must have worn off.

They stop, boots inches from his face, the scent of ocean depths and the blackest magic overpowering after nothing more than the reek of his own body coated in death.

"Well, this won't do," Wardon says, his tone dispassionate. "By the gods, I have never seen a bargaining chip in worse shape. What did those fool trolls do?"

Aiden doubts the king was truly talking to him but answers anyway. "I can show you if you desire."

"Cheeky, just like her. They could have broken you, you know. If I'd let them have her. I thought about forcing the shifter to wear her shape and then handing him over to the trolls, but you would have known it wasn't Nicneven, wouldn't you, wolf?"

He would have, for even a flawless replication wouldn't think to copy her unique winter apple scent, the one that he could follow through all nine worlds. Aiden doesn't answer though. After years locked in a cage beside Brigit's throne, he knows when to push a royal fey and when to hold his tongue.

The king turns to his companion. "Heal him."

Hands colder than the stone floor grip his face. Aiden jerks, trying in vain to pull away. The hands are strong, though the fingers were slender.

"Do you wish to trade for a Healing?" The fey asks him in a baiting way.

Aiden's eye fixes on the nut-brown features of the healer. "I've traded enough."

The creature has long stringy hair that falls over its thin shoulders and its smile is almost as predatory as Wardon's. "Not to me."

"There will be no trade today," Wardon cuts in. "Consider it your gift for my upcoming nuptials."

Every cell in Aiden's body tenses.

The Seelie king sees it and his mercurial eyes gleam in the low light. "Yes wolf, you know it's true. I will have your lover as my bride. Fear not though, I'm giving you back to her. As a pet."

The growl rumbles from his throat a second before the brilliant flash of light fills the cave. His body bows as fragments of bone knit together, swelling dispersed, bruises fade. The worst by far is the regeneration of his eye. Instead of the slow constant ache, the pain is sharp, like an ice pick being driven through his brain. The healing is the most painful thing he's endured since the trolls grabbed him.

The fey healer steps away and Aiden slumps back into the pile of filth on the stone floor. Every muscle twitches, his fingers spasm as ghosts of the intense agony slither across his nerve endings.

Wardon crouches to inspect the results. "Better, though still crusted with filth." The king snaps his fingers and icy seawater crashes over Aiden's head. His teeth chatter, but he doesn't protest the rough treatment. He should just consider himself fortunate that the Master of the Waves didn't douse him in seawater while he still had open wounds.

"You'll have to do." The king snaps again and the chains around his hands and feet disappear. Between the healing and the dousing, he's too off-balance to take advantage of the situation and lunge for the fey's throat.

"I'm afraid I don't have anything for you to wear." Wardon smirks. "Although considering what she uses you for, it's a wonder you own clothing at all. Or leave her bedchamber for that matter."

Dripping wet, Aiden raises his new eye up to lock on Wardon's. "I'm hers of my own free will. Better than any of your consorts can say."

The king smirks down at him. "Once I marry her, what belongs to her will belong to me. Perhaps I'll pass you around the troll barracks like a party favor. See if she wants what's left of you after that."

"Sire," the healer approaches on Wardon's left side. "We must go if we wish to be on time."

Wardon doesn't acknowledge the man, his gaze intent on Aiden. "Mark me wolf, you are irrelevant. To her, to me, to the world. It would be a mercy to put you down now like the rabid dog you are. Now come and witness the dawn of a new era in whatever skin suits."

Aiden pushes to his feet, his glare on the king and shifts. He isn't ashamed of his nakedness but it makes Nic uncomfortable and being the wolf gives him advantages of speed and strength over most of the fey and all trolls.

"Good." Without warning, Wardon snaps a collar around Aiden's neck.

His instinct is to struggle, he is no pet to be led about. But Nic is out there, waiting for him. So, he allows it and follows the king, all the while plotting the man's death.

Now

I WATCH them lead Aiden from his cell, Wardon and the long-fingered fey who appears more tree than man. My hands clench into fists as I stand on the cliff that is to be our seaside meeting place as I observe the wolf. He's walking, which I take as a good sign. He's wearing some sort of collar, black and hardened like cool lava. I try to catch his eye but his gaze is focused down. Harmony's words of prophecy haunt me.

Neither will be as you remember them.

Aiden has already endured so much in his life. The son of a fire deity, risen from the ashes of a golden life, cursed and yet somehow still able to give of himself. What would it take to alter him irrevocably?

And Nahini. I have yet to catch sight of her. How badly did they hurt her that such a hard warrior will never be the same?

Bard and Harmony are in place, standing with their backs to the rising sun. Though never one for prayers, I can't help but send out a mental plea that I can trust my new allies not to betray me, that Aiden will have faith in me and not give the scheme away.

And most of all, that clever, power-hungry Wardon is arrogant enough not to see the deception coming.

"The rest of my people?" Bard calls out, his voice a perfect echo of my own. It's like looking in a mirror, even if the reflection moves independently of me. Not only is he wearing my skin, but the shifter also has my squared-shoulder, chin-up stance, my look of defiance. He wears the same set of jeans and hoodie that I'd had on earlier, claiming my scent still clinging to the fabric. He insists that will help him own his role. He even picked up my backpack on his way out of the door.

I, in contrast, feel nothing like myself. Beneath the large

gray cowl that hides my face, I curl a finger around one of the dyed locks. It's a dark brown, almost mahogany, provided by the wardrobe. Between the color and the shapeless granite colored sack that passes for a religious robe worn by Wardon's temple sworn witnesses, even the aunts wouldn't recognize me.

"They're nearby." Wardon stops a foot away from Bard and takes his—my—hand. "First, a question. You are, Nicneven, future Queen of the Unseelie Court and heir to the Shadow Throne?"

I see him study my face—Bard's face. He's looking for a trick, some sort of doublecross. I, the human girl, can tell a lie, but most any fey capable of taking on my form could not.

"I am," Bard says, voice clear and unwavering.

He can do it because he has taken on my identity, has essentially *become* me, at least until the part is played out and he moves on to his next identity. According to Bard, even though many know what he and other entertainers can do, they didn't know the why or how of it. A trick of the trade. One he had let us in on.

A low growl rumbles from Aiden, but it cuts off in a high-pitched yelp of pain. Bard's gaze shifts to the wolf. "What's wrong with him?"

"His new collar appears to be chafing." Wardon puts a hand on the wolf's head. Aiden ducks away but not before I see the bright red blood that streaks the king's fingers.

Did the collar do that? I try again to send a mental message to Aiden. He doesn't so much as twitch.

I see Bard's hands clench into fists, an exact replica of my own beneath the long sleeves of the stolen robe. "Take it off him."

"And have him kill us all? I think not. For you see, my lovely, I know exactly who you've been bedding all these years. And there are those who would pay handsomely for him."

As though she'd been waiting for a cue, The Hag of the Ironwood opens a portal by his side and steps out as though stepping through a doorway.

I hear Aden's warning growl, but it is immediately cut off in another yelp of pain. As though the collar isn't just restraining him, but *disciplining* him somehow.

The giantess is once again pared down to a more standard size, though power radiates from her. She turns to Wardon with a raised eyebrow. "I specifically said he was not to be harmed."

"Apologies," Wardon's tone holds no regret. "But we had to take precautions. He's a wanted criminal in Asgard, after all. How could a few fey cope with that sort of power?"

The red-haired giantess stares down at the Seelie king like he's something she scraped off the bottom of her boots.

"What's she doing here?" Bard asks. "You promised to turn Aiden and the others over to me."

"And I will, my sweet. Just as soon as you keep your end of the bargain and marry me."

Aiden lunges, murder in his leaf green eyes. But then collapses three feet from where he started.

Right in front of me.

I want to bend down, to place a hand on his neck, to rip that gods damned collar off, but I can't. I signed on for the ruse and I need to see it through.

"The lovely giantess here has agreed to keep an eye on your pet until after you pass the gauntlet. After you become my wife."

I don't react outwardly, and neither does Bard. It is Harmony who speaks up.

"That is a mistake, my king. The giantess has no intention of returning the son of the flame."

Wardon raises a cynical eyebrow as he turns on Angrboda. "I know. But she will swear a blood oath to me, as will my betrothed. I believe the terms of the oath are universal, for anything living can also die."

"I will do no such thing." Angrboda chin lifts, her posture arrogant. "We had a deal. The wolf for your magic. I have upheld my end."

"That does present something of a conundrum." Wardon circles the spot where Angrboda stands. The giantess doesn't flinch but turns her head to track the king's movements. Suddenly water sprays upward from the cliff below us like a geyser erupting. It follows the circle Wardon made around the giantess, trapping her inside. I see her hands come up, her fists pound on the wet prison and a look of pure astonishment crosses her face when she doesn't break free.

He used her own magic against her. "Nicneven, if you will be so kind."

Oh no. I stare at Bard, who's gone blank-faced. Oh *shit*.

"I beg your pardon?" The mimic raises a sardonic eyebrow. Good cover, though it won't help him in the long run.

"This creature wants to take my gift to you. Give her your own special kiss and send a message to all in Underhill that you are not to be crossed."

The performer's eyes—my eyes—round. No matter how much he looks like me, how much he believes he has *become* me, Bard is not the Unseelie queen of the Shadow Throne. He does not possess the Goodnight Kiss. And as soon as Wardon realizes it, he will retaliate.

"I have no quarrel with the giantess," Bard tries. "What good will come from her death?"

"She ruined your consort's family. She wishes to take him away. That should be reason enough." Wardon smirks, knowing he holds the winning hand. "But if not, here's one more. Either the giantess dies here and now, or I will gift her the wolf and slaughter all your other companions before your very eyes."

A test. He's even more paranoid than I am. In the distance the waves start to churn. Then swirl, creating a whirlpool in the middle of the sea. The ocean splits, revealing a trench beneath and inside the trench are my missing souls.

And Nahini.

She coughs and chokes, trying to dispel water from her lungs. How is she even still alive?

All eyes are on me, the fake me. I risk a step forward, brushing my toe against Aiden's side. He doesn't stir.

"So, what will it be, Nicneven?" the Seelie king asks. "A small demonstration of your greatest power? Or should I trap your lost souls back in their watery prison until the seas dry up?"

Bard sends me a fleeting look. Anyone other than Harmony would believe he's staring at Aiden. I have no way to instruct him, there is no path I can set him on which will bring us all out safely on the other side.

We are trapped.

CHAPTER 15

AN OATH FOR AN OATH

"My patience grows thin," Wardon's face is like stone. "Make your choice. Or I will choose for you."

Bard takes a hesitant step forward, then another. I risk a quick glance around, but only Harmony is looking my way. Crouching down beside Aiden, I slip my fingers beneath the collar, its texture more like stone than leather or even synthetic. The fur of his ruff is matted with blood. I run my fingers around the edges of the collar, looking for a seam or a fastener. Something sharp pricks my skin. I pull my hand away to see my fingertips coated with blood. My blood. And on the back of my hands more blood, Aiden's. The collar is full of glass shards. Wardon had been essentially bleeding him out before my eyes.

If I can get him free of the wretched thing and back on his feet we might stand a chance. But if he's lost too much blood too quickly….

Angrboda's eyes grow wide as Bard approaches. Is that panic on her face? Does she believe her end is near?

Her water prison recedes down to her waist, keeping her

hands and legs bound while enabling Bard to reach her. A flash of triumph crosses Wardon's expression as Bard stands up on tiptoes.

Angrboda says something, too soft for me to hear and shakes her head, just once. Bard catches her face in a firm grip and then presses his lips—my lips—to hers.

She sags against the restraints. Wardon throws back his head and laughs aloud.

My lips—my actual lips—part as Bard steps back, hiding his shock.

I switch my gaze to the spirit landscape, wondering if somehow, in some way, Bard managed to snag my ability. Could it be possible that he not only killed her but to tether her soul to the Hunt? But I don't see Angrboda's soul floating free or drifting toward Nahini and the others trapped in the trench. No, it's still where it belongs, inside her body.

She's faking it then. The question is, why?

At my feet, Aiden stirs, a soft whimper escaping him.

"Sash," I say, partly to reassure him, partly so that he doesn't wake up at the wrong time and ruin everything.

"A deal is a deal," the Seelie king waves a hand and a rush of wave surges toward Nahini and the souls of the Wild Hunt. I expect to see them disappear beneath the crush of water, but instead it lifts them up, carrying them to the shore as though they are riding a parade float.

"And my wolf?" Bard asks. "I want that collar off."

"First the blood oath." Wardon lifts his palm and a silver knife appears within it. "Repeat after me. I, Nicneven, will wed Wardon, Master of the Waves and ruler of the Gray Throne. I will do so as soon as I have reclaimed the Shadow Throne and established myself as the monarch supreme of the Unseelie Court. I have agreed to this union of my own volition and will hold to it, upon penalty of death."

Bard repeats the words with the utmost sincerity and

then Wardon cuts a line across his—my—palm, drawing blood.

Wardon makes a cut in his own palm and vows an oath of his own. "I, Wardon, Master of the Waves, vow to release Aiden, Nahini, Harmony the seer and all the souls gifted to me by Queen Brigit into the custody of Nicneven, the one true queen of the Unseelie. I will do so immediately and without hesitation."

"And you will never capture or harm Unseelie subjects again." Bard prompts.

Wardon starts, but then, sensing no trap, adds the phrase before the penalty of death bit.

Three drops of blood from each hand merge in a silver chalice. The liquid smokes doubles and then double again until the cup overflows with a red fog. Wardon extends it to Bard. "Ladies first."

Bard takes it and sips before returning it to the king.

Wardon's lips turn up as he lifts the chalice to his mouth. I can't help holding my breath, waiting for something to go wrong, someone to shout out a warning. But he merely tips the chalice back, draining it dry.

Immediately I feel a surge of power, one I had been missing for months. It's my missing members of the Wild Hunt, back under my control once more. I stare at the beach, urging the spirits to gather Nahini up. She's drenched, seaweed clings to her clothing and her eyes are closed. At least she is breathing. I see her brother kneel beside her. Though unable to touch her, the spirits of the Hunt can influence the physical world in small ways. He reaches out a hand as though to cradle her head in his.

I want to howl with triumph. It worked. The king just agreed to marry the shifter, even as he returned control of the souls of the Hunt back to me, to the real Nicneven.

Serves you right, you bastard. I narrow my eyes on the

Seelie king and make a silent promise. One day soon, I will make him pay for the suffering he has caused.

"We'll be going now." Bard squares his shoulders, lifts his chin. "There's much to do. Remove the collar from my companion."

"All business. I admire that about you." Wardon snaps his fingers and the collar around Aiden's neck vanishes. The wolf doesn't stir, doesn't even open an eyelid.

I shake him gently, and he groans but doesn't wake.

"What's been done to him?" Bard demands in an imperious tone.

But before Wardon can answer, slim hands grasp him from behind, lifting him up off the ground.

"You thought to betray me?" Angrboda's eyes are like blue flames, her bloodred hair whipping about in an unholy wind. "Turned my own magic against me?"

Wardon gargles, as though trying to speak. His gaze is on Bard though.

I don't wait to see what happens next. With the full strength of the dead of the Wild Hunt back in my grasp, I reach out to the souls I have claimed and bid them to obscure us from our enemy's eyes.

They fan out, a rolling fog of death. Trolls fall before it, twitching in pain as limbs are removed, hearts pierced. The witnesses to the blood oath scream and flee. Bard and Harmony dart down through the crowd as Nahini's body drifts toward me on billows of vapor.

Her face is bloodless, her beautiful jet hair streaked liberally with white as pure as newly fallen snow. Extreme shock or terror can do that, leech all the pigment from a person. Her chest is rising and falling and there is a steady pulse in her neck. She'll survive if I can get her away from this wretched place.

"We need to cross back to the mortal realm," I tell them.

"The souls can reach the tear in the veil, but I don't see Nahini's horse and Aiden is in no shape to float us up to it. Any other suggestions?"

"Send a soul through the tear to alert the rest of your Hunt to your whereabouts," The words come from Nahini's brother. "Send me."

I look up into him, the murderer who my third had sacrificed her life to stay near. He may not care whether the rest of us live or die, but he would do anything for his sister. "Go quickly. We'll head inland, away from Wardon's territory. Tell Freda to meet us there."

He nods once and streaks into the sky like a comet going in reverse.

The Valkyrie I bound comes forth. "They are all dead or fleeing, my queen. Less the giant and the king. They escaped through a portal."

I nod in acknowledgment then look about the blood-soaked beach. The fog has formed into ranks of the souls again, standing in perfectly ordered rows. Dead trolls and a few of the unluckier fey are scattered all around us. A shiver steals through me as I gaze upon the carnage. I ordered them to do this. Their blood is on my hands just as if I'd kill them myself.

One look at Aiden's slumped form, Nahini's gauntness and my heart hardens. It was them or us and if I had to choose over again, I would still choose us.

"We need to fashion some sort of sled, to carry them." I nod to first Nahini, then Aiden.

Bard, back in his powerful lidless resting form nods toward the cave. "There might be something in there we can use, a door or some rope."

"Help him," I urge Harmony. She nods and then follows the shifter.

The souls of my victims surround me as I crouch beside

Nahini. I sense their worry. Nahini is their caretaker, the living being who commands them but who also watches out for them. Some of the stronger or newer spirits can speak directly to me, but most are trapped in silent service. Even the dead need someone to care for them.

She is breathing, though I don't like the greenish cast of her skin. Her pulse is light and quick and reminds me of a bird trapped in a cage, beating its wings in rapid succession. Aiden still isn't waking up, still not responding to my mental probes. What had Wardon done to them?

Bard and Harmony appear, a heavy driftwood door dragged between them. Bard also has rope the color and texture of seaweed slung over one arm.

"Good to know Wardon stayed on theme even in his dungeon." I quip and stand up before looking at Harmony. "Is it safe to move them?"

She nods. "They won't die on an inland journey."

I don't like the way she phrases her response but decided not to ask. Instead shifting my attention to the door. "That looks heavy."

"I can handle it," Bard says. He drops my backpack at my feet and then changes.

I watch as he shifts, becoming a large troll. After tying the seaweed rope to the door, he hoists it over his midsection so to drag the thing while Harmony and I load Nahini and Aiden on to the sled.

I pick up my pack, glad to have it in my possession once more. Something about its reassuring weight on my shoulder makes me feel as though I can face anything.

The sun is fully up by the time we find a smooth enough path inland for the sled. The terrain shifts from sand to rocks and clay, though it turns greener as we travel with larger trees and lush grass. No sign of a road or cars anywhere. It's nature, wholly unspoiled.

"Is Wardon dead?" I ask as we make our way up a rolling hill, the last of the sea breeze at our backs.

Though I meant the question for Harmony it is Bard who answers. "No. I can still feel the throb of the blood oath. Whatever Angrboda has done to him, she hasn't ended him yet."

"I want a crack at him first," I say, with another worried glance at my people. "Stop over that next rise. Let's try and get some water into them."

Bard pauses beneath a leafy oak. I crouch beside the sled and open my backpack. Sure enough, my metal water bottles are secured right up top. I lift one out, take a small sip, then crouch beside Nahini.

After a bit of coaxing she swallows the water. I check her pulse again. Still too light and fast for my liking, but at least it's no worse.

I turn to Aiden, still in wolf form. How best to get him to drink? It's not as though I can roll him onto his back and pour the liquid in and we don't have enough on hand for trial and error.

I decided to try and wake him again. He'll need food as well as water for a rapid recovery.

I put a hand on his head and call his name. Once. Twice.

A green eye stares up at me, no sign of recognition.

There is nothing human in that gaze. Only the wolf.

I don't have time to get out of the way before he lunges at me, going right for my throat.

I GET an arm up a second before his big fangs can sink into my jugular. The thick robe tears like wet paper beneath his onslaught, the flesh beneath it shredding. I hear Harmony's cry and the pounding of great feet as Bard charges for us.

"No!" I shout. "Stay back. He'll kill you."

"And he won't kill you?" Bard asks, though he does cease his charge.

I don't bother answering him, my entire focus is for the wolf. For it is the wolf now, with Aiden nowhere in sight.

"Hey," I say to the creature before he can lunge again. "Remember me? You know me?"

The only answer is a growl, low in the back of his throat. No hint of recognition in his leaf green eyes.

I try to gather my wits enough to contact him mentally, but nothing happens. It's like bouncing a tennis ball off a brick wall.

"I'm not the one who hurt you," I tell him, keeping my voice soft, unthreatening. I do my best to hide my terror, though it isn't easy. I've faced off with the wolf before, though that time he'd been wearing a human body. I've touched the wolf before too, with Aiden in control. But with him standing over me, teeth bared and no traces of the man in sight, I can fully appreciate why the Vikings feared wolves.

"Let me change into you," Bard suggests. "Confuse him and lure him away."

"No," I answer, not looking away from Aiden's hypnotic stare. "He'll know the difference, in scent at least."

His growl intensifies. He should have stood down by now, seen that we are not a threat, even if Aiden isn't in control. I shift slightly and he snaps at me, those massive jaws clicking shut inches from my face. A warning. Last time, the wolf had backed down when I held his gaze, because it recognized me as its mate. What am I doing wrong?

Another mistake could mean death.

My brain whirls frantically. Aiden had been taken, imprisoned and collared. He'd scolded me last time the wolf had taken over about holding his stare. Said his wolf might interpret the act as a challenge to his dominance.

Quickly I lowered my lids. Okay, he gets to win the staring contest. What else?

Submission. Though it goes against every fiber in my being, I need to demonstrate my submission. So, he knows I won't challenge him.

My mouth is dry and I hold my breath and stretch my neck out, trying not to think of his teeth shredding the vulnerable skin there, piercing my jugular until I bleed out on the ground. A small whimper escapes and it isn't part of my act.

The massive black head moves closer, until his nose presses against my skin. He sniffs. Then backs away.

I let out a breath on a *whoosh* of air and slowly, sit up. The wolf—it's almost impossible to think of him as Aiden after the close call—lopes off toward the trees.

"Are you hurt, my queen?" Bard moves forward, Harmony half a step behind him. "Your arm."

"It's not bad," I lie. Blood soaks the sleeve of the robe, turning it a brownish-red. Gingerly, I push the sleeve up and stare at the punctured flesh. It could have been so much worse. The wolf could have torn the limb free and unlike him, I wouldn't regenerate. I'd felt the strength in that powerful body.

With the adrenaline fleeing my system in the wake of the attack, the pain increases. "Get me the water bottle and my pack."

Harmony does and helps me clean out the wound, smear my arm with an antiseptic ointment and wrap it with gauze pads and more purple vet wrap. It's the same color as her skin.

A half-hysterical laugh escapes. It's either laugh or cry at this point.

"My queen?" Bard prompts.

"I'm fine." My gaze fixes on the spot where the wolf

vanished into the woods. Did I just set a dangerous predator loose on the local population?

"Should we go after him?" Harmony sounds dubious.

I want to. I just got him back and don't like Aiden being out of my sight when he's not himself. But even with him right in front of me, I couldn't get through to him. If we chase him and he turns on us, I might not be able to stop the wolf from hurting someone. And Aiden would be the one to suffer for it. Slowly, I shake my head. "No. We need to keep going. Aiden will find me when he can."

If he can.

CHAPTER 16

LOST

"Over the river and through the woods," I grumble as I sit down beside the fire Harmony tends. "To grandmother's house, we go."

"What's that?" The seer asks, confusion in her gray eyes.

"Nothing. Just a song about taking a trip. The terrain today reminds me of it."

We had indeed crossed a river and trekked through the woods. The scenery is picturesque, like something out of a storybook. Unfortunately, what with Nahini's still being unconscious and Aiden's disappearance, I'd been in no mood to appreciate it. My arm throbs with every heartbeat and I debate taking another pain killer. There are only two more in the first aid kit.

"Do you have any idea where we are? Either of you?" I raise my voice to include Bard in our conversation.

Harmony shakes her head but the performer shifts his attention from the pack.

"Vaguely. About two days ride from the border of King Soladin's land. It's getting on to harvest time there." He sighs theatrically and adds. "I performed in his court during harvest a few years ago. It is a magical time, full of food and dancing and frivolity."

"You know the other king?" I raise one eyebrow. Curiosity and apprehension fill me. "What's he like? Will we be safe crossing into his territory?"

"Safer than we are staying in Wardon's realm," Bard assures me. He plucks an apple from my backpack and offers it to Harmony. She accepts with a small smile and he resumes his digging.

My stomach rumbles but I don't make a move for my own dinner. I'm glad we stopped when we did. Night is creeping in, the shadows beneath the trees deepening and fuzzing around the edges as twilight gives way to true darkness.

There is no sign of the glowing green eyes I long to see, yet the wolf is out there, somewhere. Watching us, watching me. All the small hairs are up on the back of my neck. Again, I try to call out to him mentally and again, my thoughts rebound. It's as though Aiden isn't on the other end of the line anymore. What's happening to him?

I wish I had some way of contacting his grandmother. The giantess, Laufey knows Aiden better than anyone. She might be able to devise a way for me to get through to him. But Underhill isn't exactly known for stellar cell reception.

"Any idea where Freda might meet up with us?" I ask the seer.

Harmony shakes her head. "I can't see decisions beyond the Veil."

Of course not. That would be too helpful. I cast another glance at Nahini. Despite the crispness of the wind, sweat beads her forehead. She shifts restlessly, caught in the grip of a dream. I desperately crave her advice. Maybe it's ridiculous to think she would do better in the same set of circumstances, but I can't help imagining it.

Bard offers me a choice between a second apple and a protein bar. "Our supplies are running low. We should keep on the lookout for game or possibly a house where we might secure supplies."

I nod and accept the bar, though I don't offer comment. Other than the courts, many of the fey who dwell in Underhill are starving and will have nothing to spare for us.

Again, my eyes wander to the tree line. Is Aiden hunting out there? I could see his ribs even through the thick pelt of fur. He has a rapid metabolism and is always hungry, even if he's just eaten an enormous meal.

Will he find food? Will he ever turn back into a man?

I harbor no doubt that the wolf can fend for himself. I've seen the survival instinct in those glowing irises. He will kill where and when he sees fit, leaving nothing but carnage in his wake. My arm throbs where he bit me, a painful reminder that the wolf in question can take care of business.

But the man... the one left to clean up, to live with the consequences of whatever Wardon's trolls did to him. Aiden's despair has led him down some dark paths. Can he come back from his imprisonment without help?

Neither will be as you remember them.

"You want to go after him, don't you?" Bard's voice is soft. He settles down across the fire from me, adding his lumpy troll silhouette to our flickering shadows.

I stand, feeling the pull of my wolf like a magnet tugged to true north. "I think he needs me."

"Should we wait?" Harmony sounds reluctant, as though I'm asking her not to take an offered treat. The seer has never been beyond the bounds of Wardon's territory and her eagerness to explore is palpable.

I rest a hand on Nahini's forehead. It's cool now, no fever. I extract the remaining full bottle of water and two-thirds of the protein bars from my pack and set them on the pallet beside her.

I look to Bard. "You know Soladin, you've been to his court before. Will he offer help to Nahini? Will you be safe in his lands?"

"Safer than you will, my queen."

I glance back to the trees, then rise, collecting my backpack. "Okay. You should head for the border then. The Dead of the Hunt will protect you."

A nod from Nightweaver in acknowledgment of my orders, but otherwise the phantoms hold their piece.

"With luck, Freda will create a crossing in your path, one you can't miss and I'll see you on the other side."

"Safe journey. I will wish to hear all about it." Bard gives me a nod.

Harmony's purple face is grave, but I don't ask, not really wanting to know what the future holds. Instead, I turn my back and head into the dark.

The thick leafy canopy of chestnut and pine swallows me up. A few feet in, I set my pack down and dig out the flashlight. The small white circle of light it casts highlights the thick bed of leaves on the forest floor. The scents of untouched nature, clean air tinged just a bit with wood, of natural decay and rich soil reminds me of home, of the farm.

My footsteps are slow, steady, careful to avoid jutting rocks or the roots that snake across my path. There is no birdsong of course, the darkness would see them all safely tucked up in their nests. But there are no other sounds either, not the hoot of owls or the flap of bat wings or even the droning buzz of mosquitos.

In fact, I have seen no signs of life since we left the coastline, not insect, animal or fey. That makes no sense. The soil is hearty and would yield incredible crops. Yet I didn't see a single tilled field. If people are starving, why not take advantage of natural resources?

The gurgle of a nearby stream warns me before I step ankle-deep into the creek. Though I'll have to boil the water before I can drink, to kill any parasites that might live within, at least I have something to refill my empty water bottle.

I haven't gone far in the dark, maybe a mile from camp, though I can no longer see the light from their fire. After scraping a small pile of dried pine needles and collecting some sticks, I stoop to wash my face in the creek before filling my bottle.

The quiet is eerie and unsettling. I can survive out here. I've been camping a few times and while I'm never going to be the sort to live off the land, I can handle a few days of roughing it.

With my fire burning low, I rig a crude basket of green-wood sticks to place my newly filled bottle in then set it above the flame. One advantage of metal over plastic water bottles, I don't need a separate container to boil the water.

With literally nothing to do but wait for water to boil, I turn and stretch my back and take stock. If I ration my haul, I have about three days' worth of food in the bag. And if I don't find Aiden by then? By daylight, I'll scout along the trail for familiar-looking nuts, berries or even mushrooms.

Of course, this is Underhill, the land of trickery and deception. What might be benign where I come from could be toxic here. It's not like I have a guide to the wilds of the fey realm.

Aiden had been my guide before. And would be again if I can find him. If he wants to be found.

Not for the first time, I wonder what Wardon and his brutes did to my wolf. Torture of course, but of what sort? And why hadn't Aiden's wolf killed them all and escaped?

They must have drugged him. Maybe that collar had

some sort of toxin that repressed his abilities. But the thing had been off for hours. Aiden's magic should have returned.

Using my flashlight, I check and see that the water in my canteen has boiled, then kick damp dirt over the fire. No sense borrowing trouble. I will find Aiden and then I'll find out exactly what needs to be done for him.

Through the Wolf's Eyes

HUNGER. It is an ever-present thought. The churning need to feast on meat gnawing at him the way he would gnaw on a bone to get to the succulent marrow within. But there is no game in the woods, no delicious prey to sate his need. He wants to lie down. The lack of sustenance is making him weak. He pushes on, trotting through the woods at a steady lope.

He's known hunger like this before. The wolf doesn't interpret the passage of time. He simply is. A sensation is new or it is familiar and the hunger is familiar. He first woke with it centuries ago and feasted on the small game he'd been presented with.

Not game. The words are angry and come from the man within. The man who grieved and raged even as his hunger receded.

The wolf does not understand this creature. They share their flesh, two beings living as one, yet the man does not value life in the same way. He would have turned to ash and bones long ago if not for the wolf. He wanted to die, to fight the instinct. He intentionally starved the wolf to weaken him.

The man had left their mate in the time before, left her

undefended. Their pup had died because of his foolishness. Did the creature have no instincts, no sense of protection? Only this recrimination and guilt. Useless, weak feelings that did nothing, changed nothing.

If the man stood in his path, the wolf would kill him and feast on his pink flesh. And the man would do the same, he has no doubt. He feels the fires of rage that well within the man. Sometimes directed at the wolf, sometimes at his own weak self. There is only one thing the two both value, one bit of common ground to share.

Our mate.

The image of her makes the man curl up, his thoughts disturbed. The wolf needs to find her, almost as much as he needs food. His to protect, his to provide for.

He hurt her earlier, he knows this though he feels no regret or remorse. She was too close, came upon him unaware when he was injured. Mates need to learn, to be taught if they were to survive. She has no claws, her teeth flat, blocky things. No built-in defenses that he could detect. Her flesh is weak and easy to tear.

Yet she is brave. She faced off against that thing that had collared him and had set him free. He admires her boldness, her loyalty even as he curses it. He'd set her down hard in warning. Her blood as sweet as any he'd ever tasted and fear of those who would take it from her had him in a lather. She must learn not to tangle with a creature that could kill her.

The man had howled in rage as her blood hit his tongue, demanding he get away, to leave her behind. And the wolf had gone. He needs the man's cooperation. For to truly have her as his mate, he requires the man's body. She is his but not of his kind, her hunter's soul trapped within the pale pink flesh. He must use the other.

Unworthy. The man thinks at him, feelings of shame, of guilt, making him retreat deeper. *We are not worthy of her.*

The wolf doesn't understand. He will kill any prey she wishes and lay it at her feet. She need only point. Why would he be unworthy?

The man tries to explain, but the wolf cares not, the need for food blotting out the noise of this internal struggle.

He lifts his nose into the air and sniffs.

There is something, many miles off. In the opposite direction from his mate. She has followed him into the woods, he can scent her, but his temper is hot, the hunger sharpening it to a razor's edge.

He will kill the prey, take the edge off his hunger, then drag it back and lay it at her feet. She will see he is worthy. And then perhaps the man can be coaxed forth to join with her, to bind her to him.

The wolf will have her. But first, he must feed.

By morning I am tired, hungry and once again out of water. Not to mention lost. Part of me wants nothing more than to find a little nook where I can lie down and wait for the wolf to find me. But aside from the worry that something else might come on me unaware, a sense of unease has me putting one foot in front of the other.

It's odd, but with nothing else to focus on but him, I get a sense of the wolf as a being separate from Aiden. I flashback on the spirit scape, the way he'd appeared as two different souls in one flesh. I've seen him in control of Aiden's human form before, but I never thought of him as Other.

After a night of reaching out for his mind, I know it's not Aiden on the other end of the connection. There are no words coming back at me, it's more like I'm following him by instinct. I have no idea why the wolf attacked me and even more troubling, if he'll do so again or if Aiden can wrestle control back in time.

A sharp gust of northern wind carries the scent of burning. I inhale deeply. Not wood smoke, or not only wood smoke. Whatever is on fire is much larger than a small blaze to keep a few travelers warm.

There's another aroma, lighter and almost hidden underneath, a fecund scent of grain newly harvested. The wolf is a carnivore but where there's a harvest there are beings doing the harvesting.

And the wolf is hungry. His hunger is a living thing, jabbing him from the inside. The need to hunt, to kill. Not out of any sort of anger, and not even only for survival. Because it is what he is made to do. In a way, I understand this creature better than I do his man-shaped counterpart. And I envy his freedom to be true to his nature.

I turn north, toward the burning and whatever else is beyond it and pick up my pace to a run.

I see the plume of smoke as I emerge from the trees. Sure enough, the land is sectioned into fields, not flat but sown into a gentle slope to help with drainage. The earth has been tilled and prepared for the coming winter. A large creek meanders down the center, a perfect position to help irrigate the crops, and spills into a large lake. On the far side of the lake, sits the village. There are several squat fieldstone buildings forming a semicircle, the tallest building no more than two stories. It is that one, the tall building at the center of the community that is the source of the smoke. Shouts and screams carry across the water and fields, sounds of panic and terror.

Is it Aiden? Has the wolf somehow tapped into his godlike power, preferring his meat to be cooked? No, if he had all the buildings would be burning. Judging from the rustic setting, it's more likely that someone panicked at the sight of the big black wolf and knocked over a candle or dropped something too near the hearth.

I scan for a way down. There's a path off to my right, no more than a goat trail. It bypasses both the fields and the water though and I sprint for it, heart pounding, palms sweating.

The smell of civilization, bread baking, laundry being washed, is overpowered by the acrid stink of burning. Though the building is stone, the roof is thatch. Flammable and judging from the rudimentary setup, many of the things inside are made of wood or cloth.

Several of the villagers have formed a makeshift bucket brigade stretching from the lake to the two-story building. However, the conflagration is already too large. Flames lick out of windows, hungry for more.

I glance around, hoping for any sign of my missing wolf. A spike of terror goes through me like an icicle jabbing into my gut. I almost double over as it spears through me. It's not my own, but his.

Where are you? I think to Aiden.

No response. I run faster, drawn to the flames like a suicidal moth.

The villagers, male and female alike, are naked. Not so unusual in Underhill. From the front, they appear completely human. But as they work to put out the fire several turn to grab buckets and I see they have tails.

Actual freaking tails.

Some are long and tufted at the ends, like a cow's tail. Others are bushy and resemble a fox. And their spines are covered with what appears to be tree bark.

I give myself a full minute to absorb the strangeness, then focus on my hunt for my wayward wolf. The fey creatures are making little progress as the fire devours everything in its path. From the snatches of conversations that drifts to me,

I can tell the tactic has been changed, the goal no longer to put out the fire but to keep it from spreading to the other buildings.

"...empty?" A willowy female with one of the brushy red tails shouts with a nervous glance at the building.

A nod of confirmation from one of the squat burly cow tailed males hauling water. "Made it..."

Where is Aiden? Another stab of fear from somewhere nearby, there and gone.

"...just the wolf." A deeper male voice grunts.

My heart beats so hard I think it is going to leap out of my chest. I whirl toward the speaker then identifying the thin man with the foxtail, I sprint for him.

"Good riddance," another female with an uppity nasal voice spits. It's become clear from their remarks that no one is willing to go out of their way for Aiden.

Up close, the creatures are even more unnerving. I focus on the man with the booming voice who'd mentioned the wolf. "Where?" I wheeze, "Where did you see the wolf?"

Luminous dark eyes reflect the firelight and his tail passes the water bucket it's holding into his beefy hand. He scans me from head to toe, noting my clothes and lack of a fifth limb, no doubt. "In the cellar of the inn. Locked it in meself."

"You mean he's trapped in there?" I whirl back toward the building, hunting for a door or access hatch of some kind. No wonder the wolf is panicking. "Is there a way inside from out here?"

A cow tail wraps around my wrist before I can take off and an autocratic female voice demands, "Why would you want to let it out?"

Not bothering to respond, I shake off the unsettling touch. "Is there another way inside?"

When no one answers me, I glance back at the front door, smoke billowing through the open entrance like the nostril of a dragon. Beyond, the inferno rages and somewhere in that hell is my wolf.

I don't think, don't hesitate for an instant, propelled forward by that same instinct that kept me walking all through the night.

I secure my backpack and sprint into the burning building.

CHAPTER 17

TOO STUPID TO LIVE

I drop to the floor immediately, avoiding as much of the choking black smoke as I can. The roar of the fire is deafening and consumes the cries of the astonished townsfolk. I can't blame them, it's a dumb move on my part, one that might finally prove I am too stupid to live. And the Darwin Award for 2018 goes to Nic Rutherford, for not realizing that you're supposed to run *out of* a place on fire.

I can see the Internet memes already. Would laugh but I don't want to waste the oxygen.

The stone floor is cool beneath my palms. I crawl on hands and knees through the unfamiliar layout. There are no flames on this level, the smoke rolls down the stairs from the second story. I chance a glance up, eyes burning from the ash. The floor is wood. Not good. No telling how long I have until the conflagration eats its way through and collapses on my head.

The stairs also lead down to what must be the cellar where Aiden is trapped. I spare half a thought, projecting it to him that I am on my way to free him. There is no response, no sensations from the wolf or words from Aiden. Not a good sign.

The smoke grows thicker as I approach the stairs. I belly crawl across the stone floor like a snake, balancing the need for quick action with the need to keep breathing on a razor's edge. A *snap* and behind me a beam from the second story crashes down. I scramble away a second before being pinned beneath the massive blackened timber.

More coughing and the tears stream steadily down my face. I scurry to the lower staircase, heart pounding at the knowledge that the only exit is now blocked. If I can get to the wolf, get through to Aiden, he can shift us to sparks. We can float out of here unscathed.

"And if ifs and buts were candy and nuts we'd all have a Merry Christmas," I grumble a saying of Addy's. More likely, I'll die in a fiery inferno, either choked out by smoke or between the jaws of a feral wolf.

I half slither, half fall down the stairs into the cellar. The good news, there's less smoke down here. The bad, no light just a bunch of dark shapes, probably unused furniture.

"Aiden." My voice is no more than a weak rasp, throat dry and scaly. "Wolf. Where are you?"

I strain my ears, listening, willing my eyes to hurry up and adjust. There is no sound, no sign of him. Panic wells. I've seen his leaf green eyes glow in the dark, the light from his inner fire lighting from within. Maybe he isn't here. Did I make a fatal mistake?

"Aiden," I push forward, away from the stairs and the suffocating smoke. "Please. Help me find you."

I bump into something, a stack of chairs and send them crashing to the floor. There is a yelp and then a whine to my left. He's here and he's still alive.

"Don't kill me," I mutter and weave through the furniture wreckage. "You'll be really pissed at yourself if you kill me."

Another soft whine helps me adjust my course and then my hand connects with cool metal. Bars. Locked in, the fey outside said. They'd locked him in this cage.

My hand is shaking. It trembles as I push it determinedly between the bars. Will he bite it off my wrist? My palm connects with thick fur. "Hey there. I've been looking for you."

He nudges my hand. The big body shifts until his nose rests against my palm. He's not a dog to lick me or demonstrate affection, but I can tell he's glad I'm here.

Personally, I wish neither of us was here. "Are you hurt?" I cough, wondering why he's so still.

A soft whine is my only answer, which I take for a yes. The villagers must have hurt him somehow. It's the only way they could have caged him. And the fact that he's no longer fighting, struggling to get free worries me more than anything else.

"Listen to me," I choke, cough. "I need you to let Aiden out."

The head jerks beneath my hand. His refusal.

"It's the only way. Aiden can get you out. Can get *us* out."

A green iris cracks up at me. His eyes are always so expressive, but now the light is dull.

"Don't give up." Under normal circumstances, I might feel foolish for stopping to have a one-sided conversation with an animal in the middle of a burning building. But the smoke is getting thicker and the roof could collapse at any time. "If you don't give Aiden control, we'll both die. I know you don't want that."

The green eye peers at me and I see something shift. Then it shuts, the big body beneath my hand heaves an enormous sigh.

And then goes still.

Through the Wolf's Eyes

CAN YOU HELP HER? The wolf asks the foolish man-creature who is once again fighting for control. No part of his body doesn't hurt. The wounds the Huldra inflicted for him eating their livestock are not slight. *She thinks you can save us.*

I can. The voice is sure, steady. *I can get her out. Get us all free.*

Free. It is what he craves, the openness of the sky, of the forest. Away from the stink of fey, the reek of magic made flesh. Still, the wolf is reluctant. The man couldn't free him before. He hates to relinquish his grip on the body. Being trapped within the man's skin, having no control, no choice of where to run, where to hunt, is his own torment.

But there is no enemy to fight, even if he had the strength. The man within can do more, can save his mate.

Our mate. The man vows. *She's my mate too, and I will protect her with my life.*

It is the first time the man has acknowledged the connection. The wolf wouldn't share a mate with another, but the man is him.

And she's in danger. He hears her breaths—the air being ripped from her lungs as the poison smoke fills the space. She will die, they will all die if he continues to fight.

For her to survive, he must surrender.

Save her, he tells the man and then recedes into the nothingness in between.

Through the Man's Eyes

Nic.

Aiden senses her hand on him as he regains control of his body. He doesn't bother taking inventory of his injuries or shifting out of the wolf form. Instead, he sends two words to her. *Hold tight.*

She coughs then grips his furry scruff with both hands. Thank the gods.

Aiden dissolves, his body and hers turning to embers.

It's more difficult to transport Nic without his having a hold on her and he's careful to collect all of her and her beloved pack. Together they rise, up and up and up. Through the choking black smoke, back up the flight of stairs to the first floor. The door is engulfed in flames, but that is no barrier to him, not as he is. Nic's grip on him feels slack like she's barely holding on, about to lose consciousness. He must get her out into the fresh air. Even still, he takes the time to seek a second exit, one that won't land them in the center of the huldra village.

The chimney is to his left and after the briefest pause, he heads in that direction. Up and up and up again, through the sooty bricks, away from the confining space. His body is weak from lack of food, but his fear for Nic keeps him going.

They clear the chimney stack, clear the roof and then he surges forward and makes it to the space beneath the pine boughs, well out of sight of those in the town square, behind the burning inn.

He pieces her together first, her small body coalescing from his sparks. Then he's beside her, naked and cold, covered with bruises and ash.

Nic coughs, expelling the soot from her lungs and offers him a weak smile. "There you are. You look terrible."

His throat feels tight, though it's from emotion more than smoke. "Why did you come after me?" He isn't sure if he means when he was imprisoned, into the woods or into the burning building. All foolish choices on her part.

Clear blue eyes, the color of a winter lake peer out from her soot-stained face. She holds his gaze with her characteristic frankness. "Thought you might...need me," she wheezes an instant before her eyes roll up in her head. All the pride that usually holds her stiff drains out along with consciousness.

"I do," Aiden tucks her dyed hair behind her ear. "I always do."

Fatigue rides him hard, the sustained injuries and consequent imprisonment are piling up, taking their toll. He checks her pack, finds water and a few energy bars. He takes a little of each, just enough to sustain him. He needs to get her away from the village before the fire is put out and the bloodthirsty huldra realize they weren't barbequed inside.

After repacking her bag, he lifts her over his shoulder and starts off into the woods. Skyclad, barefoot, but his course is set.

He won't fail her again.

THE CRACKLING of the fire seeps into my nightmares. Burning, everything is burning, the world in flames around me. There's no way out, no one left to help me. I shout but there is nothing.

And then the fire goes out, leaving me in the gloaming. There is no sun, no stars, but a hazy gray light illuminates the world around me. I am on the farm, but it is unlike the farm I left. No green of growing things or blue of life-sustaining water. The trees are nothing but skeletal black stalks, buildings collapsing in on themselves. Rocks coated with soot. The streams dry down to their beds, littered with the bones of the animals that died there. The far-distant hills are covered with ash. Not a soul left alive. No animals, mortal or immortal.

There is only the wind. It sends ash into my face, clogging my senses with remains of life extinguished.

Ragnorok. Armageddon. Judgment Day. No matter the name it is called, it all signifies the same event.

The end of the world.

I look down at my own hands, realize they are nothing but charred bones. And as I watch, the ash flakes off, pulled apart and scattered in the wind until I am no more, spread to the corners of the dead earth while my consciousness is left to drift alone across the barren landscape for eternity.

And in the distance, I hear a man's manic laughter.

I wake screaming and staring down at my hands, heart thundering in my rib cage, the scent of fire still in my nose. I scramble back, away from the scent, the burning that will end everything.

On the far side of the fire, there is movement and then he comes around, backlit from the flames. Hands grip my shoulders holding me in place when I would have scooted back farther from the fire. "It's okay."

I ignore the reassuring voice and stare down at my shaking hands. Dirty and covered with ash, but the flesh is still visible underneath. Not burnt.

"Nic," he says my name again and grips my chin. "Look at me. You're all right. It was just a nightmare."

"No," I say, and shake my head stubbornly. "I saw it. Ragnorok. I heard him laughing."

Aiden swallows. "You mean my father."

At my nod, he curses, then pulls me into his chest. "Not yet. It's not here yet."

But it's coming. He can't pretend he doesn't believe it. After the dream, I believe it, too. "He wants to destroy everything. Even you? Your mother?"

"We don't matter to him, not really. Nothing does, except his vengeance. He's destined to die, too. Be just like the selfish ass to take the rest of us with him." He swallows and then breathes. "That's all I've ever been to him, collateral damage."

I hold him tighter, willing the shaking to stop. His heartbeat is steady, his grip on me reassuring. His hair is wet and he smells of my soap. I cling to him, glad to be in his arms and have nothing else to do at this particular moment.

It is Aiden who releases me. One second I'm in his arms and the next he's up and across the fire. He wears nothing but a thin blanket from my pack. "Are you hungry? Or thirsty? There's a stream nearby and I already boiled water for you."

"Water sounds good." I scowl, wondering at his sudden retreat. It's not like Aiden to give up a chance to hold me.

He stalks to the side of the stream and lifts two bottles out of the water. "I put them back in the stream to cool it off."

Always so thoughtful, considerate. Being with him makes me realize just how selfish a person I truly am. "Thank you."

His gaze dips to my arm and then he crouches again, lifting the limb to examine the healing bite mark.

"I did this, didn't I." It's not a question.

"How much do you remember?"

He fingers a strand of my dyed hair. "There were two of you. The shifter…?"

"Bard. He's on our side. He took the blood oath for me."

"So, you won't marry Wardon." Is that hope I see in his green eyes.

"Never. But I would be happy to kill him." If Angrboda doesn't do it first.

His gaze falls to my arm again. "I'm sorry."

"It's not your fault. You warned me. I caught the wolf off guard."

He releases me and runs a hand through his hair. "Don't make excuses. I hurt you."

"It was an accident."

He grunts and gets up. Paces to the far side of the camp, does an abrupt about-face and then returns.

"Aiden?" I study him closely. "Why are you out here?"

He laughs but it is not a pleasant sound. "I should be asking you that."

I'm getting a crick in my neck from looking up at him. "I followed you."

"You shouldn't have." He shakes his head, his movements stiff and jerky. "Not until after the gauntlet. It's not safe for you."

"We'll cross back over as soon as we reconnect with Nahini."

He rounds on me. "What the hell were you thinking, coming after me like that? Do you have any idea where we are?"

"Roughly." His tone has me narrowing my eyes at him.

"Not good enough. Not nearly good enough." He waves his hand encompassing the darkened trees. "This is the Desolate Realm. Notice there's no birds or squirrels."

"I did. So?"

He glares at me. "Did it ever occur to you to wonder why?"

It hadn't but damned if I'll admit it. He'll most likely tell me anyway.

"It's because everything that grows here is poison, fed from the tainted spring, *Hvergelmir*. The water is from Niflheim."

That sounds familiar. "Niflheim is one of the nine worlds, right?"

Aiden nods in confirmation. "It's older than Underhill, dating back to the time before the gods or giants when there was only *Ginnungagap*, the great nothingness. Beneath the ground here, every blade of grass, every mushroom, every berry. No food that won't kill you. The soil itself is blighted."

I frown. "But...the village. There are fey there. They're growing crops."

"Poison crops," he counters. "And those were huldra. Didn't you see the tails?"

"They were kind of hard to miss. Why would anyone grow poison crops?" Then it dawns on me, the obvious answer. "Wardon."

"An army marches on its stomach and it's a cheap way to reduce numbers to your favor. The goods come in from the coast to feed the village and they export the grain to kill the kingdom's enemies. That's why the huldra knew I was a threat. After traveling for days across the Desolate Realm, they knew I was starving. Hell, it was just as likely they would make a meal out of the two of us if given the opportunity. Wardon provides them with enough to live on but there isn't much to spare."

I swallow. "So, were you going to eat them first? Is that why they trapped you."

He shakes his head. "I wasn't after the huldra, only their livestock. The wolf was so hungry and distracted, I didn't hear them come up behind me. Took three shots with a cattle prod and when I woke up...."

"The place was burning down around your ears," I say. "You could have died."

"Not by fire." He shakes his head. "Gods, do you know anything?"

I rear back, as though the words could cut me. "I get that you had a shitty few days, but there's no call to take it out on me."

Another of those hollow laughs escapes him. "You're kidding, right? It has *everything* to do with you. Everything I do, it's all for you. And it's never enough."

I stare at him in the dim firelight. "What's that supposed to mean?"

He turns his back on me. "Nothing. I don't mean anything. Ignore me until you need to use me again. It's what you do best."

"That's not fair—"

He rounds on me. "You know what's not fair, Nic? That once again, I was fool enough to let you dictate the terms of our relationship. Last time I was your consort. This time you tell me no sex, that I'm not your boyfriend, that I'm not anything to you. Fine. I could live with that. Except for when we get dosed with pixie dust or Underhill messes with your hormones. Then all bets are off. I'm supposed to go back to servicing your needs, but only until the crisis is past. When it does, then you're back to eyeing me with suspicion, to treating me like shit. You want to know why I ran? Because I'm sick of being your sex toy!"

His words gut me, mostly because he isn't wrong. "I'm not a fucking Volkswagon, Aiden. Who asked you to service me? No one. You keep volunteering, trying to change me. You think I like this situation? Like having all these...*feelings*?" I spit the last word out like it's poison on my tongue.

"Nic," his chest is rising and falling rapidly.

I hold up a hand. "No, you had your say. You tell me I'm using you. But aren't you using me, too? I never wanted this. Never asked for the responsibilities, the relationships that come with being Queen of the Shadow Throne. The more I try to untangle it all, the more snarls crop up. So, tell me, since you know everything. If I'm so awful, why are you still here?"

"If all I am is a snarl, then why bother saving me?" His hands clench and unclench at his sides. "You knew it was dangerous. You had no way to track me. Yet you stumbled off into the unknown. The huldra could have killed you or trapped you and delivered you to Wardon. That's what they do, seduce foolish mortals and lead them astray."

"Well, I didn't find them all that appealing. Now you tell me. Why did you bite me and then run away?"

Something shifts in his eyes. The wolf. "It wasn't me, not really. The wolf had taken over."

A chill goes through me. I'd thought it had been the wolf, but hearing Aiden confirm it... "So then why did *he* bite me and run away? I thought I was his mate."

Still can't get my mind around that one.

Aiden snorts as if he realizes how absurd the notion is. "He does, but that's no

guarantee he'll be gentle with you. Tenderness is not the way of the wolf. It was a lesson, as well as a reprimand. He wanted to scare you, to make sure you wouldn't keep taking chances."

And I'd gone and done the opposite. "Why?"

He doesn't answer, can't hold my gaze. "Because when a wolf is hurting, he wants to be left alone, to find a safe place to lick his wounds."

Something about the way he says the words makes me realize he isn't just talking about physical wounds. It's in the stiffness of his posture, the way he clutches the blanket, concealing the nakedness that he usually ignores. The air of shame and guilt and impotent rage a miasma surrounding him. The way he's avoiding my gaze, my touch. Dread coiled in my gut even as I asked the question I didn't want to be answered. "What did the trolls do to you?"

"Whatever they wanted." He swallows, looks toward the night darkened water. "And I let them."

CHAPTER 18

NAKED AND AFRAID

The words land with the impact of a meteor in my hollow stomach. I flinch, biting back the impulse to ask why. Why he'd allowed the miserable creatures to hurt him. The marks from the beatings are obvious. Even in the campfire light, I see the swell of one cheek, the cuts on his neck, the black and blue bruises on his bare calves. His body will recover, as soon as he eats enough to promote the healing. I've seen the miracle of his metabolism firsthand.

But the physical signs of his torment are literally only skin deep.

"Aiden," I swallow and move closer so I can touch his hand. I need the contact, need to know he's really right in front of me. He seems so far away, like he's still lost in the dark woods. "What exactly—?"

"They took my eye."

I stare at him, horrified. "What?"

"It regenerated. Wardon brought a healer to me." He pulls the blanket tighter around himself. "I killed them, or rather, the wolf did. The ones who did it. I didn't think it would bother me so much, to be imprisoned and tortured."

The last word falls between us with the weight of an anvil. I flinch at the impact and because I am touching him, he feels it and jerks out of my grip.

"Aiden," I reach for him again but he shies away.

"I'm going to the stream to wash," he turns and stalks down the embankment, leaving me alone by the fire.

My hands clench into white-knuckled fists. I would have liked to end them for him. And I wouldn't have done it with my Goodnight Kiss either. No way would I tether the souls of the bastards who had hurt and humiliated him to the Hunt. No, I would impale them on a spike and then roast them slowly over an open fire, giving him the choice of whether to turn the spit.

They are dead though, killed by Aiden's own hands. But if he could overpower his captors, why had he endured the torment? If he'd let the wolf out sooner, he could have saved himself the pain, the humiliation. Why allow himself to be put through the abuse?

I want to cry, want to rage, to scream, to kill something. More than anything else, I want to go to him. I stay where I am though. The bitter words we flung at each other still hang in the air. He'd said he needed to wash, even though it was obvious he'd already been to the stream. The only reason he'd have gone back was to avoid me.

To lick his wounds in private.

Five minutes pass, ten, fifteen. I sit like a particularly useless bump on a rotting log, trying to convince myself that I'm doing the right thing. It's what I would have wanted if I were in his place. Space to piece myself back together, a bit of distance and time.

I frown and chuck a twig into the fire. But that was the wolf's decision. And mine. Not Aiden's. He'd wanted my touch until I'd recoiled. The ugly reality wedging itself between us. It was only then he had run off.

243

Misery fills me as I recall Harmony's words. *Neither will be as you remember them.*

I'm not sure I believe in the seer's predictions, but Nahini's white hair and Aiden's tormented soul....

Again, I glance toward the stream filled with a sense of wrongness at being separated from him, feeling like he needs me.

For what though? What can I possibly say or do that would make any kind of difference? Vengeance has been met. Physically he's okay. Aiden is immortal, he's endured untold horrors inflicted by monsters of all shapes and sizes and survived, come out forged stronger by the fires he's walked through. I have every confidence he will get past this as well.

The fire dances before me, the heat and light sinuous but offering no comfort. I wish he would come back, just so I can see for myself that he's all right. I pick up a stick by my boots and poke the wood beneath until the teepee of branches collapse, sending a rain of sparks up into the darkened sky.

Go to him. It isn't Aiden's voice I hear in my head. I recognize it as part of myself even if the sentiment is foreign.

I argue with it, this fractured bit of self. Tell it things it should already know. I am not the sort of girl to offer comfort to anyone. I'm cold, calculating. The Ice Bitch. I kill people. It was easier to run into the burning inn than to find the words that would make Aiden all right again. Words aren't something I can stalk through the woods, or run to ground. They can't be captured or killed and they always manage to escape me.

He's always stuck by you. Been there for you to talk to no matter how awful you are or how many times you've shut him down.

"That's different," I speak aloud, aware that I have crossed the official line into talking to myself.

Yes. He does it because he cares for you. You don't because you're selfish and scared. You use him, just like he said.

I don't like this small voice coming from inside me. Don't like how it shines a light on the thick black shadows that hide my secret truths. And I really don't like that it might be right.

Aiden always wants to be near me. He would sleep in my room, at the foot of my bed if I let him. Maybe he doesn't need space as much as he needs me.

Go to him.

I chuck a piece of the stick I've been fiddling with into the fire. What if I make it worse?

There is no response. The voice has said its piece.

Getting to my feet, I make a decision. If he tells me to back off again, I will without argument. But I will at least make the offer.

The slope down to the water is steep and away from the light of the fire my eyesight is poor. Moonlight spills through the trees though and after a moment I spy the blanket on the shore.

I half stumble half slide down the bank to where the blanket lays, then cast about for any sign of him. He's standing in waist-deep water, the silver-white current bubbling around him. The air is chilly but steam rises from him. He's just…standing there. Not washing or moving, bathed by water and moonlight. And regrets so thick they might as well be fog.

I don't think, just like when I went into the burning building. My actions might lead to disaster but as a hunter, I have learned to trust my instincts. Without giving myself time to deliberate, I strip down to my underwear and walk up behind him.

The water is icy at first and I shiver. How can he stand it? The bottom is rocky, the sharp stones jutting up to poke my tender soles but I doggedly make my way to where he waits. I'm not noiseless. I don't have his ability to move through the water like a wraith, so I know he hears me, but still, he doesn't turn.

About a foot away from him the temperature increases. I take another hesitant step. Warmer still, like the difference between tepid bathwater and a hot tub. It's him, I realize. The son of fire warming the glacial stream. My breaths come in harsh pants but at least my teeth stop chattering. I wonder if I take another step will I boil alive?

Slowly, giving him enough time to pull away, I reach for him, my hand landing on his shoulder blade. His skin is hot, though not the heat of fever. Words, those slippery little buggers, still elude me. I can give him this though, the feel of my skin against his, a subtle signal that he isn't alone.

Stiff as petrified wood, his skin is hot to the touch. He smells of cedar, sage and Aiden.

There is a pause, the kind of silence just before impact.

"Don't I disgust you?" he murmurs.

"Why would you?" I take a chance and move closer, sliding both hands around him in a sort of backward hug, partly because I don't have anything in my arsenal to combat his demons, and partly because I just want to touch him.

"Because…." He shakes his head as though not sure of how to finish.

I swallow and take the final step until I'm pressed flush against his back. "You don't disgust me, Aiden. I don't think you ever could."

I feel his every breath as his lungs expand and deflate. "I'm sorry."

"For?"

He laughs but there is no humor in it. "All of it. Running away. Getting captured, not escaping. Putting you in a difficult situation, then yelling at you. Mostly yelling at you."

I press my cheek against his back. "Do you really feel like I'm using you like some sort of sex toy?"

He's quiet a moment. "Sometimes."

"Then why are you still here?"

Beneath my palms, he tenses. He takes a quivering breath. "The trolls would have hurt you. Tortured you in front of me. I thought I could endure it. The wolf wanted to fight, but I knew if I did, they would have hurt you and that I knew I couldn't stand."

He had fought for my sake. Had let himself be maimed all to save me enduring the same. I don't say anything, just hold him tighter, moving one hand up until it covers his hammering heart.

He puts his own hand over it, his grip almost painful. "You know what I dreamed about that last night at the farm? That you let me hold you all night. Nothing else. You just wanted to be close to me. Without magic, or hormones, or anything else compelling you. That you just…want me."

I do. The words stick in my throat. I squeeze him tighter.

"I should have fought them." His throat bobs. "A true warrior would rather die than let himself be captured."

"The last thing I need," I say dryly. "Is another dead warrior on my hands."

He laughs, the sound almost strangled.

I press a kiss to his shoulder blade. "I doubt I'll ever understand you, but I like you as you are. Alive and well."

"Same," he murmurs and turns in my grasp. "Nic?"

I shiver as he presses into me. Where his flesh touches mine, the heat seeps in, chasing the last of the icy grip of the water away. "Yeah?"

Slowly, his hands come up to cup my face as he lowers his forehead to mine. He's naked and I'm the next thing to it, our bodies just a few inches apart. Though our conversation isn't conducive to romance, it occurs to me that physical comfort can take more than one form.

"I'm still not ready," I whisper. "I don't know if I'll ever be ready."

He takes a deep, shuddering breath. "Just let me hold you." His hands brush a few wayward strands that broke free of my braid away from my face.

He's frowning, though I don't think it has anything to do with my hair. His lips part, but before he can speak, his eyes go wide and he points at something behind me. "Nic, look out!"

I turn and spot the rush of water barreling down the cliff in our direction. It overflows the small bank of the stream, a river charging in, taking over, Aiden lunges for me and I make one step toward the bank but then it's there, knocking us off our feet and dragging me beneath the icy water.

Through the Man's Eyes

THE WALL of water sucks Nic down under like a rag doll, her fingertips a hairsbreadth from his own. Aiden lunges for her but the current steals her before he can grip her hand.

He doesn't pause to think, doesn't brace for the impact, but allows the surge to take him, too. Wherever she's going, he'll follow and that's all there is to it.

The water tosses him off his feet. His head dips under but there is breath in his lungs. He kicks, breaks the surface, sucks in another lungful of oxygen. The sheer force of water isn't the only threat. Century-old trees have been pulled free by the deluge, and they are part of the charge. Roots stick up above the churning water with great clods of dirt still clinging to them. If Nic hasn't drowned already, one of those could crush her with as little effort as he might swat a fly.

The wolf is back at the threshold that separates man from beast, scrabbling to break free, to *find* her. The wolf can track her across the Abyss itself. Aiden grips a nearby branch and hauls himself onto one of the logs even as he tells the wolf he, the man, stands a better chance of catching her.

Maybe there is a way to use both skills.

For her, he will ask the creature that murdered his baby brother and destroyed his life. For her, he will beg the wolf whom the gods fear.

Help me. He pours his heart and soul into the plea. *Find her for me, for us.*

And he lowers his defenses.

He half expects the wolf to seize control, the way he's always done when Aiden can't fight him back. But instead, his eyesight sharpens, his nose is flooded with the senses of the night and he can feel *her*.

Our mate. The creature sends him an image of her along with all the sensations he associates with Nic. It's a cornucopia of tiny details that make up a unique being.

With the wolf's guidance, the bond becomes a living thing. Not just a general idea of where she is, but a part of her, a part of himself that throbs and pulses with a life of its own.

Aiden fixes those details in his mind. He breathes in, sorting through the microbes of newly disturbed soil, decaying leaves, rotting wood, and fresh sap. And there, about twenty yards ahead of him he spots the icy blue of her undergarments and the paleness of her skin reflects in a shaft of moonlight.

She isn't moving, isn't flailing or trying to grip a hand-hold. Her small form is so still, lifeless. He shakes the disturbing thought away and then stands. With the wolf's assistance, his balance is more stable, his grace preternatural.

He leaps. One moment his feet are on one tree, then he's in the air, a scattering of sparks drifting above the surging river. Though he is weightless he has no control over the speed in his fire form.

Hurry. The wolf is still with him, anxious as he is to reach her.

Up ahead there's a sharp bend in the river, a great granite outcropping with a few trees growing out of the side, the knot of their roots exposed. He senses her movement halt. Either she grabs onto the roots or her limp body is tangled within them. He's been given a chance to catch her.

He makes for the bank, reforming on the outermost tree. Six feet below him he sees her, eyes open, small fists clinging for dear life to an exposed root.

"Nic," he shouts even as he clambers down through the snarl of roots and dirt to her. "Hold on, I'm coming."

"Trying," she gasps.

"You're doing great." Her strength amazes him, her training making her stronger, more capable. But she is mortal and her strength is not infinite. Her lower half is still in the water. The pull of the current demands its due. It tugs her almost horizontal, greedy, insisting she continues to travel with it.

There is an odd feeling to the water, a presence of sorts. Could this be Wardon's work? The Master of the Waves is capable of redirecting rivers and lakes. Yet the congealing essences don't feel malevolent so much as intent. The river must go somewhere and pity to those who have the misfortune of being in its path.

"Almost there." Aiden's gaze locks on Nic as he navigates through the massive network of roots.

"Hurry," Nic gasps.

The note of panic in the one word has him glancing down. She isn't looking at him, but rather a massive tree that is on a direct collision course with her.

His heart stops. The thing will crush her beneath its weight.

She looks up at him, back to the doom barreling towards her and then once more at him. Her eyes meeting his, blue and bright with unshed tears. A calm seems to wash over her.

"No!" Panic grips him at that look. Terror for her urges him to get to her, to save her, or at least to take the blow for her. The tree won't kill him if he can just *reach* her. Sparks. He can come apart, then mold together grab her and they'll drift out of the river. There is no time.

"Aiden, I can't." He hears tears in her voice.

Somehow, he's become hopelessly trapped within the roots. He starts ripping at them, uncaring if he goes plunging into the water. "Don't even think it. Just give me time!"

"Aiden," she sniffles and then, with the ring of command in her voice orders him, "Stay safe."

"No," he bellows. The wolf is frantic, clawing at him, begging him to do something. But his muscles freeze in place. She can't be doing this to him again, not now. "Don't make me watch you die!"

"I'm sorry," Nic releases her grip.

The river swallows her up.

CHAPTER 19

AMONG THE RIVER SPRITES

I come to with lungs burning, a stab of fire in my side and the urge to vomit. It isn't a conscious decision to roll onto my side and expel what feels like half the river onto the solid ground beneath me. I cough and choke and wheeze, trying desperately to replace water with air. Pain makes the world around me hazy.

Ground. There is dirt beneath my cheek. My shallow breaths bring me the rich scents of soil and the sweet decay of falling leaves. I hear sounds too. The patter of rain on leaves and somewhere not too far off, the rush of water.

I don't think I'm dead, no matter that I'd intended to die when I let go of that branch. I flinch away at the memory of Aiden's devastated expression when I'd ordered him to stay safe. Though I stood a better chance in the water than against that massive tree, I still hadn't expected to survive.

Yet survive I did. Somehow.

For a long while, I don't move. Maybe I can't stay curled in the fetal position forever, but the will to get up is nowhere nearby. Slowly, I crack one eyelid and take in the world around me.

The ground beneath my damp cheek is different than what we'd been trekking across. It feels alive, hearty. As if to illustrate my point, two squirrels scurry across the forest floor, retrieve an acorn apiece and scramble up a nearby tree. More proof that I've left the Desolate Realm behind me. The land *feels* different. Like it's ready to yield life, not steal it away like a thief in the night.

The leaves beneath my prone body are all rich reds and gleaming golds, fiery oranges and earthy browns. Tentatively I reach out and grasp a handful of them. They aren't dried out and crunchy but soft, newly fallen.

Autumn is here. Wherever here is.

Panic grips me. Has Samhain already passed in the mortal realm? Time moves differently in Underhill. Am I too late for the gauntlet?

"Be at ease," a soft feminine voice chirps. "Time is still with you."

"What? Who?" Heedless of my battered body, I surge upward, the colorful world around me tilting precariously. I hadn't realized anyone was nearby.

Idiot. Who do you think pulled you from the water?

I brace on all fours and close my eyes, praying that everything else will quit moving if I do.

"Who are you?" I shift very slowly.

I hear whispers, soft and low, no words discernible.

"My name's Nic," I say, offering up a piece of information in the hopes it'll coax my rescuers into doing the same.

"We know who you are, Queen of the Shadow Throne." It's a different voice, masculine and richer in tone than the first. "The river brought you to us."

"Oh. Well, thank you for saving me." I chance cracking an eyelid and when nothing moves, I open both eyes.

There before me is a cluster of gray-skinned beings. They have large gray eyes the color of storm clouds and hair paler than my natural blonde. All are naked and have three fingers on each hand, three toes on each barefoot with three joints apiece. Their odd coloring stands out against the brilliant hues of the forest.

"What are you?" I rephrase. The question sounds mildly rude, but there's no taking it back.

A male, older in appearance than the others, his skin sagging on his bones reminiscent of a soup chicken, steps forward and offers a small bow. "We are the last of the River Sprites. King Soladin has allowed us to dwell on the banks of this river since the time of your assassination."

Though I think I know the answer, I want to be sure. "To which court do you belong?"

"To yours, my queen." It is the female this time, the one who told me that I still have time. "The river sprites were once legion across Underhill and the mortal realm. One of us for every creek and stream, for where water flows downhill, a sprite is needed to see it reach its ocean home."

"And yet this is all of you that are left?" I take a quick survey at the small group. Maybe a dozen of them.

The older man nods, his expression grave. "Queen Brigit feared our numbers for only water can destroy fire. She imprisoned all those she could reach. We sought asylum with the Lord of the Land and we have sworn never to take up arms against him or his people."

I hear his unspoken message. That while they may have once been my subjects, their loyalties are divided.

"What's your name?" I ask the leader.

"I am called Fjord. This is my granddaughter Cascadia."

One by one, each of the river sprites steps forward, offering me a courteous bow, One, Wade, who seems the youngest and most curious of the group, actually darts forward to examine my hand. His gray eyes are huge in his face. He flashes me a quick smile before darting back into line.

"Come," Fjord says. "The harvest is in and tonight is a wedding feast for my eldest son and his new bride."

The thought of food has my gorge rising. No way can I stomach anything in my present condition.

"Are you injured?" It's Cascadia, her eyes luminous, who comes forward.

"My arm, I think it's broken." Normally I wouldn't admit the weakness in front of anyone, but with my backpack gone and no way to know when or if I'll make it back to Addy, I'll take whatever I can get.

"Have you asked Underhill to Heal you?" Cascadia bends down to my bare midriff to examine the injury.

"Dare airson aisling." I repeat the Gaelic phrase that Aiden had taught me. "I'm not so sure it's a good idea that I use magic right now."

But Cascadia is shaking her head. "You misunderstand. *Dare airson aisling* refers to a punishment or reward for wielding magic. But Underhill will provide a healing to her inhabitants upon request. Let me show you."

She holds her long pale hands out over my injured arm. She chants something, words I can't quite make out, but it seems a sort of tribal song with the chorus chanted over and over. I stare down at the ugly purple and blue bruise, the irregular shape lumps waiting for something to happen.

When it does, it isn't visible. No glowing light, like when Aiden's grandmother performed healing. No sparks of heat or flashes of color. One second I'm trying not to fall on my face in the dust and the next….

"The pain's gone," I breathe easy for the first time in days. "How did you do that?"

Her gray eyes twinkle. "I harnessed the energies of Underhill and directed them to mend your injury."

"Energies?" I poke at the spot where the bruising is fading to a little red patch of skin.

Cascadia's long silver hair billows in a phantom breeze as she nods. "They are always there, connecting all the fey and binding them to this place. Some, like myself, know how to focus them to accomplish some small healings. It's not magic, more akin to a mortal's faith healing."

"And there are no...unpleasant side effects from harnessing these energies?" If there is one thing I've learned about Underhill it's that the fey realm doesn't give without taking something in return.

Even though my question is for Cascadia, it is Fjord who responds. "You know about the laws of thermodynamics, do you not?"

"Vaguely," I say, wishing I'd paid better attention in physics class. "Matter and energy cannot be created or destroyed, only transformed."

"Correct." The wizened water sprite nods. "So long as what we do follows those laws, there is no price. It's only when we wish to do something that *defies* those cosmic mandates, to either create what isn't or destroy what is, that Underhill extracts her due."

That explains how Wardon had done so much magic. But then I frown. I hadn't created or destroyed anything when I'd brought that storm to shore. I'd just rerouted it. So, what was up with the hormone overload?

Ignorant to my shifting focus, Fjord beckons me forward. "Now come, you'll wish to prepare for the wedding feast."

With my broken arm no longer my top concern, I realize that I am all but naked, standing in front of a bunch of bare-assed strangers in nothing but a lacy bra and matching boy shorts. "I don't suppose my clothes or pack washed up with me?"

This inquiry is received with blank looks all around.

Head still swimming, I cast a glance back at the river. "While I appreciate your help and the generous offer, I need to rejoin my companion as soon as possible. He got caught up in the flood with me." The grief and fear in Aiden's eyes as I let go haunt me.

"We will send a search party to find him," Fjord says with absolute conviction. "Be at ease, my queen. Your journey will resume when the time is right."

I open my mouth to argue, then close it again. Aiden, or at least the wolf, would be able to track me as soon as he manages to escape my command. And Fjord said we are in Soladin's lands, the same place where Bard, Harmony, and Nahini were headed with the dead of the Wild Hunt. In the wake of the Healing, bone-deep weariness seeps in. I'm tired of running, of chasing after something or someone. The river sprites are fey, they can't lie. They've already saved my life, treated my hurts. They are my subjects. I'm as safe in their midst as I would be anywhere else in Underhill.

"Cascadia," Fjord holds out an arm to his granddaughter. "Bring our queen to the women's house and see she has what she needs."

"Yes, grandsire." She offers me her three-fingered hand. "My queen?"

After only a brief hesitation, I take it. The tri digit grip feels odd but reassuring. She dips her head and pulls me forward through the autumn woods. Behind us, the rest of the river sprites scuttle back to whatever they'd been doing before finding me on the riverbank.

Outside of the Hunt, I haven't met any of my Unseelie subjects before and am curious about them. In the distance I can hear the sounds of hammering and sawing. "I've never seen a fey age like your grandfather before. Is that typical of your people?"

"No." There's a small smile on her lips. "Grandsire gave up

his gift of immortality when he wed my grandmother. She was mortal."

A fey married to a human? "He must have loved her very much to sacrifice his youth."

"Grandsire says that he gained much more than he lost. Have you found your forever one?"

"Ummm…." Eager to change the subject I ask, "What is it you all do for Soladin?"

"We help guide the rivers and streams to irrigate the crops and fell trees for the Seelie fey to use." She releases my hand and points with her three-knuckled forefinger to an oversized log building and a churning waterwheel. "See there? That is the lumber mill. Every fall we remove the trees that will not survive the coming winter and they are used to build homes and heat them through the bitter months. It is the same service we once performed for the Shadow Throne."

Wood for the winter. "I can see how that would be very useful." I hesitate a moment and cautiously ask, "Why is it that you didn't approach Wardon for sanctuary? It seems as though your gifts are more in line with his court than with Soladin's."

"We did," Cascadia says but doesn't elaborate further.

We walk on in silence, following a winding path away from the water. The sounds of life are all around us now, children laughing and playing. A dog barks. Another answers. The cracking of twigs beneath running feet and the creak of wheelbarrows as they are pushed down the street.

"It's a bountiful harvest this year," Cascadia murmurs. "Underhill be praised."

"You talk of the land the way some mortals talk about a god," It's a casual observation on my part.

She blinks as though I've surprised her. "Underhill is a

deity. To host life one must possess life in abundance, have the ability to create life, whether mortal or immortal. The Lord of the Land and his fey recognize this, that in order to thrive they must not try to master Underhill, but to live in harmony with her."

It sounds like some serious hippy woo woo to me, but I keep my mouth shut.

The town has the same semicircular layout as the town in the Desolate Realm. Three buildings jut out like spokes around what appears to be a marketplace. Dotted in between are smaller structures, though they are too small to be private residences. Cascadia leads me to the building on the right and several goggle-eyed girls follow us inside.

The women's house is a long log ranch-style structure with a thatched roof and window coverings made out of what looks like a steady waterfall. From the outside there's no way to tell what goes on within the space. Once we cross the threshold, however, I can see clearly out into the village center where food, fabrics and all sorts of other sundries are on display.

The building's layout is one long open room with several fires burning in rock pits dug out of the earth along the center of the walkway. The fire pits provide heat and light. Stalls with no doors align either wall stretching the length of the house.

"This is the women's house, for sleeping and communing with others of our gender. No male over six winters is allowed within these walls for any reason. You can have your pick of compartments. Most of them are empty." She gestures toward the stalls.

I step inside the nearest one. It's set up like cells in a Catholic convent. A single simple cot, a lone candlestick in a clay holder, an earthenware jug and washbowl on a low table beside the bed. A colorful hand-stitched quilt is spread across the mattress.

"So, river sprites don't sleep with your men?"

Cascadia looks at me as though I've lost my mind. "Why would we?"

"Boy, am I the wrong person to answer that," I mutter then retrench. "Do your people not marry? Where do the children come from?"

She picks up the empty jug and then turns to me with a frown. "From the water, of course."

Right. She had said something about a water sprite for every spring. "But don't your people...um...interact?"

"We share meals of course. And chores." Her manner is calm, implacable.

"That's not...oh never mind," My cheeks heat and I feel like a grade-A pervert.

Her face lights up with understanding. "Oh, you are referring to sexual coupling?"

I nod, cheeks flaming higher. "It's just if the men sleep in one space and the women in another then when—?"

"Whenever they wish, so long as it's not in the town green or the women's house. Even those who enjoy the same gender as their own are not supposed to couple in the sleeping lodges. It's unseemly around the young and inconsiderate of those who have lost a lover. The women's house is for companionship, for compassion and understanding. In the past, it was not uncommon for our elderly to not leave its sacred walls." She waits patiently as though in anticipation for my next invasive question.

Embarrassment outweighs my curiosity and I look away.

"Do not be ashamed, my queen. We do not expect you to know of such things any more than we would know how to rule the Unseelie. I will get you some water for washing." With one final smile, she backs out of the compartment.

Not wanting to soak the bed, I follow her only as far as the nearest fire and sit on one of the log benches. Cascadia's comment about knowing how to rule rings in my ears. The sad part is, I have no concept of how to rule the court. From what I remember of my past life, all I managed to do was whore myself out to a bunch of would-be Unseelie nobles, alienate Aiden and die leaving all those under my protection to the tender mercies of Brigit.

Is it arrogant to try again? To believe that I will manage to do better this time around? Royals are supposed to be trained from birth on court politics and procedures. I'd been taught to stalk and hunt and kill. Hell, I didn't even clean up after myself, that always fell to the Aunts. If anything, I'm *less* prepared in this life. I hadn't even known about the energy healing thing.

Aiden was right about my needing more education. Not just what I could learn in my mortal high school, but from life in general. I'd been sequestered by Chloe and Addy. Protected and kept ignorant, only brought out to serve my killing purpose.

Looking around the long space that is obviously meant for more sprites than there are, a deep weight settles on me like a blanket. These people needed protection, and where was I? Dead at Brigit's hands because I'd driven Aiden away.

Resentment coils inside me, a venomous serpent ready to strike. I didn't ask for this destiny, didn't want these responsibilities. If the path to the Shadow Throne involves assassination, maybe. But even if I did reclaim it and win the Fire Throne too, how would I rule? Every decision I've made to date has caused an avalanche of new problems. For myself and those around me.

I kill people, but I also hurt them. One I can live with but the other…

I shiver as their images appear in the flickering flames.

Aiden, Nahini, Freda and Jasmine, Chloe and Addy. The people in that apartment complex that the Valkyries had decimated. The river sprites, the few who survived. Any who called me Queen or support my claim to the Unseelie are in the line of fire and might die at any time.

I stare into the leaping flames, searching desperately for a way out but seeing the only answer I ever have…death.

Whether mine or theirs, I don't know.

AFTER WASHING, I bundle up in the pretty quilt and lie down on the narrow bed. Though all my worries still pressed down on me, I sleep deep and dreamless until just after sunset. The sounds of laughter and music float through the waterfall windows, beckoning me to come out.

Aiden? I call out with my mind. I can feel him nearby, at the edge of my consciousness, but he doesn't reply. I hope he's not trapped at the riverbank, frozen with the same look of horror he'd been wearing untold hours ago when I'd ordered him not to follow me into the water.

His agonizing expression haunts me. I should proceed out, see how wild the river sprites shindig will get. If only I had something to wear other than my pale blue undergarments. Then I spot the fabric lying across the foot of my bed. The dress is gold and shimmers in a ray of the late day sun. The cut is simple, just a knee-length sheath with spaghetti straps. It's elegant and the material is smoother than any silk I've ever felt as it slips between my fingers.

"Do you like it?" Cascadia peers at me through the open door of the sleeping compartment.

I trace the bodice which shimmers with an almost iridescent quality. "It's lovely. What's it made from?"

"Spider silk. It's a gift from King Soladin."

My head jerks up at her words. "He's here?"

She frowns at my obvious distress. "Not yet, though he sent word with the messenger that he will arrive midmorning tomorrow. Is something wrong?"

Only that the last time a Seelie king had given me a pretty dress, it hadn't ended well. "Did the messenger happen to mention if my traveling companions will be with him?"

That Soladin knows not only where I am but that I need clothing is telling. And though I don't know how far the river sprite village lies from the heart of the Seelie Court, I doubt word of my arrival reached him through conventional channels. No, more likely he's gleaned the information from a seer. Namely Harmony.

"He didn't say. Get dressed and you can ask him yourself." With a reassuring smile, Cascadia leaves me to ready myself.

The spider silk glides over my skin like a cloud. I would have expected it to be sticky, but evidently whatever the curing process is to make spider silk fabric, involves the removal of the adhesive. The fabric clings enticingly to my breasts and hips. Not wanting to reveal either bra straps or panty lines, I take my undergarments off and rinse them out in the basin, then lay them on one of the empty logs near the fire. I have no shoes, so I pad barefoot out into the town green.

In the time I spent sleeping, the village has morphed from common marketplace to an outdoor celebration. Like the other river sprites, the bride and groom are completely nude, except for garlands of autumn flowers braided into their long silver hair. It's almost impossible to tell age in a population that shows no physical signs of the ravages of time, but something about the male's expression seems...seasoned. Then again, with the tribe of river sprites being evicted from their homes and reliant upon a Seelie king, they probably all have a bit of experience.

"How old is your uncle?" I ask out of curiosity.

"About a century. His new bride is the first river sprite born of the Nile, an elder of our tribe. Several centuries older. She has been waiting all this time for love."

I gape at the ageless seeming woman. Old as the Nile River? She hardly appears it, laughing with her head thrown back. "Why would they wait so long?"

"Because," Cascadia says simply. "They weren't ready."

They may not be young lovers in rabid infatuation but they grin at each other in a way that makes it clear they are the newly married couple, his left hand bound to her right with a length of vine twining into what looks like a Celtic knot.

"Did I sleep through the ceremony?" I ask.

Cascadia shakes her head. "The ceremony comes later, at the claiming. The two wishing to become one bind their hands before all and at sunset, they will retreat into the forest to unite their bodies and sanction their union in the cradle of Underhill."

Heat scalds my cheeks. "You mean they are going out into the woods to have sex?"

"Of course. My uncle has already selected the place where he will claim his new bride."

"Maybe she'll claim him," I mutter and Cascadia laughs.

"I believe she already has."

I watch as the new couple strides off into the trees, three crows watching their progress interestedly.

Long log tables are covered with trenchers of food with even more passing between the beings milling about the green. A massive bonfire blazes in the center of the common area, directly across from the third log house.

And then there's the music.

It's a light tune, a song with no lyrics, just an enchanting melody that seeps into my skin, sinks into my bones until it becomes a part of me. The drumbeats make my heart pound, the flutes lift my spirit, the strings have my bare toes tapping. Fey dance about it in wild abandon. With a start, I realize there are more than just river sprites in the group.

Some have wings, others claws. Several are taller than the roof of the buildings, many more no larger than the acorns that lay thick on the ground. Green and gold, brown and red, they are the colors of the falling leaves, the colors of harvest. Twilight dapples the sky, the setting sun bathing the still clinging leaves and dancing people in a golden light.

There's something wild in the air, something that calls to a deeply buried part of me, a part that yearns to break free and run as fast and far as I can. To lose myself in the shadows of the night, to get lost in sensations, the music. To shut off my damn cold calculating brain and just *be*.

"It's like the revels of old." Fjord appears at my elbow.

I turn to face him, studying his expression. It appears almost wistful as he turns to me. "My granddaughter is too young to remember but there was a time when the fey revels were so exuberant the music could be heard across the Veil. The celebrations between the changing of seasons to mark the shift of power between the Fire and Shadow Thrones would go on for days."

"When did the others get here?" I ask, gesturing toward a mottled brown fey with horns.

"They've been arriving since shortly after you did. Most are from the nearby villages, though some have traveled from Unseelie lands to the North." He points with one of those three knuckled fingers.

The music is making it hard for me to think, to keep a clear head. "Were you expecting them?"

Fjord shakes his head. "No, but all are welcome. Word of you has traveled from the giant's keep to the west and in from Wardon's coastal cities. They come seeking the Queen of the Shadow Throne."

My lips part and I send a hasty glance around. Sure enough, several of the fey are staring openly at me. Under the scrutiny, I'm doubly glad I had another option than to emerge in my skivvies. "But why?"

"Because they want to make themselves known to you in hopes you will remember them." His expression is sad. "Would you care to address them?"

I shake my head. I can't stomach being the center of so much attention. Most of my work is done in the shadows, and there are rarely witnesses. Talking to a boisterous crowd of revelers, all of whom are looking at me with an air of expectation…just no.

Fjord appears disappointed.

I ask, "Has there been any word from the party you sent to search the riverbank?"

"No, but it's only been a few hours. I'll notify you the second they return."

"I'd appreciate that. Cascadia mentioned a messenger from the king. I'd like to speak to him."

Fjord glances around and then beckons Wade over. "The queen requests an audience with the king's messenger. Do you know where he went?"

Wade blushes. At least I think it's a blush, considering his gray skin tints with a blueish hue. "He was with some of the tree nymphs the last I saw."

"Were they dancing?"

The color grows even darker. "In a manner of speaking."

Fjord smiles and leans heavily on his walking stick, moving forward toward one of the tables. "To be young. Go and see if you can pry him away at his earliest convenience. And you," he says, turning to me. "You should dance."

"I'm not much of a dancer," I admit even as the song from

the revel fills me with longing. That pressing urge to be free in body and spirit gnaws at me.

Fjord waves my excuses away. "You are of fey blood. All the fey can dance, if given the proper motivation." He picks up my hand, presses it to his silvery lips and then holds it aloft.

Almost instantly, someone else takes it and whirls me out into the stream of dancers. I spin, shocked and exhilarated at the sudden movement. My partner, another of the river sprites, grins and twirls me again. I feel my hair fanning out, skirt whirling up and then he pulls me into the steps.

My feet find the rhythm all on their own and before I know it a laugh escapes me. My partner spins me once more and then hands me off to the next in line. This male is shorter, stockier and covered with some sort of blue-black pelt. His black eyes reflect the firelight and though he isn't as skilled as the river sprite, he guides me through the steps of the dance well.

I change partners again and again, losing myself in the madness, the whirling energy of the dance, high on the good-will emanating from the fey. I forget everything, my worries for Aiden and Nahini, Harmony and Bard and the Wild Hunt. The gauntlet, the forces warring over the Unseelie Court, the enemy I made in Wardon, the meeting between Rodrick and Soladin. None of it matters in the moment of absolute abandon.

Part of me feels as if I could do this forever, could so easily lose myself in the dance until I become part of the melody. The desire scares me but not enough to stop. *Just one more song*, I tell myself as I spin and dip, am lifted and traded. One more turn and I'll be done.

I recognize it for the lie it is, but the knowledge doesn't stop me from continuing into the next set of arms, the next smiling face.

"You're a fantastic dancer," The male murmurs in my ear. "My queen."

I beam up into his handsome face, feeling lighter than a feather, freer than I've ever been.

Until a fist crashes into the side of his skull.

CHAPTER 20

WHAT'S EATING HIM

"A iden," I gasp, relieved to see him, even if he is currently trying to shred my dance partner into sushi.

The two go rolling across the ground. Thank the gods that Aiden is still a man, for the wolf would rip the river sprite's throat out in the first minute. Then again, the wild look in Aiden's eyes tells me he'll gut the fey with his bare hands.

They tip a table over. Food and drink go flying and I decide enough is enough.

"Aiden, stop."

He doesn't.

Frowning, I repeat the command and am once again ignored.

The music cuts off with a screech of strings as the fight takes on a life of its own. The fey who were dancing moments before scatter like leaves in a gale before the grappling men. Desperate, I reach down to grip Aiden's shoulder, to pull him off and make him see reason before he kills the male, but he turns to me, teeth bared in a warning.

My heart lodges in my throat. The green eyes of the wolf glare back. Whether he wrestled control from Aiden, or the man gave it over willingly, I'm not dealing with a rational being. Instead, there is one who thrives on punishing those who cross him.

And the river sprite had just been holding his mate, whispering in her ear. Jealousy, as I've learned firsthand, is a harsh and demanding mistress. And the wolf exists on instinct. After days of travel, torment, starvation, and fear, Aiden's defenses are down. Though the fey and I didn't do anything more than talk, it doesn't matter to the wolf. A literal green-eyed monster had been unleashed.

And as long as there is a fight, he won't relent.

"Quit fighting him and bare your throat," I call out

"Are you insane?" The river sprite is streaked with blue blood, his gray eyes large with terror.

"Just do it," I bark. "Before he kills you."

He is barely holding the wolf at bay. I can see the sweat on his forehead, the shaking of his limbs. Aiden's green eyes blaze, his teeth gnash as he holds the other being down.

With a murmured prayer, the sprite lifts his chin and bares his throat in submission. A snarl creases Aiden's lips, his hands going to the other male's throat.

I lunge forward, wrapping myself around Aiden's bare back, holding tightly to him and praying I'm right. That the wolf isn't completely gone with bloodlust or hunger.

That deep down, he doesn't crave the kill more than he yearns for the feel of his mate.

Around us, the revelers are motionless, their faces masks of horror and fear. Do they know what Aiden is, what sort of threat he poses if he has a full-scale meltdown?

I can't think about that though. Instead, I tighten my grip on his chest and hold him close and repeat the only words that come to mind. "I'm here. I'm alive. No one hurt me. They won't hurt you, either. Aiden, can you hear me?"

"Yes," he speaks, his tone guttural and not wholly human. But at least I know he is listening.

"He's no threat to you," I tell him. "Let him go and come with me."

He inhales once, then blows out a long stream of air. He shoves away from the river sprite so quickly that I lose my grip on him and stumble back. Shoulders tense, he stalks up the hill, leaving the valley silent.

There is a collective sigh from the fey. As bloodthirsty and unforgiving as these beings are reputed to be, none of them relished the idea of a male being torn asunder during the party.

I glance down at the injured river sprite, waiting to offer him a hand but afraid to touch him. "How bad is it?"

"I'm fine." His voice quavers slightly on the word, but he stands and offers me a steady smile.

I pivot, but instead of following Aiden's trail, I veer toward the buffet table. Everything looks and smells delicious and my stomach growls at the scent of roasted squash, stewed apples, and fresh-baked bread. I load a trencher with food and then pick a secluded spot at the top of a nearby hill. Inconvenient enough that none of the fey will approach, near enough to call out for help in case I need it. I sit down with my back pressed up against a big spruce tree and take a bite.

Five minutes pass before he appears, holding, of all things, my backpack. I raise a brow in surprise that he's bothered to go back for it. He sets it down beside me and then steps away.

"Hungry?" I offer him the tray of food.

"Always." He doesn't make a move to take anything though. "You handle the wolf better than I do."

"I was lucky," I tell him honestly. "You really didn't want to hurt him."

"Oh, but I did," he breathes, surprising me. "I still do. For having his hands on you."

"It's not like that. You know I don't feel that way about anyone." I lick suddenly dry lips. "Why didn't you obey my command?"

Instead of answering, he reaches into the backpack and extracts a familiar glass vial. The one that held the potion his grandmother and her lover had made to break the bond that forces him to obey me.

My eyes go wide. "You took it?"

He nods but doesn't speak.

"Why?" He's been so adamant about not taking it, his honor demands that he uphold the oath he'd made to me when I was still in diapers.

He crouches beside me, his eyes still on the ground. "Did you know the Vikings believe oath breakers get a special sentence in Hel? Their bones fed to Nidhogg, the dragon at the base of the world tree. To be forever consumed by the great beast. I thought about that every time you asked me to break my oath. Swore I never would. And then you forced me to watch you die."

"But I didn't die," I whisper "Aiden, I'm right here."

He stares down over the hill toward the green. The music and dancing have started up again, the valley bathed in flickering firelight. But Aiden appears to see none of it. "I was livid. So angry it scared me. I'd been so afraid for you, imagined all the different ways you were injured or even that I'd find you dying. And after the relief of finding you unhurt faded, all I felt was the rage. Have you ever thought you should feel one way but instead, you feel another?"

"I am right now," I reply honestly.

He looks at me and waits.

"I've been bugging you for weeks to break that obedience bond. And now that you have, it feels like…."

"Like you lost something," he finishes for me.

We have, I realize with a pang. The bond hadn't just been about his promise to obey me. It had also been a tangible symbol of his trust in me. Trust that I wouldn't push him too hard, that I wouldn't use or abuse him the way so many others had done. That I wouldn't ask for more than he was willing to give.

The way I had done in my last life. And the way I had done when I ordered him to stay safe.

"I'm sorry," My eyes fill with tears. "I didn't want to break us."

He doesn't deny that I did. "So am I."

I sit, staring up at him while he looks down on the festivities. He's right there, inches away from me and yet he might as well be on the dark side of the moon.

"Have I ever brought you anything but pain?"

He scowls. "You know you have."

I think back to the easy mornings on the farm, the way he would slip into my room, wake me with a tender caress. Laughing and holding hands at school. It's like another person's life, a scene from a movie viewed long ago.

"Are those few moments of peace worth all this grief?"

"I don't see any other way—" he begins.

"You can leave. Without the oath, all that compels you to stay is the wolf. And without the oath, there is no way to stop the wolf if he decides to maim anyone who gives me a second look."

He turns to face me, his eyes glowing in the dim light. "You want me to go? I thought we'd gotten past this."

"This is different. I don't want you to go because I'm

scared of how you make me feel. I want you to go because I don't want to hurt you anymore. And that's all I ever seem to do."

His lips part.

"You're a god, Aiden. I'm mortal. We have history but no future."

He swallows, "After you go through the gauntlet—"

But I shake my head. "I'm not going to enter the gauntlet."

"What?" He frowns at me. "When did you decide this?"

He is beautiful there in the moonlight. His skin glows in the soft light, his hair blending with the night. He glows with health and vitality. And here I am, his Kryptonite.

"I never wanted to be queen. Or to be immortal. And I certainly don't want to be a bargaining chip for Wardon or any other power-hungry being that rears up."

"What about the Hunt? The Unseelie Court?" he asks. "You're just going to abandon them?" I see the real question in his eyes, the fear that lurks there. He doesn't have to ask it for me to hear the words. *You're going to leave me?*

I gesture to the valley below. "Brigit is dead, Wardon is M.I.A. I have yet to meet Soladin but I believe he is a good and decent ruler. According to the river sprites, he took them under his wing and protected them. For the first time in history, Unseelie fey are living with and working beside members of the Seelie Court. I'm not a unifier, not like that. You've seen the conditions most of them live in. Naked, half-starved without means to try for a better life. I have no idea how to give them any of that."

"You haven't even tried," he argues. "You don't know what you're capable of until you try."

But I shake my head. "I know how to stalk and hunt, to punish evil and rip it out at the roots. It's past time that I got back to that destiny."

"You don't want to rule. I get that. That doesn't mean you should send me away."

"I should because we don't have any sort of a future together, Aiden. You're immortal and I only have a couple of decades left. And I'm...toxic to you."

"You're not—"

"I am. I make you feel badly about yourself, put you in danger, give you nothing." I stop, overcome with emotions. "I don't want to gamble decades of my life for a chance at immortality. Judging from most of the immortals I've met, the price is too high."

"You're just going to go back to the farm and pretend none of this exists?" He shakes his head. "I don't buy it. What about the Hunt?"

"I'll negotiate on their behalf. Brigit is gone and come tomorrow I will turn command of the Hunt over to Soladin, on the promise that he never sets them on your trail again."

"You have it all figured out, don't you? One problem, you haven't even met Soladin and you're just going to turn over control of the most powerful force in the world to him?"

"I can't lead them without being queen. I don't have what it takes to be a competent ruler and I refuse to be a bad one. Not again."

"So that's it? You're just going to go home, drop out of school and spend the rest of your limited existence alone hunting rapists and murderers?"

"It's what I was born to do." I stare out over the distance and can feel his eyes on me.

"Nic—,"

"I'm sorry." I can't hold his gaze. Instead, I reach for my backpack and heft it up over one shoulder. "I don't have a choice."

"You say that, but it isn't true." He makes one more plea,

his voice thick with desperation. "Please, don't send me away."

Tears shimmer in my eyes. Real tears because I know this is the end. He reaches for me.

I flinch.

I see it there on his face, the shock and disappointment. He thinks I fear him now. It's what I intended, to see that light of hope flicker and die in his eyes. So why do I feel so wretched?

"Goodbye, Aiden."

Blinded by tears, I stumble down the hill until I'm inside my compartment in the women's house. Where is the relief I'm supposed to feel for doing the right thing? Aiden is officially free of me now, free to go out and live his immortal life in peace. No more sacrifices for a foolish mortal, no more trading his own wellbeing for mine. No more teasing or being used. Sure, he will have to wrestle with his wolf, but at least he'll be alive, thanks to my lie.

The gauntlet will kill me. It's a reality that is part of me, that is imprinted on my marrow. I don't want immortality badly enough to survive Underhill's test. And Aiden being Aiden, will do everything in his power to see me through the ordeal.

I won't make him watch me die. Or let him die for me.

The only choice he left me with was to reject him, to convince him I want my old life more than I want him. That I'm afraid of him.

To make him believe that I don't love him.

HOURS PASS but sleep eludes me. I toss on the narrow cot, the music from the fey revelry drifting in through the open door.

Is there anything worse than hearing the sounds of a party when you're miserable?

"Nicneven?"

"I go by Nic, actually." I turn and see her there, an unfamiliar woman.

"Who are you?" I ask.

Her smile is soft and a little sad. "I'm your mother."

CHAPTER 21

THE GAUNTLET

I sit up, my head reeling, unsure which of the million questions that are jockeying for position in my mind I should ask first. I don't know anything, how to feel, what to do, if I should speak or pinch myself or scream.

My *mother*? "You're my mother? As in, the woman who gave me life?"

"Yes." She nods, once. "At least I was in your immortal life."

Aiden had told me my mortal mother had died and I'd shut him down before he could tell me any more about my first mother.

The woman who this stranger claims to be.

I scrutinize her features, looking for something familiar. She doesn't look old enough, though as one of the forever young, looks aren't a true indicator. But she doesn't look like any sort of fey that I've seen. Her figure is voluptuous where I am small, her skin has an olive tint, her eyes dark as pitch. Long and unbound midnight hair, even darker than my dye job, falls to her rounded hips. Her curves are accentuated by the purple robe that falls to the arches of her sandal covered feet. The hem is stitched with golden thread. The garment is fitted to her form, belted at the waist by a length of golden cord. A far cry from my dirty, disheveled self. Of course, looks don't mean much in a world full of beings decked out in glamour.

"Are you fey?" My heart pounds in rapid succession.

She shakes her head, a small smile playing on full lips. "I'm as human as you, Nicneven."

"How did you find me?" *Where have you been all my life?*

She shakes her head, long raven locks tangling in the breeze from the open door. "We don't have time. I'm here to fetch you. You need to enter the gauntlet."

"What?" I blink at her as though she's crazy. For all I know, she might be. "I can't go now. Soladin will be here tomorrow, I need to meet with him."

She takes a step forward, reaching for my hand. "The Seelie king won't come to this place for a long time yet. Come, Underhill awaits."

Panic seizes me. The moment of decision is here. Do I want to be immortal, to reclaim the Shadow Throne badly enough to survive the trial ahead? The doubts that had been plaguing me for days break free. "I can't, I'm not ready."

"You've dismissed your court, done your best for them, correct?"

I nod.

"Then follow me." She turns and exits the compartment.

After the span of three heartbeats, I follow.

Every step is like a death knell. Who is this woman and why is she only appearing now? Why not come to my side a week ago, a month, or better yet, when I was six years old, on my own in the Black Forest?

I want to say something to her, something to fill the awkward silence. What the hell can I say, I'm not even sure I believe her. The fey can't lie, or shouldn't be able to. Yet

Brigit had. And this woman—I hesitate to call her mother—had said she was mortal, as I am.

So how does a mortal give birth to a fairy queen?

And it's not just her. My last exchange with Aiden haunts me. Regret fills me to the brim. I wish I could take it all back, all the things I'd said to hurt him, all the times I shut him down when he'd offered intimacy and acceptance. He'd suffered for me and I'd thanked him with lies.

She stops and turns her face up to the moon, the pale oval glows unearthly in the reflected light. "All will be well."

"And you know this...how?" What if I haven't learned enough? What if I'm missing some critical skill? I won't come out again. It hurts to swallow.

There is a rustle of skirts and then a soft hand on my shoulder. "Underhill has shown you mercy in the past, has she not? You are in her good graces."

"You speak of Underhill like she's a person." I gulp past whatever is lodged in my esophagus. "Is she?"

Her eyes are dark and mysterious. "She was...once."

"Will I meet her?"

"If you want it badly enough. Trust yourself."

I shrug her off, agitation zipping down my spine. The one I don't trust is her. Or Underhill for that matter. The fairy realm is both fickle and duplicitous and as for the stranger who claims to share my blood....

She brought a killer into the world. How trustworthy can she be?

"Are you ready, Nicneven?"

I tip my head to the side to take her in, curious in spite of my ire. "What do I call you?"

Her ruby red lips turn up. "I suppose mother is out of the question?"

"You suppose right." My tone is flat.

She nods, her smile a little sad. "You may call me Pharaildis."

"Pharaildis? All right then. Let's go."

The sound of the wind picks up. Her hair blows across her face. In the space of a heartbeat I'm standing in front of a door. It's painted with a white X.

Pharaildis removes her hand from my shoulder. "Feel better?"

Oddly, I do. Less fatigued, stronger. But I don't say anything to my companion.

Blackness surrounds us, no stars or lights, not even torches on the wall. There is no light source to speak of, but the door seems to pulse with a sort of living energy.

"Where are we?"

She nods to the door. "The entrance to the heart of Underhill. What lies inside is what we call the gauntlet. Once that door closes behind you, you will remain within until you find your own exit. Some never do."

"Why not?" I swallow hard. "What happens to them?"

"That's something that only Underhill knows. She will play with you as a cat plays with a mouse, she will tempt you and trick you into forgetting your purpose. You must be unbendable at the same time you are flexible."

"I have to want it badly enough." I blow out a breath and consider the door. "No one will tell me what's in there."

"Underhill's heart is full of secrets. She shares what she will with those she chooses. It's a trust not to be taken lightly."

I hear the warning she doesn't speak. "Why are you here?"

Pharaildis smiles, but it doesn't reach her eyes. "You needed an escort to reach this place. I volunteered."

"But why now? Why not approach me when I came to Underhill the last time? Or even a few days ago."

"I'm a servant of Underhill." Pharaildis lifts up her skirts, revealing the silver ankle shackles that tether her legs together. "I am not free to move about on my own."

"You're a prisoner?" I whisper and stare in horror at the chains. "For how long?"

"Since before you were born. You had a great destiny, to be Queen of the Shadow Throne. To rule The Unseelie Court for half the year. The ones who bound me took great care in hiding your origins from everyone. I never even got a chance to hold you." Regret is etched on her face.

I swallow thickly. "Who is my father?"

Her lips turn up in a sad smile. "You wouldn't believe me if I told you."

"What's one more unbelievable fact on the heap of them?"

Her chin lifts. "If you make it out the other side of the gauntlet and can find me again, I'll answer any questions you have."

I study her a moment. "Is that supposed to be added incentive?"

"Do you need some?" she counters. "I thought you were a survivor."

"I am." I take a deep breath and reach for the wrought-iron handle. "See you on the other side then."

Not waiting for a reply, I push open the door, cross the threshold and enter the gauntlet.

I'M NOT sure what I'd been expecting. Hellfire maybe, or giant slavering beasts barreling toward me like I am next on the menu. A horde of demons armed to their pointed teeth.

What I see instead is my farmhouse, bathed in the deepening shadows of a purple twilight.

"What?" I say, spinning in a circle. "How?"

But it really is the farm that surrounds me. All the leaves

have fallen from the trees and the branches revel naked in the embrace of the north wind. They click and rattle like dried finger bones, happy skeletons welcoming me home.

The air smells of snow, and I feel the charge, the excitement of the seasons changing. And something else. Smoke. A wood fire. Someone's in the house.

Just as I think it, a light comes on in the kitchen. I see someone moving around, rooting through cupboards. Home. I take two steps, eager to see if it's Chloe making a batch of her golden hot chocolate.

I frown and search the scene again, feeling as though it's a painting, instead of my real home. What's off? As the light falls and the shadows stretch like a great lazy cat, I consider the landscape again, trying to put my finger on it. There is definitely something off.

And then it hits me like a ten-ton anvil. No cluster of tents. No tethered horses, no baying hounds or screeching falcons. No sounds of laughter or battle, no sign of armor or weapons.

The Wild Hunt is gone.

"Freda?" I call out, hoping my second in charge will appear wearing her winged helmet and let me know they've moved the camp to a more secure location. That it's just over the next rise. "Jazz?"

No one answers. Not even the bark of one of Alric's hounds or the cry of a bird. I run for the house, not for cocoa and comfort but for answers. Where is the Hunt? Is this real, have I managed to cross the Veil somehow? Or am I caught in some illusion spun by the great spider that is Underhill?

The door swings open at my approach. I pause and, just to be sure, switch my vision to the spirit plane. I sigh in relief when I spy the white energy signature unique to my aunts.

"Chloe? Addy?" I call out as I cross the threshold.

But the woman inside is neither. Her back is to me and at

first, I see only the spill of golden hair. It flows in a molten river of golden curls. If I hadn't already checked her aura, I would have confused her with Freda.

Then she turns and looks at me with dead eyes.

"Little Nic, all grown up and deadlier than ever. Through no fault of mine." A dry chuckle rasps out.

I take an instinctive step away from the door. "Who...?"

The door slams shut behind me, the sound of the bolt being slid into place by invisible hands.

The Fate that is not one of mine moves closer, the white dress she is wearing covers her feet entirely. She makes no sound as she approaches in an odd floating motion. "Don't recognize me, do you? We spent so much time together."

It's the riot of blond curls that jolts awareness through me, what I'd once thought of as a lion's mane. Horror twists my gut. "Lachesis?"

"You always called me Sissy." Her lips are cracked and bloodless, like that of a long-dead corpse.

I want to deny it. To refute the crippling memories that have been creeping back, slowing me when I need to be fast, snagging my attention when my focus ought to be elsewhere. I want to deny her the satisfaction of knowing that she had any impact on my life. "What are you doing here?"

She ignores my question. "You should have stayed dead. Never come back, never challenge fate. What gives you the right to decide who lives and who dies? Are you a god?"

My head is shaking back and forth, tears threatening. "You're not real. You're dead."

She reaches for me with one hand the texture of shriveled apples. "Come now, Nic. You know that even death isn't as final as some believe. Especially in Underhill."

Swallowing past the tightness in my throat I ask, "Why are you here?"

"For good or ill, I represent your past. A past you must

come to terms with. Ask your question, the one that's setting your soul on fire."

My throat's gone dry. I have dozens of questions, hundreds. I understand so little. But only one has been dogging my steps, gnawing at me since I found out the truth. "Why did you leave me?"

She lifts her chin haughtily, a queen in her own right. "Answer me this. How many beings have you killed?"

I swallow. "Why?"

She tilts her head, waiting.

I count back. I can see all their faces. My victims. "Sixteen."

"Sixteen lives that you unknowingly claimed for the Wild Hunt. Sixteen souls who will never get to move on."

I'll be good.

It's not in your nature.

She walks around me in a slow circle and leans in to whisper, "I left you because I thought the world would be better if you weren't part of it. I left you because your wolf never should have brought you back. Your very existence tampers with the natural order I swore to uphold."

Each word is like a splinter shoved under my fingernails. I can't stifle the flinch.

She laughs and it isn't a pleasant sound. "Will you kill again to get what you want? Or would you choose to lie to me again."

I back away from her toward that locked door. "I only hunt those who hunt me."

"You make it sound so noble. As though you get nothing from the exchange, no pride, no satisfaction in murder. Tell me, you've seen those souls you recruit for the Hunt. Do you honestly believe they deserve such a fate?"

I stare at her, chin raised, hands clenched into fists. "Yes."

"A destiny of service. Is that to be your fate as well?

Service to Underhill and the fey? To kill for them instead of for yourself? You ran from this life before, hid from it. What's different this time?"

"I'm different. I'm not Nicneven. I wasn't born a fairy queen. And I have people who will help me."

"Truth. A boon then," Lachesis holds something up, something small, and coated with dirt.

My diary. The one I'd buried outside my bedroom window before Aiden and I had crossed the Veil the first time. Before I'd regained my memories.

"Your trophies." She extends the book to me.

The familiar cover sends a pang of longing through me. Not for the contents, but for what the book had once represented. My identity, whole and complete. I step back and raise my hand. "I don't want them."

"You may regret that choice." Her eerie eyes don't move but I can feel her searching my face. "Then what do you want?"

"Answers."

She waits.

"Did you ever regret it?" I will the words to come out sounding strong and sure, a queen's command. Instead, they are pitiful things. A child's broken-hearted plea. "Did you feel remorse for leaving me?"

She tilts her head to the side. "My only regret is that I couldn't bring myself to kill you outright. That I'd grown weak, as my sisters have grown weak. You are a monster, Nicneven."

I swallow. Exhale. Then look at her. "Maybe I am. But I'm the monster the Unseelie Court needs."

"Perhaps." Lachesis tosses the book onto the fire. The pink polyester fabric ignites and I watch the pages curl and blacken to ash.

"Why are you here Sissy?"

"You know that immortals cannot lie, not even to themselves."

"I'm not lying."

"So, you want to be imprisoned by your crown, your subjects? It was a life you detested before. Your time, your choices not your own. Is that really what you desire?"

It isn't, she's right. I'd been miserable for weeks, doing things I believed a queen should do. Practicing my weapons training, searching for the missing members of the Wild Hunt, going to school, trying to fix my mistakes.

"What do you want, Nic?" she repeats.

"To make it right," I say. "All the things that I've screwed up."

She moves closer. "What things? Be more specific."

"The tear in the Veil."

"The Unseelie queen of the Shadow Throne can repair the Veil. But why should that queen be you?"

I hunt through the landscape of my mind searching for the right answer. What should I say? What can I say?

"The immortals speak only the truth," I mutter. And if I want to become one of them, I have to do the same.

But telling her, this reanimated corpse of the Fate who'd abandoned me and left me to be raped and murdered, left me vulnerable. I never exposed a weakness to an enemy. To do so was foolish.

But she wasn't about to let me by without telling her.

I swallow and put it out there. "Aiden. I want to undo what happened with Aiden."

"And is the need to fix what's been destroyed worth the sacrifice of your own life?"

I swallow and choose my words carefully. "If I knew that he could live an untroubled life? Could get over his past and forgive himself for the things he'd done? Yes, I would make the trade."

Lachesis turns back to the fire. "Truth."

The fire leaps into existence, burning not just the logs in the hearth, but the mantle itself. Where the flames touch, blackness emerges, the deep void of starless space.

Lachesis, the measurer of life, points. "Go, before it's too late."

I take a step then turn to her feeling the need to say something. For all that she'd done, all that I've feared my past and the part she played in it, she was still one of my adoptive family. She'd known me as a child, is sister to my aunts.

"For what it's worth, I'm sorry for what happened to you."

Her dead eyes hold no emotion. Not regret or remorse. "I tampered with Fate. Don't make the same mistake if you wish to survive."

"Do you want me to pass on a message to them? To your sisters?" Her executioners.

She turns away so I can see only her ghastly profile. "Tell them…" Her tone is halting, unsure. Then she looks over her shoulder as though compelled. "Tell them, that I understand."

I blink. They'd killed her, their own sister. How could she possibly understand that?

"Go," Lachesis points. "Before it closes."

Shaking off the stunned sensation I look to where she's pointing. The burnt void is shrinking, collapsing in on itself. Is this how people get trapped? By ignoring the openings that will propel them through Underhill?

With a yell, I fling myself into the void…

And land with a bone-rattling thump on a floor of solid rock. The breath explodes from my lungs. Struggling upright, I study my surroundings. I'm in a cavern of sorts. Beneath me the unyielding icy stone. Water drips from rocks and the scents are musty. A far distant yellow glow is my only illumination, like torches flickering against the rock.

Then I hear the roar. It's a terrible, gut-churning sound.

Aiden.

I push myself up to my feet and follow the echoing cry of agony. It can't really be Aiden, can it? He hadn't entered the door with me, had been nowhere near me. Perhaps Underhill lured him inside to play some part in my trial.

There's no way to respond to that heart-wrenching cry.

I hear laughter then, male laughter and another of those roars of anguish. The shadows dance on the walls. I creep forward and with each step, the light grows brighter. The low murmur of voices and a hoarse shout. There is so much emotion in that sound and I feel it all with him. The agony, the shame and rage and fear.

I have a horrible feeling I know what I'm going to see when I find him. Find them.

Dread prods me on and I reach for a sword that isn't there. I don't even have my backpack, having left it at the women's house. I still have my Goodnight Kiss and whatever magic reserves are in my tank. It will have to be enough.

Skidding around the last corner and the vision before me is worse than any I've anticipated.

Aiden is bound by the wrists and hanging from a large metal hook suspended over an open pit.

He is naked, covered in dirt, bleeding from several gashes on his arms and legs. A few toes are missing. He's battered, bruised and at their mercy.

My heart stumbles in my chest like an old man tripping over a rock and crashing to the ground. He still has both eyes. Did Wardon escape Angrboda and recapture him? Or, even more unsettling, had Underhill somehow transport me back in time? I can smell the sea air, hear the crashing waves. This cavern is where he was kept by Wardon.

Where the trolls had mutilated him.

Correction: Were *going* to disfigure him.

Is this what my wish has wrought? The chance to protect him, to undo the horror that's been done to him?

That wasn't what I'd asked for. I'd wanted to fix what *I* had done to Aiden, in my last life. Give him closure. So why had the portal brought me here?

"Should we bring her down here? Would you like your girl to see you like this?" One of the trolls uncoils a long bull-whip from his shoulder, letting the thin end dangle free on the ground. It is coated in inch long barbs, the tips already glistening wetly in the torchlight.

Aiden doesn't answer. The whip-crack makes me jump but he barely flinches as it shreds the skin on his left shoulder, laying it open to the bone. A hoarse sound escapes his throat, raw and desperate. He's immortal, the son of a god. He'll regenerate. But knowing that doesn't make it any easier to watch.

Why isn't he fighting back?

Then it hits me. He thinks he's protecting me. Their threats, that they will drag me down here and hurt me the way they are hurting him. He believes that by enduring the punishment he is keeping me safe. But Aiden has the wolf on his side. If he wants, he could have brought the cave down around their ears and crawled through the rubble.

If he wants.

He thinks he deserves this.

I don't know whose voice I hear, it isn't mine, or Aiden's or even Underhill's. But it's sad, so sad it breaks my heart. And it's right.

Nari. Everything Aiden does, everything he's ever done has been to punish himself. The wolf the Norse gods had brought forth in him had killed his little brother. Nari's blood is on his hands. He may have feelings for me, but he doesn't believe he deserves any sort of happiness. That's why he stays, no matter how badly I make him feel. Not because I control him, but because he's using my indecision about our relationship as another form of punishment.

My heart hurts as I look at my poor wolf with new eyes. I want Aiden to live an untroubled life, a content one with someone who will treat him how he deserves. But he thinks he deserves…me.

Bile rises in my throat.

I'd been willing to die for that chance to fix the wrong I'd done him, the trickery. But seeing him like this, I know the truth of him. It isn't my fault, at least not all of it. Aiden will never live in peace, not until he forgives himself for the unforgivable.

Another crack of a lash and Aiden slumps into unconsciousness. My hands clench into fists. Anger courses through me, anger at the trolls, the gods and yes, at Aiden for not having a greater sense of self-preservation.

I've killed people. Ended their lives in the blink of an eye and tethered their immortal souls to the Wild Hunt. I've taken their free choice, their bodies, their spirits. At the time, I believed they deserved it, deserved me, because they hurt others. Many people will say that was wrong, that I am wrong to do it, to be judge, jury and executioner. But how many have I saved because I'd acted, used my gift to hunt and kill?

I'd had to learn to live with myself. Aiden needs to do the same.

The troll drops the whip—no fun flaying an unconscious man. He grips Aiden and the heavy chains clink as they drag him over the floor. "I know what'll wake him up." He removes a blade from his belt.

"You're sick, you know that, Dav?" The other laughs as though it's a great game.

Help him. The voice begs. *If you care for him, then stop this.*

The urge to retch increases. I want to, gods I want to kill

them both. To lay their corpses at his blood-soaked feet. I don't think I've ever craved a kill the way I do in this moment.

But then what? Sure, the trolls will be dead, and Aiden will leave this cave with both eyes intact. Yet if I really did travel back in time, my actions will affect the future. The bargain with Wardon, our escape from his lands. If I help him now without making Wardon's trade I might never get Nahini back. Even if I do, what would become of the tortured wolf? It's not like he'd go on his merry way or live happily ever after.

With a sinking feeling, I acknowledge the truth. Aiden will engineer a way to end up in this same situation time and time again. He will come back to me, for another hit of our toxic relationship because he doesn't believe he deserves better.

With tears blurring my vision, I turn away as the troll bends over by my poor wolf, prepared to blind him. And spy the portal in the door behind me.

I have to go, to leave him behind to be disfigured. If I don't, I'll be stuck here in this cursed place forever. But I can't just go without trying to help him.

Fight back. I mentally beg him. I have no way of knowing if he can hear me. If Underhill has transported me back in time to before Aiden broke the bond, he should be able to hear me. Then again, I can't hear him. I have to try though, to let him know I want him to fight, to end this. He got out of here before, and he can do it again. *Aiden, fight them. Kill them. You don't deserve this. Let your wolf out and fight back.*

There's a sound, like the shattering of glass as I run for the exit as the first hoarse bellow fills the small space.

It isn't until I'm through the portal that I realize what the sound was.

My heart, breaking into a million pieces.

CHAPTER 22

THE HARDEST PART

The landing is just as rocky with this passage, knocking the breath from my lungs. Keeping my eyes closed, I roll onto my left side and pull my knees up to my chest. I'm not even curious where Underhill regurgitates me this time or what horror I'll have to face. I want to bury my face in my hands and sob. I left him there. Left him to be mutilated. What sort of heartless monster am I?

"I'm sorry," I whisper, tightening my arms around my drawn-up knees. "I'm so *so* sorry, Aiden."

"Why did you do it?" A soft voice asks. A familiar voice. "Why did you leave him?"

Looking up, I spy the pale oval of a woman's face. She's slender and swathed from neck to feet in blue robes. Her face is lovely in an earthy, girl next door kind of way, with honey blonde hair and apple cheeks with a smattering of light freckles sprinkled across the bridge of her straight nose. But her deep blue eyes hold a well of fathomless sadness.

Pushing myself up, I wipe away the tracks of moisture with the back of my hand. "Who are you?"

"Tell me why." There's something desperate in her tone, a fierceness that one might miss at first.

Then I see what she's holding. A large wooden bowl. She holds it straight out over the prone form of a man bound by glowing chains. He's asleep, his chest rising and falling with a slow steady rhythm. His long red hair is a filthy mess of tangles, his clothing hardly more than rags. And above his head, directly above the bowl, a snake is coiled. A sickly yellow-green substance drips from the snake's bared fangs and lands in the bowl with a soft plop.

My lips part. I know this scene, have seen it depicted in my book of Norse Mythology. The punishment of the god, Loki.

"You're Sigyn." Disbelief courses through me, but deep down I feel the truth. "You're Aiden's mother."

"I named him Vali." She stares down into the depths of her bowl, sadness emanating from her. "But he no longer goes by that name."

My lips part. Her confirmation means the sleeping man on the slab is the trickster god himself.

She lifts her chin and glares down her nose at me. "I thought you were going to be different this time, that you care for him."

"I do."

"Then why did you abandon him to torment?" Her tone is condemning.

Suddenly, it's all too much. I stand and face her, my hands balling into fists at my sides, temper fraying to the breaking point. "Why did *you*?"

She shakes her head. "I must stay here."

My gaze focuses on her unbound legs. "I don't see any chains keeping you here."

"You don't understand."

"You're right, I don't. You chose to stay here. Stay with

your unfaithful prick of a husband. You're the one who let those other bastard gods drag him off to be killed. You decided that Aiden, who did nothing wrong, didn't matter as much as his father."

"Done nothing?" She stares at me, incredulous. "You know nothing about us, about our lives."

Gods, what is wrong with these people? "Maybe not. Just like you don't know anything about him, the man he is now so don't judge me for leaving him behind when you turned your back on him first. Do you know he blames himself for Nari?"

She looks away. "That wasn't his fault. I wanted to tell him when he came back for it."

"It?" I ask, not following.

She swallows visibly and chokes on the words. "Nari's heart."

The one that now beats in my chest. My hand raises up, covering the beating organ protectively. "It would mean the world to him to hear you say those words. He can't forgive himself. I can't save him until he realizes that he's worth saving."

"And you think he is?" She tilts her head to the side.

When I nod she glances toward her sleeping husband as another drop of venom lands in her bowl. "I couldn't have stopped them. The gods were too powerful, too determined. I couldn't protect them."

I stare down at the bound and sleeping Loki at the glittering chains made from Nari's entrails. The ones the Aesir had used to trap him. Eventually, the bowl will be full and Sigyn will turn away to dump it out. Then the venom will strike him. I can see the red blisters on his skin. Still healing marks from the last time she had done so.

"Okay, the past is what it is. Maybe you couldn't have done anything else. But you can now. Did it ever occur to you to go find him? To tell him that what happened to Nari wasn't his fault?"

She jerks her chin toward the bowl. "How can I leave him?"

"How can you stay? After everything he's done to you and your sons? All he will do? Aiden was an innocent. He's hurting. Go to him, convince him that he really isn't the monster he thinks he is."

"The wolf—" she begins, but I'm sick of excuses.

"Is an animal. It was scared after being bound to an immortal being. It lashed out as any cornered beast would. You can't blame it any more than you blame Aiden, yet you choose this bastard over your last living son."

She looks down, the hands holding the bowl are shaking. "I need him."

There it is. The same damn excuse emotionally abused women have been using to justify staying in shit situations since the dawn of time. Some people will blame the men for being bastards. And they aren't wrong. Yet the old adage is true —it takes two to tango. She could have easily left Loki to his miserable fate at any time. Left the trickster to suffer alone. And even as I detest her choice to put her faithless husband above herself or her son, I can't help but be impressed at her compassion. Is this where Aiden's undying loyalty comes from?

I swallow, looking around for my exit, ready to be away from this sad, sorry woman and her miserable existence. But the portal is nowhere in sight.

"Did you bring me here?"

She shakes her head "Underhill did."

"Why?" I stare at the inert figure on the stone slab with new consideration. From my reading I know that Loki will one day break free of his punishment, that he and his monstrous children will bring about the end of the world.

But he can't break free if he's dead.

I'm a killer. Lachesis asked me if I would kill for Underhill and the fey instead of just for myself. Did Underhill bring me here to stop Ragnorok before it could begin by killing the trickster?

And the bigger question is can I actually do it? Kill Aiden's father? With his wife, a goddess in her own right and a woman who's sacrificed everything for her man, sitting there watching me?

Would Aiden *want* me to? I didn't save him from the trolls, but maybe this would be a bigger, better sort of salvation. One that would stick.

But is it right, for me to kill his father? He'd spoken fondly of Loki. Said that he was a fun dad who had taken him and Nari fishing, taught them how to laugh. That laughter had been stolen from them both though because of the trickster's ambition. In Nari's case, forever.

Damage has been done, but is it the sort of damage I was sent to deal with?

Heart beating at a frantic pace I take one step toward the bound trickster god, then another.

He's brought this suffering on himself.

Sigyn's grip on her rapidly filling bowl tightens. "What are you doing?"

"Seeing if he's one of mine." Could I even kill a god with my Goodnight Kiss? I'd roll the dice if it means I have a shot at preventing the end of the world.

Yet as I study Loki's inert form, I don't feel the telltale pull that I do to the true monsters of the world. He may have sired the wolf Fenrir, the half-dead Hel, and the world serpent Jormungand and set events into motion for the twilight of the gods, but he isn't pure evil. He just…is.

I start when his eyes snap open, the same brilliant green

as Aiden's, and fasten on my face. "Release me, pretty dead queen."

Beside my Sigyn shifts her weight. Is she worried I'll free him? "Thanks, but I sort of like you where you are."

Those green eyes grow distant. "He is the beginning and the end, the slayer of all."

"Who?"

"The fire demon. He has but one purpose, to stand at the edge of the blaze clutching his fiery sword, and wait for the signal that Ragnorok has come at last. It will envelop the nine worlds, consuming the mortals and the dead, even your Wild Hunt. There is no escaping him. The fire will devour all. All that remains will be ash."

I stare down into those eyes and see it there, the hysteria, the madness. Was he like this before or did centuries of torture bring out the worst in the trickster?

Out of the corner of my eye, I spy the swirling vortex and move to catch it.

His hand shoots out, grabbing my wrist. "I have a riddle for you."

Pretty dead girl
How will you die?
First fire, then water
And the stab of a lie.
Pretty dead girl
What will you gain?
Knowledge is power
Unless you're not sane.
Pretty dead girl
Third time will do it
The wolf at your bosom
Will be sure to see to it.

I HATE RIDDLES, I really effing do. They're morbid and creepy and I'm just not a fan. The trickster must be losing his edge. Wolf at my bosom? Obviously, he means Aiden, means to sow discord between us. Why the hell is he calling me a dead girl? Sure, I died once, at the hands of Brigit, Queen of the Fire Throne. I know that. Okay, so there's fire. But water and a lie? Is it some sort of message about Wardon?

I study him. His is the face of a man who will watch the worlds burn and dance on the ashes. After tugging my wrist free, I turn back to Sigyn. Her expression is pure defeat, her bowl almost filled to the brim. The loyal, broken-hearted wife Loki hasn't even acknowledged. She knows what he is, what he will do. And she stays, bound to him as though she too is tethered by the cursed chains that had destroyed both her sons.

She will die for the sake of her love.

"Think about my offer," I say then throw myself through the waiting portal. Behind me, the ground shakes as Sigyn turns away to empty her bowl and the venom from the serpent drips onto the trickster god's waiting face.

THE PORTAL DEPOSITS me on a familiar hillside. The grass is brown and sports a thick layer of frost. The trees overhead are bare. The farm. I'm back where I started, or at least where I entered. Up ahead the water from the pond ruffles with the chill winter wind and the tire swing spins around and around as though it's been recently vacated. The spot by the pond, the one where I used to come to swim with Sarah.

The place where we buried her.

My gaze goes unerringly to her grave marker, the cross

made of grapevines. Jasmine had woven flowers through the vines and they'd bloomed all summer. Now though the marker appears as barren as the rest of the winter landscape.

I haven't been back since the funeral. Though not a day has gone by without me imagining coming here. What I would say to her. Deep down, I know the Sarah I knew is gone, that she's been reborn and has a shot at a happy life. It's only her body beneath the frozen ground, the corpse decaying.

Now that it's upon me, I still don't know what to say. So, all I can utter is the unvarnished truth. "I'm sorry."

"What for?" The voice comes from behind me.

I whirl around. Where a moment ago the swing had been empty, now there's a slender young woman seated within, smirking at me.

"Sarah?" I whisper. "Is that really you?"

"In the flesh, so to speak." She's wearing ripped skinny jeans and a leather jacket, though her feet are bare. As I watch she starts to twist the rope clockwise. "You didn't answer my question though. What are you sorry for, Nic?"

How is this possible? Is she really here? Are any of the things I've seen since entering the gauntlet real or has my mortal brain gone off the rails? "That you're dead because of me."

"No, I'm not. I'm alive because of you." When she can barely touch the ground anymore she lifts her feet straight out. Around and around she spins, head thrown back, dark hair whipping in the winter wind.

"I'm sorry I didn't kill your stepfather." I take a step closer to her, wanting to touch her, to see if my hand will pass right through her. "I could have helped you."

The rope twists past the neutral point but she continues to spin. "You did. Just by being there, by listening to me, helping me escape."

My hand goes right through her hair. She plants her feet on the ground, halting the swing. Tears sting my eyes. "I should have done something."

There's something in her eyes I don't recognize. Regret maybe? "Nic, it was my fault. All of it. I should have never taken Brigit's deal. You were a better friend to me than I ever was to you. That's why I'm here now. It's my turn to help you."

"Help me how?"

"I'm not fey, but neither am I an untethered spirit. I have a new body, it's about five months old. Though when I dream I can travel to places like this." She waves her hand around encompassing the hillside. "It's here I met Underhill."

"Met Underhill?" I shake my head in disbelief. Pharaildis had said as much but I hadn't believed her. "She really is a person?"

"Of course." Sarah shrugs. "Or at least she was. Now she's something more. And she needs your help, Nic."

"Is any of this real?" I ask, heart in my throat. "Or is it happening only in my mind?"

I'm praying she'll say no, that I really haven't met Aiden's parents, that I didn't leave him unprotected in the custody of the trolls. That the fey realm isn't asking for my assistance.

"All of it is real, Nic. Some of it has happened and other things are not to you yet."

I shake my head. "I don't understand."

She waves her hand at the mammoth oak tree and glowing symbols appear. "Do you recognize these?"

I stare at the glowing lines. "They look just like the ones in Addy's journal."

"They're Viking runes, symbols that passed from the gods to mortals. Only these particular symbols are lost. Sort of like the original Ten Commandments. The messenger destroyed them, believing them to be too powerful for mortal hands. Only your Norns and a few select gods possess the knowledge of them now."

I crawl to the base of the oak and trace a glowing line that looks like a jagged sideways A with my fingertips. "What do they mean?"

"That is time. See the way it branches? The choices we make create new branches. This," she points to what looks like a down-facing double arrow. "Is resurrection. Bringing the dead back to life."

"What?" I recoil before my hands can make contact with it. "Why would anyone want to do that?"

She offers me a sad smile. "Don't you want to go back, Nic?

I stare at her. "What do you mean? I'm not dead."

Sarah leans back in her swing, hair trailing across the barren ground. "That's what I said, too."

I Call a Do-over

I SCRAMBLE up and back away from her. "I can't be."

She sits up, a sad smile on her lips. "How did you get out of the river, Nic?"

"The water sprites…" I begin.

"Are all dead. Why do you think you stopped hearing Aiden's voice in your head?"

I shake my head. "He took the syrup. Broke the bond."

She rolls her eyes. It's such a Sarah move that I almost laugh. But there's nothing funny about what she's telling me. "Do you really think he would do that?"

My lips part.

"Think about it. That Aiden, the one who attacked the river sprite? Didn't he seem…off to you?"

"Yes, but he's been through a lot."

"You mean you put him through a lot."

Can't argue with her logic there.

She pushes off the ground easing the swing into gentle rocking. "You died right in front of him. Let go before he could get to you." She waves her hand and a bubble rises from the icy pond. Inside it, I see an image of Aiden reaching for me as I release my grip on the branch and fall into the water. The juggernaut of the downed tree barrels toward me, crushing my body against the rocks.

A slick of red melds with the inky blackness of the frothing river and Aiden screams, tearing himself free of the tree roots so he can dive in after me. There is no sound, no change for several minutes and then he surfaces, dragging something up out of the water.

My lifeless body.

His eyes are wild, his motions jerky as he hauls me to the shore. I can see steam rising from his throat and his hands are everywhere, desperate to fix all that is broken in me.

But he can't. I was born mortal and my body is too fragile. I'm not just broken, I'm pulverized, unrecognizable.

An unearthly sound tears from him, and the ground quakes as he bellows in fury. The same way it had for his father. His sharp claws punch through his fingertips and he shreds his own skin, great gashes opening across his body as he tears at himself as though he can claw the hurt free.

"Stop," I turn away, unable to witness his grief. He'd lost me again. Had watched me die. And now there is no sacrifice he can make to bring me back.

My heart is pounding and bile churns in my stomach. "So much has happened since then. The river sprites, Aiden, my mother. How could I have all these memories if I'm dead and they didn't happen?"

"Everyone you've met since that moment is dead, Nic."

Tears sting my eyes. "No, Aiden can't be—"

"I told you, time moves differently here. Some of the souls you've met are at this moment, alive like I am. Like Aiden is. We enter this place with our unconscious minds. That's why he was different, you were dealing with the seething angry inner Aiden, the one he tries to hide from you. The unconscious self has no filter, no social etiquette. When we wake, we will continue on their path. Our interaction with you nothing more than a vivid dream. Aiden will awake from his nightmare of you and dismiss it as a figment of his imagination. The bad news is, he'll be waking to a world where you are dead."

"And the others?" Like the river sprites, like Sissy. And like me. My knees start to shake. "How?"

"All you need to know is Underhill pulled your mind into the gauntlet before your body died. That's why you can see the dead, why you can talk to them in your mind."

I need to sit down. Can it be true? Am I really dead with my consciousness preserved by Underhill somehow? "Why would she bother?"

"I told you, she needs your help. You had to learn some things. That's why she's been moving you around, testing you, preparing you for what's to come."

"Like what?" I ask.

Sarah answers my question with one of her own. "What have you learned?"

I swallow and think about my trials. Seeing Lachesis, realizing why Aiden had let himself be hurt, not killing Loki. "I can't control it, any of it. It's not just about what I do or don't do. Other people's choices impact the outcome."

She nods. "There's a difference between leading and controlling. You have to set an example, not dictate."

I stare at the glowing runes. "Can I go back then? Will Underhill still make me immortal?"

Sara's bare toe points to a branch on the jagged A rune.

"Here is where you made your choice to let go. And here," she indicates a branch further down the letter, "Is now."

"Can I see them?" I whisper. "Like the way you showed Aiden to me."

Sarah's smile is knowing. "Wondering if they're not all better off without you?"

I'm having a rough time swallowing past the lump in my throat. "Are they?"

She waves her hand again and another image rises from the water. Freda on horseback, her blonde braid trailing from beneath her winged helmet. She's riding through a field alone and from the way she's bent down low on her horse's back it appears as though she's in a hurry.

"Why is she alone?" I frown at the image. "Where's the rest of the Wild Hunt?"

"Dead."

"Not possible. Freda would never just abandon them."

"She's on a mission, her last."

I swing my gaze to her. "What, how?"

As I watch, a wall of fire billows out from behind Freda. She hunches low in the saddle. Her horse flies over the ground but even the mighty steed bred for the Wild Hunt can't outdistance the wave of flames. With a mighty surge, the fire overtakes her, burning all in its path.

In its wake, there is only ash.

"No," I breathe.

The scene changes and I see the aftermath of a terrible battle. The sky is nothing but a wall of ominous black clouds and bodies litter the scorched landscape. Trees jut from the ground looking like burnt toothpicks. The only bit of color is a spot of brilliant flame, the man wielding it has hair of the same red gold. Loki, he's free.

"Ragnorok." The word falls from my bloodless lips.

Sarah nods. "The end of the world."

My stomach twists but I need to know. "What about Aiden?"

She points, wordlessly as a wolf charges from the trees, hurling himself at Loki.

He never makes it. An army of corpses rise up from the ground, their bony hands gripping him. He snaps and twists but the horde is relentless, pulling and tearing at him. On a distant hillside, barely distinguishable stand two figures with swirling silver eyes. I gasp, recognizing Chloe and Addy. "Why aren't they doing something?"

"The Norns can't interfere with a set course. You know that." There is an edge of resentment in her voice.

"Stop," I breathe but he can't hear me. He yelps in pain as the hands seize him, but continues his hopeless fight, snarling, and tearing. The light of hatred in his eyes winks out seconds before the corpses' hands tear him apart.

A tear slides down my cheek as his blood coats the dead earth. There'll be no regenerating from that. He's dead.

High above his father's laugh of madness rings out across the barren landscape as his army continues to rip his son to pieces.

"Turn it off," I bark, sickened yet unable to look away from the horror.

"There's more you must see" Sarah's tone is light but insisting.

A demon emerges from the mist, and beside him a great wolf. Fenrir. At the edge of the massive plane, a wall of water crashes to the shore, the writhing shape of the world serpent rearing up. To stand by its hideous family.

Then the rainbow, a blaze of color in a now colorless world. They're coming, the gods of Asgard. Odin to die in Fenrir's massive maw, Thor to kill and be killed by the world serpent. Heimdal and Loki to destroy one another. They're coming to stop the inevitable, to face their own doom. It's fate, playing out the hand it was dealt.

But my gaze reverts to where Aiden fell. I know Death in all her forms, but never has seeing her in action felt so final. Why hadn't he waited for the gods, worked with them to stop this?

I must have spoken aloud because Sarah turns to me, her lips a rueful smile. "You know why."

I did. "Because the gods used him, cursed him with the wolf."

"Maybe if he had a fey queen to talk reason into him, he would have waited. But Aiden has been set on this path since the moment you died."

Mercifully, I can't see anymore because my eyes are full of tears. He can't die like that, alone, fighting an unwinnable battle. At his own father's command. I round on her. "This hasn't happened yet. Tell me I can stop it."

She does a palms-up gesture. "It has happened. It will happen. There's no stopping it."

"Then why show it to me?"

"Because all is not predetermined. Some things can be changed. Your wolf isn't marked for death, he *chose* it. Because he lost you." Her lips turn up in a slow smile. "But it doesn't have to be that way. You can change things, for everyone."

"Great, one problem though. I'm still dead."

She points her toe to the glowing runes on the tree. "If you intersect this rune with the other, you can go back as an immortal, at the moment of death, if that's what you want. Careful though, if you only use the resurrection rune you will become Draugar."

"Draugar as in Viking zombies, guardians of the grave who move with the mist and can grow to be the size of a house?"

"Or larger," Sarah adds. "And let's not forget that Hel is the one in charge of them."

I grimace. Aiden's half-sister is one of Loki's three monstrous children and guardian of the ignoble dead and the gloomy world that holds them. I doubt she would be kind to me if I accidentally fell into her service.

I stare at the pulsing runes. "And if I don't? What happens if I don't go back?"

Her toe drops back into the dirt. "Then you can go on. Become part of the Veil or be born again, the way I was. Ragnorok will happen exactly as you foresaw."

My heart pounds. "So, it's either reclaim the Shadow Throne or leave everyone I love to their fates?"

She nods. "This is the hardest part. You get to choose what path to take. This one," she points to the lower branch on the A "Onwards to rule the Unseelie Court of Alba and witness the end of the world as you know it or this one," her toe moves to the higher branch, "To whatever awaits."

I swallow. "If I go back, will I die?"

"All things die. But you get to choose how you want to live. This is your time, Nic. Consider all your options carefully."

I let out a breath. If what Sara is saying is true, Aiden had already felt my loss. Our bond is broken not because of his choice but because of mine because I'd let go. And his self-destructive course would see him ended in that horrible way. But the question is, can I stop it? Can I convince him not to make that suicidal run that will end in his being torn to pieces?

"One more thing," Sarah says gently. "If you choose to go on, you won't remember any of this. Not your life as a fey queen, not being a teenage serial killer. Nothing. You have a true *La Tabula Rasa*. A blank slate. No more Goodnight Kiss or fey powers. No more deep secrets or bodies to bury. A simple human life."

Could I move on, let my soul serve another purpose? It sounded restful. No more hunting. No more killing. No more being asked what to do, having people turn to me for answers I didn't have.

No more Aiden.

Did I want to go back badly enough?

Sarah is winding the swing up again. "Think about it Nic. Cookie dough and quinoa and top ten on the radio. Maybe we can be friends again, grow up together, go to the same school, have sleepovers and stream old episodes of *Star Trek* on Netflix."

I pull a face. "You almost had me until that last part."

She meets my gaze. "No, I didn't."

"No, you didn't," I agree with no little regret. "I want to go back."

She nods. "You love him that much?"

I shake my head. "It's not about him."

"Stubborn to the last. Is that why you leap at every chance to leap on him?"

"I don't—"

"Don't bullshit me. You were all over him in Wardon's sandcastle."

"That was Underhill. The price for using magic."

Sarah looks at me as though I'm incredibly naive. "Cascadia told you there is no price for using your own natural gifts. And yet you practically tackled that wolf."

My lips part. Is that true? Had those feelings been mine alone? "But why did it come over me all of a sudden like that?"

She shrugs. "Probably because you've been repressing those urges. You always were the Ice Bitch."

I roll my eyes, though my stomach flutters.

"Take it from me, babe. Lie to others, but never to yourself. Do you really think you would have run into a burning building for just anyone?"

She lets go and the swing starts to spin. "This is our last goodbye. Don't forget me, Nic."

My throat's gone dry. "I won't."

But the swing is empty once more and I'm alone in the clearing.

I turn back to the tree, where the glowing runes wait. With one hand I touch the point she indicated, the moment where I died. With the other I reach for the second symbol, the downward-facing arrow.

My hands connect and there is a bright flash of light and the clearing is empty once more.

"DON'T EVEN THINK IT. Just give me time!"

I hear his voice first, the pleading in it. Then the cold registers, the water icy and rushing past the lower half of my body. My arms burn where I hold on to the tree roots.

I look upstream to where the massive tree is barreling toward me like a freight train.

It worked. I've been here before. I died here before.

Not this time.

"Don't let go!" He's frantic, green eyes glowing with a wild light. "Nic!"

"I won't," I swing back and try to pull myself further up, to reach for his hands. I'm stronger than I remember being, but not strong enough to break free of the current. "Hurry!"

He doesn't respond but in my mind, I sense his panic, his determination and almost sob with relief. It's back, our bond is back, clear as a bell and stronger than ever.

And I'll be damned if he will watch me die again. Some things I can't change. But this I can.

No consequences for using my own gifts. I fling out my hand and a gust of air rushes from me, sending enough force to stop the log in its tracks. It spins there in the current not five feet away.

"Gotcha," Aiden grunts as his hands close over my wrist. He drags me up through the snarl of roots, just as the air disperses and the log crashes into the space my body occupied seconds before. "Damn, that was close. Woah."

The last is in response to me throwing my arms around his neck. "Aiden!"

"It's okay. I've got you—" The last of his sentence is cut off because I seal my lips over his in a ravenous kiss.

Not just a kiss, I *devour* him. My hands are in his hair, my body pressed flush against him and my mouth claims his. Nothing held back, every feeling that I've experienced since encountering Aiden is right there, out in the open at last. I can't get close enough. I can't help but absorb him like air and water and all the good things in the nine worlds.

To his credit, he doesn't waste time asking stupid questions, like what prompted my sudden desire. His arms band around me. Holding me close, his hands gliding along my back, following the bumps of my spine. The heat from his body radiates through my soaked underwear, warming me, igniting the secret heart of the Ice Bitch.

The way only Aiden can.

"Sorry to interrupt," A droll voice says from not too far away. "But I just threw up in my mouth a little."

I'd know that snide tone anywhere. "Freda?"

It's her, winged helmet gleaming in the moonlight, *Seelenverkäufer* strapped to her hip.

I scramble upwards and behind me, a naked Aiden does the same. I throw my arms around her, feeling a bit like

Ebenezer Scrooge getting a second chance to find the people who matter and make amends for past misdeeds.

"Ummm...?" Freda stands frozen in place.

"It's so good to see you," I tell her.

"You as well, my queen."

I step back, grinning like an idiot up into her confused face. "Freda, for the love of the gods, call me Nic."

"All right my—Nic. Forgive the delay. We would have come to you sooner but I had word that the Unseelie forces are congregating outside the underground palace."

"Word from whom?"

"From me," I turn and spot the Spriggan.

He kneels down, head bowed low. "Forgive me for leaving my post unguarded. My father—"

"Get up," I haul him to his feet. "It's okay. I understand."

Alric frowns. "You do?"

I nod. "It's your sister. You had to go."

A wave of dizziness washes over me. I see the underground castle, the seat of power of the Unseelie Court. And bodies withered to husks. Heaps of them, piled everywhere.

No longer a palace but a tomb. My knees buckle.

"What's wrong with her?" Freda asks as Aiden catches me before I can face-plant in the dirt.

I swallow, my gaze going unfocused. On the far side of the river, I see Cascadia, Fjord, and the rest of the river sprites. The light around them is an unusual golden hue. Cascadia blows me a kiss and the wind seems to sigh her message for me alone. "Don't forget us."

I blink down at my palms, at the two runes that have been inscribed there. Time travel and resurrection. The conversation with Harmony comes back to me. *The ability to see the future is earned, not bestowed...crossing into the underworld and returning...you have to die to earn it.*

And then there's Loki's poem.

Pretty dead girl
What will you gain?
Knowledge is power
Unless you're not sane.

HAD IT HAPPENED? Had any of it really happened? Am I seeing the dead because I'd been among them? Or am I losing my mind?

"Nic?" Aiden's tone is full of worry.

"I'm okay." The lie tumbles easily from my lips.

Sarah's words. *Lie to others, but never to yourself.*

My chest feels as though it's been hollowed out with an extra-large melon baller. "We should go home."

Freda draws her sword and slashes a hole in the Veil. Beyond I can see the farm, the farm I had left in early autumn, not the one from Underhill where I'd run into Sissy. Into Sarah. Where my mother had deposited me.

Unless you're not sane.

Aiden makes as though to carry me but I shake my head. "I can walk."

He squeezes my fingers in his and I have to fight to keep my expression calm and neutral as I recall the final lines of his father's eerie ass poem.

Third time will do it. The wolf at your bosom will be sure to see to it.

CHAPTER 23

HOME SWEET HOME

The sounds of home surround me. The wind in the trees carries the scents of turning leaves, apples ready for picking, dust and pollen so thick it clogs the sinuses. Fallen acorns crunch underfoot as we stride up the hill to the farmhouse. Distantly I realize Freda is talking.

"The traitor Rena was captured. She's the fey who was guarding the tear when the Valkyries crossed into our world. I have her confined in the barn. I've questioned her but thus far she refuses to speak."

I'd forgotten all about the traitor. "Good. That's good."

"Nic are you sure you're all right?" Aiden places a solicitous hand at the small of my back.

It's a gesture of support, but I can't stifle the flinch as his hand connects with my bare skin. I try to cover it with a smile. "Just cold."

"Let me take you directly to your room." He reaches his other hand toward me, clearly intending to shift us to sparks.

"No." The last thing I want is to be alone with him. "That is…um, I need you to watch the fairy hill."

He frowns. "What?"

"Yes." I nod, warming to the idea. "If Alric is right and the Unseelie are massing an army to march on us, you can get back here faster than anyone else.

He stares at me for a beat and I keep my fingers crossed, hoping he won't question my motives for wanting him gone.

"As my queen commands." Aiden nods in acknowledgment then shifts to sparks and drifts away on a gust of north wind.

"Alric," Freda snaps. "Since the queen's been so generous as to not have you punished, you'd best go look after your beasts."

"As you command, First." Alric bows once then strides off down the hill.

"I still say we should punish him." Freda shakes her head. "To run off like that…"

"Tell you what, you punish him in your own special way." I cast her a wink and she grins.

"So, everyone's returned? How's Nahini?" I ask, sobering.

Freda removes her winged helmet, the gold gleaming in the sun. "Nahini is awake and eating, though she hasn't spoken. Her brother is with her, as well as that Valkyrie spirit. They're guarding her night and day. I'd give it another day before you approach her though."

"What about Harmony and Bard?"

"Fine. I have them housed in with a few of the troops, living of course. Harmony is a big hit with the soldiers, helping them cheat at cards and dice. Having a seer will be an asset to us. And Bard is exceptionally popular. He's doing his level best to spread the tale of the brave mortal queen who outsmarted Wardon, the greatest strategist in Underhill."

I can imagine. The shifter was a one-man USO show. "How much time has passed here?"

"Less than a day. You left last night, the Valkyrie came to

315

me mid-morning, and Alric, Nahini and those other two strays you picked up were back by noon."

Judging from the position of the sun, it was somewhere in the late afternoon now. "I did it. I passed through the gauntlet."

Her eyes round. "You're immortal now?"

"I guess so." Though I can still lie. "What changed for you, after you passed it?"

"Nothing. In fact, everything just sort of stopped the way it was. No heightened senses like the fey, no superspeed or even enhanced abilities that I already possessed."

"Then how did you know it worked?"

"My hair stopped growing, and my fingernails. It's almost as if I just froze at the point when I came out."

That sounds anticlimactic as hell.

"There's one surefire way to tell if it worked," Freda says. "Try to tell a lie."

I look up into the bright blue of the summer day. "The sky is purple."

Freda blinks. "You're sure you went through?"

No. I might be losing my mind though. "I sort of maybe… died first." I hold out my rune-covered hands.

Her lips part. "How…?"

"I don't know. And I saw things—"

"You can't speak of it." She shakes her head.

"Why not?"

"Didn't Underhill tell you not to speak of it, as part of the bargain?"

"I never met Underhill."

Her frown deepens. "You can lie and made no vow. To my knowledge, those are both unique occurrences. Though I am no record keeper."

"Maybe there's a reason I can still lie, a reason I can talk about what happened. Maybe Underhill knows I will need those skills so she didn't extract the price."

But Freda shakes her head. "You don't understand. The gauntlet isn't just a test, it's an accepted truth, the cornerstone of the fey way of life. If people find out that you're given a different set of rules to live by—that you can lie, that you can talk about your experiences, they might rise up against you."

I turn to face my first and put a hand on each of her shoulders. "Freda, I am standing here in my underwear, saturated from the river and half-dead from cold, fatigue and hunger. Is there any way you can stop anticipating the next crisis for the night?"

She bows her head. "Of course, my queen."

I blow out a frustrated sigh. "Call me Nic."

"All right, Nic."

I follow her up the steps and into the farmhouse. Jasmine is sitting at the kitchen table, a reading primer opened on my tablet. She jumps up when she sees me and wraps her arms around my waist. "Nic! You're back."

"Hey, Jazz."

Freda clears her throat and Jasmine backs off hurriedly, though her smile remains in place.

"I'm glad. I need you to help me pack for the sleepover tomorrow night."

"Sleepover?" I blink.

"Remember, Kayleigh Hamill's sleepover party?" She wiggles around like an overexcited puppy. "She called to say that it's still on, even though school won't resume until late next week. Because of the tornado."

At least I'd get a reprieve from homework, if not queenly duties. "Okay, kid. We'll get you squared away first thing tomorrow. Tonight, I need a little R&R. Where are the aunts, by the way? The clinic?"

She nods. "Chloe said we'd make mint chocolate chip brownies tonight for me to bring tomorrow."

"Knowing Chloe, she just wants an excuse for mint chocolate chip brownies. I'd love to stand here gabbing, but I need a hot shower and a good night's sleep."

Jasmine nods. "I'm glad you're back safe. You too, *Jord.*"

"Nice to know I'm an afterthought." Freda ruffles her daughter's curly hair, but her expression remains troubled. "Sleep well...Nic."

I shuffle into my bedroom, sure to lock the door. Then, moving to the window, I slam it down and toss the locks before drawing the drapes. There will be no miscommunication tonight.

It isn't until I'm safely camouflaged in the shower, that the sobs break free.

Through the Man's Eyes

THERE'S something wrong with Nic. He paces by the fairy hill waiting for something that may or may not emerge from within. Had she sent him on a fool's errand? Why would she?

To be rid of me.

He thought they were past that, that she was going to accept him fully. Another circuit as his bare feet leaves scorched earth where he treads. He needs to calm down before he starts a wildfire. He can't help but think about the last time he was here, with Nic. When she wrapped herself so sweetly around him, her lips as hungry as his own.

Not unlike the way she kissed him when he pulled her from the river. That particular kiss bordered on desperate, her eagerness due to more than simple relief.

But then something had shifted. Shadows hid in her blue

eyes along with a lurking suspicion. Is it directed at him? Aiden has no way of knowing. All he knows for sure is that she'd emerged from that river…changed.

And he doesn't like it. Neither does his wolf. It feels as though she is turning to sand before his very eyes, slipping bit by bit through his fingers.

The ground begins to shake.

Aiden whirls, flames blazing up in his hands, ready to face whatever emerges.

But when the green door opens his flames dissolve, stunned at the sight of the figure before him, wrapped in a blue drape, gold cuffs on her arms. The mark of her imprisonment.

"Hello, Aiden." Underhill purrs.

"You can't have her," he lowers his head but not his hands.

"She's my daughter." She can't cross the threshold not in form or with magic. Nic is safely out of her grasp.

His hands clench into fists. "Nicneven was your daughter. She died. Nic belongs only to herself."

"She is still Nicneven. A better, stronger Queen of the Shadow Throne. Already the gods thrash about in their slumber, knowing she will be their downfall."

"She will do nothing to assist you. She doesn't know who you are."

Her lips, so like Nic's, curl up. "Oh, but she's met me."

He shakes his head. "No, I was with her the whole time."

"Except when she died."

His lips part. Underhill—Pharaildis—to those who'd known her in her mortal life, was the first human turned immortal. For her crime against Nic's father, she was bonded to the land of the fey, to Underhill. Essentially, she *became* Underhill. And like the fey that dwell there, she couldn't lie.

"I would have felt it…." He shakes his head. "It isn't possible."

"Oh, but it is and you did feel it. You suffered, even more this time, rending your clothing, hair and skin. You were wilder than your wolf because this time you didn't just lose your mate. No, this time, the woman you loved *chose* to die, to leave you behind." Her lips turn up as though savoring a treat. "It drove you quite insane."

Something twists in his insides, her words like a fork twirling in a plate of pasta. "Nic wouldn't—"

"Oh, but she did. I returned her to you before it ever happened, with the help of some of the forbidden runes." She grins and it isn't a pleasant expression. "If you don't believe me, check her palms. They are etched there."

"You can't have her." Aiden shakes off the uneasiness her words conjure. Underhill is as tricky as any of the fey, she'd been watching them for millennia.

"That's her choice, not yours Vali Sigynjarson."

He flinches as his true name tumbles from her lips like water cascading down the falls. She did it intentionally, to remind him that she can wield power over him.

Trapped as she is in the doorway to the fairy hill she smiles as though she holds all the cards. "We needn't be enemies. We both want the same thing."

Aiden shakes his head. "I don't wish that. Not any longer."

"Unlike me, I know you can lie, wolfling. Tell me the rage doesn't eat at you, as she shares a roof with those who have wronged you, wronged *her* so abominably."

In the mist behind him he sees a young girl, blue eyes bright with tears. "Don't leave me. Please, I'll be good."

His heart cracks wide. Nic, as a young girl, scared and facing abandonment.

The blonde woman whose skirt she clutches shakes her off as though she were a gnat. "You don't have it in you. It's not in your nature."

She falls to her knees, heartbroken.

The urge to bellow out his fury, to rend something is pure response to the frightened six-year-old he would give his life to protect. His Nic, rejected and left to fend for herself.

He'd known it, but seeing it happen….

His wolf is fighting, clawing for control. He can't lose it now, not when facing down the scheming Underhill.

He pants, "That was Lachesis—"

Underhill's tone is as sharp and hard as diamonds. "It wasn't Lachesis who almost killed your grandmother. Who never even apologized. Lachesis wasn't the only one that punished you, your brother, your mother who never did a thing wrong. You were innocent. I know that, and Nic knows that. You were all collateral damage in the punishment of your father."

"I have no quarrel with Addy and Chloe."

Underhill's eyes gleam. "But we both know there's more than the two of them, do we not? Those fates may be the most powerful but all of them are tethered to the same source, The Well of Urd."

A chill goes through him. "What does any of this have to do with Nic?"

"You'll see. Although it would be best if you keep this conversation between the two of us."

"And why would I do that?"

"Because I have a gift for you." She reaches behind her into the dark depths of the Unseelie catacombs and pulls at something.

An elbow. It's attached to a woman, a familiar woman with hair the color of dried blood.

"Angrboda," Aiden stares across the gap to the bound giantess.

"She broke the magic pact when she sent those Valkyries through the tear in the Veil cloaked in glamour. She is hereby banished from the fey realm. And she's yours to do with as you will if you give me your word that you will remain silent."

"And if I don't?"

Her smile doesn't reach her eyes. "Then you'll never get the answers you seek from the Hag of the Ironwood. For I will kill her right here and now."

He stares across the void to the woman who'd wrecked his life. Well, one of them. But though the Fates had played their part and others had broken his heart, Angrboda had been the first. By seducing his father with promises of power and vengeance, she had turned Loki away from his family.

He yearns to know why, desperately. Why she had been so frantic to get him that she would barter magic with Wardon and sacrifice mortals to a nest of Valkyrie.

But does he want those answers badly enough to betray Nic?

Nic who'd sent him away sent him here. Who won't accept him, won't let him in.

He looks into the giantess's dark eyes, eyes that are swollen red but too damn prideful to shed a tear and makes his choice.

CHAPTER 24

DATE NIGHT

"**D**o I look okay?" I frown at my reflection, wondering if the classic LBD is all right for my date with Aiden. Or all wrong. I have no idea where we're going and thus, how to dress for it. "He's probably taking me bowling or something equally casual. I should change into jeans."

Jasmine looks up from my bed where she'd been watching me dress. "You look beautiful. Like a fairy princess."

"No, like a fairy queen," Chloe says as she saunters in, smelling of freshly baked bread. "An immortal one at that. You should wear your hair up."

"Aiden likes it down." I pick up a hoop earring, frown at it and set it back in my jewelry box.

She rolls her eyes. "Which is why I said wear it up. He likes you too much already."

Addy wanders into the room behind her carrying a freshly baked mint chocolate brownie. "Are you all packed, Jazz?"

Jasmine nods. She's rolled and rerolled her pink and gray color block sleeping bag fifty times at least. I bought her a brand new pink flannel pajama set and she raided my nail polish stash and has the choicest bottles lined up neatly in a shoebox at the bottom of her backpack. That plus the chocolate fix is sure to make her a hit.

"Jazz, go check in with your mom, let her know we'll be leaving in about ten minutes." This is the first time I've had a chance to talk to Chloe and Addy at the same time and I want to say what needs to be said in private.

Jasmine hops off the bed, ponytail swinging.

"What's up, buttercup?" Chloe snitches the end off Addy's brownie and gets a withering look for her efforts.

"Close the door and have a seat." I wait until they do what I've asked before pivoting from my makeup stool to face them. "When I was in the heart of Underhill, I saw someone. At least I think she was real."

"Who?" Addy asks, her dark brows pulled down behind her glasses.

"Your sister. Sissy."

Chloe sucks in a breath and Addy goes still as a statue.

As succinctly as I can, I explain what had happened, at least what I think happened. I show them the runes on my palms. In my head, I'm still struggling to figure out the details of what was real and what had been part of Underhill's illusion.

"I asked her if she wanted me to relay a message to the two of you. She said…that she understands."

Tears track freely down Chloe's face. Addy closes her eyes and wraps an arm around her sister.

"I'm not sure that it really was her," I caution.

"It's her." Addy whispers. "Thank you, Nic."

Though it goes against my nature, I move across the

room, reaching out to embrace them. "I love you both, so so much. I just…need you to know that."

They are both still. We aren't a family of huggers and the PDA's can be awkward as hell. But slowly, they reach forward and wrap their arms around me until we are engulfed in a three-way hug.

"We love you, too," Chloe whispers.

I pull away before I start crying and ruin my mascara. "Enough of the mushy crap. Where are the brownies again?"

When in doubt, eat something chocolate.

I just swallow the last bit of brownie when he knocks.

"Be nice," I warn the aunts.

Chloe makes a snorting noise and Addy just gives me her patented droll stare.

"Or at least, don't be complete shrews." Licking the last bit of chocolate from my fingers I tug the door open.

And my jaw drops.

The Aiden on my doorstep isn't one I've ever seen before. He's all poise and polished, his suit—suit for all the gods' sakes—is black on black with a black shirt, unbuttoned to reveal his tanned throat. His hair, while still shaggy and unkempt lends him a devil-may-care air.

And he's holding a single red rose, his lips tipped up in a small smile.

Oh, the son of the trickster knows exactly what he looks like.

Behind me, I hear Chloe hiss like a teakettle, "Hot daaaammmmn."

"He's good." Addy agrees. Then louder, "Nic, be home by midnight."

"Queen of the Shadow Throne here." The words come out sounding a bit strangled. "Besides, my house, my rules."

More grumbling but she doesn't lodge any further protest.

Aiden extends the rose to me. "You look amazing, my sweet."

Not my queen. My sweet. Somehow, I like that better. I take the flower from him, careful of the thorns. "Glad I decided not to change."

"You're perfect as you are." Reaching for the hand that's not holding the flower he leads me down the steps. "Is the lady Jazz ready to go?"

"Thank you for this," I whisper to him. It had been my idea to drop Jasmine off for her sleepover at the Hamill's so Aiden and I can double-check that everything is on the up and up. I still harbor suspicion about Gretchen Hamill. Call me paranoid, but after all that has happened, I'm not taking any chances with those closest to my heart.

Jasmine gives Freda a final squeeze and Aiden holds the passenger door to the truck open for her first and then for me. Nothing like starting a romantic night out with a chattering preteen on the way to her first sleepover in the car.

The Hamills own a large sprawling Victorian on the far side of town. I smile at Aiden over the top of Jasmine's head and he catches my eye though his smile seems a little unsure.

I've decided to tell him. All of it. Everything I experienced in Underhill. It's too much for me to sort out on my own. I need someone to help me navigate through the confusing quagmire between real and not real. And even with the haunting words his father uttered to me, I still trust him. There is no way Aiden or his wolf will be my demise. It was just the trickster doing what he did best—stirring the pot.

I have complete faith in Aiden. Not because his wolf sees me as his mate or because he brought me back from the dead. More than anyone else, he's been honest with me. He's shone a light on his deepest shame, shared his darkest secrets. Bared his tattered soul to me.

I can do no less, not if I want this—us—to work.

And I do. During a night filled with grief and relief, I reached a decision. I want Aiden by my side. Always. Caring about him isn't a weakness, as I'd believed. Sarah had been right, I'd been my best self, charging into that burning building for him. He provides me with a bottomless well of strength that I've drawn on to help see me through.

I can't rule alone. And what's more, I don't want to.

Aiden pulls into the circular drive in front of the Victorian and I slide out, with Jasmine hot on my heels.

"Want me to walk you in?" Aiden offers.

I roll my eyes. "Not unless you want a passel of twelve-year-old fangirls creeping on you for the rest of the school year."

He tips his head to the side and winks. "My crazy jealous girlfriend wouldn't like that."

He's teasing, yet I see a shadow of regret. He's expecting me to deny the label as I did on the first day of school.

"No," I say simply. "She wouldn't." Then I shut the door on his astonished face.

Do I know how to make an exit or what?

Jasmine practically levitates up the steps and stands on the front porch, quivering with excited energy. She looks to me and hesitates.

"You'll do great," I encourage her. "Better than I would."

She sucks in a deep breath and rings the bell.

The black door with shiny brass fittings swings wide revealing an equally excited girl with a vague resemblance to Gretchen. Behind her, I hear squealing and shrieks. Maybe adding more sugar to the mix isn't the smartest plan.

"Hi, Kayleigh. This is my...this is Nic." Jasmine blushes at her almost slip up.

"I'm a friend of your sister's. Is she around?" I taste the air but other than a miasma of prepubescent hormones, pizza and cosmetics there's nothing funky emanating from the house.

"Not sure. She spends a lot of time at my grandmother's house." The girl barely gives me a second glance.

"How about your mom?" Someone must be watching these kids.

"She's in the kitchen. Mom, someone wants to talk to you! Come on, Jazz, we're all set up in the living room."

"Bye, Nic." Jasmine gives me a final wave before she disappears and the squeals hit a fever pitch.

"Hi there," A slender woman with blond highlights drawls. She has more Southern honey on her tongue than either Kayleigh or Gretchen. She's dressed casually, wearing yoga pants and an oversized cable knit sweater and carrying a glass of chardonnay. She's what Sarah would have termed a "quintessential basic bitch."

"You must be Jazz's older sister," she croons at me. "Well, I'm Marla and don't you worry none, honey. The girls and I are gonna have lots of fun tonight."

Marla is, without a doubt, human. No fey would ever be so cookie cutter.

"Okay, my cell number is in Jasmine's phone in case you need it, and of course Gretchen has it. We're in the same grade at school."

"Bless your heart," she says.

I can't take anymore and slowly back up from the door. "Have a good night."

Another round of squealing follows me down the flagstone path and back to the truck.

"All clear?" Aiden asks.

I nod. "It's a good thing we left you in the truck. Something tells me Marla would have taken a shine to you." Especially if that wasn't her first glass of Chardonnay.

Aiden's laugh is low and husky and he pulls me over the bench seat until I'm wedged up against him. Draping an arm around my shoulders, he sighs. "That's better. I don't want anything between me and my girlfriend."

"Like that, do you?"

He nods slowly. "I like anything that means you're accepting me."

The night air is cool and I snuggle against him, glad for the warmth as much as the intimacy. "Do I get to know where we're going now?"

"Soon." He turns the key and then puts the truck into reverse. Once we're cruising through town he asks, "You said earlier you had something to tell me."

This wasn't how I imagined it. "We can talk about it later. I don't want to spoil our date."

"Nic." He brakes for a red light and turns to look at me. "This isn't about playing pretend. We're still us, complications and all. You won't ever ruin anything by being honest with me. I want you to tell me everything without fear or censoring, okay?"

"Okay." I take a deep breath and then dive into it, head first.

I tell him about letting go of the branch, awaking in the river sprite village. Aiden showing up, with the bond broken. He listens when I tell him how I sent him away. He asks no questions when I reveal meeting the woman who called herself Pharaildis and claimed to be my mother. Confronting the dead aunt who'd abandoned me, leaving him to lose an eye, encountering his parents.

He says nothing when I repeat the riddle. Or tell him about the future Sarah had shown me or even when I talk about the runes and seeing the dead, not just souls I've tethered to the Hunt with my Goodnight Kiss. But all those who have died.

Aiden stops the truck, turns the engine off. He's facing forward, his knuckles clenched on the steering wheel.

I let out a shaky breath. "So much for not killing the mood. Of course, it wouldn't be a night out with me if I didn't kill something."

He shakes his head.

I want to beg him to say something, but I just dumped a whole truckload of grief on his doorstep. It's not my place to make demands.

Instead, in an effort to distract myself and let him digest it all, I look around. Night has settled around us and we're parked on an unfamiliar dirt road, though we haven't driven far. "Where are we?"

"My place."

I swing my gaze to him. "What do you mean your place? Since when did you have a place?"

"It's just a piece of land at the moment, though I plan to build on it." After extracting the key from the ignition, he pops the door to the truck. "Come on, I'll show you around."

I take his hand and let him lead me out of the woods and up a small hill to a clearing. With a snap of his fingers, torches that had been standing cold a second ago flare to life, as does a pile of wood in the center of a massive fire pit. "This will be the hearth. I'll be building bookshelves on either side. The great room will have a vaulted ceiling with exposed wood beams. Skylights on either side with automatic shades so we can look up at the stars."

"We?" I ask. What exactly is he asking me here?

He turns to look at me. "I know you have your own place. But the farm gets crowded. I thought this would be nice, to escape. Whenever you need a break."

He paces out a dozen strides, shows me where the kitchen will be, explains details of the built-in booth that he'll make instead of a standard dining room table. The island counter with a Viking stove that he'd already bought off Craigslist. The bathroom with a rainfall shower and sunken tub, big enough for two. I'm blushing before he gets to the spiral staircase leading up to the single bedroom.

I can see it all, every step he's walking me through. "It sounds amazing. But, who's going to do all this?"

"I am."

I snort. Then blink when his expression falls. "You know how to build a house?"

He nods. "I've done it before."

I want to ask more, but he leads me around to the far side of the fire. "This will be the front porch. Check out the view."

I stare out at the endless rolling landscape lit only by moonlight. It's otherworldly, peaceful. He picked a glorious spot.

The firelight reveals a picnic blanket, a basket and plush pillows for sitting. Aiden takes the rose from the dashboard of the truck and carries it over to a crystal vase set up on the blanket before turning to me.

"Your farmhouse is about two miles that way. The next mountain top over." He pulls me against him and points over my shoulder. "I come here every night after you go home, near enough that I can be there in an instant if you need me, but far enough away so I don't interfere. The property came on the market earlier this summer and I bought it."

I stare at the lights barely visible through the leafy canopy. Come winter when all the leaves fall, the long-range view would be virtually unobstructed.

"How long?" I ask, not daring to move. "How long did you watch me from here?"

"Since the Fates moved you here. When you were six."

I swallowed. "I thought Brigit kept you caged all that time."

"There are different kinds of cages," his words are cryptic

and full of pain. "You're right about me, you know. That I've been punishing myself for Nari."

"Aiden—" I turn to face him but he looks away.

"There was a point where I thought I felt you there. In the caves with me. I chalked it up to hallucination but maybe, maybe Underhill really did bring you back there."

It feels as though my insides are being crushed. "I hated leaving you. I'm so so sorry."

But he's shaking his head. "You were right to leave me there. Though I can't promise that I learned any great lessons or that I won't wind up in a similar situation." His posture is tight, his hands buried deep in his suit pockets.

"It didn't feel right. It felt like a betrayal. If our places were reversed I wouldn't have understood if you stood by and did nothing to help me."

His lips twitch. "That's because I would never do that."

I shove him and he laughs, catching my hand and threading his fingers through mine. "So clearly you are a better person than I am?"

His other hand comes up to cup my cheek. "No. It means you have what it takes to be a queen. An underfed queen at that. Come on, let's eat."

I'm half expecting a box of open stale cheese crackers and a few bottles of mountain dew. Again, Aiden surprises me.

Our picnic is a combination of all my favorite foods. Spinach artichoke dip, baked apple cobbler, fresh fruit, bread and cheese. And weirdly a platter of pancakes.

"What's with the pancakes?" I quirk an eyebrow at him.

Reaching into his suit pocket he extracts a familiar vial. "Goes better with syrup."

"Is that…?" I reach for the vial, my heart pounding.

Aiden nods. "I'm ready, if you still want me to break my oath to you."

Oath breaking is a big deal to him. I recall what the dream version had told me, about the corner of Hel reserved for oathbreakers, where the dragon Nidhogg gnaws forever on their bones.

I swallow past the lump in my throat. "You were planning this, even before I told you about the gauntlet."

He nods. "This choice has been before us all along. I wasn't ready for it before."

"Why not?" I whisper and step closer to him. "What are you afraid of?"

His green eyes are guileless. "Without my oath of obedience, that lacking the ability to command me, you'll send me away."

As I'd done in the heart of Underhill. I breathe his name and put my arms around his neck. "We're past that."

"You did it in my dreams," he points out.

"To *protect* you. I didn't want you to watch me die. Again."

"I know and that gives me hope." He pushes some hair behind my ear, intent on doing it just so. "Nic. We'll be in uncharted territory. You won't be able to control my wolf."

My fingers curl into the soft hair at the nape of his neck. "I don't want to control any part of you. But don't drink this for me."

His green eyes narrow. "I thought you wanted this."

"I do. But I want *you* to want this. Drink it because you believe in us. Drink it because you believe you shouldn't be ordered around by anyone for any reason. Drink it because you trust yourself and in the hope that maybe one day you will forgive yourself."

His hands shake as he fumbles with the cork.

I step back, giving him room, vowing that if he dumps the syrup out on the ground, I won't ever ask him to break his oath again. His choice, this must be his choice.

He stares at the vial then up to me. "This will change everything. I don't know what will happen to the mate bond without the oath. If we can still communicate mind to mind."

I swallow past the lump in my throat. "I guess we'll just have to see."

Green gaze locked on my face, he upends the vial, swallowing its contents in one gulp.

Heart in my throat, I study him, waiting for some sort of sign. There is no light, or explosion of magic.

Aiden? I think at him.

Yeah? It's an automatic reply, as though he's distracted.

"I can still hear you," I breathe. "Did it work?"

Maybe the magic in the syrup expired. Or we missed a step.

"One way to find out." His green eyes are practically glowing in the low light. "Tell me to do something."

"Kiss me, Aiden," I order.

A slow smile spreads across his face and he doesn't even twitch. "No Nic, you come here and kiss me."

"Gladly." I move into him again, claiming his lips with my own.

"If I'd known I'd be this well fed, I wouldn't have snitched that brownie." I lay back on the blanket, my hand curving over my bulging stomach.

"I'm glad you liked it." Aiden stretches out alongside me. We're both seriously overdressed for an outdoor picnic in the wilds of a North Carolina night, but neither of us mentions it.

The citronella torches keep the bugs at bay and the fire pit adds just the right amount of heat and light to make us comfortable. I stare up at the night sky, stars so familiar and yet I know nothing about them.

Aiden of course does. "That's the constellation Virgo. People born under that sign tend to be neurotic as hell."

I laugh. "What, are you an astrology expert too?"

"You're a Scorpio. Fun fact, most serial killers are born under that sign."

"Good to know the universe has a plan. What about you."

"I'm older than most known constellations."

I sigh and then turn to face him. "Can I ask you a question? Why did you buy this property?"

He exhales, his gaze still trained on the stars. "Because I wanted a place where I'd always belong. It's something I haven't experienced since I left Asgard. That sense of belonging."

I scoot closer and stare down into his eyes. "You belong with me."

He quirks a brow. "Not to you?"

I shake my head vehemently. "No, Aiden. *With* me. I figured something out while I was in Underhill. I kept trying to do things to protect you, to keep you from getting hurt. Most of the time, no matter what I tried, things only got worse. And the only way they could get better is if you made your own decisions. I don't own you, but there will always be a place at my side for you if you want it."

His brows draw together and he looks as though he's in pain. "Nic, there's something I—"

My phone rings.

I retrieve the device from where I stashed it at the corner of the blanket and frown at the display. "Sorry, hold that thought. What's up, Jazz?"

"Nic. It's me. Er…Gretchen. Can you come back here?"

I sit bolt upright. "Is everything okay? Why are you calling me on Jasmine's phone?"

"Just hurry." There's a click and then silence.

"Did you hear that?" I ask, anxiety spiking.

Aiden is already on his feet. "Sparks or truck?"

"How long by conventional means?"

"Ten, maybe fifteen minutes."

"You go on ahead. Make sure Jazz is all right. I'll take the truck. Call me if you find out anything."

He reaches out and douses all the flames as easily as he had lit them, then hands me his suit jacket. "Keys are in the pocket."

I barely catch it when he dissembles into sparks.

"And things were going so well too," I grumble as I dash for the truck, keys in hand.

Bitching keeps me distracted from freaking out over what Gretchen might possibly want. I can't shake the feeling that I'm being led into some sort of trap.

"Gretchen is human," I say as the truck fishtails off the dirt road. A Toyota swerves as I fight to right the wheel and force the truck into my lane. The other car barely misses my left quarter panel and I hear the driver shout something as I zoom past. Probably calling me a crazy bitch.

I blow him a kiss in my rearview, then focus on the road.

All the tranquility I'd experienced on the peaceful hilltop is long gone. One night off, hadn't I at least earned one night off from all the craziness? But my bitterness can't overtake the worry I feel. If anything has happened to Jazz....

I skid to a stop at the mouth of Gretchen's driveway and see she and Aiden already out front. No firetruck or ambulance or police cars. Gretchen is wearing a long nightdress and her feet are bare. Aiden's got a dark scowl on his face. Jasmine is nowhere in sight.

"What?" I ask "What's wrong? Is Jasmine okay?"

"She's fine." Aiden moves to stand between us. "But we have a problem."

"What sort of problem?" I frown, looking from him to Gretchen and back.

Wordlessly, she hands me a manila envelope.

The first photo is grainy, obviously taken from a distance probably with the zoom-in feature on the phone. My face, however, is easy enough to identify, bent as I am over a fresh corpse.

"Shit," I say, recognizing the guy I'd offed on my last night out with Sarah. Something Anderson. From the angle of the photo, it looks as if I'm picking his pocket, which I had been. For my I.D. collection.

"There's more." Aiden's tone is grim.

The next photo is of a wolf skulking through the trees. Nothing bad, except the one directly after that is a naked Aiden, his face shown in profile.

I start flipping through them faster, my brain whirling through damage control scenarios. How much does Gretchen know? There's me and Aiden, half-formed in a shower of sparks. There's Chloe, oh gods no, with her eyes swirling. When was that from?

Freda in her helmet and Nahini with the ghosts. The Wild Hunt in all their unnerving glory. Us and the Valkyrie nest at the trashed apartment complex. Damn it, I knew someone had been in the woods.

And then photocopies of my diary. I recognize the picture. Paul freaking Anderson.

She has it all, enough evidence to convict me, to lock me up and throw away the key.

"What are you?" Gretchen asks, eyes round, tone incredulous.

I exchange glances with Aiden.

One kiss and it could be over. I'm not sure if the thought is his or mine. We are both thinking it though.

Could I really kill an innocent to keep my secret?

One thing is for sure. The next few minutes will change the course of all our lives.

~End of Book 2~

Will Nic kill Gretchen to protect herself and Aiden? Click and start reading Wolf's Mate *The Unseelie Court Book 3 right away to find out!*

Bound by Fate....

Nic Rutherford has a big problem. A magical problem. A classmate has unearthed a deadly secret and is using it to blackmail her. Will she be forced to kill an innocent to protect her supernatural life, including her boyfriend, Aiden? Can she live with herself if she uses her power to destroy a pure soul?

Forever Apart....

Aiden's been keeping secrets of his own. For a shot at vengeance against the woman who destroyed his family, Aiden has agreed to keep his mate in the dark. Though Nic is all he could ever want, the past stalks him with every beat of his heart. Will his silence cost Nic her life magic? Will he ever be enough for his mate?

One Final Chance to Save All....

Two selfish hearts must learn to beat as one. To trust and accept not only each other but themselves and destiny. For if Underhill is allowed to rise to power, the mortal realm will fall. *Ragnarök*—the end of the world is at hand.

Keep reading for a sample from Wolf's Mate.

I really don't want to kill the nice girl from my American History class.

Gretchen Hamill's life is just too damn sad. Her outgoing little sister is hosting the junior high event of the season—a massive sleepover not twenty yards away from where we are standing. Her mom, the supposed adult supervisor, is busy trying to recapture her misspent youth one glass of Chardonnay at a time. While smart and sweet, it's clear Gretchen doesn't fit in with the rest of her family. She's a plus size girl living in a size double zero world. I'm the closest thing she has to a friend. Cutting her life short would transform her unhappy existence into a tragic one.

Plus, there's the fact that she didn't do anything wrong. Curiosity killed the cat, but it shouldn't be the undoing of a teenage girl. Her tenacity and dedication will serve her well as an adult. One day she might cure cancer or reverse climate change. She's got the makings of a hero.

I, Nic Rutherford am the villain of the piece.

And Gretchen's got the evidence to prove it.

I stare down at the photos Aiden, my partner in crime, had just handed over. The pictures will raise too many questions. Me, in a short skirt and slutty make-up going through the pockets of a corpse. A decent lawyer could argue that I didn't kill the man in question. Perhaps I was just a lowlife who'd stumbled across his body and gone through his pockets looking for money. Except Gretchen also has photocopies of my diary, which contain the dead man's driver's license, as well as the ID's of all my other victims.

And it stands to reason if she has the copies, she possesses the original as well. The fluffy diary with my unique and highly identifiable fingerprints all over it.

Fuck fuck fuckity fuck *fuck.*

Aiden stands a foot away, waiting for me to decide what to do. His hands are loose at his sides, his anger fully contained. Some guys act like monsters. Aiden actually has one trapped within him. I've seen the wicked claws punch through his fingertips like something out of a Marvel movie. His wolf is probably howling that he ought to *take care* of Gretchen in the classic mob boss sense of the phrase.

It's my call to make though. I'm his queen, an uncrowned queen, but still head honcho. For now, Aiden stands beside me looking sexy, still dressed in the black on black suit from our date. The male equivalent to my little black dress. His dark hair ruffles against his neck in the cold breeze while his leaf green eyes assess the threat. We look like two normal teenagers out on a special evening, not two magic wielding immortals contemplating murder.

"What are you?" Gretchen repeats her question.

She has compiled more than enough evidence to not only send me to prison, but to have me studied in a lab by scientists with questionable ethics. Maybe I've read too many physiological thrillers, but I can easily imagine being vivisected by creepy guys in white coats who want nothing more than to figure out what makes me tick.

And Gretchen's knowledge endangers more than me. She also has photos of Aiden. Maybe not as damning as mine, but someone somewhere would probably wonder at his ability to travel in the form of embers and shift into a wolf. Then there are the pictures of my aunts, Chloe and Addy, who literally hid the bodies of the perverts I'd offed after said perverts attacked me. My friends, Nahini and Freda and her daughter Jasmine, the teenage half-nymph at the slumber party inside. Plus, several other members of the Wild Hunt, the ethereal army from Underhill that is currently camping out at my farm. All their destinies hang in the balance.

Buy Wolf's Mate now!

IT'S NOT MY WORDS THAT COUNT.
IT'S YOURS!

Please consider leaving an honest review for this book. Reviews help readers like you find books they enjoy, or warn them off from ones they won't. Reader reviews help the authors you love sell books and help them put money toward the next title. Even a sentence or two can mean the difference between a series that continues and one that flops. I found one of my favorite series from a two star review. So if you want more, tell the world.

Thank you for reading!

ABOUT THE AUTHOR

Gwen Rivers is the changeling of a *USA Today* bestselling author Jennifer L. Hart. When not writing urban and rural fantasy with kickass heroines, you can find her poring over Norse mythology, dicing with the Fates, cavorting with werewolves or hunting for fairy wine in the deep, dark woods.

Want exclusive behind the scenes access to what she is working on next? Become a Patron today!